## ASSASSIN JULIA HAMPTON QUIT THE GAME AND RETURN TO HER SCHOOLTEACHER ROOTS — ONLY TO LEARN SHE'S MARKED FOR DEATH.

Primary teacher Julia Hampton's quiet life in Oregon upends with the murder of her parents and sister. Julia seeks revenge against those responsible, and against all odds, she succeeds. Her success is noticed by an organization dedicated to the same task on a grand scale: eliminate anyone importing and selling narcotics. Julia accepts assignments as a contract killer for The Company and makes a name for herself as J.

Settling in rural Idaho to live alone as a substitute teacher offers a low-profile base for assignments. Dawson Pelletier owns a nearby farm and looks after Julia's place when J is away. All goes well until she's wounded and barely makes it home. She finds her neighbor is much more than a gentleman farmer when only one of his many hidden resources is to become her expert caregiver.

Her thirst for vengeance sated and faced with her mortality, Julia notifies The Company that the assignment she barely survives is her last, and she'll return to teaching fulltime, but her resignation is rejected unless she fulfills a final contract. Against previous rules of engagement, her target is outside US borders, and she must leave her familiar firearm behind and find alternate means to terminate a giant ex-athlete responsible for importing tons of drugs stateside each week. J must take on a brute three times her size if she is to have a chance to return to the quiet life and budding romance wants.

"Pitts is a highly skilled storyteller. Riveting - action filled - yet woven with love and unforgettable characters. Can't wait for the next one!"—*Judy Schwartz, Educator*

"Pitts is one of those authors who makes readers feel as if they have lived all their lives in the settings of what he writes, and can move from an exciting, dangerous scene on one page to a sensitive, personal, and touching moment on the next. His dialogue always rings true."—*Jim Tevis - Professor and Historian*

i

*My initial dispatching of the Sanchez woman and three of her henchmen were as routine as my daily practice knocking bowling pins off fence posts, but no drill can prepare a person for an actual gun battle. For the first time in my life, I felt the shock of a bullet. My hand explored my stomach and slipped through wetness before pain set in. Dropping to one knee, I exchanged my nearly empty magazine. Two men remained who planned to end my life. I needed every round now in my gun.*

*Hearing the telltale sounds of magazines ejected and the fumbling to reload in the dining room, I stepped through the doorway with my eye locked over the sights. Both men looked in my direction, clumsily releasing their slides to chamber rounds.*

*Diligent practice with the nearly silent and recoilless Mark IV .22/45 behind my house paid off. The men wanting to kill me now became no more than wobbling bowling pins, and I simply squeezed the trigger once, then again. Both men fell faster than I can tell it. None of the seven were moving, and I took the extra seconds needed to shoot each one again. I was down to one round in the chamber when I reentered the kitchen to deal with a prime witness before my escape.*

# HITWOMAN

## Jeffrey A. Pitts

Moonshine Cove Publishing, LLC
Abbeville, South Carolina U.S.A.
First Moonshine Cove edition September 2019

ISBN: 978-1-945181-689
Library of Congress PCN: 2019912141
Copyright 2019 by Jeffrey A. Pitts

Edited by Chase Nottingham; cover illustration by Ryan Lanz (AWP, A Writer's Path), back cover, interior design, and additional editing by Moonshine Cove staff.

## Dedication

To my beloved wife Jodi whose support and encouragement is the dream of every author. Pat and Terry, your belief in me was incalculable. My friend Chase whose patience and teaching abilities were stretched to their limits. Tyrel and Terin who backed their father without fail. Amy, Judy, and Jim for their valuable feedback and insights.

## About the Author

Jeffrey A Pitts is the author of *Hitwoman* and other novels. Growing up on farms in Oregon and Washington, Jeff spent  most of his time in whatever backcountry he could reach on horseback or afoot. Now, this dedicated storyteller's characters walk in the same tracks. Seldom does he utilize a wilderness setting he hasn't hiked, camped, fished, or hunted. Jeff loads, tests, and maintains important ballistic data of his own ammunition, because the harvest of wild game is more than a hobby. It's a way of life.

After graduating from high school, Jeff worked as a carpenter, log home builder, logger, and heavy equipment operator. Fascinated by the roughest wilderness areas the US has to offer, he's spent much of his life exploring the wildest country possible, sometimes living off the land as he traveled. From the Goat Rocks Wilderness of Washington state, the Bob Marshall of Montana, to the Frank Church River of No Return Wilderness of Idaho, he's hiked thousands of miles on and off trails.

After the loss of a special German shorthair pointer, he filled the void with wirehair pointers and adds dogs into much of his writings.

An avid powerlifter, Jeff enjoys the big loads of squatting, benching, and deadlifting. He is married to Jodi, his childhood sweetheart, and they have two children, Tyrel and Terin, and three grandchildren, Noah, Hayden, and Kody.

A lifelong reader, he began writing stories when they could no longer be contained in his head and spilled over onto paper and computer screens.

Jeff derives pleasure from a slow rural life, enjoying friends and family, crafting his stories, growing a garden, and living off the grid in the Pacific Northwest with wife, two German wirehairs, and a flock of chickens.

# HITWOMAN

Chapter I

"You've been asked to work further up the food chain, J. This is a game changer...for both of us." The pleasure in Manny's voice was obvious. He was my handler and as such received twenty percent of my net pay. He was my partner, and my understanding was he had no other, making it imperative I provide for him and any family he might have.

"How much? You know my rule, Manny...I don't leave the mainland for any amount of money."

Most of my clients were so far down the ranking of victims that they almost didn't have names. After fulfilling any contract, a big payday was fifteen-grand. Most averaged in the twenty-five hundred to five thousand range. A good living, but I wasn't getting rich nor younger. A little more than three years of my life was spent harvesting guppies to eke out a living. Not until my skill was noticed and appreciated did I begin a slow crawl upward in The Company. I needed to contact a minimum of two clients each month to account for my partner's bills.

"Importers."

Christ, Manny wasn't kidding. I wasn't simply taking on a better clientele. The top of the food pyramid was in sight. My heart jumped into my throat, and I calmed it with speed developed in my profession. "Tell me you're not joking."

His answer was immediate. "How soon can you leave?"

I needed to think. "It depends on where I'm going and when I need to make contact with our client."

"Indianapolis, Indiana. The contract should be signed within fourteen days of midnight tonight. He'll be receiving an international shipment in forty-eight hours. You've also been given the green light to take control of the merchandise before it leaves his office. There is a fifty percent bump if you secure the load."

"Base pay?"

"A hundred." The excitement in his voice was controlled but evident.

Suddenly my mouth was too dry to spit. My retirement—one way or the other—was flashing before my eyes. "Plus fifty?" I worked again to control my heart rate.

"Plus fifty if you come through with the merchandise. This is only the beginning, J. I saw a list following this client if you can sign him." His voice lowered. "This is just a drop in the bucket."

"I'll talk to my neighbor about watching my place while I'm gone. I can be in Missoula tomorrow at noon. Text me my flight information." I ended the call, but Manny was already gone. The job seemed foremost in his mind, and I guessed he was already calling for a seat.

Jake strolled in, silently watching me pack. Although the time frame was fourteen days, the referencing of the initial forty-eight hours wasn't accidental. Our employers hoped I could fill my end of our verbal agreement in less than seventy-two hours from the moment I left my house. It was a Saturday morning, and I needed to call my neighbor to see if he was even home.

The phone rang twice before it was answered. A deep voice speaking in a slow cadence recognized my number. "Hidey-ho there, good neighbor." My acquaintance enjoyed reruns of 'nineties sitcoms. "What can I do you for?"

"Mr. Pelletier, may I ask a favor?"

"Sure," his bass said. "But ain't it pretty early for a Saturday morning?" The reverberations went beyond my eardrums and into my core.

"It's already six seventeen. What are you...some daisy spending the morning in bed?"

"Nope. Been up over an hour. Could we get to this favor? Got biscuits in the oven and need two hands to keep from burnin' myself."

"I would be happy to explain if you could stop by for a few minutes after you eat."

"Be there in a half-hour." He ended the call without another word.

My bags were packed, and I was eating breakfast when Dawson Pelletier parked an aging F250 in my driveway. It didn't appear washed since its purchase. I found myself irritated. He blocked me from leaving—should I wish to—or anyone from arriving. The man's abrupt nature bordered on rude and hadn't changed since my move here.

Neither did his appearance. Perhaps six-two without his thick leather boots, he was lean without being thin. His hair, black as night, was gathered loosely at his nape and extended down another four or five inches. A short, heavy beard complimented a no-nonsense look. As a neighbor, he was a good one. No pestering with frequent visits, and neither of us caused problems for the other. Our fences were high and strong, and while I didn't run cattle or horses, his never broke through.

Although we lived in eastern Idaho between North Fork and Gibbonsville, he was the only person I saw carry a gun fulltime. Enough of the revolver protruded from a crossdraw holster to be readily identified as a Colt Anaconda. In .44 Magnum, it was a powerful yet smooth handgun. Outside of police, Fish and Game officials, and hunters during season, I never noticed anyone armed. The area could not be considered a bastion for terrorism. Rifles and shotguns were in the rear window of most trucks, but no one else walked around with a handgun strapped on. One of the reasons I moved to the area…it was a remote location with more than its share of quirkiness.

Scraping the last of my scrambled eggs onto a piece of toast, I folded it over, making a half sandwich. I walked out with Jake on my heels as Dawson stepped from his truck. Perhaps because he was a pointer, Jake rarely barked unless he didn't like the person. I chose Dawson as my go-to simply because my pal and bed-buddy was fond of him.

My neighbor ambled along as slowly as he talked. I enjoyed little of his stroll from his truck to my porch and finally sat to eat my sandwich as he mounted the steps. "Hey there, Jake." It was as if they were old buddies. My German shorthair pointer had only been around our neighbor a half-dozen times but greeted him like an old friend.

"Mr. Pelletier." I nodded as if he addressed me.

"Howdy, neighbor. Want a calf pulled or a field cultivated?"

"Nothing quite so strenuous. I have to leave for a week…two at most…and need someone to take care of my animals. You've done it before. Would you like me to show you the ropes again?"

"Anything changed?"

"Not much. Both my doe rabbits have litters, but you've been around them before. Don't let them run out of food or water, and they should be fine. There's plenty of feed in the chicken coop. Please gather the eggs and take them home. I'll leave out some cartons."

"Sounds easy enough. You want me to ride herd on your place? Check on it a few times each day?"

I nodded. "Please…although it should be fine. Mostly take care of Jake. He's my best boy, and I'd hate to have anything happen." The sleek pointer sneaked a guilty look at me. Dawson was giving Jake's ears all the attention he wanted.

"If I got it all, I'll be getting. I got errands to run before dark." He turned to leave, and turncoat Jake made a move to follow.

"Thank you, Mr. Pelletier. I'll call when I'm on my way home." He grunted and waved over his shoulder. It was no wonder a curt manner made him a single man, although I would put his age only eight or ten years beyond mine. Thirty-one would be in the rearview mirror before I returned home.

***

A call to Salmon Air secured an early Sunday morning flight to Missoula. It didn't matter they charged double for the day and early hour. Manny picked up my expenses from the time I left my front door until I returned and pulled it closed behind me. My '84 Jeep Wagoneer was left behind a gated fence while I was gone. I was promised my only set of wheels would be ready and waiting for my return. I left the keys and asked if someone would take it in for an oil change and tune-up. My employer spent a C-note for a tip, while I paid for the actual work.

My place onboard the 737 was in row fifty, seat A. Rather than a large man taking up his space and much of mine which had happened, I was next to a frightened girl who never flew before. It was a place I preferred, enjoying watching at the rear of the jet's engine. I found it amazing as the wings flexed during flight. Reading a thriller written by a budding novelist from the Pacific northwest, I settled in for the ride. My scared neighbor attempted to interact with me, giving up after receiving only grunts in return. Instead, she talked nonstop to the third in our row, a man in his mid-forties. Much more taken with her wide-eyed innocence than me, he kept the girl entertained until our landing at Indianapolis International Airport. I could ill afford losing my focus at the job at hand.

Manny always came through. Although never meeting my partner in person, he was thorough, making sure I suffered no want. Where he lived was unknown to me. Hell, I didn't even know his last name—he was a voice on my phone. Conversely, as far as I understood it, he didn't know where I lived, outside of my flights originating from Missoula. Seldom returning the same way, I preferred instead to fly into Spokane, Washington, and take a commuter on my own dime. Sometimes to Challis with a hopper home—occasionally, directly to Salmon.

The transportation Manny provided was a new Ford Expedition, my SUV of choice. I wanted a large and heavy vehicle, able to carry as much or little equipment as my job required. For my Indianapolis client, a carry-on and checked bag was all. Tossing them to the backseat, I drove to the Best Western where Manny reserved a room for me off Interstate 74, not far from the Motor Speedway. My client owned a warehouse close to the track and employed twenty-eight. Our dealings dictated I meet him at his place of business after hours.

Rather than check into my room, I stopped the engine across the parking lot and watched. Being a people person is a weakness of mine. It is interesting to watch their comings and goings—from a young family with squalling kids and how they censored them to an old man who struggled to cross to his car.

My arrival time was twelve ten—I was driving away from the airport at twelve forty-five. I spent until three watching outside the motel until checking in. The staff was efficient, and after reaching my room at three fifteen, I called to touch bases with Manny using an expendable phone.

"Manny here." When I used a number he wasn't familiar with, my partner was even more impersonal.

"J." My working voice was dispassionate with a hint of cruelty.

"Hey. Are you checked in?"

"Uh huh. Details, please."

"Your client is a Caucasian, age forty-eight. He suffers from male pattern baldness and keeps his head shaved. He's easily recognized with a heavy salt and pepper goatee. He's married with three children, ages sixteen, thirteen, and nine…all girls. His wife is a stay-at-home who spends money as if it's losing value. His name is Clayton Young, wife Sarah with an h, children Sam, Julie, and Sara, without the h." I wondered about the similarities in the wife's and youngest daughter's names. "The client is six-four…heavyset…with a propensity toward wearing black."

"Nonathletic or athletic?" It made a difference to how I might approach our meeting.

"He played football in both high school and division-three college. His knee blew out during a pickup basketball game in his thirties and soon after put on weight."

"Women?"

"Yeah, they're a weakness for him. He prefers them very short and thin, the opposite of his wife. She's six-foot and on the heavier side. Right now, he's seeing two women outside his marriage…one a customer…the other an employee. He also has one child out of wedlock his wife knows nothing about."

Although most of the information wasn't required, his weakness for women could help seal our deal. If needed, blackmail is a powerful weapon when employed correctly. "Anything else?"

"His business hours are from eight to five. We expect him to take possession of the shipment about nine tonight. He will drive a two-ton flatbed to the airport, where it will be loaded by forklift. After returning to his shop, the material will be dropped off. It will have been dispensed in less than seventy-two hours."

"His mistress' names?" A mouse clicked furiously in the background.

"Customer is Anne Bolt. The employee is Janet Muir. Both are short and very slight. Do you need their personal information?"

I took a nap after we ended our call. Business dealings were notorious for wearing me out. I needed all my faculties to fulfill my end of the bargain. Gaining the smoothest deal possible would lead to better and more lucrative work in the future. My eventual retirement rested on a successful transaction with Mr. Young.

I woke at seven and dressed for success after a shower. Dealing with a man like Clayton Young meant casual attire. I wore jeans and a long, hooded sweatshirt reaching my thighs. The spring evening was cool, and I didn't plan to become chilled. On the off chance I could wrap our deal up in one night, I left my packed bags inside the door. Opportunities come at the strangest of times. Glancing back into my room, the only evidence I could see was a slight depression in the center of the bed. Even the wet towel I'd used would be dispensed with. It was in a large Ziploc bag next to my suitcase.

After a lazy meal at a nearby McDonalds and three large coffees to go, I drove to Young's place of business. It was surrounded by a chain-link fence. I withdrew binoculars from my bag after parking next to a building and settled in to wait. A few minutes past eight, I ducked when headlights came around the corner. A pickup stopped at the gate. It was remote controlled and opened without anyone showing a face. I watched as it closed and locked securely after the truck pulled forward.

Taking note of the heavy gate moving slowly on its track and the dumpster outside for garbage pickup, I smiled to myself. Finishing my last cup of coffee, I slid down when the warehouse entrance opened. As Manny indicated, a flatbed truck idled out. The huge door wasn't automated. Young was forced to physically close and lock it before continuing to the perimeter gate. I shook my head when he activated the closing mechanism and drove away.

He returned at nine forty-five. It seemed incongruous that he worked alone with such a valuable commodity. As he passed the dumpster, I stepped out, leaped to the truck's bumper, and pulled myself onto the bed. Lying flat, I waited for the truck to stop twice—once to open and the other to close the warehouse door. After hearing it lock, I risked raising my head enough to see.

Young was exactly as Manny described: a large man—I would guess his weight close to four-hundred pounds. He walked with a limp from both an injured knee and his incredible mass. Passing the truck's bed, he hurried around to the cab and pulled the vehicle forward.

The warehouse was enormous. Perhaps fifty thousand square feet—I felt stupid in forgetting to ask Manny the size. I would think to ask in the future. A small upper floor occupied one side. Even from a distance, I could see an *Office* sign and another reading *No Admittance*. Glancing about, I wasn't surprised to find no obvious cameras mounted inside. Without indication of anyone else in the building, I was ready when the engine stopped. My hood was on, hiding a face covered by a ski mask. Even my hands were covered by gloves.

When Clayton Young stepped from the cab and turned to close the door, I shot him in the temple from less than ten feet. My suppressed Ruger .22/45 hardly made a sound outside of the clacking bolt. He never knew I was there and dropped to the floor without sound. I leaped from the bed. From three feet away, I shot him another four times in the head even though blood was already pooling. The empty cartridge casings were caught inside the custom netting connected to my ejection port, making cleanup of evidence moot.

I released the partially loaded magazine and inserted a fresh one, watching for movement from my client or anyone I might have missed. The idea of killing an innocent was revolting, but I was prepared if necessary. So far—after signing fifty-six clients—I hadn't yet neutralized a bystander. If it happened, I would have little help from The Company. It was our job to take care of ourselves.

"Manny here." He answered on the first ring.

"Young's been signed. I need an address. I'm driving away with the shipment as we speak." My client's body remained where he fell—with both gates closed and locked behind me. The truck was big and unwieldy, making me strain to tame it.

"There's a golf course nearby. Have you noticed signs?" I found no indication of terseness in his voice and forced myself to remain calm.

I did notice the manicured links, although golf was something I didn't particularly care for. No, not entirely accurate. It wasn't that I didn't care for it. I simply didn't have any interest in the game. Manny gave me directions. When I arrived, a frightening man waited along with a taxi. He nodded when I stepped out and handed him my

SUV keys. The Company would take care of it. He drove the big truck I had procured into the country club and disappeared. No words were exchanged during our brief encounter.

My job a success, I relaxed in the taxi ride to the Best Western. Manny lined up a return flight by the time I checked out with my bags. Ninety minutes later, I was flying toward Spokane. It was a late departure—twenty-five percent full—and I took my customary row fiftieth seat.

Finding a hop out of Spokane to Salmon was difficult. It was made harder without Manny doing it for me. I slept in the airport while waiting for a 6:00 a.m. flight and boarded with my eyes full of sand. The boys were ready with my Jeep when I landed. The powerful V8 started with its customary purr, made smoother with a fresh tune-up. Smiling and waving, I pulled away. Both Jim and Ken waved back.

Jake was happy to see me. It's funny. No matter how upset a dog becomes, all is forgiven the moment its owner returns. My pointer was no different. He mauled me the instant I walked through the door. He'd obviously been well taken care of. Food remained in his bowl. He was a browser rather than a gulper, and his water container was full. Despite it being before noon, Dawson obviously stopped early to take care of my animals. Leaving my bags in the living room, I hurried to my office to go online.

A quick check on a secure server showed one-hundred twenty-thousand deposited in my offshore account. The full amount—minus Manny's twenty percent—was moved not long after I delivered the shipment of drugs on Young's flatbed truck. My heart swelled with pride, knowing not only another piece-of-shit drug dealer met his end, but the poison he dealt was off the street. Did I feel sorry for his family? Somewhat—not because he was dead. Only that they lost a husband and father. In the end, the world was a better place for me having signed another client.

When my phone rang, I took it after seeing Manny's name. "J, here."

"Have you checked your account?"

"I'm looking at it now, Manny. All I can say is thanks for what you do."

"No, thank you. For everything *you* do and for a job well-done. Our employers were impressed at your speed and cleanliness."

He couldn't see my shrug. At least I hoped he couldn't. "The opportunity arose, and I took it. Besides, I'd rather not spend any more time away from home than I necessary. My bed is more comfortable than any the Best Western has to offer."

He chuckled. "I don't doubt it. I'll be in contact when another contract is tendered. How soon will you be ready?"

"Give me a week or two unless it's an emergency."

"You've got it. Rest and relax, J. We're not going to run out of clients." He ended the call abruptly.

I didn't have time to finish my shower before the shakes hit me. It wasn't something I would ever become used to, but once I returned home, I paid a physical price for the stress of taking a life—no matter the sort of bottom feeder the target may have been. It began with trembling which increased quickly, followed by vomiting and diarrhea. Anything eaten in the previous twenty-four hours would be lost. Sometimes I feared a lung or my stomach would come up. Naked, dripping, and on my knees in the bathroom, I clung to the toilet while my body ridded itself of the toll. After I was sure it was over, I crawled into bed and dragged the blankets to my neck. Always worried when I became sick, Jake curled next to me after sitting and watching my purge. Still in the throes of a response to my chosen profession, I drifted to sleep.

***

I stretched and reached out after awaking at four in the afternoon. Jake was ready and put his muzzle in my palm. I rubbed his noggin and scratched both ears before rolling to face him. "You're a good boy, Jake." Lying with his front feet crossed, my sweet guy looked down upon me as if he were royalty. "No matter how superior you are, I know you'll love me forever." He put his chin on my abdomen, reminding me of a full bladder. I stroked his head and took it as long as I could before finally racing for the toilet. Jake hadn't moved when I returned.

Slipping into clean underwear, jeans, and a tank top, I found my slippers before checking the refrigerator. No food miraculously appeared in my absence, disappointing me. I sighed before finding a can of chili. While it heated, I toasted two pieces of bread and buttered them when they were light brown. Laying one on my plate, I covered it with the hot chili, before stacking on other slice of toast and covering it, too. Over the top, I sprinkled more cheese than was healthy.

I filled Jake's dish full of dried food before sitting to eat. Having little milk left after pouring myself a glass, I softened his 4Health with the last of it.

While I instinctively craved fresh vegetables and fruit, my belly was stretched when I finished my dinner. I should have stopped at the store before leaving Salmon, but I hurried for home, knowing what the next few hours would bring. Perhaps one more day of solitude—then I'd take Jake for a ride where we would secure all the sweet carbohydrates I could eat.

Jake's ears perked up before mine. Cursing myself for forgetting to call, I took my glass of milk and walked to the front porch. Both my bags were where I left them outside the door. Somehow, I didn't want him to see them and tossed both inside. Perhaps sensing my melancholy mood, Jake sat next to me rather than running to meet his friend.

"I see you didn't take the time to call."

"An apology is in order, Mr. Pelletier. The meeting with my client went quicker than we anticipated. I've been operating on very little sleep. Quality sleep."

"Congratulations are in order then, I suppose."

Leaning against the bannister leading up to my porch caused Dawson's revolver grip to jut from its holster. It neither frightened nor worried me. A gun will only do what its user asked of it and nothing more. Mr. Pelletier didn't seem the type to murder less-than-innocent neighbors. Even those who forget to call.

"Thank you. I've done nothing but sleep since arriving home. I was finishing dinner when you parked."

"Your job appears stressful." He was right. I'd caught sight of myself in the bathroom mirror. My eyes had sunk deep into the sockets with dark rings around them.

For the first time, Dawson didn't seem in a big hurry to leave. Alarm bells went off until I corralled my paranoia. We'd been neighbors for almost eighteen months, and he'd been nothing but a gentleman, staying out of my business.

"It can be. Although this time my meeting was a slam dunk. It was over before we knew it." I almost laughed aloud, having nearly said the job was over before *he* knew it. My sense of humor was becoming macabre.

"What is it you do, exactly?" His dark eyes appeared devoid of suspicion.

My story was well-rehearsed. "I work for a company which sends me out to sign clients. The heavy lifting is done before I arrive. My specialty is to work out any last-minute kinks and ink the deal. Once the contract has been secured, my job is finished until the next time I'm needed."

"Well, sounds a bit more complicated than a farmer like me can figure out. I reckon it's good there are people in this world who do what you do."

I felt myself harden. Yes, what I did was good for the world. My job was to make sure fewer brothers and sisters, aunts and uncles, parents and even cousins became statistics in the brutal drug trade. I was the grim reaper without a conscience. Each time I swung my sickle, retribution was garnered.

"Mr. Pelletier, I was struck by a thought while flying home last night. Do you own a tractor with a plow?"

"Well…" God, I could tell his answer was going to take forever. "…Farmers seldom plow these days. Once a crop is harvested, it's disked under before planting the next. Our topsoil isn't lost like back in the old days."

"Oh," I found myself disappointed. "No one owns a plow any longer?"

"Sure, almost everyone around here does. Few use them anymore. Why? Are you thinking of plantin' your farm?" He didn't have to smile. I could see the humor in his eyes where they crinkled at the corners.

"I own twenty-six acres. It wouldn't amount to much of a crop, would it?" My mouth was a flat line as I gave him my best look of disappointment.

"No, not as most farms go. What exactly are you asking?"

"I never seem to get enough vegetables. I've been thinking of putting in a small garden. I've never raised one, but I had in mind somewhere near the garage or old machine shed." I gestured in the general direction.

"Well…" I wanted to scream when he stopped to remove his Stetson and scratch the back of his head. "I reckon what you want is a tiller to come in and bust up your topsoil. Then you need some cow-shit tossed on and tilled in. It's kind of a late start for this year, but yeah, I could at least start the semblance of a garden." He brushed an imaginary spot from his Stetson before replacing the beat-up hat on his head. Didn't take much forcing to admit it looked good on him. The sides of the brim were rolled up and the front pulled low over his eyes.

"Is it something you can do? I would be more than happy to pay for the job."

"I can do it, but don't ask me to take cash money. Around here, neighbors help out when they're needed. Someday, I'll need your help, and you'll pay me back the same way."

I kind of doubted it—unless there were speed freaks or cocaine dealers nearby. In that case, I would be more than happy to help. A bit of freelancing outside The Company as it were. A killer moonlighting as a killer. Although I smiled inside, Mr. Pelletier was none the wiser. "With all the deer and elk around here, I'll need a fence." I noticed most gardens in the area were surrounded by high structures. "Do you know anyone I can hire to build one?"

His stare made me squirm. I'd said something wrong again. Eighteen months of living in the area, and I'd yet to make a friend. It seemed I needed someone to teach me the local customs. "I reckon you misunderstood me. Putting in gardens, buildin' fences, those are the sorts of things neighbors do for one another. We don't charge for it. You buy the fencing, I have the posts, and we can get old Bill Platt down here to punch 'em in with his tractor. My attachment needs work. Once I have the ground busted up and get a load of steer-shit tilled in, we'll get the fence built. It has to be deer- and rabbit-proof."

"I meant no disrespect, Mr. Pelletier. There are fencing companies around. I thought perhaps it best to hire one after having already asked you a couple of favors."

"You can if you want to, ma'am…Miss Hampton, I mean. Except, we all worry about a woman like you out here all alone. If you hire a bunch of men, you're kind of off the beaten track. You are a tiny woman, ma'am. Unless you got some way of defending yourself, well, you're at their mercy."

By the time our neighbor left, we'd set up a day and time for him to begin work on my garden. I showed him where I thought it should be, and he managed to explain why it was a poor choice. In the end, we compromised with his promises my garden would produce all the vegetables I needed, even in the first year. Finding myself smiling while Jake and I returned inside and closed the door, the reason suddenly dawned on me.

I might be small, flat-chested, and built like a boy, but Dawson Pelletier finally noticed I was a woman.

Chapter II

Julia Marie Hampton is the name on my birth certificate given to me by my folks. If they thought it important enough, I would never consider changing it. I am thirty-two. Born and raised in northern California, my childhood was everything most Americans dream of. My parents were well-off, although not rich. They were also loving and hard-working. Gerald was a forester, and Beth was a high school assistant principal.

I was the oldest of two. My sister Meghan Alise was nine years younger. Mom called her their wonderful surprise. When I was fifteen and could think of little other than boys, Meg was almost seven and a pest. Looking back, I am horrified at how shabbily I treated her. She was a little girl who simply wanted to be near her sister, even though plenty other girls her age lived in our neighborhood. It drove me crazy to have her hovering nearby when I was talking to a boy.

Meghan was going on ten when I graduated from high school and went on to community college. After earning my AA, I transferred to Saint Mary's College of California. Meg was eleven when I moved away, and already we could see something was going on. During my junior year, I received a call from Mom. Meghan was becoming more than an unruly handful—she ran away from home. At age twelve, she was already hellbent on becoming a juvenile delinquent. Mom and Dad already received court summons to explain why Meg didn't go to school often enough. They were threatened with jail time and were at their wits end.

I worked the previous summer, but between my junior and senior years, I moved home to help with Meg. Our parents were right—she was more disobedient and self-destructive. Many times I caught her trying to sneak out at night and finally went through her personal items. I found both joints and crystal meth. My baby sister was in trouble.

She turned thirteen before I left for my senior year. I still remember the night we lay out under the stars and just talked. I learned she was no longer a virgin and lost her innocence not long after I left for the university. Meg admitted she'd developed a yen for drugs and traded sex for them. Sick with fear, I begged her to stop or at least talk with Mom and Dad—they could get her help. She agreed to speak with them, but it was to be the last time we had a sisterly connection, and I never saw her again after leaving for school.

Megan Alise disappeared when she was fourteen. Reports were forwarded to us she was seen on the streets of LA, hooking on corners. My parents and I drove there each time we got a new report, but we never saw her nor made contact. Finally, she was arrested for soliciting, possession of narcotics, and distribution. Somehow, she was bailed out before our arrival, and we missed getting hold of her once again.

Four years later, I was teaching second grade in Astoria, Oregon, when I received the call. Mom and Dad had been murdered. Worse, they were tortured, presumably for information. They never confided in me; however, police said my parents lodged several restraining orders again men who threatened them. It seemed my folks' visitors lost some of their property. Unfortunately for us, their chattel was Meghan.

Dad was a competitive shooter in trap, skeet, and IPSC, which represented practical shooting with a pistol. It was established to promote marksmanship, and because of it, he involved me in all three, too. The shooting sports were something I excelled at and enjoyed very much. It was hard to believe as the excellent shooter, man, and father he was that he would allow himself to be held hostage by people wishing his family harm.

It wasn't until later I read police reports of why Dad said and did little in defending himself. The men searching for my sister threatened not only Meghan when they caught her but my life, too. A real man will do whatever he believes will best protect his family. His decision ultimately led to his and Mom's brutal deaths.

Meg not making an appearance for our parents' funeral didn't surprise me. I put the family home for sale. When it sold, I split the proceeds and secured my sister's share in a separate account. Their savings and insurance plans were also split with Meghan's part held in escrow. Mom and Dad were extended further than I dreamed. After their deaths, I learned it was because of all the money they spent searching for my sibling. Little cash remained after they were buried.

I was twenty-six when the call came. As the last surviving member of my family, it was my duty to identify her body. When I did not recognize the emaciated form lying so white and still, DNA proved it was my baby sister. It was a devastating blow I wasn't prepared for.

With my parents' money going to me and battling a growing rage, I quit my teaching job to move back to California. Names were provided, and I made absolutely certain who the guilty parties were. Mohammed Kwanzas and Allen Park were the ones searching for Meghan and threatening my parents. Although it couldn't be proven enough to prosecute, I was certain they murdered my family. Ultimately, my sister, too. The two detectives were also sure—off the record.

Having in my possession all my family's firearms, I took Dad's Glock 17 and drove to Los Angeles. With only basic information in hand, I rented a cheap room to sleep, shower, and shit. Kwanzas and Park were my targets, and I refused to stop until they were as dead as my own family. Occasionally, I would see one or the other while surveilling but never both.

After learning where each lived, my decision was made to take Kwanzas first. He seemed to have approximately twelve prostitutes working for him and spent most of his time at a strip bar. More than once, I followed the man inside, searching for the proper place to end his life. My problem was twofold—I needed to kill him but stay out of jail long enough to also take Park. Having spent years tagging along with my father on hunts, I made my decision to treat it thusly. They were nothing but prey—dangerous prey—and I was there to hunt and kill them.

My opening came almost without realizing it nearly six months into my stalk. While nursing a beer and surveilling Kwanzas, Park came in, taking a seat at his partner's table. He was animated and angry. When he stood to leave, Kwanzas followed. Not sure what might be going on, I waited for them to return. When they didn't, I left in time to see Kwanzas' 'nineties era Cadillac pulling away from the curb. Both men were inside, and I sprinted for my car. They almost lost me, but the lowered silly pink Cadillac stood out like a beacon.

After they stopped at a street corner where one of their whores worked, Kwanzas stepped out. Following a few seconds of angry words, he punched the woman, knocking her to the ground. I watched in surprise as others standing or walking nearby refused to raise a hand. Instead, they turned their heads and ignored it. When he beat the whore to the sidewalk a second time, he dropped on her stomach with one knee. I watched with both interest and anger when he reached inside her bra and withdrew a fistful of cash. How many times did the same thing happen to my sister? After pocketing the money, he lifted the woman by the hair and threw her into the Caddie's back seat. I tagged along when Park resumed driving.

If either pimp paid attention, he would have seen the older sky-blue Honda Accord behind. Instead, through their rear window I watched as Kwanzas reached back to slap the cowering woman. Trailing them off an overpass, I continued past when they stopped underneath and parked. I pulled to the side after rounding a corner about a hundred yards away, leaving my keys in the ignition.

They were out of the car beating the hell of the woman again. I crept to within twenty paces and watched as they knocked her to the ground and began kicking. Each shouted and warned her about withholding money. The way I saw it, she was dead if it continued.

Kwanzas finally noticed me when I was within thirty feet of them. "Bitch, what you doin' here? Get your skanky ass gone, or you can have a taste." My hands were in my coat pockets as I watched them killing the woman.

"Don't you know me?" My time had come, and I wanted— needed—to savor each moment.

"Never seen you before, bitch."

I hate few things. Dislike with a ferocious intensity but seldom hate. I loathed the word *bitch*. Call me anything else, but even on good terms with me, someone using that name will earn a loose tooth or two. The traffic overhead was loud, and I used it to my advantage. The whore lay still on the ground, yet I could see her eyes open and moving about. I wanted their undivided attention, and there was only one way.

Drawing the Glock from my coat pocket, I shot Kwanzas and then Park in their knee caps. It went faster and smoother than any competition I attended or participated in. The double-tap sounded almost as one. Legs literally shot from under them, they dropped like the sacks of shit they were. Kwanzas reached for the gun under his shirt. I motioned for him to toss it when he saw me aim a follow-up. It landed ten feet away, and I darted in to kick the gun away.

"Bitch, why you go do this?" They were both struggling to put pressure on their wounds.

I shot Kwanzas in the other knee for using the word again. He screamed, and his eyes rolled back.

"Oh, shit…" Park was rocking in pain, holding his own injured leg.

"Let's start over again, shall we? I asked if either of you knew me."

"Hell, no, bit…" Kwanzas saw the muzzle sweep upward, causing him not to finish his thought.

"Does the name Hampton ring a bell?"

Both men stopped rocking for a split second before resuming. "I know lots of Hamptons." Kwanzas' teeth were gritted in pain. "Why you be shootin' me, bitch?" He worked hard to earn the next round— who was I to withhold it? It was fired at his right ankle, and the high-pitched shriek proved my bullet flew true.

The whore started to scoot away. Having her notify someone before I was ready wasn't something I wanted. I needed more time for my questions. "Stay." One word and a gesture from my gun stopped her movement.

"Don't know no Hamptons. You gotta believe me, lady." One-hole Park was a little smarter than his triple-hole partner.

"Meghan Hampton. Ring a bell?"

Both men froze for a moment before shaking their heads in tandem.

"No, we ain't knowin' no Meghan Hampton, do we, Mo?"

"Our mother was Beth Hampton. Gerald was our father. Are you sure you don't recall them? We're running out of time. If you're going to remember, you have to hurry."

Long years of contempt for women—even one with a muzzle trained on him—took over his agony-addled brain. "Goddamn it, bitch. We said we don't know 'em!"

My next went into Kwanzas' groin. One to his left hip, then the other before two more to his stomach. His eyes protruded as if attempting to escape their sockets. His breathing labored. I moved closer to be the last thing he saw on earth. We made eye contact, even though I'm not certain how cognitive he was while going into shock. My next two went into his chest and then I emptied the remainder into his head. When the action locked back, I ejected the spent magazine, rammed my spare home, and released the slide. Kwanzas' body continued to spasm while I turned my attention to Park.

"Goddamn it, lady, I'm sorry. I knew Meghan. She was hooking for Mo. I don't know nothing. She was just a crackwhore lookin' for dope."

"You killed her." I wasn't asking a question. It was a statement. "My sister...you killed her."

"Mo did, lady." His eyes searched for the whore not far away. "She was holding out on us same as this one." He jerked his chin toward her. "It weren't the first time, and he killed her when she tried to run."

I'd read the autopsy report. "One of you strangled her."

"It was Mo. I wasn't around when it went down."

"His story true?" I turned my attention to the woman who watched us, silent and wide-eyed. More whites showed around the pupils at my question, and she looked at Park before she shrugged.

"What? You're worried about this guy?" Her eyes went from me to him before returning. My next four from the new mag broke his ankles. After the first, he squirmed and made breaking the second harder. "Don't worry about your job. You're officially unemployed." It was difficult to make her hear over his screams.

"They both killed her." Her voice was deep and melodic. At one time, she may have been a beautiful woman. Now, she was used up, hard, and worn.

"My folks…what possessed you to kill my parents?" It was the biggest question haunting me.

"We didn't…" I aimed for the joint, and my next bullet shattered his hip.

"Okay, she was skimmin' from her tricks." He could barely speak over the intense pain. "When she had enough and bolted, we both figured she was going home." He made a crazy laugh sounding more like weeping. "Your dad was such a pussy…he kept crying and begging us to leave the old bitch alone." I guess he figured time was short, and he wouldn't pay a price for the word I disliked. Wrong again. He found himself with a broken elbow, and his screeches took a long minute to dissolve into whimpers. It was my mother he disparaged. *My mother.* My hate was all-consuming, and I wished I had a dull axe handy.

"So, you killed them, even though they didn't know where Meghan was." My voice was flat. Our time together was reaching its conclusion.

"We needed her back. She was a money-maker—a young, good-looking blonde."

"You didn't have to murder them. We never saw Meg again between the time she ran away at fourteen and when you killed her." Tears threatened to spill over. "You didn't have to kill them," I repeated. I ran a sleeve across my face. I didn't want my eyesight compromised.

"We were pretty sure they didn't know nothin' in the end, but hell, who cares about white folk in suburbia?" His wounds became numb enough for him to brave another laugh.

I had gained my pound of flesh. He knew his time ran out when our eyes locked. I emptied the second magazine into his head. Both men looked as though a tractor ran over their skulls. I experienced no feelings of elation nor satisfaction—no guilt, no nothing. I observed both bodies while dropping the G17 into my pocket. Not planning to where I survived my attack on the men, it was surprising to find I felt as empty as the Glock. Perhaps it would change later.

The whore was in good enough shape to drive. She sped away in the Cadillac, going in the same direction we came from. My feet were dragging as I walked to my car, realizing I was out of ammunition.

I'd thought about killing the girl. She knew my face and family name, yet she swore she was going home to see her folks. After fishing through their pockets, she left with the same cash they took from her and a bonus I'd earned for her.

Without any recollection as to how I got there, I somehow found myself closing the door of my rented room. I convulsed and collapsed to the floor. It was as if I were having a seizure while I spasmed on the dirty worn carpet. Then came puking, and such a purging it was, wetting and shitting my pants in the process. Not having eaten much, I was vaguely aware of surprise when my stomach brought up partially digested food. The vomiting continued until I lost consciousness.

Without family or close friends, I had nowhere to go. My folks' home sold…the memories of it soiled. I possessed little outside of an apartment and a comfortable bank account. The idea that my harebrained scheme of retribution would work wasn't something I seriously contemplated. Vengeance needed to be extracted for my family, but never did I expect it to spare my life.

Waking sometime later—I didn't know whether it was minutes or hours—I found the sickness gone from my body. Dragging myself upright, I disrobed and struggled into the shower, coming out only after the water turned cold. Both the vomit and my clothes were left on the front room floor. I crawled into bed naked and passed out again.

Banging on my door woke me. It was light inside my room, telling me either I hadn't slept long, or I'd slumbered until the following day. Stepping into sweat bottoms and pulling on a matching hoodie, I decided to answer, if only to stop the banging. Inserting another magazine into my Glock, I pulled the slide back and released it, chambering a hollow point. I slid it into my thick pullover's ambidextrous pocket, and my nose wrinkled when I stepped around the vomit. It was soaked into the old carpet and what remained was dried, telling me a day passed. Checking the peephole, I saw a man facing the door, looking down. He wore a gray sweater and seemingly uninterested in anything around him. I didn't think he looked official, yet he was knocking on my door, and a whore who witnessed killings knew my name.

"Yes?" The door was secured with a heavy chain, and I cracked it open but wasn't prepared for what came next. Putting his shoulder into it, the man easily broke through with wood exploding inward. It threw me backward. I landed in the half-dried puke, the Glock falling from the loose fabric to land beside me.

"Don't touch it." The warning in his voice explained more than the three words. I didn't have to look up to realize he would kill me.

Closing my door while never taking his eyes away, my visitor faced me. In his hand was a gun like none other. I knew the action and frame to be a Ruger MKIV, yet I'd never seen a business end like was on it. From a normal barrel, it brandished a big muzzle. It finally dawned on me the gun had a silencer threaded on. His eyes flicked around my rented room. With no reaction to its dinginess, he took a seat on the tattered couch.

"You're welcome to sit." The man gestured with his assassin's weapon to my single wooden chair. "Leave the pistol. I'm not ready to kill you…yet."

I wasn't surprised. He'd invaded the motel room to end me. To be perfectly honest, I was ready. Everything I loved in life was gone. It astonished me how quickly I accepted my impending death. Following his direction, I got onto the chair. "If you're here to murder me, go ahead and get it over with."

If ever I saw a gray man, he sat across the tiny room from me. Perhaps five-eight or nine, he didn't weigh much more than a buck fifty. His features were bland and unremarkable. With mousy brown hair cut neither long nor short, he wore a standard baseball cap with no logo. In blue jeans, a long-sleeved gray sweater, and standard black tennis shoes, no one would ever notice if he passed by. Even his eyes were the neutral achromatic color of slate. He chuckled at my statement. "Whether you live or die is up to you. You'll make the decision…not me."

"Then get the hell out of here and leave me alone."

His smile didn't reach his grayish eyes, and I learned what the old saying really meant. It ended at the corners of his mouth, and he seemed more predator than human. I felt he was measuring where to drive a bullet into my body.

He could have passed for a machine. "Julia Marie Hampton, age twenty-seven. You grew up north of here, south of the Oregon border. After graduating from high school with a 3.9 GPA, you went on to earn your associate degree at the Yreka campus of the College of the Siskiyous. You finished with a bachelor's degree in education from Saint Mary's College of California. After hired at an Astoria, Oregon, primary school, you taught second grade four years. You had one lover and lived with him fourteen months before he was hired to manage a salmon cannery in Juneau, Alaska."

I stared openmouthed. Not even my parents knew of Samuel. He and I had a relationship of convenience and little else. Offered a job he couldn't turn down, we wished the other well, and I'd not seen him since. We didn't even kiss goodbye. Instead, I shook his hand at the front door after his car was loaded.

"Your parents, Gerald and Bethany Hampton were murdered. Not long afterward, your sister Meghan was also found murdered. Having a problem with drugs, she ran away at the age of fourteen and became involved in prostitution."

"Are you a detective?" I could think of no other reason he would know so much about my family and life.

"In a way. I like to think of myself as a hunter." His gaze never left mine, and I felt my skin crawl. I was little more than an insect to be glanced at, while he decided whether to step on or over me. "Perhaps an exterminator would be a better explanation."

"Look, asshole, if you're here to exterminate me, do it now. Otherwise, you're boring me to death." It was difficult to maintain anger after accepting my demise.

"You began searching for Mohammed Kwanzas and Allen Park almost six months ago after quitting your job and moving to Los Angeles. Yesterday afternoon upon the conclusion of your hunt, you terminated both. Their manner of death indicated extreme retribution, rather than efficiency. Have I missed anything?"

I felt a burst of satisfaction. "The whore. You missed the whore."

His lips finally pulled back, and I saw teeth reminding me of a shark. His chuckle held no humor.

"Miss Paula Kaine currently resides in a Los Angeles mortuary. I miss nothing." The double entendre was obvious. His great white teeth remained in the open, and I felt the sudden need to run screaming from the room.

"You killed her?"

"When Miss Kaine left you, presumably after making a promise to not go to the police, she drove to the nearest precinct." My eyes widened. This man knew much more than I could imagine. "She was picked up before going inside and helped into the next world…one I hope is much kinder to her." His predatory teeth were hidden again, and I wondered if it was because of regret. "Rest assured your secret is safe."

My mind was reeling. "I don't understand. What is it you want from me?"

"What I want is irrelevant. My employers would like to hire you."

"I still don't understand."

"I was hired to do the job you performed admirably yesterday, albeit sloppily and with a little too much…shall we say, exuberance? During my hunt, I discovered someone else was tracking them. After reporting it, I was ordered to back off and observe. I did, and now here we are." His face didn't change expressions, yet I was distinctly aware of his smug inner pleasure.

"Yes, and now here we are."

"You're wondering who I am, who I work for, and why they wanted your victims dead." It was as if he reached in and plucked the questions from my mind. I didn't answer for a moment, trying in vain to gather my thoughts. Finally, I gave a curt nod. "I work for a large group of wealthy businessmen who are tired of the government allowing the drug trade to prosper. Businesses ultimately pay for it in lost revenues from shoplifting, break-ins, and strong-arm robberies. A day finally came when a saturation point was reached, and a syndicate…for lack of a better term…was formed to tackle the issue. There are different departments inside this cabal which address the separate aspects to the drug trade."

I shook my head, having difficulty absorbing what he was trying to explain. "I don't get it."

"There are the bottom feeders…the ones who deal their poison to reduce the costs of their addiction. Then come the smaller dealers who can almost make a living but never quite do. They tend to dabble in both pornography and prostitution, such as the two unfortunate souls you sent home yesterday." Shark teeth were exposed again. "Above those are the real distributors…the ones who take large quantities and parse them out to the smaller dealers. However, at the top are the importers in whom we are most interested. Seldom do we go out of country, though it sometimes happens, and there is a department for it."

"What does all this have to do with me?"

"It is very simple. After coming to our attention, I'm here to offer you a job."

\*\*\*

Unlike most occupations, I had no application process. Instead, they watched me from afar, and the way I dealt with Kwanzas and Park was my informal interview. My employers didn't conduct any formal training—I was paired with a faceless person on the other end of the phone. In a way, I was lucky. Manny was mine from the beginning. I hoped he had another livelihood of some sort, because my first jobs were the bottom feeders outliving their usefulness. Their lives were worth less than five thousand, sometimes only twenty-five hundred. Manny called me with their names, descriptions, places of business, and home addresses. If caught, there was little chance of me giving up any important information. Should I be unfortunate enough to know something, it was clear I wouldn't live long enough to become a threat to The Company.

My guts were churning after I received my first appointment to sign a client. Manny was dispassionate and simply recited the needed information. It came only a few weeks after meeting the gray man. I never learned his name. Upon verbal agreement to join their organization, a Zurich bank account was provided for me. I was taught to access it and found they started me with ten thousand seed money. I encountered personal costs, and they paid them all. I only needed to call in the amount. From plane tickets to gas and food costs, anything having to do with signing a client was covered. My word was good. They didn't want a paper trail. Even the expense of firearm purchases was covered along with ammunition. I was encouraged to buy and shoot exorbitant amounts, and I followed through.

For a moment after my phone rang, I thought my guts were going to spew my recently finished breakfast. I answered using the name I decided to work under. "J."

"Manny here. San Francisco, Albert Price, male, aged thirty-two. African American, five-eleven, approximately one-hundred-forty pounds. He's covered in colorful tattoos from his ears to the tips of his fingers but not his chest or back. Place of residence is 212 Booker Avenue, Southwest, in San Fran." A beep on my phone indicated a picture.

I caught my breath. "When?"

"ASAP." He took pity on me, because Manny suddenly sounded human. "J, this piece of garbage is only a bottom feeder. Still dangerous, so be careful, but he's a lowlife without any real family nearby."

"Thanks, Manny. I'll call after I've signed him." I didn't have the chance for more. The call ended abruptly.

I drove to the bay area from where I rented an apartment in the outskirts of Petaluma. Not sure what to do, I drove directly to 212 Booker Avenue, SW. Across the street was a dilapidated home with many of its windows boarded. No one lurked nearby, and I took the time to find a place to eat. I wasn't particularly hungry, so I ordered a half sandwich and a cup of soup to settle my queasy stomach. I picked at the sandwich and finally tossed it into the soup when I saw it almost dark. The time to act had arrived. I paid my bill and hurried to my car.

Driving past the house on Booker Avenue, I was surprised to see my client seated on the front porch under a single hanging bulb. Perhaps he waited to make a drug deal, but the reason meant nothing to me. He was an easy mark from sixty feet away. Glancing up and down the street as I passed, I stopped to screw the suppressor on my Ruger 10-22. It wore an adjustable scope I turned to four-power before inserting the magazine and working the action. Using standard velocity lead ammunition, I was ready.

I swung around the block and idled back. One pedestrian strolled along on the sidewalk behind me. My client was still there and watched me with interest. I lowered the passenger window after parking on the opposite side of the street. Without a light inside my car, there was no way he could see me raising the rifle to my shoulder. Centering the crosshairs above the bridge of his nose, I squeezed the trigger without thought or remorse. This was the same sort of bastard who introduced my sister to the drugs that ultimately led to her and our parents' deaths. The only sound my rifle made was the clacking of the bolt extracting the empty and slamming another cartridge home. No one beyond ten feet away could have heard it.

Leaned back in a soft chair, my client's only movement was his jaw relaxing to drop open. Seeing an opportunity, I placed the crosshairs in the center of his open mouth. Four more shots, and each one drove through to either his brainstem or spine. I wasn't sure of the exact angle while shooting slightly uphill. Seeing no motion, I drove away, satisfied with my marksmanship and taking another predator off the streets. I made the call after I was on the freeway driving north.

"Manny, here."

"J. Our client is signed." The telltale click followed by dead air told me the message was received.

The shaking hit me after I walked into the relative safety of my apartment and set my work tools on the kitchen table. Not expecting it, I collapsed sideways to my couch as I shook uncontrollably. My stomach rebelled the moment my muscles relaxed and gave me a chance to race for the bathroom. I crawled into the shower and turned on the water, letting it pelt my clothes. The water worked to wash my vomit into the drain. I certainly didn't want to lie in it again. I eventually disrobed while still in the shower and rinsed myself. Sleep overtook me the moment my head touched the pillow.

My dreams, rather than filled with death or butchery, were instead of my parents and Meghan. They were good memories of years gone by and sheer happiness. I woke smiling with chills of how real they were running down my spine.

Hoping for the best but fearing the worst, I logged into my secure server and checked my Zurich account. Exactly as promised, Albert Price was worth forty-five hundred, less Manny's twenty percent. It was deposited not long after I made my call. I suppose my smile was shark-like and very similar to that of the gray man.

Perhaps I found my niche in life.

Chapter III

I asked my favor at the beginning of May and was surprised to find Mr. Pelletier finished my garden plot before month's end. I wanted something small, perhaps twenty feet by twenty feet, but he swore I'd soon want it enlarged, so he made it twenty by forty and grumbled when I stopped him from doubling it again. He capitulated but insisted I was "a quarter bubble off plumb."

Manny gave me three weeks before ringing. I was watching my neighbor come up the drive with a trailer filled with what he called farmer magic, when the distinctive tone identifying my handler interrupted. "J, here." My voice was monotone as usual.

"Manny. Are you ready for more work?"

"When and where?"

"This one is big. Please take a few days to give it thought before accepting or discarding."

"Agreed." I continued observing Mr. Pelletier back the flatbed with short wooden sidewalls holding cow manure to the end of my garden.

The way he wedged it in between buildings and vehicles was impressive, yet I didn't appreciate his ability as I should've. My attention was on Manny: "A car dealership in Laredo, Texas, is boosting its bottom line by importing agricultural imports. Enormous quantities of cocoa and poppy seed." Manny's euphemisms for cocaine and heroin didn't require rocket science to figure, yet I understood the need for obscurity despite the secure line. "The owner needs signed; you have third right of refusal."

"Sounds easy enough, so what's the catch?" Mr. Pelletier jumped onto the trailer without a glance toward the house.

"This client is a woman. Do you have qualms signing a female? She has four kids between the ages of six and eighteen. Two others have turned it down."

I wondered if the gray man still worked for The Company. Killing a woman didn't make him blink. I shuddered when I remembered the way he'd casually mentioned the whore wouldn't turn me in—only because he got to her before she talked. "No," I said slowly. "Makes no difference to me. If our firm deems a client should be signed, who am I to dispute sexual equality?" I took a deep breath and hoped I was right.

"Are you sure?"

"As you suggested, I'll take a day or two to sleep on it, all right?" The call ended with my answer. No reason for idle chitchat—we would never be besties at a luncheon.

Mr. Pelletier didn't look when I jumped to the bed of his trailer to help shovel. I worked hard, but I couldn't come close to his level. He was so much bigger and stronger, my efforts were little more than token next to his. When we finished—probably in less than a half hour—I was drenched in sweat, and my blouse clung to my back.

"You're a pretty damn good worker, ma'am." Dawson pushed the last of the manure from his trailer with a shop broom.

"Thank you. I'm fairly sure tomorrow my muscles will remind me what we did." I was most worried about my hands, even inside a new pair of White Ox gloves. I certainly didn't want blisters when I was preparing to ink a client.

"You need to eat, lady. I'm not sure I've seen anyone quite so skinny as you. Instead of pickin' at food, you need to treat steaks and sandwiches like they did you wrong. Hell..." He squinted at me. "...you barely break the five-foot mark, and I'll bet you've never seen a hundred pounds in your life, have you?"

"I'm five-one and a half I'll have you know." I raised to my tiptoes and stretched my neck upward. "And I've been over ninety-five more times than I can count." I gave him my haughtiest sniff before dissolving into a giggle. The girlish laugher almost made me sick. It sounded like it came from a lovesick schoolgirl, and I was nothing of the sort.

"A veritable giant, ma'am. I'm sure bugs and small rodents give you a wide berth." His tone was light, and I appreciated his attempt at levity. If only he knew. I was more of a monster to those who were the scourge of mankind than to bugs and rodents.

"Would you like to stay for a glass of sun tea or cup of coffee? Perhaps a sandwich?"

"No, ma'am, but thanks. I need to till this shit in and load my tractor, so I can start on my own place."

I felt bad immediately. "I've kept you from your own garden?"

"Not really. It's still a few weeks early to be planting. I need another load of manure. I'm ready after it's tilled in. It was a mite bit more important to get your ground busted."

When Mr. Pelletier descended my driveway with his tractor loaded securely on the flatbed trailer, my mind was no longer on him. It was already fifteen hundred miles south in Laredo on the Mexican border.

***

I waited from Sunday until Tuesday before I made the call.

"Manny here."

"J. I'll take it."

"Are you sure?" His tone changed one hundred eighty degrees. Suddenly no longer a business partner, he tried to dissuade me. "This is like when you see something bad and wish you didn't. You can't unsee this, J." He was begging me to reconsider.

"I have my reasons. Tell me more. Is this a big payday?"

"One-eighty-five with a twenty-five percent bonus if done before the end of the week." My eyes opened wide, and I swallowed at the amount. It was difficult to remain cool in the face of so much money. "She's valuable because no one can get close. The sheer volume of agricultural products the woman imports is staggering. It seems the Mexican government or someone high up is giving cover and keeping her safe."

It was already Tuesday, allowing two and a half days to meet with the client and sign the contract. The payoff was larger than I could have imagined. It was twenty times what most bottom feeders brought in. The Company must be pleased with my results.

Dawson didn't seem bothered when I asked him to take care of my animals for a few days again. I was almost jealous of the way he and Jake were bonding. Manny purchased my ticket from Missoula to San Antonio while I drove to Salmon. Once in Texas, I would pick up my rental and drive to Laredo.

I finally learned what made Mrs. Arnold Slade, aka Monica Slade, worth so much. She was a mini television celebrity on both sides of the Rio Grande, singing, dancing, and selling her cars. I watched a few—some had all four daughters singing with her. There would be an uproar if I were successful.

I wasn't sure what to expect and took my reliable and suppressed .22/45. If I were lucky, it would be one shot, in and out, flying home with a fatter bank account. Manny could easily rearm me if circumstances on the ground dictated that I needed a different firearm. Six hours after leaving my Idaho home, I was driving away from San Antonio in an F250 diesel. It was a four door, and the truck provided all the room I needed. I set the cruise control on sixty-five in an area posted seventy and drove south on Interstate 35.

Manny booked me for a week at the Red Roof Inn near Laredo International Airport. It was cheap and clean on the bottom floor with easy ingress and egress. I made myself comfortable with a box of KFC for dinner. Mr. Pelletier articulated what I knew intimately— my bodyweight needed to increase. It was difficult to admit to myself that I'd never cracked ninety-six. After he left, I weighed, and the scales hovered over ninety-one. My collarbones and hipbones stuck out, and I didn't even need a training bra. I resolved to find a way to eat until I broke one hundred. It would be nice to actually have boobs. Men liked boobs. Someday, if I caught one without shooting him first, I might have something to jiggle for him.

I was eager to start the chase. My resolve to take a shower and retire early evaporated the moment I finished eating. I figured the greasy dinner would quickly make its way through my system and napped until it was time to race for the toilet. After inserting a loaded magazine into my pistol and chambering a round, it was time to scout the lay of the land. The hunt began.

***

Two days of learning my quarry brought me no closer to a solution. Monica Slade lived in a McMansion inside a gated community. Her husband, Arnie, would have been a slam-dunk to sign. He drove the youngest two girls to school. The older pair had their own personal vehicles. I would not have considered either Mustang appropriate for young women. As near as I could tell, Mr. Slade did little except chauffer and spend the rest of his time working out at a local gym. Perhaps my employers wanted to offer him and his kids a chance at a safer—if not better—life. More's the pity I'd not been offered the opportunity for a true double.

Very little inroad was made into inking a deal with my client. I followed her once to Nuevo Laredo over Juarez-Lincoln Bridge. After closing within range, I found she had two daughters with her. They stopped before crossing back and entered a beauty salon. I wasted three hours of watching and complaining to myself before they went straight home. Depressed over staying longer so far from home, it was time to change tactics. I called Manny and discussed it with him while sitting outside the dealership. It was almost dark, and my client was still inside. I didn't dare get closer. Cameras were the bane of my existence. "Manny here."

"J. I'll be past the bonus phase soon. There hasn't been an opportunity yet."

"The Company can call in a different employee if you're not certain about this client. There's no shame in it." I got the feeling he really didn't want me to do it.

"It's not that. The fact she's a woman doesn't bother me. She's always surrounded by others. I've had one opening so far, but she had two daughters with her. I wasn't going to sign her with kids present."

"Good girl." I heard the satisfaction in his voice. "Don't worry about the bonus—her signature is everything. What can I do for you on this end?"

"How long would it take to find an M4? I want it scoped and suppressed." A keyboard clacked in the background as he searched. A light came on outside the showroom, and I perked up when I saw a new Mustang leaving. Only one person drove it to work. "Hold that thought, Manny. I'll call you back in five."

I put on my hazard lights and popped the hood latch. It was a heavy son of a gun, taking all my strength to lift until I climbed onto the front bumper. If lady luck smiled, the quarry would come to me. My pistol was stuffed down the back of my jeans with the grip protruding.

Monica Slade came out of the dealership in a hurry. The car fishtailed when she shifted, the tires barking and leaving rubber marks behind. She wouldn't have stopped if I hadn't run onto the centerline, waving my hands. Dropping gears hard after seeing me, she screeched to a stop only a few yards from where I waited. She revved the engine and backed away. The car was loud, and I couldn't hear her when she lowered the window, forcing me to shout. "Can you help me?" No others were inside when I used the opportunity to squat and look.

"Don't you have a phone, you silly bitch?"

Even if I weren't there to sign her, my least favorite word coming from her mouth would've been enough. "Are you Monica Slade?" I put as much excitement into the question as I could muster. Where we met was a hundred yards from a main thoroughfare. Any driver trying to pass would have to turn around at the dealership gates. It wasn't likely after hours.

"Yes." Her face twisted with distaste. "Now move your ass so I can…"

I drew my gun and held it at my side where she couldn't see anything but the muzzle. My shot went into her temple or very close to it. She seemed surprised before letting her last breath out. She'd already been leaning in my direction and died slumped against the door. Four more taps to the top of her head, and my client was signed. While she spasmed, I slammed the hood and started my truck.

I love speed dial and punched it the moment I was driving north. "Manny here."

"J. Get me a plane out of San Antonio, Corpus Christi, or even Victoria if you have to. The ink on the contract is still dripping."

"Good work. How long until you're packed and ready?"

"Give me fifteen."

"I'll call you in sixteen. She's signed within the allotted time. Congratulations."

He couldn't get a flight from San Antonio, and I flew out of Corpus Christi instead. I stopped by a dumpster on the way to my plane and tossed a bag containing my wig. An hour wait followed check-in, but soon enough I was riding high in the night sky in a 737. I was forced to catch a connecting flight in Portland on the way to Missoula, putting me in Montana past midnight. After a quick call to Manny, one that made me realize he was human, I had a room waiting a few miles from the airport. For the first time since working together, it was obvious I woke him. He needed a moment to gather his thoughts. I was chuckling about it at home when the shaking and puking started.

***

I had tossed the numbers around in my head, yet I was stunned to see them. Signing my client paid one-eighty-five, the bonus a little less than fifty. I was left with the original amount after Manny took his cut. To sit in my robe with Jake by my side and see it in my account was exciting. I leaned back after logging off and sipped my coffee while I considered.

I'd not spent anything deposited into my offshore account. Every nickel of each contract still collected interest. Before my last two clients were signed, I was drawing interest on three-eighty-five. After adding another one-fifty and one-eighty-five, I was looking at a number I could never have imagined: Over three quarters of a million dollars. Interest brought it very close to eight hundred thousand. The Company promised to help with repatriation when I retired or needed to dip into savings.

When my folks were buried and their place sold, a little over three hundred thousand remained. Their house was worth almost a million, but they'd refinanced it in the search for Meghan. I expected The Company knew why I wasn't bothering with my Zurich account. They probably knew my personal account balance better than me.

I needed a place to call my own after hired by The Company. One very private and quiet. Few neighbors were good—none would have been better. In my search, I found what might be considered perfect. Twenty-six acres halfway between the wide spot of North Fork and Gibbonsville, Idaho. The property included a small house with a detached garage, a leaky carport, and a partially caved-in machine shed. The former residents were unable to make their payments, and I purchased it from the bank in Salmon.

The asking price was within reason. I offered, they counter offered, and I countered again with cash. After putting my name on the dotted line, I slid a cashier's check over for one-fifty. The payment depleted my savings, but not a penny was owed to a bank. Afterward, I loaded a rented U-Haul for the trip, because only a few mementoes and possessions remained from my previous life. It took me six weeks for the move, during which I cost myself and Manny money with lost clients.

The house was small but larger than any apartment I'd rented. Only my folks' place—where I'd spent my childhood—was bigger. My new home was a little less than twelve hundred square feet, old, with dingy wallpaper. Even the windows were ancient, and I learned the hard way they didn't keep the cold out. It came with two bedrooms and one bath. I took the largest, and the other sat empty with only a bed.

I speculated about the kitchen while I drank my early morning go-juice. It was a place with older basic appliances, cracked linoleum, and torn wallpaper. If better clientele were going to pay more, it might be time for refurbishing. Perhaps even tear it down and build a new home. Even so, like the gray man, I wanted no curious eyes drawn to me. I hoped to teach again after I retired. Living on my parents' dwindling money, I pinched pennies wherever possible. A job would give me something to do along with a visible income to show the feds.

The living room was small and the kitchen smaller yet. The more I considered it, a wall could be torn out, making the area seem much larger. It would still appear as a dilapidated home from outside. Appearances—or lack thereof—meant everything in my line of work. If I could find the proper contractor—one not local—perhaps it was time to gather bids.

*\*\**

It was time to begin working my garden. The weather warmed, and from what I'd read, root crops could be planted. Dressing in jeans, tucked in blouse, and hiking boots, I loaded Jake into the Jeep. I wore Dad's G17 on my belt, covered with a light sweatshirt. Mr. Pelletier mentioned the feed store where I bought animal food also carried seeds in the spring.

It was easy to pass for a boy if dressed correctly. Before leaving for town, I dragged a brush through my thick, unruly, dirty blonde hair and plopped on a baseball cap. Unless I used eyeliner, it was difficult to see my eyebrows or eyelashes. My hair was short enough to barely show from under my hat, so it didn't hurt my feelings when the clerk offered assistance. "Can I help you, son?" I was looking at their potato bins and racks of seed and turned to smile, causing his eyes to widen in recognition. "Oh, shoot, ma'am. Can I do anything for you?" he stammered.

"I'm putting in a garden this year. It's my first, and I need someone to steer me in the right direction."

"What are you hoping to grow?" His face was still crimson.

I handed him my list. Potatoes, onions, carrots, lettuce, spinach, peas, and rutabagas—my list was lengthy. Included were raspberry and strawberry plants, two of my favorites.

A man from the back was loading the feed I purchased, when a familiar voice sounded from the porch. "Howdy, neighbor."

I turned to see Dawson about to enter the store. "Mr. Pelletier. I can't thank you enough for taking care of my animals while I was gone...especially Jake."

"Just bein' neighborly, ma'am."

Before he continued inside, I had an epiphany. "Mr. Pelletier, if you haven't eaten, I'd love to buy dinner to show my gratitude. Knowing Jake has someone who will be there for him takes a lot off my mind. Please, it would make me feel as if I've repaid you in some small way."

"Well..." I broke into a smile while he took forever to make up his mind. "...I ain't ate yet, so yeah, I'll take you up on the offer."

"Excellent. We'll eat anywhere you prefer."

He strolled across the boardwalk to stand next to my Jeep. Jake's head was hanging out the window, and Dawson took time to pet him. "There's a good little deli just down the street a bit." He seemed hesitant.

"Not sandwiches, Mr. Pelletier. A place with steaks and man food." I made a muscle with my biceps. "You tell me I'm skinny, so how can you expect me to eat smoked turkey and bean sprouts?"

"You're right, ma'am. There's one helluva steakhouse servin' good beer across the river on the right. It's called The Jumping Salmon. I'll pick up my feed and meet you there."

\*\*\*

He was right. The steaks were good, the beer cold, and the ambience exciting. Sawdust and hulls littered the floor, and a bucket of peanuts graced each table. After cracking them open, we were to discard the remains underfoot. The local band was pretty good, but I didn't like how it made conversing difficult. We were sometimes forced to shout to make ourselves heard. "Do you come here often?" I repeated my question before he understood.

"Not anymore, ma'am. I tend to stay closer to home."

"I wish you'd call me by my given name instead of 'ma'am,' Mr. Pelletier."

He frowned for a moment. "What the hell is your first name...um...ma'am?"

I gave what I hoped was his last formality a smile. "Julia. Julia Marie Hampton." I thrust my hand across the table. I'm pleased to make your acquaintance, Mister...?" I knew it but made him introduce himself anyway.

"Pelletier...Dawson Pelletier." He took my hand firmly and shook it like he would a man. "Friends call me Dawson."

I pulled my fingers back and forced myself not to rub them. My neighbor possessed a grip of iron. "How long have you lived in the area, Dawson?"

He was quiet a moment. "All my life, I reckon...with a few years gone here and there.

"Is there no Mrs. Pelletier, or do you not wear a ring?" I'd called his cellphone a dozen or more times. A woman never answered, but I was curious.

"Nope, ain't no wife at my house. How 'bout you? Ever been hitched?"

"No men in my life." I took a pull from my beer mug and glanced around the room. "My job makes it difficult to have any sort of relationship."

"Kids? Nowadays folks don't get hitched to have cracker crunchers."

"No kids, either. A child would be a bigger hindrance than a husband."

"Not feeling the ol' clock tickin?"

I instinctively pulled back. "How old do you think I am?" I struggled to hide how offended I felt. It was the first time someone posed a question about my age.

He shrugged, unconcerned. "I dunno. Thirty…maybe thirty-five?"

"Thirty-two not long ago." I took a long pull on my beer mug. "How old are you?"

"Thirty-eight next month."

"Christ, we're both getting old." Dawson's eyebrows raised when we ordered our steaks. He wanted his medium rare. I asked mine to be cooked rare. He and our server laughed at my request. "Just knock off the horns, wipe his behind, and chase him across the griddle."

The meat was cooked perfectly when it came. My neighbor wasn't sure he didn't see mine squirm when I cut into it. Nor was he shy in telling me. The steak was better than it had any right to be—the flavor excellent. I could see myself coming back often if all their chefs were so proficient.

"Been holding out on us, Pelletier?" A man younger than Dawson spun a chair and sat on it with the back facing our table. "Where did you come up with this good-looking woman?"

Dawson gestured with his fork. "Julia Hampton, Scotty Rich." He pointed his utensil directly at our intruder. "Try to tone it down. She's new to the area. Last thing we need is you scarin' her off."

"I'm not going to scare her. Hell, she's sitting with you and not running away screaming, is she?"

I held my hand out. "It's nice to meet you, Mr. Rich. Have you known Dawson long?"

Scotty grinned at my dinner mate after he released me to eat again. "Huh. Manners and everything and still not fleeing for her life. To answer your question…" He made it a point to look at my left hand. "…*Miss Hampton*, I've known this mangy coyote since I moved here." He clapped Dawson on the shoulder. "What's it been? Fifteen, twenty years?"

"Seems longer," my dinner companion said, ignoring everyone while he worked at making his meal disappear.

"What is it you do, Mr. Rich?" I caught him watching with morbid fascination as I ate the bloody steak.

"I own the Wannabe Rich? guide service."

"Wannabe Rich? Really? Did I detect a question mark? Where do you guide to?"

He moved his chair around the table so we could hear better. "Fish on the Salmon. Deer, elk, bear, goat, sheep, and moose back in the Frank Church Wilderness."

"Sounds like fun." I meant it. To spend time in the wilderness to harvest big game animals seemed like the perfect life.

"If by fun you mean a lot of work, then yeah. Especially when I have an agreeable client." My smile was meant to be internal, but judging by his reaction, it must have slipped out. If only my clients were more agreeable to being signed. It would make my life much easier. "What is it you do for a living?" Scotty was not only uninvited but paying me too much attention, hanging on my every movement and word.

"I work for a large corporation. They send me to meet customers our company has interest in. It's my duty to take care of any potential bugs, then sign them."

"You've got to be kidding. Sounds too easy. My clients bitch at me when *they* miss a shot."

"Yep, that's it. Sometimes finalizing and getting their signature can be difficult. There are always some who have to be dragged kicking and screaming to the dotted line." Even though a verb rather than a noun, I gritted my teeth at his utterance of the word I disliked so much.

"Would you like to dance?" Scotty said.

Sitting back in my chair, I took the young man's measure. He was shorter than Dawson, perhaps an inch or two under six feet. Thicker and more muscular than his friend, Scotty wore close-cropped sandy blond hair. He, too, wore a Stetson, although it appeared to be a Sunday go-to-town hat. I found it difficult to judge his age. Where my neighbor was dour and quiet, Scotty was as chatty as a child.

The idea gave me butterflies. "I'm not really one for dancing." Besides, Dad's G17 was belted to my waist.

"You don't have to do much but hang on if you don't know the steps." Scotty wasn't begging but made it clear he was hopeful.

"Maybe next time. Also, I'm not sure you're old enough to be in a lounge." My grin took the sting away from his hurt look.

"Lady, I'll bet you a hundred bucks I'm older than you."

"What if I don't have that much?" It made me sick to hear the coy note in my voice. The woman sitting with these two men wasn't anyone I'd known for years.

"Then you have to give me a kiss." Oh, my. This one was forward. "Right here on the cheek." He pointed directly to where he wanted it. "And a dance. Just one, and you get to choose the tempo."

"It's a deal." I stuck my hand out, and we shook again. "I turned thirty-two at the beginning of this month." Seeing his surprised look, I waited for my money.

"Not so fast, Miss Hampton." My heart sank as his smile grew. "I turned thirty-two in February." If his grin got any bigger, I feared the top of his head might fall off.

I looked to Dawson who moved out of the way for our server taking our dishes. He merely grunted and nodded. When I turned back to Scotty, he'd anticipated my request. A driver's license was already in his hand. I scrutinized it, finding he wasn't lying.

"Okay, you win, Scott Robert Rich. I guess at this point..." I handed his ID back. "...my only question is why aren't you an organ donor?"

The band chose that moment to go silent in preparation of their next song. Scotty and Dawson burst into laughter. Every head in the lounge turned to us, trying to see what they found so funny. A few chuckled at my table mates, while I watched them with a raised eyebrow. The friends hooted at my expense.

"Nice try, but you aren't going to change the subject, ma'am." Scotty was still laughing, gripping his chair as if to keep from falling. Dawson's elbows were on the table, and he was holding his head.

"You lost fair and square, Julia." My neighbor seemed to be siding with his friend. Bros before hos, I guessed.

Our server swung by to leave the check. Although Dawson reached for it, I was quicker. "This was my treat, Mr. Pelletier." The check was for almost seventy-five. I dropped five twenties on the table before standing.

"You're not leaving, are you?" He wasn't going to let me off easily and stood when I did.

"I'm afraid I am."

"What about our bet? You aren't welching, are you?"

"I don't remember anyone saying I had to pay up right now." A smile and the fluttering of my eyelashes were enough to get a grin back. I was in no mood to kiss a strange man nor make a fool of myself dancing. If possible, I could find a better way to make it up in the future. Maybe hire his guide service. A few thousand dollars would likely sooth any injured feelings, plus satisfy my curiosity of about the surrounding wilderness. "I pay my debts; maybe not exactly how you're hoping, but you'll be adequately recompensed."

"As long as you aren't planning on beating me out of it."

"No, this old lady needs her beauty sleep. Otherwise, I'm a fright to look at."

"I can't imagine such a thing, Julia." He took his hat off and seemed suddenly shy. "I'll bet you're a wonder to behold in the morning."

My sudden laughter caught even me by surprise. "You're right. I am one hell of a sight." I was still chuckling when the door closed behind me. It opened again before I had a chance to cross the porch to the stairs.

"Are you sure I can't talk you into just one dance?" Scotty Rich was persistent if nothing else.

"Not tonight. My buddy Jake probably thinks I'm lost as it is."

"Jake?" His voice was weak and flustered.

"Yeah, that's why I have to go. The cute guy I live with depends on me. I'll see you some other time, Scotty." I waved and left him standing on the lounge porch, watching me buckle in. I started the engine and relished the powerful V8 roaring to life. A cold and wet nose nuzzled my neck. "Don't worry, old buddy. I didn't forget about you." I backed out after patting his head and looked for the exit as my phone rang. Seeing the number, I pulled to the side and answered, my voice cold and dispassionate. "J, here."

"Manny. We have a problem."

"More customers to sign?" I wasn't mentally prepared to go on assignment so soon.

"No, this is real trouble. You need to go online and see for yourself."

"See what?"

"There's a picture of you not far from where Monica Slade's body was found."

Chapter IV

Manny was right. My face had been broadcast from every television station in and around Laredo. Personally, I thought it difficult to recognize me. The wig covered much of my cheeks and forehead. When I drove through Slade Motors lot during recon, my image was caught on a camera through the truck windshield. A glare caused them to miss my rear plate. Authorities were having difficulty identifying me or the truck. Nothing was mentioned about a rental. One reporter noted homicide detectives following other leads and persons of interest, but I was considered their most interesting lead. Taking a hard look at the photo, I thanked my lucky stars I went to Texas as a smoky-eyed blonde with contrasting dark arches penciled over nonexistent brows. For my next job, I decided to wear long false lashes and blue contacts behind glasses and top it off with a curly red wig.

Monica Slade was a big deal in south Texas. The investigation ran rampant. What could be seen of my face in the hazy photo had been posted on social media sites. Manny was right. I needed to sit back, keep my head down, and wait for her drug affiliations to come to light. After the visit to Salmon for animal feed and groceries, it would be months before I needed to leave my place. Longer, if my garden produced.

Potatoes poked through the soil before the second week of June. For the first time in years, I felt the need to tell or show a personal experience. Without anyone to take an interest in my life, I used the time to sit back, eat, and relax. Four rabbits needed slaughtered before they were too big, and the distasteful job fell to me. They were almost too old for fryers by the time I forced myself to take care of them. The little bit of meat I purchased would go much farther with my home-raised bunnies.

I am not inhuman. I'm who and what I am because of circumstances. Another life might have seen me as a fulltime teacher, perhaps even a housewife. I cried when it came time to butcher my rabbits. I sobbed before I started, during the deed, and it continued afterward. I used a heavy stick while holding the hind legs, hitting them as hard as I could on the backs of their heads to stun and kill them. My first thought was to use my .22/45. I simply couldn't bring myself to use a tool meant to stop those guilty of spreading drugs on innocent rabbits. Their deaths required more honor. Three went into the freezer. I left one in the refrigerator two days before feeling good enough to eat it. As it turned out, I cooked and ate two pieces over three days and froze the rest. It surprised me a rabbit could produce so much flavorful meat.

Mountains grew from the back of my property and rose to heights I could hardly imagine hiking. From what I understood, they were almost unbroken until reaching Highway 12 a hundred miles to the north. To the east, they ran into Montana. Where I lived was a veritable jumping off place into the wildest country the lower forty-eight offered. Thinking of Scotty and what he said about his guiding business, I again considered hiring him for a few weeks. A pack trip into the backcountry might be what I needed. Better would be if I could swap business for our bet.

My next call from Manny gave me reason to breathe a sigh of relief. My masquerade as a dark-eyed blonde with unknown height and weight was still a person of interest, but officials were uncovering Monica Slade's drug business. Situated on the border with Mexico, attention turned toward suppliers in our southern neighbor. From what Manny could discern, they initially uncovered only the tip of her iceberg. Her husband had lawyered up to protect himself from blowback. If they could prove he took part, Mr. Slade would be heading to jail for a long time. If not, I was more than willing to take him on as a client. In the near term, Manny explained, I was on vacation. Long term, The Company couldn't wait for me to work again. He also put me in touch with a money manager to diversify my overseas portfolio. I utilized The Company's server and made contact to answer questions about my goals and expectations. Once finished, I felt good about the security of my financial future—even if I didn't add another penny to the account.

I am a relatively fit woman. Skinny but always with wiry strength. Early in life, I learned my body thrived on running. Not long endurance courses but shorter and faster sprints. Since joining The Company, my body was the most effective weapon I possessed. I needed to keep up with the demands of signing clients, or it wouldn't matter what lethal mean I employed. So, I ran, jogged, tumbled, rolled, and jumped—much of the time with a firearm in my hand. Basic strength movements like free squats, pushups, and chins weren't forgotten twice per week, whether I wanted to or not.

Never disregarded was basic marksmanship. It's important to be capable of hitting a stationary target at two hundred yards with a rifle offhand. Yet it is equally or even more crucial to have the ability to engage multiple targets at close range. Although I'd never been in a firefight, the possibility was drilled into me by Manny. To date, every client I signed had been incapacitated with a single bullet. More were added as an insurance clause.

Three weeks into June, Jake and I received a visitor. After finishing my morning workout and target practice, I was searching my growing garden for errant weeds with Jake keeping me company when he looked toward the driveway and set to barking. He would have been quiet and excited if it were Dawson. Standing and stretching my back, I wiped my hands on my jeans. Wearing only my Levi's and a sleeveless top stained with sweat and dirt, my Glock was exposed on my right hip for an easy draw. Fully loaded with eighteen rounds, it gave me peace of mind. On the left were two more magazines holding another thirty-four. The weight tugged at my belt, but as the saying goes: it is better to have a gun and not need it, than need a gun and not have it. I cinched the leather belt tighter and lived with the added burden.

I didn't recognize the pickup that rattled to the side of the house and parked. It was an older standard cab Chevy with tinted windows and could use a good washing. I heard the door grind when it pushed open, and Scotty Rich stepped out. Putting his hands upon his hips, he grinned while looking around. His eyes stopped roving when they got to me. "I forgot about this old place. My dad played with some boys who lived here when he was growing up." He held a hand out for Jake to smell before petting him.

"How did you find me?" I closed the garden gate and leaned against a post ten feet away. He seemed nice enough, but who knew what lurked in the hearts of men?

"I stopped by Dawson's. Bastard gave me the third degree before he agreed to tell me. It wouldn't surprise me if he doesn't find a reason to stop by to check on my intentions before I leave. I was damned near forced to show him a picture ID, leave my driver's license, the deed to my house, and sign over my first born." Where his friend was quiet and reserved, Scotty was a natural talker.

I got a whiff of me and hoped he wouldn't get close. "What can I do for you?"

"Maybe start by explaining all the hardware?" He pointed to my holstered gun and reloads.

"Snakes. It's getting hot out." I knew in my heart the smile at the corner of my lips didn't extend upward. While not yet making me nervous, his questions raised alarms.

"You can hit a snake with a damned pistol?" Scotty's eyebrows raised, and he seemed unconvinced.

"I'm a terrible shot. That's why I carry eighteen rounds." My smile softened, if only a little.

"Give me a rifle any day. I might as well use a handgun for a boat anchor for all the good it does me."

"You still haven't said why you're here." I winced at the way my question sounded.

"It's two weeks until the Fourth of July. The town puts on a parade and a bit of a show, then fireworks after dark. Later is a dance on Main Street. Would you be interested in going?"

"Oh." I hadn't been asked out on a date since...I couldn't remember when. My mind went into overdrive searching for an excuse to say no. I decided to put it off. "Would you like to sit on the porch while I see if there's any sun tea and biscuits left?"

Rather than sit next to him as he did with Dawson, Jake elected to follow me into the house. He sat in the kitchen where he could see me but positioned himself to stare at the door. I poured two glasses of tea, drank one, and then refilled it. Weeding was thirsty work. I had biscuits left over from the night before, and I found a new jar of orange marmalade along with the butter dish. Scotty was seated and waited for me to appear again. Jake trotted hot on my heels when I packed our snacks out. I set our visitor's drink on the little porch table—the biscuits, jam, and butter next to it—before sitting. It was an old metal chair I dragged with me from the kitchen.

"This is your seat. Trade with me." Scotty suddenly realized what I brought. He stood, expecting me to exchange.

I waved my hand. "Don't worry about it. This is as comfortable as that old chair." With my ancient furniture and dilapidated house, he must have figured I was destitute. Jake took his place at my side, occasionally leaning forward and inspecting our visitor curiously.

I found it difficult to read Scotty's thoughts. We were both quiet for a bit, while we munched biscuits and drank our tea. As a woman alone, although I was introduced to Scotty by Dawson, the G17 still rode on my hip. Men and women who seemed nice enough weren't always what they professed to be. My occupation linked me to the worst the world had to offer, and my life experiences couldn't be easily ignored.

"Do you like it out here?" He didn't glance at me, instead familiarizing himself with my front porch and driveway.

"I love it. It's quiet, and no one bothers me. Did I mention it's quiet?" I took a deep breath of the sage-flavored breeze.

His smile was quick, his eyes flashing with appreciation. "You live alone, don't you?"

The same alarm bells that would go off in any woman's head clanged wildly in mine. "Nope, I have Jake and my friend…" I patted the Glock.

"So, this is the infamous Jake." He smiled weakly. "My question didn't come out right, did it? I apologize. What I meant to ask is there's no one in your life, is there?"

As awkwardly as he possibly could, Scotty was asking if I enjoyed a romantic relationship with someone. "No, right now I'm pretty much married to my job and coworker. I haven't had time for a real life." A piece of my biscuit broke off and tumbled to the floor. Jake didn't bother to ask permission and wouldn't look back when I stared at him.

"You must do all right at it, having bought the old Marshall place."

"It pays the bills, but as you can see, not much more." I stabbed my thumb over my shoulder at siding needing a serious scrape and paint job. Let him think what he would. The interior was even shabbier.

Jake sat up, and a few moments later, Scotty chuckled. "Told you." He pointed at the Ford barreling our way.

Dawson parked behind his buddy's truck and stepped out. He appeared as always, the no nonsense man who seldom smiled. His first words were to Scotty. "Don't you have trails to clean or something?" The Colt hung from his belt as usual. Jake met him at the top of my steps, docked tail wagging furiously. Getting his ears scratched and a few kind words made him even happier.

Scotty wasn't backing down. "Don't you have fields to plow or hay bales to buck?" The two bickered like the best friends they were.

Dawson didn't miss anything. Scotty and I were still seated on the porch eating and drinking. "How's the biscuits?" My neighbor came up the steps and took one for himself without asking.

"There's butter and marmalade. I have more tea if you're interested." I left my chair for Dawson at his nod and hurried into the kitchen.

My heart skipped a beat when I assessed the last minutes. Two men stopped at my house for the first time in perhaps ever, and I can't work hard enough to make them comfortable. After watching my mother take care of guests during my formative years, the thought of following in her footsteps never entered my mind.

They were still bickering when I reappeared with another chair and tea. Dawson nodded his thanks and smiled, waiting for Scotty to finish. Dragging another chair outside my kitchen door, I put Jake between the men and me and listened to their jabs. "I thought maybe she'd enjoy a day in town with me, farmer."

Dawson grunted. "Ain't it time you were back in the hills getting horse paths ready for dudes?"

Scotty had the grace to blush. I'm not sure my neighbor saw it, but I did. "I figured to get a late start this year. The last few seasons I've begun working a bit too early. Had to fix them again before my clients arrived." If I didn't believe his story, neither did Dawson. As it was, I didn't make a commitment one way or the other. Scotty tried to collect on his bet, and I shot him down. It wasn't about a date. It was a kiss and dance if I happened to be in the right place at the right time. Showing my face at a large public gathering wasn't going to happen. Laredo worried me. "Can I have your phone number?" Dawson and I studied at Scotty after his quiet request.

"You know where I live. Isn't that good enough?" My private phone number was known by three people. Manny, my money manager, and Dawson. My neighbor only because I needed his help more often than I wanted.

"I wouldn't mind having a chance to call or text, instead of driving all the way out here."

"Faint heart never won fair maiden." I could hear the humor in Dawson's voice. As I mentioned, he was a strange sort of man.

"I don't use my phone much except for work. Leave me your number, and I might call you sometime. Fact is…I'd like to hire you before the guiding season starts and your customers show up."

Both men looked at me in surprise. "Really?" The single word came out their mouths simultaneously with equal amounts of disbelief.

"I've looked over this country on Google Earth. It'd be nice to hike and ride through it. What would it cost to have you show me the backcountry for a week or two?"

Scotty didn't look happy. "I start booking clients in about three weeks. Summer work goes until September when elk season opens for bow hunters. My busy season starts then. If you're really interested, I can see if there's an opening and pencil you in."

"That would be fine. Don't worry if you're busy. Next year would be great, too. I'm in no hurry."

Dawson waited until his friend left before petting Jake on the head and leaving without any farewell. He was an odd and taciturn man even to someone like me.

*** 

A week after the Independence Day celebration, I'd been between assignments longer than ever before, though Manny remained in touch on three separate occasions to give me updates on the hunt for Monica Slade's killer. Reliable sources said authorities considered multiple persons of interests south of the border. His ID showed on my phone a fourth time. "J here."

"We need a customer signed in Seattle. A grandfather with a large family. Are you up to it?"

I didn't have to think. "I've been going stark raving mad waiting for work, Manny. Who, where, and when do I leave?"

Actually, I acquired two clients. One in Seattle, another in a town to the southeast of the big city close to Yakima. The Seattle signee was a tugboat captain who used his boat to shuttle large quantities of drugs into the US from Canada. A father of three and grandfather of eight, I couldn't imagine what would possess him to take such chances. What if his grandchildren fell victims to his trade?

The other was the leader of a Latino gang in a community on the outskirts of Yakima called Union Gap. She—yes, another woman—imported heroin and methadone precursors from Mexico. It came up Interstate 5 after crossing the border and repackaged in San Diego. Once in Washington, the deadly product crossed the Cascades Mountains and into the desert. For decades, Highway 12 was called the black tar road due to the volume of heroin smuggled. Once a street whore, Juanita Sanchez upgraded to the wrong profession and worked through the ranks until she took over the business. It became so profitable under her leadership that she popped up on The Company's radar and was found a liability.

Jim Lockette scared me. A kindly appearing old man, he possessed a friendly smile when I signed him aboard his tug. Few clients were easier, and for several hours, I remained frightened I made a terrible error. After calling it into Manny, I found The Company was pleased with his signature and commended me. The forty-five thousand deposited into my account were thanks enough—and the knowledge my sister and parents rested a little easier with each customer I signed. A heavy load was lifted from my mind when a mistake hadn't been made. I wasn't in the business to take life from an innocent.

A late-night moon rose high above the Space Needle when Lockette piloted the *Maxine Kay* to the dock. I stood next to his berth, so he tossed a bowline to me. While I wrapped a figure eight around a cleat, he leaped from his tug with the sternline and deftly hauled the tires hanging from the port hull against the pier. When he tied it off, he pointed to a springline, and I used it to doubly secure the boat while he did the same. He was constant motion, and I was forced to follow him. "Jim Lockette?"

"Are you lost, young feller, or looking for a job? You're pretty handy with a line." For a short and rotund man, he jumped deftly aboard again without waiting for an answer. I scrambled after without a sound. My step was quick, and I pressed closely behind before he was aware of me. My heart hammered as it always did when the time came to get his signature, but my hand grew steady. He didn't bother to look—I suppose in a hurry to batten down and leave his ship. When my client dipped his head to enter the cabin, I signed him with a shot behind the ear. He fell heavily, and I leaped to straddle him where he lay. Four more shots, and I turned to leave—closing the door with a sweatshirt sleeve pulled over my hand. I strolled away with my head down in case another bad luck camera lurked nearby. Already past midnight and well after my bedtime, I drove more than halfway to Yakima. I was pleased Manny called ahead for a room in a nice hotel in the beautiful mountain town of Morton. After checking in and learning I did indeed sign the correct client, a hot shower dissolved more stress before I collapsed onto my bed.

I slept late the next morning. Following another shower and a change of clothes, I asked the front desk for a breakfast recommendation. The clerk sent me across the road to a small drive-in restaurant. I ordered a deluxe bacon burger at the counter and took a seat in the dining room. Dawson would be proud of my heavier diet.

"New in town?" The voice startled me, and I turned to see my waitress with a cup and a pot of coffee. "I'm sorry," she said. "Thought you heard me."

I smiled and moved my hand away from the Glock under my light jacket. "It's not your fault. I was a thousand miles away." I took the mug and tested her brew. It was a letdown— typical weak coffee. "Yes, just passing through."

"Are you a tourist?" With no other customers, she appeared chatty. "If you are, we have maps in case you wanted to drive up to see Mount Saint Helens."

"I'd love to see it. Unfortunately, I'm on business, and there isn't time."

I really would have enjoyed checking out the volcano. I remembered my folks talking about it erupting and the damage it caused. Exploding almost a decade before I was born, I didn't have to live through the repercussions. A ding caught both our attention, and my server hurried away to greet a customer out front.

The burger was good. Not spectacular, but good enough I would stop by if traveling through again. I took my time eating, and the young woman filled my cup four times before I left. I relished the opportunity to see a group of whom I presumed to be loggers take seats across the room from me. They were loud, boisterous, and dusty. Not understanding any terms they used, I finally understood the woods were too dry, causing an early shutdown. On one hand, they were happy to be going home. On the other, they needed a paycheck. I felt for them. None seemed as happy with their employment as I was with mine.

Driving over White Pass proved exhilarating. The summit featured snowbanks, although most were far back from the highway. I passed a ski resort and stopped to stretch my legs. Unfortunately, mosquitos drove me back to the rented Ford. They were terrible, and I continued east to my destination. Mosquitos do not bother me like some people who are allergic, but I prefer to avoid the obnoxious insects whenever possible.

I found Yakima to be a thriving desert community. It lay only an hour from the tall evergreens on the west side of the Cascades, yet the area could not have been more different, surrounded by apple orchards and sage brush. Temperatures on the eastside were dramatically higher, more than fifteen degrees. It was a hundred in the desert, and I didn't look forward to the hunt other than allowing me to return home. By then, I would have swept another destroyer of lives and dreams from the street.

Signing my client was going to be difficult. Juanita Sanchez turned out to be a hard and driven woman surrounded by a dozen men and women as brutal and dedicated as their leader. Most were family, and everyone had a job. First were the mules bringing drugs north from Mexico, not all related to Senora Sanchez. Once in Yakima, the narcotics were broken into smaller amounts for distribution. Members used their personal influence to sell to dealers. Finally, the consumer bought and used it. These were the ones I tried to save from themselves.

The drug ring thrived in Yakima, Union Gap, and Moxee. The Moxee headquarters was large and ornate, built with money only a thriving narcotics trade could provide. I wished every client could be as easy to sign as Captain Jim Lockette, yet I approached each one with dread that the encounter could prove fatal to me. Taking up a position where I could watch the Moxee home, I used binoculars to observe.

When I started, Manny suggested I use the best glass money could buy. After hours of studying the history and makers of optics, I settled on a pair of rubber armored Zeiss ten power with a 42-millimeter objective lens. They set me back over two grand, but it became money well spent. At a mile, I could watch barn swallows in flight, and human sweat showed at a quarter mile. Although more powerful and expensive binoculars were available, the ones I chose proved perfect for me. They were not only strong and clear but light around my neck. I could use them for twelve hours and not suffer eyestrain.

Two days of watching the main house netted nothing. Multiple vehicles arrived and departed, yet Sanchez didn't appear in any. Another three days of observing the Yakima and Union Gap homes earned me little more. Eventually bored enough to worry about Jake, I texted Dawson to check on my boy. *Stuck at work longer than anticipated. Is Jake and my garden doing all right?*

His reply was less than ten minutes in returning. *Watering your garden every day. Took lettuce and spinach home, tossed some to the chickens. Okay?*

At least someone enjoyed my labor. *Yes! Please take anything you need from the garden and all the eggs my hens lay. Jake?*

*Lonely. Happier than usual to see me.*

*Could you take him for a ride? He loves the wind in his face.*

*No problem.*

*Thank you, thank you. I owe you one.*

*Much longer and you'll owe me another dinner.*

He was right. My neighbor had spent an entire week of driving to my place to satisfy the requirements of everything I owned. From experience I knew every visit took an hour. Add travel time, and he lost a minimum of ninety minutes each day. Knowing Dawson as I did—however little it was—he likely spent more time than me taking care of everything. *Anything...if it's within reason,* I wrote.

His response surprised me. *Anything?*

*Within reason,* I repeated. *Do you have any suggestions?*

*Yeah, I go along when Scotty guides you into Frank Church Wilderness.*

His request caught me by surprise. Perhaps he was as curious as me about what lay behind our homes? I supposed farmers didn't spend much time in the mountains, even those who carried a gun daily. *Deal. I'll see you after I sign my final customer.*

I didn't wonder when he didn't answer. My house sitter texted more of a conversation than he held when we spoke in person, but no final goodbye was as normal as Dawson got. When a sheriff passed where I was parked on Kittitas Canyon Road, I made a production of texting. It was already late in the day. I left soon after he went by and drove back to my room in Yakima. No sense in drawing unwarranted interest of the law.

My break came on the sixteenth day. I contacted Dawson often and was reassured he didn't hold me to a time schedule. A procession of cars passed before turning into the Moxee driveway. They wound their way up the slope until parking in front of the porch pillars. The house was a giant. It looked more at home in the deep south surrounded by moss-covered cypress trees. My binoculars allowed me to see Juanita Sanchez surrounded by armed guards. She was a bigger deal than I anticipated. I made the call while continuing my vigil. "Manny here."

"J. You didn't tell me I would have to have to fight my way in and then back out."

"Come again?"

"Our client has at least eight armed thugs around her. Someone's been feeding you shitty intel, Manny. The chick hasn't been here until a few minutes ago. She arrived in the center car of a three-vehicle caravan. I'm looking at more machineguns than I've ever seen."

Manny cursed. "I don't like the sound of it. Is it possible your cover is blown?"

"No one's shot at me if that's what you're asking."

"No, it's not. J, get out of there now."

Knowing Manny as I did, I followed his instructions immediately. Before I could reach Highway 24 to return to Yakima and my hotel, a vehicle quickly caught me. Driving exactly the speed limit, I ignored the tail and my hammering heart as I signaled my turn and stopped. A car was coming, and I took the opportunity to glance at the SUV in the mirror. It had darkly tinted windows, and I was unable to see inside. It might be filled with a dozen killers or drug dealers—or a grandmother. I pulled away from the stop sign, and the Navigator followed.

"Manny here."

"J. I may have been compromised. There's an expensive SUV close enough behind to let me count the driver's whiskers if the window weren't tinted."

"Can you lose it?"

I was doing my level best to stay professional. "Doubt it. Suggestions?"

"Find a large restaurant or shopping mall with people nearby. Don't let them cut you off from the herd."

"Will do. I'm driving toward Yakima. Should be downtown in five."

Taking the first right after crossing the freeway, I pushed the speed limit and watched my mirror. I hope they weren't interested, or tailing me was a coincidence. Either way, I saw a sign for a Walmart and ducked into its parking lot. Driving to the front near the store, I found a car ready to leave. The SUV followed me in, and I sat with the suppressed pistol in my lap. I slid in and parked when the car pulled away. As the Navigator passed behind, I able to see two occupants for a moment. Both were studying me intently. Unless they wanted to conduct a daylight assassination attempt, they were forced to keep going. I watched carefully to see if they parked or left the busy lot.

Stuffing a gun inside the back of your pants as we see in movies isn't comfortable. It is also a way to have it noticed. Without a holster for my Ruger 22/45, I sometimes carried it inside the front of my pants. Cocked at an angle, it rests with the butt above my zipper and the barrel comfortably inside my jeans. The muzzle doesn't reach down my leg: it lies at a forty-five-degree angle with the suppressor making a bulge. My blouse covers it easily. I was ready to bolt for the store if they wanted my head.

Observing the SUV travel through the expansive lot, I saw them search for a place to park. They found one two aisles over and perhaps fifty yards away. Staying put and waiting for them to exit their vehicle, I breathed a sigh of relief when I was ignored. They walked into the store chatting and never looked in my direction. Laying my gun next to me, I quickly left and made a call.

"Manny here."

"J. I need a different car ASAP. A new room in another part of town would be helpful."

"Was your cover blown?"

I could hear computer keys in the background and knew he typed quicker than me on my best day. "If it wasn't, I'm the luckiest girl in Washington, my friend."

I heard him chuckling. "Oh, you're lucky. After all the clients you've signed, you've never been shot at, let alone tagged."

"I hope I never am, Manny."

"Being good is why you're the luckiest employee of The Company."

As much as I depended on my partner, the bastard should have kept his mouth shut.

Chapter V

Manny found a room at a tiny motel in Naches, a town so small you'd miss it if you blinked. It was twenty minutes from where my client lived. Clucking like a mother hen, Manny made me trade my white SUV for a black Dodge Charger. He knew I preferred a larger vehicle but feared I might need power and speed, rather than size and weight. Putting my life into his hands again, I didn't question my partner's choice—much.

My room was old yet clean. I didn't ask but bet it didn't cost The Company fifty bucks. The bed turned out to be comfortable, the sink and bathroom worked, so I didn't need much more. I stopped at a fruit stand along the highway and bought a small bag of peaches, plums, and nectarines for dinner. Spotting a pint of pickled habanero garlic, I grinned and purchased it, too. I love garlic. Without anyone around to bother, I would eat the entire jar.

My break came twenty-four hours later. Traffic was difficult, and three identical black SUVs were leaving the Sanchez home when I arrived. I continued past before whipping the car around and goosing the throttle. The tires broke free and barked, making my eyes widen in delight at the power my foot commanded. In seconds, I could see them ahead before other cars moved between us. The vehicles they drove were hard to miss and easily followed.

The convoy slowed and stopped in front of a small Mexican eatery in a poor neighborhood on the east side. When I was a young girl, it would have been an area to avoid. For a predator with a contract and gun, I imagined the setting provided splendid hunting grounds.

I gave them twenty minutes before parking a block away. Held against my panties by a thin leather belt, my suppressed pistol snugged inside my jeans. A standard round had been chambered and my ten-round magazine filled. A spare lay in my pocket, making me as prepared as possible for a daytime signing. Wearing a wig with long black tresses and bangs reaching my eyebrows behind tinted sunglasses, I hurried to the restaurant.

It had one door in front and two in the rear. As I neared the building, one in the back opened. A young Mexican man crossed the alley with a garbage sack and tossed it into a dumpster. Now I knew where one door led and assumed the other was a rear exit to the dining area. Testing the latter, I pulled gently to find it locked. Without a window in the rear wall, I couldn't locate my client until I entered. For a moment, I considered calling it off, but the kitchen door beckoned and called my name.

A dishwasher looked surprised when I stepped inside with my shades pushed up, the same young man who threw the trash out. He froze until I smiled. "I'm sorry, but I'm new in the area. Is this the entrance?" I did my best to set him at ease by showing my pearly whites.

"No." He didn't have much grasp of English. He whispered a quiet demand and pointed behind me. Spanish is a language I never learned despite living in California, so I acted stupid and pushed past. Through a swinging door to my left stood cooks applying their trade to a grill, singing along with Spanish music. The young Latino plucked at my blouse hesitantly to deter me without causing a scene.

He didn't have a chance to redirect me. A man came from the dining room and stopped short of colliding into us. I recognized him as one of the two following me to Walmart. His eyes widened as he stepped back to claw at his gun.

His was in a snapped holster beneath a jacket—I needed only to brush aside the hem of my blouse and draw from the waistband. Mine came up long before his was free. His eyes grew as the muzzle raised, and I pulled the trigger. Little sound cut through the salsa music, and only a muffled thud resulted when he collapsed to the floor. I was caught unaware when the young Mexican grabbed at me from behind. His hug went around my torso, pinning my arms to my sides. I lowered my .22 and shot into the top of his knee. Our struggle had been silent until he shrieked in pain and fell to hold his leg.

I was forced to step over the first man to sneak a glance inside the dining room. He lay motionless, and I almost missed his blink. In midstride, I put an insurance round into his temple. A series of spasms almost knocked me from my feet. Stepping aside, I caught my balance and got a good look inside. One man pushed his chair back in the small and relatively dark room, but I focused on my client. Seated and facing me, she glanced up as my bullet impacted the bridge of her nose. Sanchez slumped forward, and I fired one more into her crown for good measure. Both shots took less than a second. The room stood deathly still for only a moment before the five remaining men sprang into action.

Without a way to retreat, I continued firing. None of my adversaries were innocents, and I killed for self-preservation. The cooks took refuge inside the kitchen, eliminating them as threats. As quickly as I could squeeze the trigger, I aimed four shots into the room. The man originally getting to his feet collapsed, and so did two others. Wishing to give them each an extra round to the head, I simply didn't have time as I dodged return fire. Two men still lived, and I searched frantically for a way out of my predicament. If I left by the kitchen door, they would shoot me as I ran for the safety of my rental.

My initial dispatching of the Sanchez woman and three of her henchmen had been as routine as my daily practice knocking bowling pins off fence posts, but no drill can prepare a person for an actual gun battle. All the movies where the hero hides behind a desk or a table were full of shit. Slugs were flying through walls and breaking things in the kitchen. For the first time in my life, I felt the shock of a bullet. My hand explored my stomach and slipped through wetness before pain set in. Dropping to one knee, I exchanged my nearly empty magazine. Two men remained who planned to end my life. I needed every round now in my gun.

Perhaps most surprising was the stark silence after the shooting stopped. Oddly enough, I noticed light coming from bullet holes in the wall and telltale sounds of magazines ejected and the fumbling to reload in the dining room. I took the opportunity to step through the doorway with my eye locked over the sights. Both men looked in my direction, clumsily releasing their slides to chamber rounds.

Diligent practice with the nearly silent and recoilless Mark IV .22/45 behind my house paid off. The men wanting to kill me most likely shot their loud, jarring handguns once or twice and called it good. They now became no more than wobbling bowling pins, and I simply squeezed the trigger once, then again. Both men fell faster than I can tell it. None of the seven were moving, and I took the extra seconds needed to shoot each one again. I was down to one round in the chamber when I reentered the kitchen to deal with a prime witness before my escape.

The young man was no longer clutching his knee. Instead, he was sprawled against a counter sucking air through a chest wound delivered as collateral damage by the wild Sanchez bodyguards. It looked fatal. Hunched over with my gun in one hand and the other clutching my stomach, I limped to the Charger. I could hear sirens in the distance, but they disappeared before I reached my car. I was thankful for more pressing needs elsewhere in the city.

Pain was setting in when I rounded the block and followed signs to the freeway. Needing to be free of Yakima, I drove toward Naches and my belongings inside the motel. It frightened me to realize how dizzy I'd become and pulled to the side. Fumbling for my cell, I tapped to talk.

"Manny here."

I was never so glad to hear his voice. "J," I whispered. "I'm hit Manny. What do I do?" It took all my willpower not to cry. The thought of my handler hearing me weep almost made me bawl. I was an assassin, for Christ's sake. A killer. Not a little girl with a nail torn to the quick.

Over the following minutes, I learned how professional Manny could be. In the past, he never seemed ruffled no matter the situation. A bullet wound and possibly my imminent death didn't seem to faze him. "Where are you hit and what is your location?" He enunciated in staccato rapid fire.

"My stomach...above my belly button. I'm bleeding bad." I looked around. "Three miles east of Naches, give or take."

I thought I detected typing and talking on another phone. "We have a safe house in Prosser. Can you make it?"

"No." Not knowing exactly how far the town was, I knew instinctively it was farther than I could drive. If I could hear the anguish in my voice, Manny could, too. "There's blood everywhere."

I heard myself sob and sniffed. "And I'm dizzy…" My eyes rolled back, and I forced myself awake.

"I have an extraction team in route. Can you give me GPS coordinates?" A hint of desperation entered his voice. Perhaps a quaver. Maybe it was wishful thinking from a girl frightened of dying.

Whether I passed out or they were already close, four men were suddenly helping me from the Charger. They fastened me to a stretcher before sliding it into the rear of their Suburban. A man who looked suspiciously like a doctor waited inside. Three of the four were in the operating theater on wheels—I heard the fourth start my Charger as we pulled away. I felt bad when it dawned on me how stained his clothes would be. I wondered absently how hard the blood would be to wash it out before whatever was in the IV lines did its job.

***

"Son of a bitch! Look what the cat drug home." Dawson Pelletier appeared surprised when he noticed me sitting on my porch. My cell showed 6:24 a.m.

Even in the stifling heat of early September, he wore the Colt on his belt. Although it was cinched tightly, the style of holster canted the gun butt out at a slight angle. I was sitting in my rocking chair and was sure he hadn't noticed me until he saw Jake outside. He'd been leaving Jake in my house and taking him for a drive or run each day.

On the previous day, The Company flew me from the Tri-Cities directly to Salmon by commuter plane. I descended the steps gingerly and slowly made my way to the terminal office. The boys at the airport seemed glad to see me. I paid extra for their care of my Jeep, and an additional twenty brought my Wagoneer around and left at the front door.

I'd been flat on my back for a week before The Company doctor pronounced me lucky. I was shot with 115 grain hardball. The full metal jacket hadn't expanded, and he saved it so I could look later. It was already sitting on the mantle in the living room. A bullet dug out of my guts—even with minimal damage inside—hurt like a bastard. The doc told me it didn't exit when losing its energy after penetrating the wall. For a while, I was afraid I would never poop again. When it finally happened, I was terrified of more bowel movements.

Once he learned I was going to live, Manny couldn't wait to tell me the news. In the aftermath of signing Juanita Sanchez, police declared the massacre part of a gang war. They were searching for more than one suspect, but nothing was mentioned of a skinny Caucasian woman leaving the scene. Either the cooks were too frightened to talk, or they didn't get a good look at my face. Perhaps wearing a proper wig was the answer. After the fiasco in Texas, my face on the news wasn't something I wanted to see again. It was frightening. For a killer, I was one hell of a scaredy-cat.

I was more excited when Manny told me about our payday. Sanchez was worth ninety thousand, but The Company decided to compensate me for the other six. All played a part in the Sanchez drug importation ring. They rewarded me with fifteen grand per head for her henchmen, totaling a second ninety thousand. Manny refused money from the six, taking his twenty percent from Sanchez only. We argued about it—he saved my life, and I owed him. Unfortunately, he controlled deposits going into my account. If it were up to me, Manny would have taken half of everything. Without logging into my account and looking, I was sure the magic *one million* mark had been achieved. It was time to consider retiring from The Company and taking another job. I might settle into something more mundane like the field of education, even though when facing racing adolescent hormones, teaching can be akin to mortal combat.

It was difficult to smile at my visitor. "More like the dog played with and shook too hard." I hesitated. "Look, Dawson...I need to apologize for taking advantage. From now on, I'll find someone else who can stay here while I'm gone. It makes me feel awful knowing..."

He butted in before I could finish. "I didn't do a good enough job?"

I shook my head. "It's not that..."

He interrupted again. "It's no problem driving over here. Hell, it ain't like I got much to do anyway." Putting one foot on a step at the bottom of my porch, he leaned again the bannister. "Don't let it worry a single hair on your pretty little head, Julia. I enjoyed havin' a reason to be out and about."

I could see he was surprised at Jake lying next to me, rather than rising to greet his friend as usual. Dawson held his hand out, but my shorthair didn't leave my side. It must have seemed odd after taking him for walks and giving rides in his truck. Yet when I returned home the previous evening, Jake never left me when he realized I was hurting. He even followed when I went to the bathroom.

"All I can say is thank you. I appreciate your help, neighbor. Consider your backcountry trip free of charge when I hire Scotty to pack us in." I jabbed a thumb at the open door leading to the kitchen. "Coffee's fresh if you'd like some." I held my empty cup out as he passed.

He handed over my filled mug when he returned, taking the chair opposite of me at the small oval table I kept on the porch. "You're looking a bit under the weather this morning, if you don't mind me saying. You sick or comin' down with something?"

Staring death in the eye and not sure I would make it changed my view of the world. Dawson was a perfect example. Jesus, the man was beautiful. He was everything I liked to see in the opposite sex. Tall and rangy, not thin, with broad shoulders, and big, strong hands. When he shook mine, his fingers and palm were iron, calloused and powerful. The way he wore his long hair tied loosely at the nape was more attractive than I could have imagined. Dawson Pelletier was the first male I thought of as a *man* who I liked wearing hair reaching past his shoulders. It was straight, jet black, and thick. To picture him with another hairstyle was impossible. His mouth was wide above a strong chin, and I almost shuddered when he really looked at me. It was as if his gaze penetrated me, seeing everything I wished to hide.

"Something going on with my stomach. Doubt if it's serious…the corporate doctor gave me a thorough examination while I've been gone." I avoided looking at him, fearful he would see my lie for what it was.

My answer appeased him, and he changed the subject. "Where's the little peashooter you usually pack?"

"Peashooter?" I tested my coffee and found it the perfect temperature after noticing Dawson set his aside. "Let me empty a magazine into you and then tell me again it's a peashooter." I was halfway miffed. It was my father's gun. I tasted both blood and retribution with it.

"If you could even hit close to me from a good twenty-five paces."

I saw the crinkle around his eyes when he hid behind the coffee cup, but I could no more stop myself than a runaway dump truck. "Hit you? You think I couldn't hit you dead center from that range?"

"Why do you suppose folks carry over a box of shells in just a few magazines for those impersonal and unlovable Glocks? Most of them belong to the spray-and-pray crowd."

I knew the term well. It described those who couldn't hit jack crap like my Latino adversaries in the restaurant who hoped volume might make up for it. If he wanted to see real shooting, he should have watched my father when he was alive. Dad was one of the best shots I knew, although only in competition. He'd never stood against an armed opponent. "Someday I'm going to school you, boy." There was no sense in ratcheting up the hyperbole. I was secure in my own ability and firearms. Hurting as I was, proving my imaginary dick was bigger than his would earn me little.

"You do that. In the meantime, you ate breakfast yet?"

His change of topics was surprising. "Just coffee."

"How 'bout something more in North Fork—my treat if you're interested." Before I could answer, he disappeared into the kitchen and returned with the pot. Filling my cup and then pouring the rest into his, he set the empty carafe aside and sat again.

His offer gave me pleasant butterflies, but I grimaced at the thought. "Thanks, but I'm not really up to it. My stomach's a real problem, and I'm on a bland diet. I see you didn't take enough eggs home. The refrigerator is almost full. I could scramble a half dozen if you're hungry."

His nod appeared agreeable. "Sounds good. Don't go lookin' for bread, though. I threw it to the chickens once it started molding." He stood and offered a hand. "Need help?"

I handed him my cup. "No, but if you'll take this, I'll meet you in the kitchen."

My first inkling that Dawson Pelletier was not what I expected came when he refused to leave until I stood. It was awkward—I no longer possessed abdominal wall strength—and to rise from a seated or lying position was painful. First, I tried to lean forward in the rocking chair as we normally do, until I almost wet my pants from a stab of pain. Sitting back and gasping, I tried to control my agony before it became more obvious.

"You still turning down my help?" He offered his hand again, and I was finally smart enough to accept it. He was gentle, pulling with one hand and ready to assist me with the other. It wasn't until I was on my feet, and he was sure I wasn't going to fall that he released me. Jake stayed at my side, also ready to give aid in any way he could.

I held one hand against my stomach and shuffled inside. Dawson helped angle me to the table. Exhausted from the effort, I didn't complain when he assisted me to sit. "Give me a second to rest, and I'll get started."

I wasn't kidding anyone, let alone my neighbor. "You rest. I'll cook breakfast. Six for me. How many you want?"

I shook my head. The thought of food was revolting. "None, thanks."

The man was efficient and a joy to watch. He put on more coffee and cracked eggs into my nonstick pan. They were cooked perfectly when he slid them onto a plate. Before he sat, Dawson retrieved a yogurt cup and spoon for me. My fingers weren't strong enough to break the seal, and of course he saw it. Taking the container from me, he tore the top away, stirred, and handed it back. Eating half his breakfast before slowing, he stopped to fill our cups again. "Whatever in the hell's going on with your stomach…it's startin' to leak." His voice was calm as if mentioning the weather. I looked down to see my wound bleeding again. It seeped through the bandage to stain my blouse. "You up for a ride in my truck, or should I call an ambulance?"

"It's nothing." I tried to pass it off as normal, but my heart hammered with fear.

He nodded to my midsection. "Your nothin's gettin' bigger." Blood was seeping into my sweatpants.

"Oh, shit." I pulled my hand away covered in crimson. Once a month blood I could handle, but it was frightening coming from anywhere else. My eyes were huge when I looked at him in terror, only to find Dawson calmly finishing his breakfast.

Dawson disappeared for a moment before returning to the kitchen. Permission wasn't asked, and I was too scared to complain. Lifting me as gently and easily as an infant, he carried me to my room. A towel was on the thin comforter where he placed me.

He opened the bottom three buttons of my blouse to expose the pad. It was saturated, and two trickles ran from it. I could feel them stop at the terrycloth, making me grateful he anticipated the need to soak up the mess. After tearing the tape away, he pulled the gauze back to expose my bullet wound.

"This should be an easy fix." Dawson disappeared with the useless bandage. I heard him in the bathroom rummaging while I watched in horror as blood oozed from my stomach. The original injury had been enlarged by the surgeon but still identifiable as a bullet entry.

"You dislodged the drain tube moving in your sleep last night or this morning. Instead of draining, it caused the stitches to pull and your wound to bleed." He pressed on my abdomen and watched me carefully for signs of distress. "No pain when I push?"

"No, only when you touch the tube."

"Your stomach doesn't feel or look bloated?"

I looked down to see it flatter than ever. I'd lost a lot of weight I'd struggled to put on over the past days. Even the small pad of fat normally around my bellybutton was gone. "No."

Dawson's calloused hands looked big enough to reach around my waist and touch his finger and thumb tips. "You should probably have these stitches removed and new ones put in, or you're gonna have a noticeable scar." His voice was calm and even as if discussing taking Jake for a ride. He gave me a sour glare. "I don't suppose you give a good god damn."

"No." My answer was abrupt. "Are there any of those little butterfly bandages in my first aid kit?"

Using one hand to keep pressure with gauze, he used the other to rummage through the extensive bag. He didn't talk while working to control the bleeding. Dawson moved methodically in his own way, resituating the tube and closing the skin with the strips he located.

Another sterile pad went over, taped tight enough I'd need to wet it to peal it away. He finally stood back and looked at his work. "Ain't the best way to go, but I reckon it'll do." One side of his mouth pulled back in what I could only describe as a grimace. Even if he wasn't asking questions, Dawson wasn't happy with his discovery. "Got antibiotics?"

I nodded. "I do, and thank you." I touched his arm before letting my hand fall. "Could you lock the door when you leave?" I yawned and felt my lids droop.

I didn't hear my neighbor leave, but someone's entry woke me. When I was in my own home, no one else should be inside. Jake still lay next to me, but oddly enough he didn't bark. Stretching an arm to reach my nightstand, I quietly opened the drawer. Inside was my Glock. When the bedroom door slowly opened, my sights were trained on our intruder. The shades were partially drawn, but I recognized my neighbor.

The muzzle trained on his forehead didn't faze him. "Did I wake you?"

I took my finger from the trigger. "Goddamn it, Dawson. You were four ounces from being dead, you dumb son of a bitch." I was angry enough to hurl a loud curse, a rarity for me.

"Just wanted to tell you I brought my gear. I'll be takin' your spare room."

"What? You what?" I lowered the gun to the bed and stared incredulously.

"Unless you want to spend time in the hospital or hire a nosy nurse, I figured it was left to me to take care of you."

"No. What? No. I don't need you taking care of me. Besides, I don't have extra blankets."

"Brought my sleepin' bag, so it's time to shut your pie hole. It's gonna to be a while before you're up and about. Meantime, someone a bit more adult needs to play nursemaid."

"More adult…" I sputtered at his insinuation.

"Hey, I ain't the one laying there with a bullet hole in my guts. So yeah, more adult."

I froze and contemplated my alternatives. One, I could kill him and move on. Two, I could swear him to silence, or three, simply ignore what he said. I chose the latter.

"Two days." I gritted my teeth and dared him to oppose me. It was a mistake.

"Two months."

It was years since a man was last in my bedroom. Now one was standing at the foot of my bed. His sleeves were rolled to the elbows, and I could see forearms corded with lean muscle. They were as tanned as his face and neck. Something told me if he removed his shirt, his skin would be milky white beneath it. It wasn't called a farmer's tan for nothing, and I needed to think of something different. "Horseshit. Three days." The man had a propensity for drawing expletives from me.

"Three months."

"A week then." I was getting a hang of his negotiations.

"One month, and we'll reassess."

I sighed dramatically. "Fine, now help me up, Nurse Pelletier. I have to pee after all the coffee you forced on me."

*** 

"I knew the guy who built this house." My neighbor came in from watering the garden with a box of tomatoes. He stopped at the sink to wash them.

Trying to read the latest romance novel by my favorite author wasn't going well. Not until Dawson moved in did I remember how much value I placed on silence and my privacy. Because I owned a computer, I didn't need the noise of a television for news or movies. It was one of the reasons I chose the location. I considered him a quiet man until we were thrust together.

"You did? I thought this place was built following the second world war." I set my book aside because he finally broached an interesting topic. The price of wheat and cattle futures hadn't captivated my attention.

"It was. I met him about fifteen years ago, not long before he died…probably in his nineties."

I could listen to Dawson's deep bass all day unless I was trying to read. "Did he live here long?"

"Until the 'eighties." I could see him working at the kitchen counter from where I lay on the couch in my tiny living room. "Afterward was a revolving door of renters and owners."

I'd bought the place as a bank repossession, and the news didn't surprise me. "He lived here forty years?"

"You interested in hearin' a bit of news no else alive knows?" Even from twenty feet. I could see his devilish smirk.

"Perhaps you better tell me in case you have a heart attack during my convalescence. I'd hate for the information to die with you." When he turned in my direction, no one was more surprised than me at the way my pulse quickened. It must have been the news he was about to impart, not the tall and lithe man walking my way.

He stopped at the threshold of my bedroom and grinned. He stomped his foot and didn't stop smiling. I waited, expecting more. An eyebrow lifted, and he cocked his head, apparently expecting something from me. After a few seconds of enduring my blank look, he stamped the floor again.

"This deal with you staying here might not work out. If there's a nervous twitch in your leg, it's going to keep me awake." I hoped he thought it was dry humor rather than my stupidity.

He repeated it a third time. "What do you hear?"

"Sounds different?" My ventured guess was hesitant.

"Yep!" He planted his boot again at the bedroom door, watching where he stepped. The hardwood was old and needed refinished in the worst way. Laying a new floor was going to be a priority when I started my renovations. Dawson continued while staring intently around his feet. He finally grinned and disappeared into the kitchen. The door slammed, and I heard his pickup door close. He returned with a large slot screwdriver in one hand and a flashlight in the other. He caught my look of confusion and his smile grew. "Old Bill told me about digging a root cellar before he built this place." Dawson inserted the screwdriver between floorboards and pried. A trapdoor was connected to a chain, and he pulled it open until the links came tight with the door swung upward. "He'd returned from fightin' in Europe and didn't feel safe any longer. His aim for this place was storage and safety. Once the cold war was in full swing, he dug deeper and reinforced the walls…" Dawson shined his flashlight in the hole. "…and a ceiling."

"You mean I've been sitting on an old-time 'fifties bomb shelter?"

"Looks like it from here." Shifting to his stomach, he hung his head and swept the beam in the hole.

"Well? What's it look like?" I cursed my wound for the millionth time.

"About twelve by fifteen, I'd guess. Ceiling looks around seven feet and the room is concrete. I see a wooden ladder needin' replaced."

"Go down there and look around for me, will you?"

"Oh, hell no." Dawson looked at me like I was a crazy lady. "Who knows what sort of critters are crawling around, just waitin' for their chance at dinner?" He gave a mock shudder, then shot me a boyish grin. "But after I toss a bug bomb in, it's time to start exploring"

Chapter VI

How I wished to explore my cellar. I sulked instead, while my neighbor hurried home for bug bombs, carpentry tools, and wood. Precisely what he meant by the blanket term "*wood*," I hadn't a clue. Dad wasn't a carpenter, nor was I around builders. It was frustrating to stay on the couch while left alone, so I wrenched my attention away from the exciting discovery and went back to reading my novel.

Two hours flew past with time for a short nap and several more chapters before Jake's head lifted from the floor, signaling Dawson was on his way back. The familiar sound of his diesel stopped outside my house. I heard the screen door screech, and he was already in the living room when it slammed—a man on a mission. "Hey, can you put coffee on before you start?" I asked while smiling and batting my eyelashes, but he didn't look in my direction. My poorly developed feminine wiles were wasted.

"Yup." He pulled two canisters from cartons he discarded atop my book, then bent to open the trapdoor. "After I toss these bombs down."

Interest diverted, I glanced at large print on the side of a box: SET UPRIGHT FOR BEST DISTRIBUTION OF MIST. "Hey, wait!" But Dawson was already on his stomach with his arms hanging into the cellar. One at a time, the cans hissed and clunked to the floor below.

Jumping back, he dropped the door and quickly looked around. "What?"

"Too late." Like most men, he'd done it his way instead of reading directions.

He pulled the folded afghan off a chair and covered the hatch. "Don't want any gas seeping up here to make my patient sicker."

I traded mention of his manly *faux pas* for a domestic nag. "As long as you run it through the wash once you've finished killing those big old mean bugs, Nurse Ratched."

Dawson went blank at my comment before a smile grew. "Oh, yeah. *One Flew Over the Cuckoo's Nest.* She was the cruel villain."

"The same. I seem to be at your mercy in the short term. No frontal lobotomies while I'm down."

"I think you're pretty safe." His voice was dry. "If you don't object, I'm going to run your tomatoes, peppers, and onions to my mom. I've already talked to her about it. She's willing to preserve some stewed tomatoes, salsa, and tomato paste, but you have to provide the jars and lids."

I'd wondered if my garden would go to waste. "Yes! I wish I could watch. Canning is something I hope to learn. How much do you think will it cost?"

"Don't worry about it. I have to get feed in Salmon, so I'll pick up jars, and you can pay me later."

"Could you get my purse and do a huge favor for me, Mr. Pelletier?" I gave him my brightest smile.

He glanced around the room. "Where is it?"

"On the end of the counter next to the refrigerator." If I'd thought ahead, it was something I should have handled myself. My handbag is huge, and I kept everything in it. Everything. It's not something I'd want to carry for days or even while shopping. I have a smaller one for the necessary stuff. But when I travel, I have my bag with the essentials locked inside to survive up to and including an atomic strike. I noticed Dawson's expression changed when he handed it to me. The reason was obvious the moment I went to look in. I'd unlocked and opened the heavy zipper when I got home but failed to secure it again, and my Ruger was inside with the suppressor still screwed in place. All was exactly as I left it, including the bloodstained grips. For a moment—just a fleeting instant—the notion passed through my head to neutralize my oversight. It evaporated as quickly, but the putrid thought left me shaken. Had I really reached that point? My voice turned cold. "I think you should leave. Don't come back." My purse was open to expose the elephant peering out into the room.

"What did you need it for?" It wasn't until then I realized he'd taken a half-step back. His hand was close to that big Anaconda coiled at his hip. If I attempted to grasp the butt of my gun, he might very well kill me.

"Nothing. It doesn't matter now." Suddenly I was more exhausted than ever. Resting my head on the pillow, I covered my face with a forearm. Although I loved my home, perhaps it was time to move on.

"Sure it does." Dawson lifted the heavy bag from my lap and set it on the floor next to me.

"I was going to ask if you would buy groceries. It's been too long, and there's not much in the house." My voice broke, and I hid my weeping with both hands. I heard the screen door slam and his diesel growl away. Not since my parents died, and when soon after I was called to identify Meghan's body did I feel so alone. It was time to call Manny and ask for The Company's help to relocate. Except my damned phone was on the charger in the kitchen.

***

Afternoon wasted away to early evening when I woke to the clatter of a diesel engine. I needed to pee but reached into my purse for the gun instead. It sounded like Dawson again, but when you kill for a living, you tend to become paranoid. After having a bullet removed from my stomach, I felt every right to be worried.

Dawson stomped through with an armload of two by fours, ignoring me while making a neat stack on the floor. He disappeared, and I soon saw him ferrying grocery sacks to the table and counter. I counted six trips before he unloaded them into my refrigerator and cabinets. Finding things after he left was going to be a chore. When he disappeared outside, I figured he was done. His truck door slammed again, then my screen door, followed by water running in the sink. He reappeared to hand me a ripe peach and a plum on a paper towel. He dropped a slip of paper on my lap. "Your supplies ran almost three hundred, not countin' jars and lids for Mom which were fifty-two. I'll be eating here, so we'll split the groceries. You owe me two hundred whenever you get the chance."

I'd never been shot before, so I wasn't sure if helplessness or trauma caused all the crying. Whatever the case, sticky peach juice mixed with my tears, and the paper towel came in handy. Dawson didn't comment, though I'm sure I looked as horrible as I felt. When

81

he stood to leave again, I handed him the fruit pits wrapped in a soggy sheet of Bounty.

He returned with a battery-powered skill saw and drill. "I'm dying to know what's down there. How 'bout you?"

"Yes, but not as bad as I have to pee." Any moment there was going to be an accident. "Can you help?"

"Nurse Ratched to the rescue, huh?" He rubbed his hands together and let out an evil chuckle.

"Dawson, I'm serious. You're about to have a mess to clean if we don't hurry."

My gun was on the couch. I pulled another afghan off the back and used it to cover the tool of my trade. Rather than help me stand, my nurse lifted me bodily and rushed to the bathroom. He stopped at the door and set me upright, then guided me inside with one arm around my shoulder. Not until I was backed up to the toilet did he leave and close the door. While I sighed in relief, the muffled sounds of boards dropping inside the cellar reached me. I waited for a minute after I finished before it dawned on me that I was on my own. Using the counter to rise, I dragged my underwear and sweat bottoms up and started the trek to the couch one step at a time.

It was impossible to resist looking through the trapdoor into my cellar at a gray room lit by the harsh light of a single bulb. My roommate was nowhere to be seen, but his voice drifted up through the opening. "Holy shit!"

"If a big fat spider's trying to pack you off, I'm of no help. By all rights I should still be in the bathroom waiting for you to help."

Dawson's head appeared. "There's running water down here with a sink and toilet."

"Seriously?"

"Yep. This bomb shelter has potential. It's pretty small and the ceiling is low, but with a little work and maybe a refrigerator, it should be useful for anything. It'll make a great secret storage or hideaway if need be.

"Bomb shelter? Didn't the cold war officially end thirty years ago?"

"Technically, if more than one country still has nuclear weapons, it can't be over, official or otherwise. But this could bode well if you needed to…" His head and the rest of his sentence went below. "…well, not be found."

What he was saying was obvious. He might not know exactly what I did for a living, but events of the last few days were relatively self-explanatory. Dawson wasn't a dumb man and incapable of reading signs and tracking the truth.

***

I was walking on my own four days later with only moderate pain. Nurse Ratched only needed to help me in and out of bed and on and off the couch. He seemed as happy as me to see my stomach healing. Finding an appetite again were grounds for my cheer section to cook more. Other than leave me two hours each day to tend his own farm, my neighbor was always nearby—usually in the cellar with a saw or drill running. I asked once why he didn't use nails. He looked at me as if I were stupid. Only then did I learn how handy screws were and how easily removed if needed.

On the seventh day, I mentioned to my nurse it was time for him to move home. Of course, it was right after he'd helped me out of bed. He snorted and shook his head when he left me to work on the cellar. I felt a bit sheepish after giving it a little thought. Perhaps a few more days of his aid were needed.

The eleventh day after my return saw an end to the noise beneath my floorboards. I'd gone forty-eight hours without his help, and Dawson allowed me to see his work. It was difficult to navigate the ladder even with him below and holding a part of my weight. What a small place it was! The actual measurements were slightly less than twelve feet wide and fourteen long. The ceiling was seven feet. Buying knotty pine siding with money I provided, Dawson finished the walls with the attractive wood. One end was partitioned off with a couple shower curtains, behind which a toilet and small sink functioned properly. They were new. The old ones had left a small gouge and scrape in my floor upstairs.

Baffled at first by the lack of drainage, Dawson eventually realized the system needed a hand pump. Once he found it and understood how it worked, an order at the local hardware store brought a new one. Even though he was quiet in his explanation, I could see his pride when he demonstrated how it operated. Water lower than the floor required pumping to enter the drain and septic system. It wasn't difficult—I could operate it even in my weakened condition. I almost offered to pay him but remembered my lesson.

Halfway through September—two weeks after Nurse Ratched moved in—I gave only token help in harvesting my garden. We rolled potatoes out until heat and exhaustion proved too much. Leaving him to the job, I retired to my room for a nap with Jake, who steadfastly refused to pronounce me fit. Hours later, my caregiver was in the kitchen with boxes of canned products from his mother, mostly salsa, tomato paste, and preserved tomatoes. I was set for winter.

"I'd guess you have about three hundred pounds of taters. Not sure why you need those purple sons of bitches." Cursing my choice of potatoes, he claimed it wasn't right to have famous Idaho spuds looking like rocks. Many errors had been made in the stone-filled soil of my garden. A muttered curse seemed to go with each one.

"They're good for me, that's why." I'd wasted too much time trying to explain how the antioxidants were significantly higher in the dark tubers.

"Well, they sure as hell must make disgusting-looking mashed potatoes and gravy." He glanced out the window and swore again. "Goddamn rabbit is going to die and swim in the stewpot if it keeps nosing around."

A plethora of cottontails attempted to raid my garden before the harvest could be completed. I was thankful the job was nearly finished and made Dawson understand my gratitude. I wasn't quite so worried with most of what I wanted already stored inside and thought about his earlier comments. "Time for you to put up or shut up."

His face was dark with anger when he redirected his glare to me. "Huh?"

"You're this fantastic shot capable of snipping the eyelashes from flying hummingbirds...or so you say." He'd mentioned nothing of the kind, but I was entitled to a token amount of hyperbole.

"Yeah." Dawson's mood lightened when he grinned and glanced out the window. "Get up here and watch. If the little bastard lets me sneak out without it running off, we'll be eating stringy hasenpfeffer in a couple days."

I stood near the window and watched the great white hunter creep onto my porch. The rabbit was crouched at perhaps twenty-five yards. It was close to the nearest corner of my garden fence, and nothing in the background was in danger of a bullet. I could see Dawson waiting for foam earplugs to expand and fill his ear canals.

His shot was impressive—not nearly as loud as I feared a .44 magnum would sound, nor did the recoil seem ferocious. My nurse's draw was smooth and the sights barely aligned before he squeezed the trigger. The single shot demonstrated great skill even to one in my line of work. The rabbit sprang into the air before falling to the ground and performing its final dance. A gyration more than one of my clients—dare I say—executed. I found it interesting when he extracted a loaded round from his belt, lifted the empty, and replaced it with the live cartridge before holstering the Colt again. Dawson Pelletier was a careful man.

He allowed me outside to inspect the results. The rabbit was headshot and died instantly. A bit of damage went into its shoulders, making me chuckle. "A little far back, but not bad, Ratched."

One of his eyebrows lifted when he regarded me coolly. "A little far back? A headshot is a headshot, my dear woman." After he stalked to my water supply with the rabbit in one hand, I left him to clean it at the faucet.

*** 

"I'm not sure if you drink, but I make a mean tequila sunrise." Dawson and I were seated on the front porch after dinner, letting fried purple potatoes, chicken thighs, and creamed corn settle.

I shook my head politely. "Not often." Never sure when I might receive a call to work, drinking was something I avoided. Even when I taught—especially during those times—alcohol was an item I couldn't afford. My money was better spent elsewhere or saved.

"Would you mind if I made one?"

I didn't care and shrugged. It would allow me to see if he battled alcohol. "Knock yourself out."

Another rabbit worked its way from the brush past my garage toward my garden while Dawson was inside. My patch was mostly harvested, but a bit more needed to be gathered. I wasn't looking forward to the roar of his .44 if he chose to shoot another.

"You're missing a great drink." Nurse Ratched took his seat next to my rocking chair with a filled glass.

"Never developed a taste for booze, I guess." Nor the repercussions.

"You're up, Calamity Jane." His sharp eyes didn't miss the rabbit crouched at the far end of the fence.

I wasn't ready to kill again, especially an innocent bunny. "Let him live. He's not hurting anything."

"I don't blame you for not wanting to look bad." He clucked like a chicken under his breath.

"After thirty-two years of life on this planet, I'm not sure what there is for me to prove."

"A little far back, but not a bad shot."

I lasted less than ten minutes. The time was filled with his infernal clucking, a few swallows of booze, followed by more quiet taunts. He finished his drink and made a second before I could take no more. Dawson was grinning when I went into the house, mirth that melted away when I reappeared with my .22/45. With the suppressor screwed into place, it looked exactly like what it was—an extermination tool. With that gun in my hand, I changed from Julia to J. It was an extension of who I was. I occasionally wondered if I should bother with the sights. At times, the bullet behaved as a heat-seeking missile where my guidance wasn't needed.

My clients were larger and almost always closer. At thirty-five or forty yards, the target was tiny. Utilizing the open sights, I willed the forty-grain slug to where it was needed. The suppressed muzzle came up, and we became one. There was no loud report nor abusive recoil. Instead, all was silent but for the slide extracting the empty and loading a second round into the chamber. Using the tool of my trade, there was no excitement or exhilaration when the rabbit died. I simple *was*.

Lowering the front-heavy pistol, I turned to Dawson to see a look of alarm. It didn't approach horror, though perhaps containing a perverted degree of respect. He shook it off—or perhaps it was a shiver—and left to dress the poor bunny.

I had the gun apart to clean it along with the suppressor baffles when he returned with the carcass. He set it in the refrigerator with the other before sitting across the table from me. "I suppose you know where you hit?" He wasn't asking a question. Instead Dawson verified what he suspected.

I nodded. The bullet struck an area not much larger than a thumbnail between the eye and ear. It was a difficult shot for the distance. "I taught school about a million years ago. Did you know that?"

"Huh uh." Dawson watched with an unnatural fascination while I scrubbed my tools. Each time I performed the task, the firearm was cleaner than when it shipped from the factory.

"Primary school. Seven- and eight-year olds. Each one became my surrogate child." I sighed while making sure the recoil spring slid in correctly. "I loved it. I loved them."

His big Adam's apple bobbed when he swallowed hard. "What happened?" He worked to keep his voice casual.

Judging by his reaction, I suppose my face was bleak when I glanced. He blinked twice before his eyes narrowed. "Duty called," I said.

"Military?"

I battled anger. "No. Duty." My glare was one of defiance, a challenge to question me further only if he dared.

I could see the alcohol taking hold of his limbs, moving slower and more deliberately. "I've never watched a woman do a better job of cleaning a weapon. Hell, most men don't do as well." I replaced the bolt and barrel assembly with a familiarity that bespoke my proficiency. Working the action a handful of times, I screwed the reassembled suppressor to the muzzle after cleaning and checking the threads carefully. Speed in ease of attachment and removal was crucial. My life and signing a client might depend on it. I had retrieved an extra cartridge to replace the empty but first checked the unloaded magazine for dirt or debris. After reloading, I carefully inserted it into the Ruger magazine well and pressed it home with my thumb. There was an audible click when it locked. I left the gun next to my hand and looked up. Dawson didn't take his eyes away as I performed my routine. After meeting my gaze, he said, "What sort of plans do you have?"

I knew what he was asking, and he knew I knew what it was. My nurse didn't bother to smile when I replied. "I'm going to bed. See you in the morning."

***

The end of September brought two things: My stomach was less of a problem, and Dawson announced he was moving out. "I reckon you can get along without me. I'm heading home when breakfast is cleaned up."

"Oh." For a moment I wasn't sure what to say. Nurse Ratched hadn't given much notice our time together was ending.

"You can handle your place without my help, can't you?"

Could I? All major chores were taken care of—from shoveling chicken and rabbit manure to stacking three cords of firewood in the garage and on the back porch. After he inspected and explained how to use the old wood cookstove, I looked forward to cutting my heating bill. Money was becoming a problem, but a call later in the day would see to it. "I think so. With all the work you've done, my time is going to be spent watching it snow this winter."

Dawson dried the dishes after I washed them. Something was eating at him. It wasn't clear until he returned from the spare bedroom with his bag and asked, "Be needin' me to watch your place this winter?"

My decision was final. "No, I'm planning to look for a different job. My resignation will be tendered this afternoon. My old employers will have to find another secretary to fill the position."

While he knew my post was anything but secretarial, he didn't challenge me. "No one is irreplaceable." The tiniest of smiles played at the corners of his mouth. "You might be surprised at how quickly they forget." Nurse Ratched waved farewell after petting Jake one last time. "Don't be a stranger, you hear?"

He left a silence behind that filled my home. After waking from another nap, I found myself looking for him. Since I'd stolen a month of his life, he was likely eager to catch up on work at his own place. We were already having frosts, and he was sure to have chores to finish before it snowed.

Without extra ears nearby to catch the crux of my conversation, I rang the number. "Manny here."

"J."

"J! It's good to hear your voice. Ready to make some big money? I have two hot ones with your name on them."

"Manny…" I hesitated to say the words. "I'm calling to give my resignation."

His voice cooled. "You can't quit. It's taken a long time to work your way to the top."

"I'm sorry. My mind's made up."

"Does your decision have anything to do with stopping a bullet?" He sounded as if I were letting him down. I guess he was right.

"It wasn't only the slug in my stomach." My left index finger traced the wound. "Things went downhill after I got home. A nurse lived here fulltime to keep me alive." While my news was a white lie, it may have come to fruition had I been left on my own.

"Damn it, J. I wish you'd reconsider. I'll tell you what. Why not take the winter to sit back and relax? Work on your customer appreciation skills and rebuild any lost strength. You may look at the world differently in a few months."

My mind wasn't going to change, but I was finding it difficult to make Manny understand. We were finally catching the bigger fish where life-altering money was within reach. I gave in to his entreaties. "Good idea. We'll talk again after spring."

"I'll be in touch." The line went dead.

His disappointment was palpable. For the first time, I wondered if I would be allowed to call it quits. What of my money? Could The Company seize it until I agreed to continue? Only a hundred grand of my parents' funds remained in my personal bank account. With The Company paying most of my bills, I spent little except for my home and the move. Even the old Jeep cost less than five thousand.

Concerned, I checked my offshore account. It hadn't been touched—yet—but the total made my eyes widen. With interest and investments adding up, my nest egg was over the magic million. I shifted back in my chair, surprised to see so much. Perhaps my best bet was letting my investment manager continue to do what she did best—make money with my money.

If I planned not to touch it, an income was required. I could make my original nest egg stretch for three or four years, but expensive things needed done. Another gun or two, financing Scotty to take Dawson and me into the backcountry, and perhaps buy a horse. A good mare or gelding would mean a barn. Serious expenditures would add up quickly. Property taxes weren't cheap, and at some point, a truck would be important. I needed a job.

We got our first dusting of snow on October fifth. I woke to a cold house and built a fire like Dawson demonstrated. The stove was an old cast iron model designed for cooking, and he'd scoffed at keeping it. To me it was attractive—perhaps not the best way to judge a stove. Edged with chrome, I spent hours buffing and making it shine. The small firebox didn't hold enough wood to burn through the night. If I woke to use the bathroom, I would fill it again, but my nighttime visits didn't often happen. It was fun to make coffee or heat water with it, and it threw off enough heat to take off the chill of my small home.

After it was burning and giving off heat, I went to the back porch for more wood. It was dark, forcing me to turn on the light. Movement caught my eye, and I stood with an armload of wood to see the first flakes. The sight of snow made me shiver. Still in my nightgown and bathrobe, I hurried inside to finish filling the stove.

I'd regained my lost bodyweight and was inching toward one hundred pounds. Stepping from the shower after drying, I stood in front of my mirror and gazed critically. The angry twisting of skin above my navel stood out and always would. It could take years until the redness faded, leaving in its wake an unmistakable bullet scar. I was past the age where a string bikini was appropriate, and I blew my nose after realizing I would never wear one again.

I finally had boobs. Giving a slight shake, it made me smile to see my little girls behaving like breasts! Bouncing in front of the mirror, I brought my shoulders back to shimmy as I watched dancers do on television. Stopping my girlish antics but still smiling, I dressed and went back to the stove. It was warming the room, and I managed to stuff two more pieces inside. I couldn't wait to see how much difference wood heat made when my electric bill came.

Breakfast was a three-egg omelet, a meal Jake looked forward to. I rarely finished, so he did for me. After starting coffee, I grated two spuds into a colander and rinsed them in the sink. The pan sizzled when I dropped them in and covered it.

The eggs were added next. Topping them with green onions, fresh spinach, and chopped pineapple, I slid the finished product onto the bed of potatoes. A dab of hot sauce, perhaps too much, and a couple liberal spoons of salsa from Dawson's mom, I sat with my coffee to eat.

Jake didn't mind when I finally made it past the halfway point through my breakfast. He was grateful for anything extra after finishing his own. Giving him the part without hot sauce or salsa, I moved to the living room and opened my laptop.

It was time to search for a new job.

Chapter VII

It caught my eye the moment I scanned it. A local Christian school desperately needed substitute teachers. Salmon District 281was also looking, along with other schools farther out, but I wanted to stay close to home. Salmon was as far as I was willing to go. I searched to learn what was required to become certified in Idaho. Outside of signing clients and teaching, I had little expertise. It shamed me to have Dawson explain how to plant and garden properly—even to build a fire.

Lunch came and went before I finished. After speaking to a secretary for the Superintendent of Public Instruction, I learned it was possible to substitute with an emergency or temporary certification. Most schools across Idaho were desperate for teachers. At the root of the problem was low pay for expectations set too high by state and federal lawmakers. Teachers were no longer tasked to instruct the basics but do the work once done by parents around the dinner table.

Requirements for recertification were tests and online courses. Naturally, there would be a nominal fee. Should I wish to sub immediately, it was possible to have other teachers help me with the studies after school. I could be recertified to legally teach in the state of Idaho in a matter of weeks. It was something to be considered—rather than leap before I looked.

The stove burned down significantly. I took the time to fill it again after ending my call. Chunks could be no longer than sixteen inches and little more than four in diameter. It could be loaded from the top or front, and I found the top to be easiest. The wood Dawson hauled for me caught easily and put out significant heat. With my small pile stacked under the cover of my back-porch dwindling, I took the time to build it again.

I kept a wheelbarrow stored in the garage. I filled it six times and pushed through four inches of snow to the rear of my house. Stopping only after a tall pile was stacked, I returned the squeaky one-wheeled to storage and retreated inside. My cell rang while I kicked my boots off. Recognizing the number, I smiled when I took the call. "Are you wanting me to shovel your driveway, Nurse Ratched?" The thought made me smile. To hear him talk, Dawson's driveway was a mile long. I'd never been there.

"Nope. Just making sure you didn't die on me."

"Alive and well, thanks to Idaho's strictest nurse." Nothing could be further from the truth. He bent over backward to help me, and I couldn't imagine another gentler. A gruff and abrupt exterior was belied by his actions.

"Wait until you get the bill." His voice was dry.

"What can I do for you, Dawson?" He didn't call to shoot the breeze. If anyone spent less time on a phone than me, it was my neighbor.

"Last night, a buddy stopped by and it made me think of you. He—"

"I know I'm a skinny stick figure, but a man reminded you of me?" If only he could see me at ninety-six-point-three pounds. I'd not only have real boobs before long but a muffin-top, too. It was all I could do to not shimmy again. "No…" He sounded irritated. "He made me think of you because of a firearm he wants to sell. He's been out of work too long and needs money for his family. Problem is—it's kind of spendy."

"Why would you think of me when it came to a gun?" My voice flattened and any humor evaporated.

"High quality, portable. and unfired in the box—although it was made seventy years ago."

"A collector's item then." I owned four: My .22/45 and Ruger 10-22, both suppressed. My dad's Glock for personal protection and a Colt M4. Other than my father's pistol, all were purchased for my job. Only the rifle had yet to be used for signing clients. Did I really want a gun that belonged in a collection?

"Do you know what a Colt Diamondback is?"

"A smaller version of their Python, isn't it? Instead of .357, they were made in .22 Long Rifle and .38 Special?" I'd spent long hours poring through gun magazines. I used to joke to myself that they should be written off my taxes.

"Yep. They look like a little baby revolver compared to my Anaconda. The one Rich Shrike needs to sell is the blued four-inch version in .38. He wants it to go to a good home where someone will appreciate and take care of it."

I was no longer angry. "What's he asking?"

"He told me he'd like thirteen hundred, but my gut tells me he'd take a grand. I hate to see him get rid of it, but he has a wife and three kids to feed."

"New in the box, huh?"

"Yep. The woodgrain carton is original and probably worth as much as the gun."

"You've looked at it?" I trusted Dawson's judgment when it came to weapons.

"Like it just left the factory floor. Oh, it comes with a new set of rubber grips and a holster, too."

"Tell him I'll take it." For some reason, the old-timer piqued my interest. It would be a tiny version of the Anaconda Dawson carried on his belt. I would finally have a sidearm to carry that wasn't for signing clients. Only my M4 was virgin, but a military style rifle brought unwanted attention.

"What should I offer him?"

"He has a family, so I'll pay thirteen. I'll take any ammunition he has for it, too."

"You're sure? It's a lot of money, Jules."

"I'm sure." It wasn't until later when I realized he called me by the nickname I grew up with. My cheeks were already wet when I swore it wouldn't make me cry.

\*\*\*

Dawson offered to brave the snow and bring the revolver to me after he contacted Mr. Shrike. While I didn't keep a huge amount of cash in the house, there was always some for an emergency. Enough to purchase a flight out of the country and set myself up short term. I dipped into those funds kept inside a ratty stuffed bear Megan loved when she was little. A string loosened in its back to allow removing expensive stuffing. Sitting against the wall atop my dresser, no one would think it was filled with almost twenty thousand.

Dawson made his appearance the following afternoon. Thankfully he was alone. I guess he understood how much I valued my privacy. He carried a box under one arm as he waded through seven inches of snow. It had let up, but the weather report promised more. Temperatures were cold enough I worried about my animals. Not giving him a chance to knock, I opened the door the moment he crossed the porch.

"Rich asked you to look it over before buying. He isn't going to hold you to the offer sight unseen." He removed a flat box from the larger one.

I gasped after opening it. "Oh, my Lord. It's beautiful, Dawson."

Like the snake it was named after, the handgun coiled inside the box, ready to strike. With a four-inch barrel, full underlug, and ventilated rib, the blued steel was flawless. I removed the gun from where it lay, and found the smaller frame with a corresponding grip fit my little hands perfectly. Like my other two handguns, it came up with the sights aligned on my target, a spot on the wall of my aging kitchen. "I want it." I couldn't set the revolver aside and continued admiring its heft and lines "Rich's willing to sell all the thirty-eights he could find. He can't afford to give them away." Dawson placed boxes of Remington ammunition on the table. "There were only eight full and one partial box. They cost him around fifteen dollars each, and he'll let them go for a hundred." Dawson set the extra rubber grips and holster on top.

"Sold." I counted the cash and stuffed it into an envelope before giving it to my visitor. "Fourteen one hundred-dollar bills. Be sure to thank your friend for me."

"I didn't tell him who was buying, if you're wondering." My neighbor understood me.

Ignoring his comment, I smiled and asked another favor. "Have you ordered ammunition before?"

"Sure, lots of times. I handload, so I have my favorite companies when I buy components and factory loads."

"Would you mind putting in a big requisition for me?"

I saw comprehension in his eyes. "I can. What do you need?" His eyebrows rose when he saw the volume of my request. He felt ordering from more than one company might be best. Each year the government became more intrusive toward gun owners and shooting sports, and he wished to stay off their radar. I gave him another envelope of one hundreds and promised to make up the rest when he had a better understanding of the costs.

"Dawson…" I stopped him before he could start down my porch steps. "If your friend Rich has anything else I might find interesting, let me know. I'm in the market for one more."

"Such as?"

"I have a bird dog and no shotgun." Truth be told, I felt I was a crappy shot with a scattergun. Pistols and low recoil rifles were almost an extension of my body, yet the ferocious energy developed by a 12 gauge pummeled my tiny frame. "Perhaps something in a smaller bore."

He nodded. "I'll let him know. In true form, he left without another word.

I was still admiring the double-action six-shooter when dinnertime rolled around. Not a weapon for work unless caught by surprise, I thought it would be perfect for general carry. A couple of speed loaders dropped in a pocket would be plenty. Eighteen rounds would be only one more than a single magazine in Dad's Glock.

While Mr. Shrike had owned it unfired for his collection, I planned nothing of the sort. Before I retired for the evening, the revolver was cleaned and the old wooden grips removed. In their stead were the rubber combat version with finger grooves. Much smaller than the wooden version, the aftermarket variety fit my hand perfectly. The shoulder holster wasn't much, old and poorly fitted. I resolved to find a new one. Texting Dawson, I asked him to order one similar, except for the strong side rather than cross draw.

As I healed and was more active, the snow acted as a training partner. It quit falling when over a foot was on the ground. I took Jake along on my hikes, and each was longer than the previous. Living in California and on the coast of Oregon, snow was as foreign to me as were cold temperatures. Yet while I enjoyed it, Jake fell in love. Acting like the two-year-old he was, he ran, jumped, and rolled in it. It didn't take many excursions before game birds were encountered. More than once I found him locked on point and forced to drag him away. It seemed he had little choice in the matter—the scent of a pheasant or grouse caused him to freeze like a statue. His eyes would roll toward me while trembling in position as if asking what was happening.

Once I could travel for an hour without pain, fatigue, or general discomfort, my trips were redirected up the mountain. I knew Scotty guided big-game hunters much farther into the mountains. It made me wonder how long it would take from my house to his camp.

The snow melted back before the end of the month. Temperatures warmed for a week, enough to clear the lower elevations. On the hills above where I explored, snow was still deep. Combined with food supplies precariously low and my health better, I felt a shopping trip to Salmon was in order. In jeans, a heavy flannel shirt, woolen socks, and leather boots, I pulled my mad bomber hat over my ears and started the Jeep. I hadn't used the old girl for over a month and feared she might be obstinate, but the engine caught almost immediately.

I was halfway to town when my cellphone rang. Expecting it to be Dawson, I was surprised to see a local number—one I didn't recognize. Pulling to the side in a wide spot, I answered. "Hello?"

"Excuse me. I'm trying to contact Julia Hampton."

"Who is this, please?" The voice wasn't familiar. I glanced at Dad's Glock on the seat next to me.

"My name is Bess Mueller. I'm vice principal for the Salmon school district. How are you?"

"I'm well, Mrs. Mueller. How may I help you?"

"It's come to my attention that you've expressed an interest in substitute teaching. Is my information correct?"

"Yes, ma'am. I contacted OSPI to learn proper procedure in becoming certified in Idaho."

"Oh, good. Then you're already certified to teach elsewhere?"

"Yes, ma'am. I taught four years in Astoria, Oregon."

"Are you looking for something long term or merely substituting?"

"I'm not certain. I've bought a home in the local area and would like to find stable employment and be a part of the community."

"It's a wonderful place. Where are you located, and when could you come in for an interview?"

"My home is between North Fork and Gibbonsville. I'm almost to Salmon as we speak."

"Oh!" She sounded pleased. "Would it be asking too much to have you drop by my office while you're in town?"

"No, ma'am. Tell me where to find you, and I'll stop before grocery shopping. I must warn you, I'm dressed for the cold and not an interview."

"Won't be a problem. I'll be waiting."

***

Mrs. Mueller was an impressive woman. Perhaps fifty or older and at least six-two, she towered above me by a foot or more. Her face lit with pleasure the moment I peeked inside and knocked at her open door. "Mrs. Mueller?"

"Come in." She rounded her desk and offered her hand. I took it and found her shake strong. "Is it Ms., Miss, or Mrs. Hampton?"

"Miss Hampton, but you can call me Julia."

Bess Mueller offered me a job before I left. As many days as I wanted with the possibility of a long-term substitute position opening. She'd called Astoria and spoke to my former building principal with whom I enjoyed a good working relationship. After briefly explaining my abrupt departure from teaching, I thought the older woman was going to cry. I signed all the paperwork for temporary recertification before leaving and promised I would work hard to become credentialed in Idaho.

Bess walked me to the front where I was parked across the street off school grounds. A firearm in my Jeep, I wasn't going to break any laws by bringing it on campus. We shook again. "Mrs. Mueller, I left out something you should know. I was in an accident a few months ago. I'm still weak and rehabilitating. I'll struggle to finish every day until the end of the school year and probably won't be able to work more than two or three days per week. Will that be a problem?"

"I don't think so, other than we're shorthanded. Each hour you can give us will be helpful. Is next week too soon to start?"

"No, ma'am. You have my number. Let me know when you need me."

Dad's Glock was in my holster and under a heavy coat when I walked into the supermarket. I bought enough groceries to fill the back of my Wagoneer. Jake wasn't happy when it forced him to the front seat. My phone buzzed again as I was ready to leave. It showed Dawson's number. I tried to keep my excitement over a job in check. "Hello, neighbor."

"I understand you're going to substitute teach in Salmon."

"Did someone tell you about my meeting with the vice principal? It was an hour ago."

"No." He chuckled. "Salmon isn't very big and everyone knows everyone else's business. Aunt Bess seemed to like you."

"Aunt Bess?" He caught me flatfooted—the idea of Dawson and Bess Mueller related was surprising.

"Yep, Mom's sister." He was silent, and for a moment, I thought he ended our call. "It's nice to hear you're planning to teach again, Jules."

I was in complete agreement. "Working an eight to four day will feel good again."

"Hey, before I let you go, your order came in a few days ago. When shall I drop it off?"

His news was a relief. "Anytime. I'll be home in a half hour or so."

"I'll see you in an hour."

I was finished unloading when we heard the familiar clatter. Since his mistress steadily healed, Jake was ready to show more interest in our neighbor again. His head came up, and he hurried to sit next to the door, his stubby tail swishing against the worn linoleum. The moment Dawson reached the bottom step, I opened the door to let him in. Jake went wild, wiggling and jumping as if his best friend returned. In a way, I guess he did. My recovery freed Jake from worry, and he was able to be himself again.

It took two trips for my neighbor to bring it all in. We opened boxes and stacked the contents on the kitchen table. A case of rounds for my dad's Glock, four times the amount for my .22/45 in standard velocity lead. For the M4, I purchased a thousand fifty-five grain 5.56x45mm NATO. The rifle wasn't properly broken in, and it was time to become more proficient with it.

The Colt Diamondback was a different matter. For my new gun, I ordered a myriad of ammunition, from light bullets to heavyweights. Both standard and +P rounds. To use it as a daily carry gun, I wanted to find the most accurate load I could purchase. A .38 Special wasn't particularly powerful, and it was up to me to learn to shoot it. A proper hit with a lesser caliber was better than a miss from a cannon. I opened the last box to find it filled with a dozen speed loaders and a holster for my new revolver.

Dawson handed me the bill. He marked the money I provided, the cost of my order, and how much I still owed. Giving over another fistful of cash, I breathed a sigh of relief, knowing I wasn't going to run out of ammo anytime soon. Firearm proficiency came from properly applied rounds downrange. Sitting and thinking didn't help a shooter's accuracy. Since he still considered me working, I would submit the amount to Manny, who would see I was reimbursed.

"What did you think of Aunt Bess?"

"She seems nice. For a giant." I was grinning when I glanced to see Dawson smiling.

"Yep, she's a tall one, taller than Uncle Andy by at least four inches. Is she putting you to work?"

"I start next week if they need me."

"They will," he replied confidently. "What grades?"

"I was certified in Oregon for K through eight, but it sounds like K through twelve, considering the temporary certification they applied for."

"Can you handle a six-five, three-hundred-pound lineman? We have some big kids on the football team."

"Easy. It's the girls who are tough." I grimaced, remembering the ones I went to school with. They were brutal to one another and anyone who came between them. From fights over boys to spats between friends, they were unrelenting toward anyone they perceived as different. I fit the bill because of the shooting sports I regularly attended with my family. High school athletics didn't interest me. It didn't take long before I realized a pecking order didn't only apply to chickens. It was a way of life among high school girls. Boys of the same age were simple to deal with. "I'm curious. Is Scotty still up in the mountains with all the snow and cold?"

He grunted. "Now is the best time to hunt…late in the season with snow piling up. Yeah, he's still there and loving every minute. I don't expect to see him until after Thanksgiving unless he has cancelations. He'll take a week off to mend, put away gear, and rest up, then guide for duck and goose hunters. Hunting season will end for him in January."

"There's enough money in guiding to make a year's wages in only a few months?" The idea surprised me.

"No, Scotty barely scrapes by. He works on the river during the offseason. Why, are you interested?" He was teasing, and I took it that way.

"I don't know anyone around here or what they do for a living. The boys at the airport who take care of my Jeep, you, Scotty, and now Bess are my nodding acquaintances. Your mom took care of my canning, and I've never met her."

"You'll get to know people when you teach. Next summer, you'll be friends with half the population in the district."

I changed the subject when I remembered. "Your friend who sold me the Colt. Did you talk to him about a shotgun?"

"Yeah, he doesn't know of any. If you're interested in bird hunting, talk to Scotty. He'll know where to find a scattergun and where to have it fit to your shoulder." Dawson looked thoughtful. "Are you planning on a rifle next and becoming a real hunter?"

I know he didn't mean it that way, but his comment hit me wrong. "*Become* a real hunter?" A snarl colored my voice.

"You know what I meant." For the first time, Dawson seemed at ease with the elephant in the room.

I made myself ignore where the conversation was going and dropped it. "Would you like to have dinner with Jake and me? I was planning on a shrimp stir-fry."

Dawson shook his head. "I'm going to have to pass this time. I'm buying a rifle from Richie Shrike and promised I'd get the money to him as quick as I could. One of his boys was teased at school about wearing the same clothes from last year. Seems he's taking it harder than his son. I think they're planning on shopping—maybe this evening. I'll take a raincheck if you don't mind."

***

My first day of school was enjoyable. A sixth-grade teacher had a doctor's appointment and left behind a detailed lesson plan. Not knowing the school or where the classrooms were, I barely found my desk before students trickled in. The kids seemed surprised by such a small instructor. Most of the boys took delight in showing how much taller they were.

I'd gone through old clothes from my previous teaching position, searching for something appropriate to wear the first day. A long, dark dress and matching sweater still fit and were comfortable. Putting my hair up with bobby pins, I gave one last glance in the mirror before leaving and was pleased with what I saw—a professional who knew what she was doing. Old habits die hard, and I preferred to be someone others wouldn't remember fifteen minutes after we met—a female version of the gray man.

Although kids of that age are feeling the stirring of hormones flowing through their systems, most were helpful. I didn't ask for their input, rather stating plainly what was expected. None complained, and they were soon at work. One girl stayed in class after they were excused for lunch. "Kathy...right?" I was given a seating chart with names and ran my finger down to assure myself. She was nodding when I found her desk and name. "Can I help you?"

Kathy Sturdivant was taller than other girls in the class and most of the boys. She towered over me. A strawberry blonde with a blossoming figure, she would be heartbreaker in a few years. "I was wondering..." Her words were almost too soft to hear. "...don't you live out my house? A German shorthair usually rides with you?"

"I don't know where your home is, sweetie. But you're right. Jake goes everywhere with me."

"Out toward Gibbonsville? My family is in the big blue house on the right after you leave city limits. You live a couple miles before town, down that long road to the north, don't you?"

"Your folks own that beautiful old farmhouse? I've often wondered about it." I stood, not wanting to talk about where I could be found, although she was correct. "You'd better hurry to the cafeteria. I have to go to the teachers' lounge. You're going to miss lunch." I held the door and locked it behind us. Kathy was going to run before I cleared my throat loudly to remind her to walk.

"Miss Hampton, is it?" Another staff member opened the lounge door and held it for me. He wasn't much older than me, tall and handsome. Nodding with my brightest smile, I entered with him following. Three others were already there, eating and discussing curriculum.

"Miss Hampton, I'd like to introduce you to Marty Hart and Teresa Dotson, both fifth grade, and Donald Burgess, technology. If your computer gives up the ghost, he's the guy to bring it back to life. My name is Thomas Howell, sixth grade across the hall from you."

Marty Hart and Teresa Dotson were older, perhaps in their late fifties. Donald Burgess was young enough to be mistaken for a student. Thomas Howell was perhaps a little older than me and slicker than a mole's ear with his glib tongue. It dripped honey each time his mouth opened, and I saw the reaction of Mrs. Dotson as he spoke. Her lip tightened until I could see lines around it. He was a tomcat on the prowl, and I'd noticed a lack of a wedding ring on his finger, nor a mark indicating he wore one.

Marty Hart rescued me. He was short and rotund with interested bright eyes. He drew a chair from another table and gestured for me to sit next to Teresa. I didn't have to be trapped next to Mr. Howell if I wished not to. I didn't and accepted the chair, setting my lunch sack on the table.

Marty took the time to make me comfortable. "It's nice to see a new face, Miss Hampton. Are you new to the area?"

Lunch was more enjoyable than I'd anticipated. Mr. Hart was a funny man and seemed to know a joke about any subject. Best of all, he kept Mr. Howell from monopolizing the conversation, which I was reasonably sure he would. Mrs. Dotson was quiet with eyes missing little, and the techy entertained himself with his phone. Like Mrs. Dotson, I tried to keep quiet and answer as few questions as possible while eating a thick tuna and cheese sandwich. I finished my meal with large piece of chocolate cake made the night before. Water was from my bottle kept full by the fountains. I was reasonably young, and as a substitute should be struggling financially. To me, it was important to look the part.

My class was manageable for the remainder of the day. I left a note explaining to Rachel Boyer how well-behaved her kids were. After donning my coat and locking the door, I noticed Thomas Howell waiting outside his. I sighed while he spoke to passing students with one eye on me. "How was your first day, Miss Hampton?" He hurried to catch up.

He was as tall or taller than our principal, and I was forced to crane my neck. "I certainly can't complain, Mr. Howell."

"Will you be back tomorrow?"

"Only if the sub service calls me."

"Would you be interested in having dinner some night soon? I can help you with questions about school. Perhaps tonight?"

"I'm sorry. I have a guy at home who would be unhappy if I arrived late. He's kind of needy, and dinner is up to me." Jake likely wondered what happened to his mistress. I was let off the hook when a student needing help stopped Mr. Howell. It gave me the opportunity to hurry to my Jeep parked across the street. With a Glock and one hundred two rounds under my seat, I didn't wish to break the law by parking on school property. Mr. Howell waved, and I pretended not to see him.

Although it was an enjoyable first day, Thomas Howell could become old indeed. I sighed as I drove home. Should he continue to consider me a target of his prowling, the man needed to be put in his place. If not, it would be an uncomfortable environment in which to work.

Chapter VIII

Thanksgiving was upon me before I knew it, because the district sub service kept me busy. Except for kindergarten, I taught every grade level between first and eighth. Being pleasant and personable while staying under the radar was difficult. Mr. Howell made himself my new best friend, not giving up even after learning there was a male in my life. Far from flattering, the man left me with a greasy feeling each time we met in the halls or staff lounge.

Teaching was gratifying even without my own room and with applying other teachers' lesson plans. I not only missed my old job in Astoria but the children I barely got to know each day in Salmon. Such energy, hope, and a profound belief of the goodness in life. After reaching a girl one morning and seeing the illumination of understanding light her face, I sat alone and cried during my lunch break. My parents' murder and then Meghan's impressed upon me the evil that exists in the world. For too long, I was fixated on the removal of such terrible wickedness. It was time to live again.

I no longer celebrated holidays after the loss of my family, including my birthday. Instead, I used the time to hunt. I was at a loss of what to do without a client to locate and sign. We had an early-out on Tuesday before Thanksgiving, and my isolation struck when I returned home.

I decided to fill my time with target practice. The weather was mild after the early snow—in the fifties and overcast. The Diamondback I'd purchased hadn't been shot nor sighted in.

My back porch was small but covered. I could see to the base of the mountain and used an old table left behind for a bench to shoot from. After setting a target at twenty-five yards, I fired the first five rounds from the beautifully made handgun. I finally understood what Dawson meant when he talked about a Glock's lack of personality. The little Colt was a breath of fresh air—a thing of steel with grips of rubber and wood made a delightful companion.

I practiced until boxes of empty brass stacked up. I found the gun shot best with a standard mid-level load, the same made when the gun was built. While it wasn't particularly powerful, I felt almost as confident with it as my work gun. Although not in the same category as Dawson's cannon-like .44, good ear protection was paramount. The holster he ordered was comfortable enough on my belt. After removing the cylinder and thoroughly cleaning the Colt, I reassembled and loaded it, returning the snake to its leather den. It would also coil next to my bed with a dozen speed loaders accessible inside the drawer.

While eating dinner and watching funny clips on my computer; I made a conscious decision to check my offshore account. I could feel the concern in the back of my mind—perhaps The Company stripped my account. It was uncomfortable to view it or contact my money manager after calling in my resignation. I needn't have worried. It was all there and more. I hoped a way existed to move it onshore and into an account accessible only by me. It was time to have my manager start the ball rolling, and I fired off an email loaded with questions. It seemed remarkable I could be worth one point two-five million dollars. More if my folks' money were added. Not counting my home, I'd earned a small fortune only a few would ever amass.

A reply message waited when I checked the following morning. It wasn't until I ate yogurt with a little cereal mixed in and washed down with coffee before I thought to peek. As I suspected, my accountant didn't think it would be a problem—it would take time. No matter, a small income from teaching eight to four was enough for Jake and me. She provided a name to manage the small sum left from my parents. It did nothing in a savings account earning little interest, and I thought it would be nice to see it grow.

The morning darkened under a thick cloud cover, but Jake talked me into a hike. He was a growing boy and required daily exercise. Otherwise, he tended to find something to chew, usually an expensive item of mine. More than once, I arrived home to find him hiding with a destroyed shoe left on the couch. He knew better, and my only defense was to make sure he ran enough. I gave him my strictest look. "Are you sure, Jake? The weather doesn't look good."

I brought my Colt and dropped two extra speed loaders into a coat pocket before shrugging on my daypack. It was loaded with basic supplies—flashlight, tarp, rope, matches, a fire starter, survival blanket, and my lunch before we struck out. Within an hour, we were high on a promontory overlooking our house. A covey of grouse caught Jake's nose, and I scared the birds to relieve him of his point. The blanket of clouds was thicker when we reached the ridgetop, the farthest I'd been from home. The slope continued in the direction of an even higher ridge. After a last glance at our rooftop in the distance, I waved my four-legged friend up the mountain.

The steep climb sapped my energy. I shared a fried egg sandwich with Jake, although he probably ate more than me. I brought a small thermos filled with two cups of coffee and drank it before we continued.

The first flakes touched my shoulder when the weather wasn't far above us. It was almost two o'clock and time we turned back. The hike down would be faster than up, and I hoped to return long before dark. Another covey of sharptails caught Jake's attention. They flew, and before I could stop him, my pointer raced across the ridge. "Damn it, Jake," I yelled. "Get back here, you dumb pup!" Already two years old, he would always be my puppy. The sage on the hillside was stunted, and he ran out of control.

He sprinted after the disappearing covey, and I cringed when they glided into a canyon with Jake running full tilt instead of listening. Not sure of what to do, I followed, yelling like a maddened idiot. He vanished with the birds, and terrified over losing him in the mountains, I gave chase into the deep abyss.

When I caught him hours later, he was sheepish, frightened, and exhausted. Almost at the bottom of the chasm, the light of day gave way to dusk. Snow flurries thickened, and I knew we wouldn't make it out before dark. Instead of climbing back the way we came, I heeled Jake and followed the gorge. It took us in a different direction than home, but my goal was to find a road before too dark to see.

I saw lights long before finding a highway. As we emerged from a feeder canyon, the illumination of a distant house caught my attention. It was dark enough to make me use my flashlight. Rocks lay in wait big enough to break an ankle, and sagebrush loomed tall enough lose myself. Focusing on the distant point of light, I walked as straight a line as I could.

The house mirrored most old farm homes. I climbed stairs to the huge porch and out of the weather. Jake beat me to the deck and shook snow from his back. Knowing he was still in trouble, he stood obediently yet oddly on half point, tail wagging low in anticipation. A lone woman showed dimly through window sheers. She looked to be knitting, flickers from a television playing over her like a strobe. I knocked firmly after opening the screen and cringing at the loud protests of a spring straining to hold it closed.

Without a glass panel in the entry, I could only detect footsteps approaching. A light flooded the porch, and the door cracked, the woman appearing as a cautious silhouette. I spoke before she could. "Excuse me. My dog and I got turned around on a hike, and we were caught by dark…"

The door opened farther, and I didn't have a chance to continue. The overhead porch light cast weird shadows onto features backlit in pulsing flashes as she bent to examine Jake before straightening. "Miss Hampton? Julia?" She was taller and much older than me—in her late sixties or even seventy—and may as well have slapped my face as to address me by name.

"Yes?" My right hand crept down to assist a preemptive strike by the diamondback.

"Is everything all right, child? I didn't hear you pull in." She opened the door wider and stepped aside to usher me in, illuminating half-familiar features I'd never seen before.

I stammered, jolted because precise recognition—so key in my former line of work—failed miserably. Jake's stub tail lashed my leg. "I…I have my dog with me. Are you sure it's okay if he comes inside?"

"Jake? Of course, he can. He's been here plenty of times." She closed the door and bent to pet my dog. "Isn't that right, Jakie? Are you being a good boy? Yes, you are." Her patronizing tone would have been embarrassing if not something I did as well.

Nothing made sense. How could this strange woman know Jake? Yet my dog obviously recognized her. "I don't understand. How…"

"Dawson's brought him over lots of times while he's taking care of your place. I'm Melissa Pelletier. Dawson's mother."

"Oh, God..." My legs shook. "For a moment, I thought I'd stumbled into the *Twilight Zone.*"

Melissa burst into laughter. "I can see why. Hasn't my boy talked of bringing your dog over?" The answer must have been written on my face. "He didn't, did he?"

"No, ma'am. For a while, I wasn't entirely sure he understood English. He hardly says ten words when he stops by. It wasn't until I returned from my previous business trip and wasn't feeling well before he would hold a conversation." My laugh was rueful. A bullet in my guts opened my neighbor and me in two different ways.

"My son is only quiet around folks he doesn't know well. No one can get a word in edgewise when he's among friends and family." Her home was very warm. I set my pack aside and glared at Jake when he jumped onto Melissa's couch, turned the required number of times, and curled up. I left my coat on after remembering the Colt. "Can I take your jacket?" She was trying to be a good host, but I shook my head. "Don't worry if you tote a gun. Doesn't bother me. Robert and I raised our boys to understand they're tools for a job— no different from a hammer or screwdriver. They simply serve a different purpose." I'd never heard a woman speak so casually about firearms. Yet we were in Idaho, where common sense abounded, and PC was frowned upon.

"Thank you," I took my coat off and stood near the woodstove to absorb its heat. Melissa hung my coat behind the fireplace on a hook looking suspiciously like one in my place. I finally realized it was to dry clothes.

While she may have glanced at my holstered Colt, my host ignored the fact I was armed. "Dawson tells me you relocated from Oregon?"

"California, actually. I worked in Oregon for a while, then returned to California for a year or so. I made the move to Idaho after my business there was sorted."

Melissa clucked as she sat after moving her darning aside. It appeared she was repairing the heel of a man's sock. I wondered if it was one of her son's. He once mentioned his father passed when

Dawson was barely out of high school. "How does Idaho compare to California?"

Although she didn't come out and say it, my home state didn't seem to be a favorite. I didn't blame her. Anytime I heard about others escaping its strange self-destruction and moving to Idaho, the news caused me to cringe. "I love it here." The words came out before there was time to consider, and they startled me. Until then, I hadn't realized how much I enjoyed where I lived, especially my isolation. It was the right answer—Melissa beamed with obvious pride.

"Bess and Dawson mentioned you're working at school as a substitute teacher." I'd forgotten my boss was related to my neighbor. "Are you enjoying yourself?" When I hesitated, the giggle belied her years. "Don't worry. I won't tell my little sister if it's not good."

"Oh! Bess is your sister? Dawson told me she was his aunt." Melissa nodded. "I like the school, administration, and the kids."

"Have you met many of your coworkers?"

"A few. Most seem pretty nice." I certainly didn't want negative comments getting back to my boss.

"You've met Tom Howell." A hint of a smirk played in her grin.

"I see him almost every day."

"You've probably figured it out. He's always looking for another pretty face. Probably the closest thing to a man-whore Salmon has to offer." Her statement caused me to blink. Melissa Pelletier appeared to be a blunt woman. "Mr. Howell isn't a favorite of this household." She didn't elaborate further.

"Oh, he's pretty confident in himself." I was going to be noncommittal if it killed me.

"Enough about him." She gave a little shudder. "Tell me about yourself. Have you always been a teacher?"

Nothing in her question led me to believe Dawson shared anything personal about me. Instead, she seemed open and genuinely curious, but I wasn't ready to talk about me. "I have to thank you for preserving almost everything in my garden, Mrs. Pelletier."

"Melissa. It was my pleasure, Julia. May I call you by your first name?" I nodded. "I was already harvesting my garden and set up to preserve. My son barely had time to drop things off before I'd finished."

We spoke another half-hour before I mentioned my plight. "Melissa, is there any way I can catch a ride home…or someone I can call for help? Jake took me on a wild goose chase while we were hiking. By the time I found him, neither of us seemed to know the best way to get out."

"Oh, my. I wasn't thinking, was I?" She used the black desk phone next to her. "Honey, could you be a dear and hurry over? I have an important favor to ask." She winked at me. "No, tonight. Yes, right now, young man." My host ended the call abruptly. I saw where Dawson got it. "He'll be here in a few minutes. He sounded a bit grumpy, so I imagine he was either ready for bed or reading a good book."

He didn't live far. The familiar clatter of his pickup with the added whine of four-wheel-drive caught Jake's attention in less than ten minutes. Hoping we would leave soon, I asked for directions to the bathroom and hurried to it. I could hear Dawson's voice and his alarm when I came out. "Mom, what the hell is Jake doin' here? He should be at home with Julia."

My appearance surprised him. "Hey."

My neighbor didn't seem the cool, calm, and lackadaisical man I was getting to know when I returned from the bathroom. This one was worried—almost frantic. He startled when he caught sight of me. "Jules? I didn't see your Wagoneer outside."

I snorted my displeasure. "Took Jake for a walk, and we were pretty far back when he got into some grouse. They flew, he chased 'em, and I went after him. Now here we are."

He didn't get it. "I don't understand. How did you get here?"

"I'm not exactly sure. I eventually caught up with Jake in a canyon bottom, and we followed it out."

I could see Dawson going through my jaunt in his mind's eye. From my house, back into the hills, and then finally to his parent's home. "Christ, you really went for a hike, didn't you? I think I know which canyon you dropped into and 'bout where you came out." His lids drooped as he made mental calculations of my route.

"Yep, and no pain. It seems I'm healed, Nurse Ratched."

Dawson's mother was confused. "Who's she?"

"Someone in a movie, Mom. Just a joke." It was funny to watch my strong neighbor interact with his mother. He quickly changed the subject. "You and Jake need a ride home?"

"If you don't mind. I'm a bit tired and would rather not walk." Between the miles I'd traveled and Melissa's warm house, my eyes were gritty.

"It's too late, too far, and the temperature is barely thirty. It's snowing harder than ever. Probably a bit colder in the morning."

"I'm ready if you are." I reached behind the stove for my coat, causing Jake's head to come up. He hadn't strayed from Melissa's couch and her stroking hand.

"Do you have plans for tomorrow?" Melissa waited with my backpack, while her son helped with my coat.

"Probably catch up on sleep and recover from our roam through the hills," Dawson rolled his eyes where his mom couldn't see. He knew I ate dinner before five and was in bed and asleep around eight each evening. There was no reason to stay up late without a television. I got plenty of sleep and woke each morning at five-thirty.

"Tomorrow is Thanksgiving. If you don't have other plans, please say you'll come. We'll eat about three, but snacking will start around noon." She looked from me to her son as if he could sway my decision.

"Thank you, Mrs. Pelletier, but..."

She butted in before I could come up with an excuse. "Melissa, remember? Please, help celebrate the day with us. We would love to have you."

"I..." A good excuse after her kind rescue and welcome wasn't coming to me. I needed to think faster on my feet.

"We'll have more food than we can eat. Won't you come?" She cocked her head, waiting for a positive response.

My shoulders dropped in defeat. "I'd be delighted." I wouldn't, but she didn't need to know. "What time do you want me and what should I bring?"

"Be here at noon and just bring Jake. He'll love seeing everyone again." Everyone? Again? I had questions that needed answered. Melissa handed the pack over as her son opened the door. "Don't be late. Should I have Dawson stop and pick you up? I'm worried about the road."

"Jake and I can drive ourselves, Melissa. We'll be here as quick as we can. Thank you for the invitation." I certainly wasn't looking forward to it.

Dawson drove like everyone in Idaho no matter the weather. When I drive in snow, it is slow and with great care. It didn't take long when I traveled to Salmon each morning for a string of traffic to build behind me. All the turnouts were becoming well-known to my Wagoneer. "Is there something you've forgotten to tell me?" My voice was dry while I hung onto the door and Jake for dear life.

Dawson's face was illuminated by the dashboard lights. "Neglected."

"Fine, neglected to share."

"You were gone a long time, and Jake needed companionship. We went for a ride each day and usually ended up at Mom's. They kinda hit it off." We didn't travel far on the highway before we reached my driveway. No more than five miles.

"I *was* gone for a while…" It was a glum and wistful remark, causing Dawson to glance to me in response. While I earned an enormous sum of money, I wondered if it was worth it? Probably, but only time would tell.

The final leg of our ride was quick, and Dawson stopped so I could see my steps in his headlights. Leaving early without plans of returning late, no lights were on inside or out. Hopping from the truck and holding the door for Jake, I leaned in before closing it. "Thanks, neighbor. We appreciate it. See you tomorrow." A brief nod, but he didn't answer. Jake beat me to the front door, even after stopping to pee. Dawson left his lights trained on my house while I dug my keys from a front pocket and let us in.

The fire had long gone, and my house went cold. Baseboard heaters didn't let inside temperatures drop below fifty-five degrees. But when it was freezing outside, my place gave me the shivers. I brought in wood and built another fire. Jake made short work of his dinner. While it warmed, I took a hot shower, washing everything but my hair. As thick as it is, even my short locks take too long to dry. I planned to fall into bed immediately and followed my instincts after filling the stove and shutting it down. I felt a presence creep in and jump on the bed. Jake turned three times before groaning his pleasure. It seemed my bed was as comfortable to him after a long day as it was to me.

***

My first Thanksgiving in years wasn't as bad as I feared. Jake and I got to Melissa's house at nearly half past noon, finding plenty of space to park. It was cold, much colder than the previous day. Dawson was already there as was the car Bess drove. My hand went up to knock when the door opened, startling me. "There she is!" I saw the smile of pleasure.

I was surprised. "Scotty? What are you doing here?"

"I've been coming to Pelletier shindigs since Dawson and I started hanging together years ago."

"You're not related, are you? The more people I get to know around here, I find you're all family."

"Nope, no relation," Jake took the lead through the living room and into the kitchen. Like in most holiday homes across America, everyone gathered where the food was.

"You made it!" Her kitchen was huge, and Melissa came from behind the island to hug me. Pulling back after she eventually released me, I handed her the best white wine I owned—the sole bottle in my house. Hell, the only booze I'd purchased since moving in. Dawson was across the room at the far end of the counter and looked up when I entered. He noticed my gift, and I saw the instant humor in his eyes. He knew it was my total supply of strong drink. With a sly smile and the corners of his eyes crinkling, he tipped his chin. "Julia, you know my sister Bess." I nodded at my boss. "This is her husband, Andy. You know Elizabeth and Andy Junior?" Indeed, I did, having subbed in their middle school classrooms. Both children were mauling Jake, and he was soaking it up. "This good-looking man is my other son, William, and his wife, Susan." Susan was very pregnant, and I worried she might give birth at any minute.

"Hey, everyone." I gave a shy smile and wave to the room. "I'm from down the canyon a few miles. Don't mind me. You won't even notice I'm here if I can help it."

114

Scotty took my coat, and I was careful to make sure an open flannel shirt over a gray camisole didn't expose my gun. The sleeves were rolled up, and with it hanging open and not tucked in, the butt of my gun wasn't noticeable. He attempted to cut me from the herd and run me into the living room, but Melissa wasn't having any of it. She forced Scotty to give up and sat me at the counter on a barstool, where she poured a glass of the wine I brought. "I hope you don't mind. I was telling everyone how you and Jake made your appearance last night."

The room was still, waiting for my answer, while I took the opportunity to sample the wine. My taste buds exploded, and for an instant, I wished I'd left it at home. It was good. "Thankfully, God keeps an eye on stupid women and foolish puppies, same as everyone else." I smiled, hoping someone would jump in and bail me out. Of course, no one did. "We went on a long hike because Jake couldn't control his inner birddog." I went back to the wine after my brief explanation.

"Dawson and I plotted it on a map this morning, Julia." Scotty was at my side again. "If you hiked where we think you did, you hoofed it at least fourteen miles by the time you got here."

"Yeah, it was a heck of a walkabout." My glass got precariously low for such a crowd. At some point, I would need to find something to drink without alcohol or run the risk of falling from my perch. I seldom imbibed, and one glass would go to my head.

I was glad when the men, children, and Jake disappeared. We soon heard the sounds of a football game turned up to blare from the television. Susan, Melissa, Bess, and I stayed in the kitchen. The house smelled like I remembered Thanksgiving when growing up. The realization hit me like a runaway train. My mom was gone. I'd never taste her cooking again. Susan noticed me hiding my tears. "Julia? Is it something we said?" She appeared stricken as did the other women when they turned to us.

Melissa was worried, too. "What's going on, honey?" Bess crowded from the opposite side of Susan and put her hand upon my back. Someone handed me a tissue.

"Nothing…it's nothing," I said through hiccups.

"Unexpected tears on Thanksgiving are a lot of something." Bess's voice was as soft as her hand, making my tears flow faster.

"I'm missing my family and Thanksgivings we celebrated at home. The smells brought it all back. I'm good, ladies. So sorry," I sniffed. Christ, give up chasing bad guys, and I turn into an emotional basket case. "I haven't celebrated holidays since I was left alone."

"What's goin' on?" Dawson's voice came through tissues I pressed to my face.

"Nothing," his mother said. "Take yourself into the front room and watch the game."

"Jules?" I felt his familiar grip on my shoulder. It was the same one when he helped me around my house. From bed to the bathroom and couch to kitchen, Nurse Ratched manhandled me many times.

"It's okay. Just a little flashback to when I was growing up." I smiled through the tears after bringing myself under control and asked to be excused to the bathroom. I wasn't gone long, yet the kitchen was silent when I returned. When I saw their sorrow, I figured Dawson explained a part of my sad story. Although I didn't need help, he assisted me to the stool.

"We're so sorry, child." Melissa blinked back her tears. "Dawson explained about your folks...your family..." It was obvious she didn't know what to say.

I felt Dawson's hands on my shoulders again, providing a soothing presence and strength. I loved my family, but it was time to move on. "That's all in the past, and this is the present. Why don't we enjoy today for what it is?"

Melissa's turkey was the centerpiece from a Norman Rockwell painting. Watching Dawson take the stuffed bird from the oven almost set me off again. So many times I smiled at Dad doing the same thing for Mom. Turkey, stuffing, potatoes, and yams. Salads, cranberry sauce, and endless pies. I feared for my stomach when the day ended.

Andy Senior gave the blessing. It was reminiscent of home—we joined hands and listened to his prayer. Other than Dawson and the women, no one knew of my struggle, and I hoped it wouldn't be mentioned again. He was seated across from where I was between

Susan and Bess. Scotty was on the other side of the table, separating Andrew Junior and Elizabeth.

"Do you enjoy teaching at Salmon, Julia?" Susan made sure to steer our conversation away from the earlier situation.

"It's nice. The staff and administration are great to work with. Of course, Bess is the best of everyone there," I grinned at my boss.

"Would you be interested if a long-term sub or teaching position opened?" Bess asked the question during my interview, and she repeated it now.

"I think so. My four years in Astoria were wonderful."

"Why aren't you teaching there?" Andy knew nothing and Bess glared at him. I'm sure such discussion wasn't common dinner conversation.

I swallowed hard realizing it would eventually come out, and I decided to share. "My parents were murdered in California. My younger sister disappeared, and I was executor of our parents' will. It took time to file the necessary paperwork and sell my folks' home." I thought it prudent to leave out hunting and killing the men responsible for their deaths.

The sounds of idle conversation and silverware died instantly. Those who'd been in the living room stared in uneasy surprise.

"Did you find your sister?" Elizabeth asked the inevitable and painful question.

"No, sadly she died, too." I'd been staring at my plate. When I lifted my gaze, it was Dawson to whom I looked. His expression was calm without the pity I saw elsewhere. It was the same conversation he and I exchanged while I healed.

"Jesus," Scotty said. "Did they catch whoever did it?"

"Yes."

Andrew was as curious as his sister. "You stayed in California?"

"For a while. "I smiled. "I moved here so I could get lost and be invited to a Thanksgiving dinner." The youngster grinned at my wink.

I was stuffed when we eventually stopped eating. Another football game was on, and all except Bess were chased from the kitchen by Melissa. The sisters worked well together and quickly joined us before the game progressed far.

The living room was large with two sofas and a pair of recliners. Andy Senior sat in one chair while Scotty chose the other. Andrew Junior, Dawson, and Elizabeth sat together on a sofa, and the children motioned for me to sit with them. On the other, William and Susan had their heads together in quiet conversation. I tried to sit between the two kids, but Andrew quickly shuffled to the side, forcing me to squeeze next to Dawson. Andrew and his sister giggled, and after leaping up, disappeared into the kitchen. It was an obvious ploy to put Dawson and me together. I didn't mind. Of them all, I was most comfortable around my neighbor. I was relieved the kids didn't sing, *Uncle Dawson and Miss Hampton sitting in a tree. K-I-S-S-I-N-G . . .*

Football was a sport I watched little of. Huge men crashing into one another didn't interest me. It soon became obvious I was the only one not captivated by the game. Curling up on the far end from Dawson, I drifted to sleep, filled with tryptophan-laced turkey. Still wearing my Colt, I lay with my head positioned away from him to keep it from digging into my side. I could hear whispers and the game being played on the television in the background of my nap.

"Is anyone ready for pie?" Melissa's voice woke me as I'm sure it was meant to. She and Bess took orders, and mine was for a small piece of apple. She promised to heat it and add a dollop of vanilla ice cream over my protests. I was dealing with a stomach stretched tighter than it had been in years.

After rubbing sleep from my eyes, I used the bathroom and returned in time for dessert. I felt the vibrations of a phone call in my pocket and drew it out to check the number. Quickly setting my plate down, I stood and apologized. "I'm sorry. I have to take this." I hurried outside and into the cold on the front porch. I answered the phone and heard the door behind me at the same time. "Yes?"

"Manny here."

I wasn't ready for his call, and my tone was impersonal. "Yes."

"Can you talk?"

"No."

"Can you listen?"

I knew who loomed behind me—his quiet presence was a force to be reckoned with. "Yes."

"We have a big one, and it's right up your alley. This is no guppy. It's a shark worth more than you can imagine."

My mind was made up, and I wasn't willing to change it. "No. I said I was done…retired."

He didn't sound particularly surprised. "Your request was rejected."

His casual statement shocked me. "What?"

"You can't turn this one down, partner."

"Oh, yes, I can. Watch me."

"Not this time." He was firm, and I could hear no leniency in his tone.

"Why?"

"Because the big guys, the ones who run The Company, requested you personally."

"Me? How do they know me? I'm nothing but a lone anchovy in immense oceans. Let them find someone else."

"This wasn't to go any further than me, J." Manny was taking his time, making a decision on his end. "You need to understand you've quickly become legend." The cold made me shiver, and I heard the door open and close once more.

"I don't understand."

"From what I can ascertain, you're one of only two signing clients who've never failed. It's why they want you for the job. We need you to ink this deal."

The door opened and closed a third time before the warmth of a jacket settled over my shoulders. My shivering slowed. "What does it have to do with wanting me to take on this particular client?" I grimaced at my slip of something Dawson could hear.

"It's out of the country. I realize you've refused them, but you can't pass on this job."

"I intend to do exactly that. You know I don't take anything offshore. Where is it by the way?" The perverse side of me wanted to know how far from home they expected me to travel.

"Bahamas. It's the reason this is client is worth money. Big money."

The Bahamas? The islands weren't that far away from the shores of the US. I shook my head, surprised I was actually considering it.

"Can't do it, Manny." I squeezed my eyes closed, knowing my side of the conversation spoke for itself. He might as well be on speakerphone.

"He's worth a half million, J. You can't turn it down."

Chapter IX

My God. I'd retired and meant it, but who says no to a half million dollars? It took me almost four years to save that much. A chair sat empty a few feet from the door, and I collapsed into it. In my peripheral vision, Dawson leaned against the door frame. He wasn't looking at me. Instead, he stared out into a snowy yard. Flakes fell sporadically—barely enough to notice.

"Minus your cut." Twenty percent would be a hundred grand, leaving me with four. Still a fantastic payday.

I heard satisfaction on Manny's end. He knew I was nibbling at his bait. "No. I'm to offer you a half-million. The Company will take care of me."

I was silent, torn in two directions. Greed battling my fear of catching another bullet was only half the problem. What if this was The Company's solution of assassin disposal? I had a chance at a normal life, perhaps one filled with a mate and family. The thought swung my gaze to Dawson. Our eyes met, and his reflected sadness and defeat. If he'd shouted his unhappiness aloud, it couldn't have been expressed more clearly.

Setting the phone on the arm of my chair, I rubbed my face with both hands. In the distance, I could hear the tinny voice addressing me as J. I lifted the cell to my ear. "I'm here." Swallowing hard, I squeezed my eyes shut and was surprised to feel tears.

"You have to take this. You have to."

"Why me? Can you answer that? Why me? There must be a hundred others who could do it better and faster for less money."

"Because this guy imports more narcotics into the US than all the other dealers we're aware of combined. It's brought to the mainland by the ton multiple times each month, occasionally per week. To counteract it, we need to send the most successful employee The Company has fielded."

"Seven-fifty, and you agree to my terms. All of them." I couldn't stop weeping but didn't allow Manny to hear it.

His sigh signaled leaden sarcasm to come. "We could have the island firebombed for that amount."

"All right. If it's that easy, have it firebombed." I ended the call and pulled my legs against my chest, hugging them with my arms. I used the knees of my jeans to soak the river of tears. My cell rattled again.

"Don't answer." Dawson's deep voice was like the rumble of an approaching storm.

"I have to." I whispered, staring at the phone as though it were a deadly viper.

"No, you don't."

"You don't understand." A tone sounded when it went to voicemail. "These people hold the power of life and death in their palms. No one on earth is immune to them." It buzzed again. "They can order the death of a president as easily as yours. They send people like me to carry it out."

Dawson didn't blink. He recoiled and something in his countenance changed. It was hard to put my finger on. He took a big breath and held it for a moment before letting it out and licking his lips. "Then parley. There's something they want from you, so you're in the position of power. Use it to bargain with." He dropped to one knee next to my chair. "If you can find a way to trust me, I've got your back." He pointed again at the noisome phone. "Negotiate." The easy-going man I knew had disappeared. Even his folksy manner of speech altered.

I answered and switched to speakerphone. "J here."

"You've got it. They've agreed to seven-fifty. What other terms are you *demanding*?" Heavy emphasis weighted his last word.

"Don't piss me off, Manny. I've always considered you my friend. Let's not change that." My tone edged my benign words.

"I apologize. Please, go on."

"The seven-fifty in cash if I'm successful, delivered to an address I'll provide."

"He didn't hesitate. "Done."

My next stipulation was equally absolute. "You'll see that I'm buried with my family if I don't make it back. Not in a pauper's grave in another country. I want to be interred next to my parents and sister." Dawson's growl was the slow distinctive rumble of a tiger, low enough only I could feel it resonate in my core.

"You don't have to ask. It goes without saying."

"I need to hear your promise, Manny."

"Done."

"Are you ready for the big clause? Like the others, this is nonnegotiable."

"I already know but go ahead and tell us…me…tell me."

"When this client is signed, no one calls me again. I'll come out of retirement for this task only. But my phone never rings with another job. Not ever in this lifetime."

"J…"

No further negotiating for me. It was all or nothing. The next call would be followed by yet another and so on. Eventually an assignment would catch me, and I wouldn't come home, whether by death or arrest. While certain the duty I performed was just, my thirst for atonement was sated. I required normalcy in my life. "All I need is one word from you, Manny. Just one."

"I'll have to get back to you on this."

"Our bosses had better make the right call, my friend."

"Understood." The line went dead.

Leaping to my feet and running down the stairs into the snow, I stopped at my Jeep and leaned on the hood. My head dropped into my arms, and I wept harder than when my family died. The combination of a hefty payday and valid fear of The Company if I didn't comply consumed me. If I perished while fulfilling my final contract, I would die as I had lived my life—alone—without family or friends. I was consumed with self-pity and already worried about Jake. It was him and me—we took care of the other without question. He would be lost without his mistress.

"Jules…" Dawson's hand was light on my back when he came from behind.

I drew a shaky breath. "I'll need you to take care of my boy while I'm gone. He'll miss me." My fears came out in a rush. "If I don't come back, can you make sure he goes to a good home? Someone who'll love him like I do?" I choked on the words. "My house and property…I don't have heirs or a will. I can write something and leave it on the table. Try to take it to court if you can and fight for my place, Dawson. Please tell me you'll go to war to keep the government from confiscating it. I'll put a call into my money manager before I leave, and she can make funds available for you to fight."

He nodded seriously. "You write it up and put your John Henry on it. I'll see to it Mom and Scotty sign. Won't be a problem when I explain why. Don't worry about the money. I'll take care of it."

"Thank you," I sniffed. It was snowing harder, and I felt him turn me and wrap his strong, warm arms around my body. I felt unreasonably safe inside his embrace. It meant nothing that he could do little but hold me. He wasn't wearing a coat and had to be cold, but his internal heat carried the scent of the soap he showered with. Most importantly, his embrace gave the safety my dad once provided in times long gone.

His voice was soft. "Don't worry about Jake. He can stay with Mom. Andrew and Elizabeth visit often enough he'll get plenty of exercise." Dawson's chin rested on top of my head. "I'll take care of your place till you get back."

"I have to go." I pulled away and started my Jeep to let it warm. He was waiting to walk me back to the house. "Could you ask Bess to come outside? I need to explain I won't be available for a while." When the door reopened, she and Melissa followed Dawson to where I waited on the porch. Their eyes were full of questions when they saw my state of disrepair. "Something's come up, and I have to leave for a while. Bess, I've enjoyed working for you. If things go well…" I battled against my tears. "…if it's at all possible, I'd like to be a part of the school again." My hiccups returned in full force when it came time to face Melissa. It seemed incongruous we met only twenty-four hours before. Already she seemed like an old friend. "Dawson thinks Jake likes staying with you. Could he while I'm gone?" It was difficult to force the words out. She looked from me to her son and back before nodding. Both women were speechless while I hugged them with all my strength and fled to my Jeep. They felt more like family than neighbors and boss.

***

I beat him to my house by less than five minutes. We hadn't said goodbye, but I didn't expect him to follow. Dawson stomped in while I was in the middle of starting a fire. My phone rang while he was sitting on my couch. I didn't have to look at the number and put it on speakerphone. "J here."

My eyes locked with Dawson's when we heard the voice. "Manny. We have a deal. Consider this call a formal handshake."

"Thank you. It's the assurance I need that you know where I stand," I said. "When am I leaving?"

He chuckled, and it was nice to hear his friendly voice again. "Where would you like to fly from?"

Dawson and I were still looking at one another. He stroked his short beard while he listened. A part of my brain disengaged and watched him. "Missoula, I guess."

Keys tapped through our connection. "You're booked three-thirty in the morning on a flight to West Palm Beach, Florida, with a short layover in Dallas, Texas. Find a bus or taxi to Fort Lauderdale. Take the Bahamas Express Ferry to Freeport on Grand Bahama Island. If you don't have a passport, make sure you have a driver's license, credit card, whatever."

"Freeport is in the Bahamas?" I knew little of the area.

"Grand Bahama, yes."

"How long is this expected to take?"

"I won't lie to you, J. It's hard to say, because your client is a multi-millionaire with a string of hotels, resorts, and casinos. You can't sign him with a gun, so forget about a firearm." I winced when he said the words, and Dawson didn't blink.

"Jesus Christ, Manny. How in the hell am I expected to get his signature?"

"It's the reason we've called you. You're one of the best we have. Improvise. How you do it is up to you."

I took a deep breath. Any expectation of survival was evaporating. "You'll need to provide the usual shell company credit card, and at least ten...no...twenty thousand in cash waiting for me in Freeport. God only knows who I'll have to bribe." Dawson stopped tugging at his beard.

"The card will be with your ticket at the counter in Missoula."

"Do you have a name, description, and age for me?"

"Tyree Wiggins, forty-six."

I was going to be sick. Everyone in the western world recognized the man. Retiring from MMA fighting at the height of his career, he'd invested heavily in the Bahamas and made it big. Anyone traveling to the area wanted to stay at a Wiggins hotel or resort, and gamble at one of his casinos. They were second to none according to press reports. "Oh, Manny, why do you hate me?"

Quiet compassion filled his voice. "Quite the opposite. Like our employers, I still wish only the best for you. It may seem unfortunate at the time, but we need what is best for The Company, which directly correlates to the welfare of the US. You win, we win, and the American people win." His voice dropped to a whisper. "I'm sorry, J." The call ended.

My fire was almost out—small pieces burned quickly. I pushed what was left together, added more wood, and waited for it to catch before putting on larger lengths. Once the firebox was full, I closed it partially and retreated to my recliner. I pushed back and covered my face with a forearm to block out the world.

"You'd better pack, shouldn't you?" I enjoyed Dawson's deep voice, feeling it reverberate through my bones. James Earl Jones had nothing on this gentleman farmer. It made me sad to think I might never hear it again.

"How bad do you think Lost Trail Pass will be?" It was normally a three-hour ride to Missoula from my house. In wintertime, deep snow occasionally closed the high roads.

"It'll be slow going, but I'll get you to the airport on time."

"You?" I lifted my arm and peeked at him.

"I'm driving, so you can sleep."

"Stay home, farmer. This is my problem, not yours."

"I'm making it mine."

Something in his voice made my breath catch when his rumbled warning dropped an octave. My eyes were swollen and face covered with tears of regret, but I still had to look. Like always, his features changed little, but Dawson was as angry as me. "Nothing good can come from your involvement."

I leaned my head back to break eye contact. Fear, anger, and worry combined to exhaust me. I awoke from a short nap to sounds of Dawson adding wood to my stove. When I didn't move from my comfortable position, he went into the kitchen to make coffee. He knew almost as well as me where everything was, and I heard him fill my thermos with hot water.

"You're awake." He returned to the living room and saw me watching. "It's getting late. We need to leave soon to catch your flight." Where I was filled with sadness and regret, his eyes flashed hostility.

I heaved myself from the chair and quickly scribbled a note in case Dawson needed to take possession of my home. "I'll get a shower and pack a few things."

We left my Wagoneer in the garage, and I tossed my small carryon in the backseat of his truck. I felt naked to go to a job without my work tools. When we passed the turnoff to his mom's house, Dawson didn't bother to glance. In some ways he was more businesslike than me. The road was clear. Snowplows had been through, and we made good time until we started our ascent. Feeling an urge like never before, I fumbled for my phone and removed the battery. Technology went much further than I could imagine, and I didn't want us tracked nor anyone overhearing our conversation. It was something I should have done sooner if I were thinking clearer.

I broke the quiet in his pickup other than the barely audible diesel and tires muffled by snow. "Dad taught me to shoot. I used to compete with him when I was growing up. My sister Meghan was a lot younger than me. Mom and Dad called her their wonderful surprise. When I left for college, she was already dabbling in drugs. For the life of me, I could never understand why. She was only twelve."

Although Dawson concentrated on the worsening conditions, I'm sure he never missed a word. The tires slipped once, causing us to slide sideways. He steered into our skid and regained control without missing a beat. It seemed not to bother him, and I tried to show equal courage. "She ran away not long after turning fourteen. We never saw her again. My parents spent thousands...hundreds of thousands...looking for her. We'd get reports of a sighting and drive to Los Angeles but never found her. Reliable sources told us she was hooking on street corners for drug money."

It was a story I'd related to no one else. Certain that I wasn't coming back, the need for someone to know my family's story was overpowering. I didn't cry when I told of my parents' deaths. Neither did I withhold my satisfaction when I tortured and killed their two murderers. Dawson would never tease me again about carrying my dad's Glock after learning how well it served me.

While I confided my meeting with the gray man in great detail, I didn't disclose any of my client's names. Knowledge of that sort would only burden Dawson, rather than further my story. I finished with my client in Seattle and how I was wounded in Yakima. We'd crept over the pass and were nearing Darby, Montana, when I concluded.

"Seven…that's impressive." I guessed the recounting of my debacle in Yakima caught his attention. He chuckled. "And to think we were having a shoot-off with rabbits in your garden."

The way he stated it made me giggle, although it wasn't funny. "I'm having the money sent to your house. Is that okay with you?"

"It would hurt my feelings if you didn't."

"Act like you don't know what it is, that I'm just a neighbor. I'll say the same on my end. Tell whoever delivers the cash we all do it for one another." I didn't want to implicate Dawson.

"I don't have to act. Folks around here do it for one another."

"You know where to store it if or when it comes, don't you?"

He nodded. "I do." I wasn't surprised. Hell, he was the one who found and rebuilt my bomb shelter.

I struggled to stay awake. "If I don't come back, keep whatever you need to get my property and donate the rest to the school district."

The drone of his engine lulled, and I fell asleep before we reached Hamilton. It was less than forty-five minutes of rest, but I woke feeling refreshed when we parked at Missoula International. It was a few minutes after two in the morning. He came around after parking and opened my door. With only a carryon to worry about, I jumped down so he could close it.

"Don't come in." I dropped my bag on the asphalt and stepped into Dawson's open arms. I felt like a child inside them, safe and protected. Mine went around his waist, and I clutched at him rather than merely hug back. Perhaps if I held tightly enough…no, a job had to be done if I hoped to be free. I pushed myself away with a monumental effort. He didn't want to release me any more than I wanted to leave. Planning to turn and walk away, I only made it a few steps. "Take care of Jake, please? Love him as much as I do and don't let him forget me." I hoped in the low light of the parking lot he couldn't see tears started again. He nodded and took a step toward me, but I held my hand out. "Don't."

"Jules, do me a favor, okay?"

I nodded. "If I can."

"When you get to where you're going, remember something." I tipped my head, curious. "Things are never what they seem." Puzzled, I stared back. "I want you to repeat it to me. Things are never what they seem."

"Things are never what they seem?"

"Yep…" He grinned. "…and no matter what, don't give up hope."

\*\*\*

My ticket and card were waiting when I checked in. The plane was half occupied, and we were wheels up at three-thirty-one. Exhausted by stress, I ignored those nearby and slept until we landed in Dallas. I had two hours to endure before boarding to West Palm beach. I bought a couple of fashion magazines and thumbed through the pages during the last leg. The flight was smooth without others in my row, and the periodicals were tossed in a trashcan when I found a taxi. Twenty minutes later, I was let off at a small and old hotel. True to his word, Manny left a package for me to take possession of. Although it was light outside, I fell into bed and to sleep immediately.

The following morning was Saturday. I took a close look at myself in the mirror after a shower and brushing my teeth. My midriff looked better, although the bullet wound was still an angry red. It was above and a little right of my navel. I was sure a high cut one-piece swimsuit would cover it if I wanted to swim. Flip-flops and bikinis would be most prevalent where I was going.

Still closer to thirty-two than thirty-three. My ribs were visible even after working hard to eat more, and my belly button had no other course against rock-like abs than to be an outie. I was sure my ninety-six point three pounds dropped. Years before at the same bodyweight, I measured my waist and came up with nineteen inches. Now a little older, I assumed it thickened but couldn't see the difference. I needed to eat better and more often.

Other than clean underpants and a bra, the only clothes I brought were what I wore. I called for a taxi and went outside to feel what could only be described as the heat of summer. In Idaho, it'd been snowing heavily with temperatures in the twenties. A digital clock-thermometer down the street gave the time and alternate readings of seventy-nine Fahrenheit and twenty-six point eleven Celsius. Whatever the numbers they combined with oppressive humidity to wrap like a hot, wet blanket around me.

"What address please?" The driver waited for me to buckle before entering traffic.

"Somewhere for a good breakfast. I'm starving."

I was dropped off at a hole-in-the-wall café with directions to call when I finished. Large tips made good friends. Telling him I needed to shop for more appropriate clothes, he smiled and assured me he knew where to go.

Inside were no more than a dozen tables with a *Seat Yourself* sign near the door, and I chose a spot for two. The server came from the kitchen with a meal for another. She nodded to let me know it wouldn't be long and returned with a menu. "What can I get you to drink?"

I took the laminated folder and realized she was gorgeous, perhaps model material. A ring with a tiny diamond on her left hand told me she was married but with little money. Backing up my impression, threads were visible on her collar over a nametag proclaiming *Miranda*. "How's your coffee?"

"I don't drink it, but my customers tell me it's good. We grind our beans here if that means anything."

"A glass of water, please, and coffee in an IV bag." I gave her my brightest smile. She understood immediately.

Their breakfast choices looked like something designed for yuppies. Fruits, eggs, and potato wedges—it seemed made for someone from a diet commercial. On the bottom corner of the breakfast list, I spied what I wanted and more importantly needed.

"Have you decided?" Miranda set my cup and a carafe on the table.

"The petite filet mignon, rare, eggs staring, and wheat toast. Could I swap the potatoes for a small plate of fresh fruit?" I smelled the coffee while she wrote and gave it a taste test. "Your customers are right. This is good."

Their breakfast was, too. The steak's flavor was nice and cooked to perfection. I'd never eaten fruit as fresh and flavorful and planned to consume it often while in the area. The meal was expensive at twenty dollars but worth it. When Miranda brought my ticket, I made sure she saw I left a pair of American Jacksons. I told her no change while I pushed them to her. She was more than helpful when I asked where to shop for swimsuits, casual apparel, and shoes.

I was returned to my room by the same driver, my arms loaded with retail totes, logos on the sides. One box in a paper sack was take-out, a half sandwich and fruit from the same café. My stomach wouldn't thank me in the short term, but I couldn't wait to gorge myself.

Men are lucky. They're generally happy if their clothing doesn't fall off or split open. Most but not all men. Women? We agonize over everything. Young people tended to buy clothes a bit too tight. I was an exception to the rule. However, I was often forced to buy in the girls' section, which meant I took what I could get.

I laid my purchases across the bed and studied a one-piece swimsuit. All were cut high on the hip and covered my stomach. Three had plunging fronts but stopped above my scar. I was thankful of no exit wound because most suits were open-backed to the waist. The rest of my body was unscarred and would tan if given time. Even the most conservative beachwear available was more risqué than I was comfortable with. I nibbled at the fruit while I checked the fit of each one again. Pulling my hair high, I thought I saw in the mirror where a man might be interested. From a distance, I appeared young, but up close, worry lines around my eyes and mouth were deeper and more visible. Age and stress were catching up. I went to bed no closer to a solution on how to sign Tyree Wiggins to a contact.

***

A sign greeted us as we ferried into port Sunday morning: *Welcome to Freeport Harbour, Grand Bahamas Island.* I disembarked with everyone else, going through customs and showing my ID. The uninterested man gave my driver's license a cursory glance before handing it back. I picked up my bag and went in search of a taxi. Why did Manny tell me I couldn't bring a gun? None of my belongings were inspected. Was my assignment an anomaly?

A room awaited me at Wiggins' largest hotel on the twenty-second floor, affording a splendid view of the ocean. A slider beckoned, and I opened the curtains and door, enjoying the smell, sounds, and feel of wind. It was a Juliet balcony, no different from any other, made of steel and perhaps ten-feet wide and protruding four with two chairs. Within a hundred yards lay the shore of Silver Point Beach and beyond that, the Atlantic Ocean. To my left sprawled both Coral and Lucaya Beaches and past them more unknown sand. Yet to swim, all I had to do was step from my balcony to fall into the nearest manmade pool. Perhaps it would be better to take the elevator than dive over two-hundred feet.

My room was three floors below the twenty-fifth and final floor. Wiggins' biggest and most opulent hotel was also his home and office. From the lobby map, I could see he took the entire level for himself. Three elevators carried guests, and a fourth was private.

The top suites were for patrons with money and influence. My room was actually three, a bathroom, spacious living area and kitchen, and a bedroom. It was larger than my house. A fully-stocked bar would likely go untouched. However, I planned to make use of the king-sized bed while I was there. Manny went all out, and accommodations weren't without my appreciation. Unless I found an unexpected way to garner Wiggins' signature, my time in the Bahamas would be lengthy.

After relaxing on the comfortable couch, watching local television and napping, it was time for reconnaissance. I took a shower and chose my most modest swimwear. Primarily blue, I picked it to match my eyes. It didn't plunge as deeply as some of my

132

purchases, and I covered the bottom half with a white sarong. Not sure where I was going, I chose sandals that protected my feet better than flip-flops. I gave a last check of my outfit in the mirror, afraid if I bent forward, others could see inside my top. I tried to make it gape open, only to find it was worth the two-hundred-dollar cost. My chest would likely draw little more than uninterested glances—I did a poor job of filling out the upper half.

The lobby was huge. Perhaps fifty percent of the ground floor were casinos and three restaurants. Local cuisine was available in one, another served Italian, and the third Greek. From what I could see while wandering, all three were packed during midday. Security guards stationed themselves at the front desk and each exit, making my job more difficult. I'd arrived in back where local fauna stretched into the distance. Between the hotel and beach were a series of three pools of varying sizes ringed by lounge chairs.

I knew what Tyree Wiggins looked like. Even if I didn't, pictures of him looked down from walls all through the hotel. He'd been a heavyweight fighter and still looked the part. A tall man, his mother was Chinese and his father Moroccan. With a big upper back and long thick arms, he possessed the sloping shoulders of a mule, exuding raw power. Not even a suit could hide his physical dimensions. Staring at a photo at least twelve feet high, I could feel only despair. How could a woman barely five-feet and less than a hundred pounds sign a giant without proper tools?

The locals were friendly and constantly searched for ways to part tourists from their money. I bought a straw hat with a wide brim to keep my pale skin from burning faster than it should. Only a few hours of the first three days were spent in the pool area. My skin reddened quickly, and I retreated to either my room or one of the restaurants. Greek was a favorite of mine, and I spent almost as much time there as in my room. I was hooked on the fresh food they served. An older man worked as a server my third day, and he quickly became my favorite.

"May I help you?" The first time he appeared at my table set me at ease. Many of the servers were young men in their teens and twenties. Although they worked hard, I felt dirty after they left my table, having been measured and categorized. Butch was different.

Appearing around the age of forty, he approached the job as a professional. I noted the simple gold ring on his left hand and how it hadn't been removed for years. Something in his eyes told me he was happily married.

"A platter of fresh fruit and coffee, please."

"Will that be all, or do you need time to look at our menu?" He waited patiently.

"No, just the fruit." It was a few minutes before the lunch rush.

The platter he brought back made my mouth salivate. "Are you new here, or have I missed seeing you?" I awaited his answer while tasting the java. One can't be too friendly toward the help in my line of business.

"I started this morning, Miss." He seemed in a hurry and I understood why. Tourists were milling into a line outside. "Can I get you anything else?"

"This will be fine, thank you." Seated on a back wall, I was able to monitor the hotel lobby and through a series of windows, keep tabs on the parking area. The spot quickly became a favorite, allowing me to note patterns emerging as people went about their business. I also learned to be fifteen minutes early for the meal rush. My preferred seat was usually available and I was served quicker. I was also able to watch who ate where. My goal had been to catch sight of Tyree Wiggins and learn his daily format.

It wasn't until the seventh day that he made an appearance

Chapter X

I found the new server was employed to work six days each week. Butch Prayde and his wife had two sons, the youngest about to follow his brother to college. Proudly proclaiming them to be the first of his line to enter institutions of higher learning, Butch worked hard to support the family dream. He became a joy to watch as he performed duties with little wasted effort. Unlike most who waited tables, his hands and fingers were thick, scarred, and strong. I spent hours daily in both the Greek and Italian restaurants, building good relationships with the help.

My story went that I was spurned by my husband who ran off with a secretary and left me alone and in pain. A vacation to the Bahamas was to help me forget, so anyone asking learned I planned to spend a month before reassessing and perhaps moving to another island. A divorce left me with money enough for a modest lifestyle but little more. Each day, I attempted to purchase something frivolous: a hat, magazine, scarf, or even shoes. I was at a kiosk waiting in line for a bottle of water when Tyree Wiggins walked into the lobby.

Seeing him at such close range, I wanted my .22/45 badly. The nearest he came was twenty feet. Even from there, I could feel the draw of his persona and self-confidence. He strode like a conquering king and didn't care who knew it. I wasn't the only one who noticed him. Most of those ahead of me left their place to clamor for a signature. Others nearby did the same. It surprised me when he stopped and fulfilled all their requests. It seemed everyone was drawn to him, and I stopped after purchasing my water to watch. When I turned to leave, he glanced up, and we made eye contact. My smile made barely an acknowledgement with an upturn at the corners of my mouth. My plan was to sunbathe another hour before returning to my room. Stopping at the glass doors before stepping outside, I turned for one last peek. He was still looking—or perhaps viewing me again.

"May I bring you something?" I raised the brim of my hat and lowered my sunglasses to better see the staff member hoping to take my order. It was hot, and I was one of many sweating under an umbrella. Most were men and woman twice my age or more, and one I judged to be thrice. Apparently, only the old and retired spent time in the warm climate during winter months.

"A Sprite, please?" I hadn't met this one, and he appeared to be longer in the tooth than Butch. It made me wonder if retirees moonlighted to help defray the cost of living.

I had a better chance to take his measure when he hurried back. The man looked more a boxer than waiter. His nose had been broken and twisted in different directions. Scars were visible on his forearms and hands. It also looked as if he'd spent his life on the water or plains with tanned skin turning to leather.

"Should I bill it to your room?" He handed me a check, and I neatly inscribed J. Marie Hampton—allowing a five-dollar tip for the four-dollar soda. After a smile and word of thanks, the grizzled man moved on to serve others. I tasted it before throwing off my sarong, hat, flip-flops, and sunglasses, to dive into the pool.

I've always been a good swimmer. Not great—good. I loved springboard events and took in competitions whenever I could. Freestyle stroking the length of the deep pool three times, I climbed the ladder nearest the boards. Choosing the lowest first—a three-footer—I cut the surface with minimum splash to swim the length and back. It seemed no one wanted to enjoy the water but me, and I had the pool to myself. For my second dive, I chose the ten-foot board and was pleased with my form. After two more simple pikes, I returned to my sheltered chair and sampled the cold soda. If it weren't for the circumstances of the trip, my stay would have been magical.

"You dive beautifully." A woman not much older than me stopped nearby. Perhaps six feet tall, she wasn't lean, although not heavy, either. She wore a conservative one-piece swimsuit covered by a light beige caftan.

"Thank you. It's something I never have enough time for." When she didn't move on, I invited her to share my shade. "Would you like to sit?"

"A few minutes, I guess." She perched on the edge of the chair. "My husband and I arrived today." She held her hand out where I could see her ring. "Mandy Maj…err…Bradshaw." She blushed prettily. "We were married only yesterday."

Her hand was much larger than mine. "Congratulations. My name is Marie Hampton from Idaho. How about you?"

"Madison, Wisconsin. Mark and I used to work together…"

I hardly heard another word. Her droning continued, but my attention shifted to Tyree Wiggins who left the hotel wearing only cargo shorts. His heavily muscled torso rippled while he walked, and I was sure he was keenly aware of every eye following him. Mrs. Bradshaw may not have recognized him because she never stopped talking, although she watched with mild interest. Two bodyguards followed him, although I couldn't understand why. The man was a walking mountain—a peak that seemed an impossibility for me to summit, sign, and survive. He traveled on the far side of the pool and disappeared into the sand beyond. Thirty seconds later, I watched as he jogged onto the beach with his guards not far behind.

"Excuse me?" I realized Mandy Bradshaw asked a question.

"I wondered if you're staying long? If you are, could you teach me to dive like that?"

"I don't know why not if you have the time." The idea seemed like a good one. It would give me a respite to relieve my boredom. "Won't you and Mr. Bradshaw be busy though?" I waggled my eyebrows and grinned to emphasize my meaning.

She colored beautifully again. "Probably, but we lived together for three years. It's not like this will be our first time." Mandy glanced at her husband and turned back to me. "I'd better go. Mark was hoping to find a place to eat away from the resort."

I was about to leave for my room when the returning form of Tyree Wiggins showed in the distance. The closer he came, the more powerful he appeared, and I was sure he recognized me. Rather than walk on the far side of the pool again, he took my side as if he owned it, which he did. With my dark sunglasses and my brim pulled low, he could see little but my sarong and swimsuit top. Watching carefully as he passed, I noticed him glance in my direction. A jolt of fear ran through my body. I wondered if it was a set-up by The

Company. Did Wiggins already know and plan to toy with me as a cat with a mouse?

Butch waited on me before the dinner rush. I was early as usual, and he pulled out a chair at my favorite table the moment he noticed me. "We have turkey soup and half a beef sandwich as a special this evening, Miss Hampton."

It was a strange feeling to have a man seat me. He pushed the chair in as I scooted forward. "Sounds good to me. Could you bring a small plate of fruit first?"

He winked. It was well known that I would order something fresh with each meal. It didn't matter what—strawberries, mangos, watermelon, apples, bananas, oranges, pineapple—I was willing to eat it. He returned with a plate larger than I envisioned. It held a creative design of pineapple, raspberries, strawberries, and cantaloupe. My customary water and coffee came with it. "I'll have your meal out in a jiffy, Miss." He hustled away to seat the next table.

My plate was empty when he returned. What I envisioned as a cup of soup arrived as a bowl the size of a bird bath, or so it seemed. The sandwich was thick with beef and perfect when dipped in my soup.

Wiggins wore a suit when he strolled past the restaurant. His shaved head gleamed as if polished. A black limo idled not far from my window, and I watched curiously when he was seated in it. Both bodyguards departed with him. I wondered whether his men carried guns. If so, could I somehow secure one?

I remembered Dawson after Wiggins pulled away. It left me feeling guilty. I'd thought of my neighbor little since arriving in Freeport. Everything was blocked out while working—not allowing my personal life to intrude. Yet somehow his strong jaw, heavy beard, and long hair worked itself into my consciousness. He was tall, strong, and self-assured, and I speculated how Wiggins would measure up against my gentle farmer. The thought made me smile. Somehow it didn't seem to me the retired fighter would stand a chance against Dawson. Even without the big Colt strapped to his belt.

I couldn't finish my dinner and didn't attempt to. The fruit and sandwich, yes; the soup I only used as *sauce au jus*. Doing my best not to waddle, I left a twenty-dollar tip for Butch after putting my signature on my ticket. His shirt cuffs were worn, and it broke my heart to see how hard he worked. Before leaving the restaurant, I saw him find the money and wave for my attention. He held it up before putting a hand over his heart and dipping his head in gratitude. If nothing else, perhaps I would brighten one family's life before my time on earth was ended.

One episode left me badly shaken. I was leaving the Greek restaurant early one evening when I noticed a familiar face although I saw it once only briefly. Between blinks the gray man or his doppelganger disappeared into the crowd. We never made eye contact, and after a moment, I doubted my hasty perception. If The Company chose me to sign our client, why would he be here? To take care of a loose end named J? By the following morning, I'd invented a dozen excuses why it wasn't him.

Wiggins' pattern eventually emerged. It cost me sleep, but after a week, I was closing in on my target. He ordered breakfast at eight each morning. A bodyguard would appear at any of the three restaurants and leave within seconds. Someone was obviously calling it in early. The men were careful, not allowing the cover to be removed. His empty dishes were later returned by an older woman who I learned was a maid.

Even if I'd not used it in the past, the idea of poison intruded. Somehow, I needed to gain entry to the kitchen. After the food was plated, I would have to induce it without notice. Perhaps apply for a job as a chef? I dismissed it out of hand, knowing a beginner wouldn't be allowed in the kitchen for years. Other than contacting Manny, I didn't know where to procure a lethal dose of anything available on the island. Although a popular choice for women poison was outside my expertise.

Wiggins jogged each midday in the heat. I guessed his run to be about five miles, all the more impressive when he never slowed when kicking through loose sand. If I had my suppressed pistol or rifle, the job would be simple even with tourists teeming nearby. One shot from the brush, and I could be on a ferry for home.

A lunch was delivered to his room afterward. As fit as he was, I guessed Wiggins had weight equipment in his quarters. Outside of his run, he rarely made an appearance until the dinner hour, and then only to leave in the limousine. It was impossible to establish his route without renting a car of my own. Once I understood he left evenings until nearly two most mornings, it was time to widen my net.

Discounting an approach by sea, two ways led to his hotel: A road near the beach running east and west, and another north toward Malibu Reef. A vulnerable woman alone, I went for short walks until I discovered he always took the north route. From there, he could be going anywhere. It wasn't until I checked a map before I realized the beach road dead ended. Wiggins wasn't even close to signing my contract. Feeling foolish and out of my element, I wasn't sure what to do.

"How do you like working for Mr. Wiggins, Butch?" I was the first customer in the restaurant at six a.m.

"Technically, I work for the restaurant, but along with the resort, he owns all three. To answer your question, he seems like a good employer. I've been here only two weeks, so another worker could give you a better answer." Butch filled my cup with fresh brewed coffee. "Should I bring you a platter of fruit?"

"Make it a small one and a meatless breakfast, please." I smiled up at his bushy eyebrows.

"How would you like your eggs?"

"Glaring at me with crispy hash browns. Wheat toast, dry."

The breakfast rush didn't start until after nine, and only a lone businessman appeared several minutes before eight. I'd finished my meal and continued to read a magazine and drink coffee. According to my watch, one of Wiggins goons entered the kitchen at seven-fifty and departed seconds later. He was shorter than either his boss or fellow guard. My guess was five feet seven and at least two-hundred-fifty pounds with none of it fat.

Butch stopped by to check my carafe. "Why is muscleman in here about the same time each morning but never stays?"

"Mr. Wiggins calls in a breakfast and a guard picks it up." His lips compressed in distaste when a family arrived. I'd noticed multiple times the teenage children were rude and disrespectful.

My next question implied I couldn't keep my attention on one male at a time. "Is there no Mrs. Wiggins or someone to cook for him?"

Butch laughed. "No Mrs. Wiggins. Any of the women frequenting his room aren't there to cook. There's a maid, but she's older, married, and only cleans from what I understand." He left me to wait on the family, and I left him his customary tip, compliments of my operating expenses.

It didn't behoove me to spend time watching only Wiggins and be discovered for what I was. Bike rentals were common, and I made a show of exploring a short distance. I kept to the most populated areas where tourists frequented, so those who preyed on the weak wouldn't be tempted. I pedaled the beach road and walked where I could. Since arriving, judging by the few clothes I wore regularly, I'd gained a few pounds.

I joined a charter one afternoon to swim with the dolphins. It made me laugh when I found myself thrust into close contact with Mark and Mandy Bradshaw. As the local Brits might put it, *unbeknownst* to me, they had the same idea. If she was six feet, her husband was at least five or six inches taller. I was once again a tiny girl in a land of giants. "Hey, you two. I see you were able to tear yourselves away from your room to take in the sights."

Mandy seemed pleased. "Mark, this is the woman I met at the pool who dives so well. Marie, this is my husband, Mark."

We shook hands while I tipped my head back to look into the stratosphere where his head resided. "Mandy said you're newlyweds."

I enjoyed his grin. "It took me three years of begging before she finally gave in." Mark pulled his wife close for a kiss.

"Oh you." Mandy pushed him back and smiled. "It wasn't over a year, was it?"

He ignored what seemed a normal exchange between them. "My wife tells me you're here alone." Even at a relatively youthful age, Mark's short hair was receding. His eyes were brown, and he was graced with an easy smile.

"While you're here to start this chapter of your life together, I'm mourning the ending of mine."

His head dipped. "I'm sorry."

"When my husband ran off with another woman, there was no staying married." I shrugged. "What is, is. Once I return home, a new chapter of my life begins." My quiet declaration could not have been more truthful. If I did somehow return to Idaho, it would be with the chance of a new beginning.

"I can see it in your eyes."

"We're here to swim with the dolphins and any other sea critters down there." I glanced at the ocean as our bow sliced through it. "Let's celebrate your union and allow me to forget about mine."

Our day was long and tiring. After returning to the dock a few miles from our hotel, I offered to pay for our taxi ride. The Company coffers were unlimited. I guessed my two friends saved for their wedding getaway, and every dollar had to be accounted for.

"On which floor is the honeymoon action center?" I teased them as we trudged toward the elevators.

"We're on the seventh." The door opened, and we had it to ourselves. "How about you?" Mandy said.

"Twenty-second." I pushed their number and then mine.

"Hold the door, please." The voice was smooth as silk and masculine enough to make my bony knees wobble. I couldn't see who it was, but Mandy's eyes grew large.

Tyree Wiggins and his bodyguards crowded in. The elevator was suddenly full, and I took the opportunity to view my client. Although not as tall as Mark, Tyree was taller than Mandy. Probably an inch over Dawson. Yet he was more heavily muscled than any man I'd seen. Standing so close, scars on his hands and face showed in detail. He didn't appear cruel or uncouth. Instead, he seemed like an average businessman. "Did I hear someone is taking advantage of our honeymoon suites?" He smiled at my companions and winked at me.

"No, we have a room on seven." Mandy stood with her mouth agape while Mark answered.

"Are you newlyweds?" Wiggins tipped his head to the side, still smiling.

"Yes, about a week now. But we're on a budget and couldn't afford a suite." We stopped at the seventh floor, and the doors opened.

"Anwar, follow this couple to their room and call the lobby. I want to see them in our best suite on the fourteenth, compliments of Wiggins Hotels." He held his hand out and Mark took it. "There will be no charge for your stay." He glanced to his man. "Make sure they have a chilled bottle of complimentary champagne delivered." I saw Mandy was in tears before the doors closed, and I was fighting a lump in my throat. It was a beautiful gesture Tyree Wiggins made. I became aware of his attention and glanced up. "Did I hear you're on the twenty-second? Those are some of our nicest flats."

"Yes, sir. I'm very happy with mine." We were almost to my stop.

"Are you here on business or pleasure?"

"Neither. I'm celebrating being single again."

"Oh?" His eyebrows slid upward.

An idea for gaining his signature sunk its tendrils into me and produced an epiphany. "Ten years of wasted marriage and life." I tossed out a baited hook and waited for a nibble. "From now on, I'm living for me."

We came to my floor, and the doors opened. His man held it open while we finished our conversation. "Will I see you again?"

"That depends on you, doesn't it?" I smiled and left the elevator, turning in the direction of my room.

"Then I will most definitely see you later." He raised his voice, and I simply waved over my shoulder. I heard the door close and grinned a vicious smile I'm glad no one witnessed.

\*\*\*

I didn't see or hear from Tyree Wiggins for three days. That time was spent lounging about my room, the pools, restaurants, and gift shops. I bought a new best seller by a favorite author living very near a former client. It was an exciting read, and I used one of the two letter openers I'd purchased for my bookmark. To keep my thick hair up and off a sweaty neck, I wrapped it in a bun and used the openers to keep it in place like geisha girls used chopsticks. Each was about five inches and tapered to a fearsome point. At the hilt was a round hole big enough to fit my thumb through. They came in handy for many things, not the least of which was opening letters. Slid into my thick hair from either direction, they were neither out of place nor obvious.

"May I get you anything, Miss Hampton?" I looked up from where I was crying over the book's ending to see Allen Fryxell looking concerned. It wouldn't have surprised me if he thought I shed tears for my *lost* marriage.

As with Butch Prayde, I'd become fast friends with the older man who tended to guests outside and around the pool. Where Butch somehow reminded me of Dawson, Allen was more of a grizzled version of my father. Facial scars and a squashed nose were no longer noticed after we built an amicable relationship.

I sniffled and wiped my nose. "Allen, do you enjoy the high backcountry?" Much of the book I'd finished took place in the wilderness, where a budding romance burst into full bloom.

"I'm a city boy, Miss Hampton." He ran his fingers though short stiff hair. "Never spend much time there outside of the service." He shuddered. "Too damned many bugs and creepy crawlies."

His declaration caught me by surprise and caused me to laugh out loud. "A big strong man like you brought to your knees by a caterpillar?" I chuckled again. "Somehow I have a hard time believing that."

"Please do, ma'am. A bug…especially spiders…will have me running screaming for my wife to kill." He grinned. "Thankfully I have an understanding woman who is the family assassin."

As one who doesn't believe in coincidences, his word froze my guts. I tried to see where his smile extended past his lips yet had difficulty finding it. Perhaps it was my natural skepticism, but I thought his eyes looked cool. It was my last signing, and I wished it to be me versus Wiggins, not me against his employees.

I worked hard to keep my tone even. "It's certainly handy to have someone else to do the dirty work, isn't it?" I waited to see his reaction.

We heard his named called before he could respond. A woman held her bejeweled hand to catch his attention. "Duty calls, Miss." He waved back to her. "If you find some sort of nasty vermin that needs killing, please don't call me. I'd rather you do it yourself."

God, were his eyes cold, or did I simply imagine it, searching for a problem where none existed? Could he be a plant from The Company? I glanced almost straight up to where my room was high above. The wet swimsuit I'd hung from my balcony to dry was visible. It allowed me to locate pinpoint the location. I initially envisioned it farther toward the building's corner. Instead, it directly overlooked where I sat considering dinner.

Retiring to my room for a quick shower and change of clothing, I instead watched television and dozed. All the planning, worrying, and reading too much into everything said was wearing on me. The phone woke me from a realistic dream of riding through the Idaho mountains with Scotty and Dawson. I believe Melissa and Bess were in it, yet when I woke to the ringing room phone, I couldn't remember them.

"Yes?" I wasn't the friendliest when I answered. Being dragged from a dream of home and my few friends angered me—all while understanding it wasn't real.

"Miss Hampton?"

"Speaking." I'm sure the caller could hear the irritation in my clipped response.

"I'm calling for Mr. Wiggins." My stomach lurched at the name. "He wondered if you would join him for an early dinner before he attends to business."

"Oh!" It wasn't difficult to sound surprised and flustered. "You woke me from a nap. I would have to prepare to go out first." In the background, voices murmured. The man came back on. "Mr. Wiggins wanted you to know there is no hurry. If another day would be preferable…" He left it open ended.

I made a quick decision. "It will take a half hour, perhaps forty-five minutes to get ready. Would that be too long?" More whispers I couldn't make out.

"No. Mr. Wiggins will be at your door in forty-five minutes." The line went dead, making me wonder if he happened to be related to Manny.

*** 

I was ready when the knock came. I wore a black sundress to set off my blonde coif and fair skin. It buttoned down the front, and I fastened them to within a few inches of my collar bones. My hair was in a tight bun with ringlets in front of each ear. On my feet were strappy sandals—never sure what the night may require.

"You're ready." Tyree Wiggins stepped back, and after close scrutiny, whistled his appreciation. "Stunning…absolutely magnificent."

Even a fashion simpleton such as myself could see his three-piece suit cost thousands. I took the opportunity to whistle back. "Nice threads, Mister…what should I call you?"

"Tyree or Tye would be fine…but you, Miss Hampton…how do you prefer to be addressed?"

"Marie." I took the arm he offered and followed him to the elevators.

"Hampton. Is it your maiden or married name?"

Alarm bells clanged wildly. He was suave, sophisticated, and I had never found myself in a similar business situation. By all rights, clients should be signed from a distance. It was wrong to be wined and dined by them. My dad had a saying about people like him. *Slicker than a mole's ear.* Mr. Wiggins was all of that. "Maiden. I couldn't bear to be Mrs. Rich a day longer." The name made me feel badly for Scotty. His was the first that came to mind.

The elevator garage door opened and five guests were tongue-tied to be within touching distance of Tyree Wiggins. One of the bodyguards held the door and the four of us stepped in. Tyree pinned my hand between the back of his forearm and his other palm. Should I have been looking for a way out, escape would have been impossible. If The Company contacted him to say I was coming…I shook myself mentally. It was no time for doubting myself. Rather, he should view me as a wraith seen shortly before his death. All I lacked was a cowl and scythe to complete the picture.

Wiggins broke the uncomfortable silence. "Where do you hail from?"

"Born and raised in southern Cali." I gave him my best valley girl impression, making the three men laugh.

"You and Mr. …" He pretended to cast for my mythical married name. "…Rich, wasn't it? Where did you live?"

I could not have been more positive they were going to run a search. He needed information and that was exactly what I planned to give him. "Salmon, Idaho. Scotty still lives there after I moved away. It makes me wonder how the bimbo he left me for will like a hick town." The way I was led through the lobby gave me reason for concern. Never relinquishing his grip on my hand, Wiggins and his men hustled me out the back and into a waiting limo. One opened the door and the other slid in before us, then me, followed by Tyree, and his final goon. Both bodyguards sat across from us, and the car pulled away immediately. More than ever before I was alone without any help or avenue of escape. Smoothing the dress over my knees, I fought to keep my cool. Sitting as demurely as possible with my hands in my lap, I smiled vapidly. "Where are we going?" I'd not been far, no more than a bicycle could take me in twenty minutes. Even then I was worried about being alone on a road.

Wiggins smiled confidently. "I think you'll like it. Churchill's is one of my favorite establishments."

We arrived not long after leaving the hotel. I was gratified to escape any further manhandling, nor did he show outward signs of affection. Perhaps he didn't wish to frighten what he hoped would be another simple conquest.

Churchill's was one of the more opulent restaurants I'd ever seen. It was magnificent inside with the staff ready to seat us. Wiggins' men sat at their own table not far away, making me smile.

"You find something funny?" His eyes were alive with humor.

I had to think fast. "My husband rarely took me to a place like this after we married. It's beautiful." While not what I was thinking, it was a welcome diversion. He probably wouldn't appreciate my thoughts of his bodyguards.

"And before you were married?"

He was observant and didn't miss anything. I needed to take great care. "Like all men with girlfriends, he took me to nice places before our nuptials. Afterward, work became all-consuming, and we settled into a normal relationship."

"There is nothing normal about you. Quite the opposite. You, my dear, are stunning."

Christ, listening to him was like sitting through a cheesy movie. Doing my best to beam, I thanked him for the kind words and changed the subject. "I find myself with the great and successful Tyree Wiggins. Why don't we talk about you instead?" Before he could orate on what was surely his favorite subject, a staff member came to our table with an unopened bottle of champagne.

We'd reached the part where I was most concerned. Would someone as well off and as powerful as the man I sat with consider drugging a woman he didn't know? I watched carefully as our server removed the cork, and I could see no signs of tampering. What of the wine glass lip? Yet if I were to be drugged, it certainly wouldn't be before we ate. The waiter poured a glass for each of us and left the bottle.

"Would madam and sir be interested in a tapa to begin?"

First, who in the hell knew what a tapa was? I opened the menu to scan it. At the bottom, I found what could only be described as appetizers. This job was much different from my normal hole-up in a tiny motel and wait for the shot, eating junk food or fruit. Usually both. "I would like your Mediterranean Bruschetta, please."

"Very good, and sir?"

Wiggins didn't bother looking at their choices. "Your fisherman's platter starter, please."

Our server turned to me. "Has madam had a chance to decide on a main course?"

I handed him my menu. "I have. The pan seared sea bass. May I also have a garden salad?" If I felt the fool out of place, at least I didn't stutter.

"Very good, and sir?" Jesus, the guy was a talking parrot with only rehearsed words.

"The biggest ribeye you have, rare."

Damn, I was liking the man more by the minute. At least he knew how beef should be cooked. "You were going to tell me a little about yourself." The waiter left with our order, and I wanted the conversation to stay on my companion. In the time it took to have our starter course placed before us, I learned Tyree Wiggins was his biggest fan. The man simply idolized himself. He talked of his hotels, plans to expand, even to the US mainland. Rarely did he stop prattling unless taking a bite. Each time he needed only a gentle nudge from me to continue. While he talked, I made casual note of how his goons stayed glued to their phones. I guessed they were searching for information about me before we could finish our meals.

While not extravagantly expensive, our food was prepared by chefs who were masters of their craft. It occurred to me partway through my dinner: was this my final meal?

Although seemingly an impossible task—if circumstances allowed, I would make my attempt to sign Wiggins later in the evening.

Chapter XI

After we boarded the elevator again, Wiggins' man pushed only the twenty-fifth-floor button. I waited a moment before pressing twenty-two.

Wiggins protested immediately. "I thought we might have a nightcap at my place. Haven't you enjoyed our evening together?" He stuck his bottom lip out as though pouting. "I have business to attend in about ninety minutes. Just a drink for now?" He'd become very persuasive after years of romancing the opposite sex, and I understood how his infantile effort might work on some women.

"It's been a long day, and I'm tired, Tye. Could I get a rain check?" It was late with few people in the lobby when we arrived.

"I leave for Miami tomorrow and won't return for two weeks. Will you still be here? Or back at home in Idaho?"

The door to my floor opened, and I stepped out. At only thirty-two, I wondered if it were possible to have a heart attack or stroke, because my heart pounded loud enough to muffle sounds, making me incapable of hearing or thinking clearly. A thousand things rushed through my mind. Should I accept his invitation? Perhaps make my own? No matter the decision I made, I needed to offer an apology to Dawson through a brief prayer of contrition. We'd connected, although we hadn't taken it further. I drew a deep breath and plunged toward my imminent death. "I have a bottle of champagne in my room. Just one and then we call it a night. Right?" I held my hand out as though to receive that of a lover. A look of surprise followed by one of triumph crossed his face as he silently accepted. Taking my proffered fingers, he pulled me forcefully against his side and bent for a quick kiss. I did nothing to dissuade him and found myself ushered to my room. Was this how a whore felt?

Wasting additional time to fumble for my key, I glanced furtively around to find his two goons assuming stations at each side of the threshold. One wore a look of disgust, while the other smirked. It was not required to be a mind reader to understand their thoughts. My door swung open, and I was happy to have it close and create a barrier to their accusing eyes. The bottle of champagne was exactly where I'd left it sitting on the counter, warm and unappealing. Wiggins' greasy voice made me want a shower. "Should I call for a cold bottle, Miss Hampton?"

"If you'd like." I unfastened three buttons and let my dress pool on the floor at my feet. Standing almost naked in only panties, my skin crawled as his eyes feasted. "Except you said something about having only a little time, didn't you?"

"My God..." His greedy stares burned my flesh where they touched—I was so exposed and defenseless. "I do love tiny women..." Wiggins' words trailed off as he moved to take me in his arms. "So thin, so vulnerable," he whispered in my ear.

"Careful." His hands were everywhere, and it took every trick in the book to fend off yet not alarm my client. "Shall we take this to the bed?" I kicked my sandals off.

For such a huge man, his lips were soft and yielding, while at the same time insistent. Steering me backward, he suddenly lifted and tossed me across my bed. Before I could make myself comfortable, Wiggins lunged to land between my parted thighs. While I lay helpless and struggling for balance, he caught me off-guard and exposed. Still wearing a suit, his slacks and my panties were all that protected my virtue—a virtue he hoped to plunder over the next few minutes.

His hands were busy on my breasts with special attention to my nipples, while his mouth covered my own. In my limited experience with men, I harbored no doubt Tyree Wiggins was a master seducer. If he hadn't been a client, I could walk away satisfied from his oral assault alone. My guess was hundreds if not thousands of vulnerable women had found themselves in the same position with the imposing man. It didn't surprise me to hear someone moan with delight and felt an electric shock when I realize it came from me. He chuckled at the sounds I was making. "You bitches are all alike."

The invocation of my most despised word startled me into awareness. When I felt a hand move down my belly, it was time to change tactics. Feeling me squirm away from his explorations, he seemed to welcome it when I pressed his head downward. I used both hands to direct his mouth to my breasts. His thumb and fingers assaulted my nipples, while other thick digits worked their way between our torsos. I stretched my arms overhead, and he grinned when he supposed I relaxed to enjoy his ministrations. Instead, I slipped out the sharp rods holding my hair. When his eyes closed in concentration, I struck to ink his signature in crimson.

Sliding my thumbs into the holes of the letter openers, I gripped the hilts with my palms and slammed the right opener into his temple with all my might. It penetrated half its five-inch length immediately, and I pounded it with my fist to imbed it deeper. My weapon should have penetrated his brain, yet with the roar of a wounded beast, Wiggins reared back, staring in shock.

Seeing another opening, I stabbed my left weapon into his throat, attempting to hit his right carotid artery. It seemed to be an accurate blow when blood jetted wildly. I withdrew the opener and stabbed twice more while he continued to thunder.

It astounded me to find the thrust to his brain hadn't killed him instantly. One massive hand went to it, while the other sought to stem the flow from his neck. He didn't seem capable of grasping the opener sunk into his head, although his fingers scratched at it like an itch. The roaring didn't stop—in fact, its volume increased. Shouts sounded outside the door, and blows rained against it. Before I could formulate an escape, his men burst through.

Wiggins still hulked on his knees holding his throat. Blood poured from between his fingers, more than I'd ever seen. No previous client bled so much because they died instantly, stopping their hearts from pumping. He continued to pick at his wounded skull. Standing behind him with no escape options, I used the opportunity to seize one of my sandals and slam its heel against the side of his head to bury the opener deeper. The blow ended our battle, and Wiggins pitched forward on the bed. Like any other animal, his nervous system didn't know he was dead as he lay kicking and twitching.

While I didn't underestimate the loyalty his men brought to their job, I was woefully unprepared to defend myself. One goon stopped to place fingers on his boss's bloody neck and exclaimed, "Shit, I think he's dead." I crouched until he was close enough to strike with my remaining gore-smeared letter opener. I might have been a toddler brandishing a toy, considering the ease he disarmed me. I let down my guard in the knowledge the police would be called and prison beckoned, and I was not ready for his fist. I slammed against the wall, my ears ringing and blocking all sounds. I sensed my body lifted like a ragdoll before fists rained down on my face and then my body. Both men were taking an active role in beating me to death. I could do nothing to defend myself. My brain detached itself from the pain, and I watched my approaching demise.

I felt myself flying. Opening my eyes when I didn't impact a wall, I had an instant to comprehend they threw me from the balcony. With time slowing and only an instant to live, I asked God for forgiveness before impact.

Dawson and his family loomed foremost in my mind. His deep voice and gentle touch, Melissa willing to accept me so easily, and Bess for hiring a lost woman. And Jake, my sweet boy. A finer friend never lived. My parents, sister, and family awaited my arrival. Accepting my end, I relaxed and waited patiently.

It was violent and sudden, and the world vanished.

***

"Wake up, Miss Hampton. Oh, please wake up." Something was slapping my face.

"What…" I lifted a hand to stop the abuse only to find it not responding. Instead, it flopped.

"Get her up! They'll be here any moment," the male voice hissed. I opened my eyes to find Mandy Bradshaw hovering over me with her dripping husband watching the hotel.

Mandy lifted me to my feet. She was forced to hold me in a standing position because I had no control over my body. My head swam and ears rang while I tried to make sense of still living.

"We gotta hurry." Mark was under one arm while Mandy supported my other side, both carrying me toward the scrub covering the island. I still wore only panties as they sought to hide me.

Chlorinated water sleeted off me, and every part of my body had gone numb. By the way my arm flopped on Mark's back, I could tell it was broken. It was fascinating to watch while I felt no pain. We passed the final pool, but instead of going onto the beach, they dragged me into the brush.

"Leave her here." I felt Mark stop, but Mandy continued tugging. "This is a good spot."

"No, we need to help her farther in where they can't see her," Mandy urged Mark. "Julia, can you stand?"

"Can't. No feel...legs," I slurred. My mouth didn't work right with my tongue too thick and swollen. In my confused haze, I had a glimmer of having bitten nearly through it and should be paralyzed with fear of such grievous injuries from angry fists and a twenty-two-story plunge, but I was barely capable of rational thought.

They sat me inside the stunted growth where I could see patches of ocean about two hundred yards through the scrub. I felt my naked torso covered as Mandy squatted in front of me. She was shielding my upper body with her sarong. Mark was already walking to the beach fumbling with something in a pocket, leaving Mandy alone with me. "Stay here, Julia. Help is on its way." She administered a quick kiss to my forehead and hurried away with her husband. Help? Her words didn't make sense.

My brain remained addled from the fall. I lay in the dark and wind, listening to the pounding surf. In the distance were sirens, and I assumed emergency services were summoned. With them would be police to search for Wiggins' killer. Panic struck me, and I flailed in an attempt to stand. On one usable arm, I dragged myself through the sand. Self-preservation is a powerful motivator.

Perhaps it was the work it took to move myself inches, or a massive dose of adrenaline finally entered my bloodstream. First my toes helped push, then my knees, and I realized standing was a possibility. Using only my right hand to push myself up, I held to a piece of scrub when the landscape wavered around me. The horizon tilted crazily while I waited for it to stop.

My steps were tentative until I heard more sirens. The thought of prison made me rush headlong to the ocean. I still needed minutes to cross the narrow sandy beach and keep going until the water was deep enough to lunge forward. I held my left arm at my side, but my forearm twisted about with a mind of its own. The salty heat welcomed my body, holding it up and warming my skin. Rolling to my back, I kicked lazily, moving into deeper water. I felt the tug of current sweep me eastward. It carried me along the beach faster as I back-stroked into deeper water.

Island lights illuminated my way. Never more than half-mile out, I watched as condos, hotels, and homes moved past. Beaches names Coral, Lucaya, and then Taino gave way to ones with which I was unfamiliar. Relaxed and floating in a warm, buoyant cocoon, I fought to stay awake and not be swept farther to sea.

Only when the lights dimmed and fell behind did I kick toward shore. For a short time, I wondered if swimming might prove a fatal mistake. Perhaps I was too weak to battle the tide. I finally floated to an outcrop protruding seaward and dragged myself ashore to hobble among the ever-present clumps of brush. Air temperatures were cold, but sand heated by the sun during the day helped warm my body.

Pain from my broken arm woke me. I was cramped from lying in an odd position and struggled to sit. Trying to figure out where I was, I realized both eyes were nearly swollen closed. With my good right hand, I explored a badly wounded face. Lacerations and abrasions, along with lumps should have never been there. The flesh on my right cheek was opened probably thanks to a fist. Another serious ragged tear extended along my jawline. "God, I try to never ask for more than I deserve," I prayed. "You've seen fit to let me live...now could you help me survive?"

My arm was broken above the elbow. It wasn't compounded, but the bone was snapped. Using my teeth and right hand, I tore three-foot strips from Mandy's sarong. Not an expert when it came to fractures, my guess was I should keep it immobilized and let it heal as it would. Having watched and loved old western movies with Dad, I found three sticks and pressed them into service as splints. I tied them in place as well as I could with lengths of the salvaged cloth. It was a long and awkward process, leaving me exhausted and my body throbbing in greater pain.

Where I found myself seemed ideal. Out in the ocean within a mile were both tourist and fishing boats. Thickets surrounding me were my friends, and I made myself comfortable within them. I wore only panties, but a reasonably large piece of material remained to cover my chest. It was difficult to tie using one hand and teeth, and by the time the tasks I set out to accomplish complete, whatever strength reserves remained to me were depleted. Curling into a fetal position within the warm sand, I was soon asleep.

I came awake with two things standing out. First, how did Mandy know to call me Julia, my given name she couldn't have heard? Did I dream it? Secondly, I'd slept through the day and found it to be dark without stars. Tired enough to sleep again, I scooted out of my nest to void my bladder before resuming my position in the sand. As I drifted off, I worked on the problem of Mandy knowing my name. I eventually gave up no closer to an answer.

The night was long and morning slow in coming with daylight a sight for sore eyes. My body was reacting to the beating I took with debilitating aches setting in. My arm hurt enough I would have screamed should it have helped. Instead, I fought back whimpers and tears each time I moved. My torso complained, and I discovered my chest and ribcage blackened by imprints of knuckles. Other than soreness, it didn't tax me to breathe, indicating I wasn't suffering from broken ribs.

A crack between the lids of my right eye allowed me to see and focus, but the left was closed. Not sure what else to do, I used warm ocean water I obtained after a short crawl at the highest tide to scrub my face of blood and debris. I was thinking more clearly, and it gave me a chance to ponder my dilemma.

Beyond my injuries, I was hungry and thirsty. No fresh water was indicated in the immediate area. It wasn't until the tide retreated before I saw a way to help with hunger. Crabs were exposed, and birds landed to eat the smaller ones. I was no different than an animal and scuttled onto the exposed rocky beach to catch an armored meal. They were faster than I anticipated, and my efforts were rewarded with only cut feet.

God smiled on me when a passing gull lost its grip on one. Dropped from overhead, the crab was stunned when it landed a few feet away. Surprised, I stared dumbly until the poor creature moved. I behaved like any other starving seabird and dived on it. It was small and soft, and to describe how I ate it is something I wish not to do. I was little more than a wounded beast during those days spent in hiding. If it moved, and I could catch it, I ate it.

Cars occasionally traveled along a road not far past the brambles. It wasn't far—yards in fact—and I crawled through the scrub to view it. I was caught between the ocean and asphalt and feared the wrong passing motorist who might inadvertently notice me. I crouched in the foliage and watched for a possible avenue of escape. Across the road seemed to be miles of more scrub. If needed, I could flee and lose myself in it and from anyone who might search for me.

My biggest short-term break came when I was examining trash thrown from passing vehicles. Searching for any clothing no matter its condition, I found a partially filled water bottle. I sniffed it and could detect no odor but water. As it flowed down my throat, I could feel the cells in my body absorbing the sweet liquid. As hard as it was to do, I stopped before draining it.

My skin burned in the sun, and sand fleas and other insects feasted on my body. They plagued me with their bites while I attempted to sleep or even lie still. At times, I felt continuing to fight for life was impossible.

My broken arm stopped tormenting me. Worried about its condition, I found my fingers and hand moved, although too much, and pain started again. Between crabs and strange mollusks I pried from rocks during the low tide, God smiled on me yet again. Ready to give up the difficult task of living, I was saved when the heavens opened and rain fell. It quickly became a torrent. At first, I covered myself with a piece of plastic found along the roadway until I realized my stupidity. Shuffling to the open beach, I dug a hole and lined it with the small tarp. It filled quickly, and I took the opportunity to lie on my belly and drink until I could hold no more. When the deluge stopped as quickly as it started, my bottle and belly were filled, and the lined hole still held water. I made it last for days against other creatures needing it as badly as me.

I was alarmed after noticing a boat passing east and west multiple times each day. It didn't appear to be a fishing vessel but didn't seem to be police launch, either. I also became cognizant of a car traveling the road behind me. I say a single car because it sounded the same each time it passed. Most times, I was burrowed in the sand when it went by. If not searching for food, I was sleeping.

My error occurred when I didn't notice the boat. The tide was out in the late afternoon. Hungry and thirsty, I was crouched at the water's edge searching for anything edible. Scrambling for a fleeing crab hidden under rocks close to my feet, I fell face first and struggled to stand. The boat was floating only yards away in water barely deep enough to keep from running aground. A man dark glasses and a hat pulled low lifted a radio mic to speak into it when I looked up. I was unable to hear his words over the pounding surf, but I had no doubt they searched for me. I turned and clambered from the rocky sea floor, confused at which direction to flee. I'd gone without fresh water for two days, and my ability to think was slow and disorganized.

I scooped up my plastic sheet and water bottle and disappeared into the scrub. It was a struggle to fight my way to the road and disappear into the vast acreage beyond. Rather than use one of my trails, I lunged blindly toward safety instead. Limbs tore at the sarong covering my breasts and back, slapping at my face and legs. It seemed ages before I burst from the clutching branches and onto the asphalt, only to find a car barreling at me. I leaped from its way as it braked hard, barely missing me as it skidded past. I heard it stop after I entered more tangles of native vegetation, and its door burst open. "Jules?" The shout was deep and sharp with full-blown panic.

I stopped my headlong rush into deeper scrub. Only four people ever called me Jules. Mom, Dad, Meghan, and—who? I struggled to remember.

"Jules?" Brush cracked behind me. "Jules, it's me." Dawson. He was the fourth.

I turned and waited. If it were somehow him, Dawson stopped moving in my direction. Perhaps he didn't know where I was. What if this was some sort of ruse? Perhaps it was my own slow and plodding mind playing tricks. Yet only my neighbor called me Jules. No one else knew it. I crouched like a crab and worked my way to the voice.

"Jules? Julia Hampton? Is it you, honey?"

God, the closer I got, the more I could feel the deep, delicious rumble of his bass—a sound that fed my soul.

"Jules!" I could hear panic as he raised his voice to a shout, not knowing where I was.

"Here I am." My voice was soft and hesitant when I stepped from the scrub less than twenty feet away to behold the most wondrous sight. Dawson. It really was him. In his faded jeans, flannel shirt with the sleeves rolled to his elbows, he wore the same heavy boots as when he left me at the airport.

"Oh, God, Jules." He covered the distance between us in an instant and scooped me from my feet. When he turned, a man waiting beside the car came into view. "Open the door, Butch," Dawson commanded. "The blankets…get the blankets from the trunk. Hurry, Prayde." Dawson helped me into the back seat with great care for my left arm and slid in next.

Butch? Prayde? Was Dawson talking about…? Yes, I recognized the concerned face when Butch thrust a stack of bedding through the window. Dawson shook one out and surrounded me in the soft fabric.

"Drive, Prayde. Just go." Dawson drew a phone from his pocket and punched a number. "It was Jules, and we have her. Meet us at our place."

With the windows up and the blankets covering me, the safety I felt with Dawson was overwhelming. I couldn't control my weeping. Butch looked over his shoulder multiple times as if to assure himself I was okay.

"God Almighty, I was afraid we'd never find you." Dawson's deep mutter settled into my core. It was food of the gods, consisting of sweetness, strength, and safety rolled into one sound. I didn't try to answer, burying my face against him instead.

The island wasn't large, and it took only minutes to reach our destination. A bungalow waited away from any nearby homes or apartments. Butch parked next to it and hurried to open my door. He helped me out with Dawson's aid, holding the thick covers around my shoulders. When Dawson stood, he swung me from my feet again and whisked me into the house.

I could think of only one thing after he deposited me to the couch. "Water! I need water." Before I could unwrap the blanket from my injured arm, he returned with two bottles of the sweet elixir. Dawson opened one and offered it. Raising the plastic to my lips, I emptied it and set it to the side. "More." He was armed with another two before I finished the second. I held up a hand. It would all come up if I continued.

He collapsed into the opposite chair. "We were worried you didn't survive."

My eyes felt heavy. Relatively safe, out of the constant wind, and rehydrated, my lids drooped. The swelling in my right eye had receded, but the left was still partially closed. "What are you doing here?" I forced one open and tried too hard when they rolled back. Shaking my head clumsily, I concentrated on his voice and tried to focus.

"What did I tell you?" His tone softened and deepened further. "Things are never what it seems." His rumble was delicious.

"Yes, you did. Can you explain…" The door burst open before I could finish. When two people charged in, Butch and Dawson were waiting with drawn handguns. Instead of enemies, the anxious faces of my friends Mark and Mandy Bradshaw appeared.

Mandy rushed to sit next to me. "You're alive. Julia, I can't believe you survived. I was so sure we'd find you that night or the next day at the latest. We've been scouring the shoreline looking for any signs. Dawson's been so worried and angry, and it's all my fault."

"Your fault?" It didn't make any sense.

"I expected you to wait in the brush where we left you. It was our plan to have you out of there before police arrived. We led Dawson to where we hoped you would be, but you'd vanished."

Her words droned on, and I was unable to keep up with the conversation. Dawson's bass interrupted. "Could you help me, Mandy? We need to get her into bed." He lifted me from the couch, and I remembered no more.

***

Voices sounded from the living room when I woke. Dawson's was like no other, Mandy's was distinctly feminine, and the third probably belonged to Mark. I tried to roll over, but my splint caught beneath the covers and stopped me from further movement. They were talking about my injuries.

"What about her arm?" Mandy asked.

"With the way it's splinted, it appears she's sure it was broken," Dawson said like distant thunder.

"Can you do anything about it, sweetheart?" I was certain the third speaker was Mark.

Mandy's answer was certain. "She needs X-rays first. Then after almost three weeks, the upper arm probably should be rebroken and pinned before set in a cast. I can't do any of that without the proper facilities."

"A little help, please?" I called out. My bladder was about to burst. Footfalls of all three hurried through the door. "I have to use the bathroom."

Mandy and Dawson walked me to the toilet. He waited outside, while she helped me to sit before leaving. Worried both men and Mandy might be within earshot, my shy bladder reared an ugly head of its own. I sat forever before it released almost in tears with the relief and was an enigma even to myself—a killer who couldn't pee within hearing of others.

I had the opportunity to assess myself in a mirror. What I saw was worse than I envisioned. The area around both eyes showed black, green, and yellow, extending down my left cheek. It was split with the wound at least two inches long and only partially healed. My eyeball was spider webbed with splotches of blood. Another gash lined my jaw, longer than the one on my cheekbone.

My body was frightening—my chest little more than that of a young man. My ribs protruded along with my collar bones, and my stomach was sunken with hipbones jutting. I found the sight of myself revolting and collapsed to the toilet seat in silent sobs.

"Julia? Are you okay?" When I didn't answer, she knocked and asked again.

"No…" My reply was little more than a whisper. I bit my lip to keep from moaning aloud.

"I'm coming in." The door opened slowly, and she peeked around the edge. Seeing I still sat, she quickly shut the two of us inside. "Are you in pain? I was a medic in the Army. If you explain what you're feeling, perhaps I can help."

"I'm a skeleton," I said through sobs. "My ribs are sticking out, and I look like something from a World War II prison camp. Even my breasts are gone."

Her smile was sad—she could see the truth of my words where I sat nude on the toilet seat. "You'll be fine, sweetie. It's going to take time to recover. You've been through a traumatic experience, and only time is going to help you heal." She cocked her head thoughtfully. "Would you like to shower? I can help."

My clothing remained at the hotel, which we didn't dare retrieve, so Mandy sent Dawson shopping with a list. By the time he returned ninety minutes later with underthings, shorts, tops, a sweatsuit, and sandals, I was significantly more presentable, though I cried again at how it all hung from my body. When we emerged, I'm sure Dawson barely recognized me compared to at my rescue.

With the sweat, dirt, salt, and blood washed away, I was feeling almost human again. Mandy found scissors and removed my splint before showering. I asked her to cut my hair back to the length of a boy's. She left three inches on top, shaped the sides, and squared in back. We parted my hair on the left and combed it over. A very young male who'd been badly beaten looked back in the mirror.

Dawson was indeed surprised when I made my appearance. We found him in the kitchen cooking, and he visibly startled before smiling. My neighbor knew what I liked and needed, a cup of chicken noodle soup and a ham and cheese sandwich with coffee. I almost lunged for the tube of lip balm lying near my plate. Saltwater and thirst caused my mouth to split and bleed, producing an endless agony while speaking and eating.

My injured arm dangled at my side. A spoonful of soup, a swallow of water, followed by a small bite of my sandwich. Methodically, I worked my way through the meal. I was joined by those whom I was learning were my friends, and we ate without comment. After I finished everything in front of me, Dawson offered to cook more. Holding my hand up in protest, I leaned back and begged off. "I can't get down another bite. My stomach isn't used to so much." Other items of importance loomed. "Besides..." I made deliberate eye contact with each member of our group. "...I need to know exactly who you really are and how you became involved in this."

Chapter XII

Mandy glanced at Dawson, awaiting his response. Before he could answer, a loud knock rattled the door. Everyone but me scrambled from the table. It opened, and I breathed a sigh of relief at the familiar voice. "Hey, is anyone here?" Allen Fryxell made his appearance. It seemed impossible I knew all their faces, but I did. Mark held a fearsome-looking knife in his hand, which disappeared as did the handguns Butch and Dawson produced. Alone at the table, I had to smile at the concern on Allen's face when he waltzed in. "I can't believe it. You're alive." He ignored everyone and walked directly to me. "I heard you're a little beat up." Giving me a gentle hug, he turned to Dawson. "Don't tell me I'm late for dinner."

"Not if you like ham and cheese sandwiches and soup," Dawson said.

Allen's response was typical of a man: "Hey, I'm hungry enough to fight a starving bear over rights to a two-week bloated whale carcass." Mark groaned, and Mandy gagged. Dawson and Butch smiled. I would have welcomed such a feast only hours before.

"What did you find out?" Dawson didn't glance from where he put together a sandwich to grill for Allen.

"Forensics are still working, but the entire system is corrupted." He made it sound easy. "Even their backup and the backup's backup were tainted. I'll guarantee you…" He glanced at me. "…they'll never find her picture. To make the day better, Wiggins' bodyguards have disappeared for parts unknown. Doesn't surprise me. They know where all the bodies are buried."

"Allen was my unit's IT guy," Dawson said. "If he thinks the hotel's computer system is toast, it's guaranteed burned beyond repair. Good news about his goons."

I didn't understand. "Your unit?"

Dawson turned to me and gestured at the group. "These were the ones who had my back in the sandbox…and vice versa. We came home alive because we trusted each another."

"Sandbox? I don't get it." Did they previously spend time on a beach?

Mandy said, "Our unit was deployed to Iraq a few years after the invasion. We were a part of the surge. Dawson commanded our outfit and led us during the retaking of Fallujah." She recounted her story in a matter-of-fact manner. "I patched more than one hole in a couple of these guys. Grenades and RPGs throw out a lot of shrapnel."

"Oh, you were in the Army together!" It finally made sense.

"Ding, ding, ding! Give the girl a medal." Allen was focused on his phone.

"I still don't get it. How and why are you here? Were you having a reunion?" I looked to Dawson. He should have mentioned it when I was preparing to fly out of Montana.

Dawson set Allen's meal on the table. "They can blame me. I contacted the ones I trusted most after you left. Butch lives in Boca Raton. Mandy and Mark in Baton Rouge. Allen lives in..." He winked at me. "...get ready...Missoula, Montana."

"All of us and others not here but wishing to be owe Dawson. When the call went out, he only had to say he needed us," Mandy said.

"None of you are indebted to me." Dawson's comment was quiet.

"Sir, you let us decide who owes what." Mandy sounded firm, and she left no illusion that he could disagree. "Butch and Allen were hired by the hotel soon after they arrived. Mark and I masqueraded as guests to watch you." She smiled. "You really dive beautifully, you know. Anyway, Dawson stayed at a small hotel in Freeport for the first few days and remained in contact from there. He's the one who located this place." She gestured around us. "He couldn't let you see him."

I could only draw one conclusion. "Then all of you know." I stared at Dawson, but my question was directed at the room.

Mark said, "He had to tell us, although not until we arrived on the island. Otherwise, if we witnessed you involved in something violent, we may have inadvertently called authorities for help. Besides, everyone in south Florida and beyond knows Tyree Wiggins was a major drug importer. I have friends in Miami who tried to catch him for years." His mouth twisted, and he shrugged. "Good riddance to bad rubbish."

"Still…" I wasn't sure. These were Dawson's personal friends and companions, not mine. The old law of The Company—kill any witnesses—crept from my subconscious. I shook it off. If I wanted to retire, it was time to relearn trust.

Butch was next. "All of us have killed, Julia. While ours may have been government sanctioned during wartime, your situation isn't so different. A war on drugs is still war." I could hear the anger in Butch's words build. "I lost an older brother to drugs. Friends, too." He snorted. "Far as I'm concerned, kill every last one and let God do with them as He will." He looked as if he'd chewed on a lemon.

"Mark and I watched as closely as we could without drawing attention. We worried about blowing your cover…especially when we chartered the same boat to swim with the dolphins." Mandy chuckled. "That was an accident, not something planned. The same with meeting Wiggins in the elevator with you when he comped us a honeymoon suite."

"A damn nice room," Mark said.

"Did you really just get married? Are you even a couple?" I had assumed, not knowing if it was roleplay.

"Almost ten years now." Mark leaned and kissed his wife. "We got hitched thirty days after our discharge."

"We put the room to good use though, didn't we?" I could see her teeth when she grinned in the middle of their kiss.

"I certainly thought so."

Butch chimed in again. "Why so long to tap your mark? You had me on pins and needles waiting."

"What?" His question didn't make sense. "I don't understand."

Dawson's voice reverberated in the silence. "He's asking why it took so much time to sign your client."

"Oh…" I was pathetic when it came to the world of skullduggery. Butch was impatient. "Well?"

"It wasn't like I could sign him the regular way." God, I sounded like an idiot. He glanced from me to Dawson, who pointed an index finger and dropped his thumb. Butch nodded.

"You should see her shoot. It's nothing short of frightening." They sat up straight to give me a second look. Given the room's reaction, Dawson must have offered high praise.

"I had to figure out another way, and to get close enough took time."

"How did you do it, if you didn't use a gun and don't mind me asking?" Butch winced at my sharp look and held his hands up in mock surrender. "It's not something you have to explain if you'd rather not."

I closed my eyes to remember the intimate details of Wiggins' death. Not only his roars of pain and rage as he fought the grim reaper but the smell of his body and the feel of his lips on mine. It didn't distress me—he was an animal to be put down. One who preyed on those with a weakness for drugs. "A letter opener." I shrugged my right shoulder.

"A letter opener?" Judging by their response, those around the table seemed horrified except for Dawson. He smiled, if it could be called that, making me shiver.

"Two, actually. One went in here…" I pointed at my temple. "…the other here," gesturing to my throat.

Mandy was incredulous. "He was still able to toss you from the balcony?"

"No, his two goons almost beat me to death…then threw me over." I sat ramrod stiff in sudden memory. "You were there when I hit. What happened? I don't remember anything from the time I fell until you dragged me into the brush."

Mark and Mandy looked at each other in surprise. "You don't recall?" Her eyes were big as her memories flooded in. "Mark and I went for a walk to the beach. We were on our way back when something fell from the sky. You never made a sound and splashed down ten feet out in the pool. We ran to the edge and could see you motionless on bottom. I thought you were dead, but Mark dived in and dragged you out before you could drown. I was astounded anyone could live after a fall from that height. It was the twenty-second floor! Your arm was obviously injured or broken when we got you out. After leaving you in the brush, Mark called for Dawson's help since he rented a car. When we returned to the spot,

166

you were gone." She shook her head in obvious disgust. "I should have stayed with you."

"I heard sirens." In my mind's eye, colored lights flashed accompanied by sirens. "I had to get away or surely be caught."

"We never stopped looking…searching everywhere for your tracks. The police had the same idea, except they used dogs. According to local news, they assumed an accomplice was involved in your escape. How did you do it?" Mandy cocked a curious head.

"By swimming into the ocean and letting the current drift me east. When I thought I was far enough away, I swam to where you found me." Dawson and his friends didn't need to know of my terror when I almost didn't make it to land. Only my skill in the water kept me from being swept farther to sea.

"Jesus Christ. I really do need to take lessons."

"Figured it was something similar." Dawson nodded. "Butch, Allen, and I took turns or worked in pairs driving the beach road. Mark and Mandy rented a boat and scoured the shoreline for clues."

"Authorities are still looking, aren't they?" It was why I wanted my hair changed.

"Yes and no." Butch was still online with his phone. "Police report they have leads but aren't saying much more. They'll never find your picture on a hotel camera. All their information was mysteriously lost." He elbowed Allen with a laugh. "Even your purse somehow disappeared from your room." I'd noticed it on the counter near Dawson.

"We have to get you home," my neighbor said. "You need a doctor to see to your arm and face."

I'd been so focused on staying alive that the lacerations on my cheek were forgotten until seeing them in the mirror. I touched where they were healing. The area was a scabby mess.

"A good plastic surgeon can make you as good as new." Mandy turned my head and looked critically at the gashes. "Your arm may be more problematic. A doctor might have to break it again and put in screws or pins. Ten weeks in a cast, and you'll be as good as new." Her wink didn't alleviate my angst.

Only Dawson's question stopped me from crying. "How soon until you're feeling good enough to leave, Jules?"

"Right now." Idaho was calling my name.

Even though I was still tired and weak, I guess he expected my answer by the way he nodded. "Butch, you need to fly to the mainland tomorrow and get your cabin cruiser ready. We'll meet the day after at whatever coordinates you feel safest. Jules and I will go with you. Allen, Mandy, and Mark will return our boat to Freeport and fly out the same evening." He looked around the table. "Does anyone have anything else to offer?"

***

Mark drove Butch to the airport the next morning and returned before I was up. I was starving after a fitful night. Dawson and Mandy cooked an enormous breakfast, then shopped for me. She did a better job of sizing clothes so I would appear unisex to the casual eye. She also brought hair dye, and before dinner was served, I looked at a brunette in the mirror with eyebrows and eyelashes to match.

Mark and Mandy along with Allen rented a boat at West End the following day. Dawson dropped them at the marina, and after the boat was secured, he returned to the bungalow. It was a relief to leave decision making to others, especially Dawson who ran operation SJSA—*Save Jules' Skinny Ass*—since leaving Missoula. We packed our gear and met the boat in Bell Channel Bay. No one looked twice when we boarded for what appeared to be a pleasure voyage. With a cruise speed of forty knots, we met Butch where he waited midway to Florida. Dawson and I left our boat for Butch's and waved to Mark and Mandy. Three hours later, we were sitting at our host's table. Later in the evening, Butch left to pick up our co-conspirators from their flight. His residence was comfortable, and my defenses lowered when I felt safe.

"You kids make yourself at home. This shouldn't take long." Butch departed to shuttle the rest of our team.

My reaction to signing a client didn't always wait until I was in the privacy of my own place. It would overtake me when the worry and stress diminished, and both safety and relaxation were available. I had yet to pay the penalty for dispatching Tyree Wiggins. I felt the trembling begin while curled on Butch's couch with Dawson at the opposite end. He was enjoying a college playoff game. My stomach jolted, and my head jerked as convulsions took hold. They increased until I rolled from the cushions.

Dawson leaped to my side. "What the hell…?" He quickly stood over me.

My stomach was expressing its displeasure, and I tried to get to my feet. The spasms were hurting my broken arm, and I lay crying in pain after falling back. Jerking and twitching, I tried to huddle on the floor in a fetal position to ride it out and protect my injury.

"Jules, what's happening?" He dropped to one knee next to me, his deep bass rising in panic.

"Ba…bathroom…get me to the toilet…" I tried to stand again, but Dawson lifted me into his arms. After we reached the bathroom, he stood holding me, not sure what to do. "Toilet…going to puke…"

He didn't get me in position in time, and I vomited where we were. Down my chin and chest, it ran and soaked into his shirt. Dawson lowered me gently as if he had all the time in the world, then cradled my left shoulder and break below it. I remained on my knees, praying to the porcelain gods until only green bile came up. Quivering continued even after my purging slowed.

"Out of the way, sir." Mandy swept into the bathroom and shouldered my neighbor to the side. In my peripheral vision everyone watched wide-eyed at the bathroom door. "All of you…give the woman some privacy, would you?" Raising her voice seemed effective judging by how quickly they vanished. Dawson closed the door when he left.

"Are you all right?" She squatted next to me, putting a hand on my back. I shook my head. "What can I do for you?"

"Help me into the shower." The thought of Dawson knowing I'd wet myself and crapped my pants mortified me. I stank.

Mandy started the water while I puked again. After she adjusted the temperature, the tall woman moved to my side and assisted. I plucked at my sweatshirt, trying to decide how best to remove it. Before I had a chance, she took the hem and pulled it over my head and right arm, exercising great care with my left. I shivered violently, trying not to fall. I stepped from the sweat bottoms and underwear with her help, trying to avoid the pity I saw. My body was cadaverous and ugly and not something I wished anyone to see. I attempted to step over the tub's edge and almost fell. Mandy caught and got me inside where I folded like a newborn foal. Curled on my right side, I let the water cascade while the tremors slowly subsided. Rather than leave, Mandy made herself comfortable on the toilet lid and waited. "Can you tell me what's wrong? Is it life threatening? Should we call an ambulance?"

I finally sat up and plugged the tub after I cleaned and rinsed my rear. All the puke and crap appeared to have flowed down the drain. When she saw what I needed, Mandy cast about until locating Butch's towels. I took the proffered washcloth and scrubbed my face. "Side effects, I guess. It always happens after I have time to settle down from signing a client. It slams into me once I'm relaxed. Jerking, jumping, and puking...I have to ride them out until it's over."

"Every time?" Mandy frowned.

"Yep, every single time."

She nodded her certainty. "PTSD. I've seen it a thousand times in one form or another."

"PTSD?" I was incredulous.

"Post-Traumatic Stress Disorder." I guess she didn't think I understood what it was.

"I know what it means." I settled back, enjoying the warm water reaching my neck. Mandy turned the faucet off for me. "Why would I have it? I haven't been in a war...oh..." What she was trying to make me understand sank into my thick head.

"The hell you haven't. Each time you go out on a mission to...to..." She searched for the term. "...to sign a client, you've effectively entered combat. Once it's over, this is your mind's way to release pent-up stress." She shook her head. "If our troops could be taught to do it, we might not see the problems we do with returning soldiers."

My laugh was shaky. "You mean this is a good thing?" My mind's eye imagined thousands of fighting men and woman doing the cathartic dance afflicting me for so long. It certainly wouldn't be pretty.

"It's what has allowed you to keep your sanity since starting in this line of work." Her positive view made sense.

170

Once I was clean, Mandy left me to dry myself while she got me a change of clothes. They were dirty but cleaner than what I took off. She started the washing machine as I dressed, and returned to find me crying again. The larger woman took me into her arms. "What's wrong?"

"I'm so embarrassed. I can't go out there."

"Hurt and sick are nothing to be ashamed of, Julia."

"I can't face Dawson."

"Why?"

Her question made me cry harder. "Because I pooped my pants while he was in here with me," I wailed. "This purging ritual has never happened while anyone was around."

Mandy pushed me back to sit on the toilet and seated herself on the tub's edge. Her eyes were misted. "I was with those men in there the first time we came under direct fire." She jerked her thumb in the direction of the living room. "We took up defensive positions and prepared to be overrun, and there was only a dozen of us. I was embarrassed when it was over, because I'd messed myself." Mandy smiled sadly. "You know what? It wasn't just me. Many of them did the same."

\*\*\*

Mandy was correct in her medic's assessment of my arm. Over the course of the next week, I was scheduled for surgery, my arm reset, and pins inserted to hold it in place. Somehow Dawson paid for my care, and I promised to reimburse him. My face—already partially healed—was something I left for nature to deal with. The scars would be wide and long, reminders of a past not to be forgotten. I left the hospital with my arm in a cast and spent two more days sleeping at Butch's home. Pain medication and antibiotics were my constant companions. By then, Mark, Mandy, and Allen departed with my thanks. I was forced to plead with Dawson's team to accept payment for their outlay of cash. They eventually accepted, laughing about the fun it'd been. What they found most amusing was when I promised a check would be in the mail. They considered the old gag hysterical. They wouldn't think it was so funny when they saw I paid interest, too.

\*\*\*

Afraid to fly and show my face in public, Dawson rented a big King Cab Dodge diesel in four-wheel drive. My cheekbones and chin still showed tinges of yellow where I was beaten. But with the swelling gone, it was nice to see out of both eyes. My condition would draw unneeded attention, and my cast extending from shoulder to wrist wouldn't help. I didn't mind leaving Florida's muggy heat but parting with Butch was difficult. He and I bonded more tightly than I might have expected. More than any of the others, we'd talked at length before my opportunity to sign Wiggins presented itself. It didn't matter his story was mostly fabrication—so was mine.

Dawson seemed to like the truck he chose. "What direction do you want to take home?" We'd passed a sign for Okeechobee sixty miles ahead.

I knew my neighbor took care of his mom's place as well as his own. "Are you in a hurry?"

"I plan to drive until my eyes cross while we break every speed limit each day, if it answers your question."

"Don't get the law on us. It's the last thing we need."

"Yes, Mother." He didn't smile, but I'm pretty sure I saw his crow's feet crinkle a little.

"Since most of the north is locked in snow and ice, wouldn't it be nice to stay south where it's safer and warmer?" Nothing felt as good as signing a client in a southern state during the dead of winter.

He paused, obviously considering. "You mean travel along the gulf coast and then through New Mexico and Arizona?"

"Yeah and cut north through Nevada into Idaho."

"I like the way you think, girl." He was trying to figure out the cruise control. We both felt it catch, and he glanced at me with a sly grin. "I have *got* to get me one of these." I doubted it. He seemed to have a fond place in his heart for the old Ford he drove.

We left Butch's at eight in the morning. Tallahassee was in our rearview mirror by three. I know, because Dawson woke me to eat since I fell asleep not thirty minutes after leaving Butch's home. Pain medication combined with fatigue kept me drowsy. Always one to rise early, I found myself sleeping constantly. When I'd complained to Mandy, she explained my body was traumatized, and sleep was its repair mechanism. Once she delved into the molecular processes, my eyes glazed over, and I dozed off to her chagrin.

"I expect you have to use the restroom," my chauffer said loudly to wake me. "Why don't we go inside, and I'll order while you use the facilities?"

Dawson wasn't joking about driving until his eyes crossed. He was finished with his meal and helped me back into the truck when I returned. Four large coffees occupied the drink holders, and I looked at him with a raised eyebrow. "Are you planning to drink all that?"

"Except for one for you. Now start eating and don't stop until it's gone."

Peering inside the bag, I saw it was filled with greasy burgers and fries. None of it looked fit for human consumption if I were to judge. I held my nose and ate anyway.

It was almost ten in the evening when we stopped at a motel outside of Baton Rouge. Judging by the way Dawson stumbled when he stepped down, his declaration came true. Perhaps his eyes *were* crossed. He paid for a room with two beds, and we each collapsed on one.

I'd fallen asleep again not long after we stopped for food. Every so often, I would wake, only to dig out another burger and eat. Now that we were in a motel, I was concerned about sleeping after spending little time awake. The moment I fell on the bed, I knew it wouldn't be a problem. Dawson merely tossed his bag to the floor next to his bed, kicked his boots off, and went to snoring. Waiting until after using the bathroom, I undressed to my underwear and a clean shirt and slipped beneath my own covers. If I snored, I knew it could not equal my roommate.

*\*\*\**

"Boxers, huh?" Sometime during the night, Dawson undressed to his underwear and a sleeveless t-shirt. We'd slept until almost eight, when I heard him slide from beneath the covers. Watching him pad silently toward the bathroom, I was struck by how much more muscular he was than I might have guessed. I earned a grin and a wink from my observation.

We were showered, dressed, and leaving the motel in less than thirty minutes. Dawson noticed a restaurant the night before, and we stopped for breakfast. "We should be in San Antonio by three or so this afternoon. We're making good time," he declared, cutting into his steak.

"San Antonio? We have to go through there?" I must have grimaced.

"You got something against it? It's on Interstate Ten and difficult to avoid."

I pushed a waffle around my plate, wishing I ordered the same T-bone and eggs meal Dawson chose. "There was a client nearby, and I used the airport. It wasn't a good trip."

"You weren't successful?"

"I never failed to get their signature." My tone was sharp and my glare sharper.

"Sorry." He raised his hands in his familiar gesture of surrender and turned his attention back to breakfast.

I took a few moments to assess my reaction. "No, I should apologize." My injuries and lethargy made me tired and irritable. "It was difficult to secure."

"Your visit to San Antonio was recent?"

"Yeah. Not the last time you watched Jake and my house for so long, but the one before." I was no longer hungry and pushed my plate away.

He stayed quiet longer than I might have expected. It became increasingly clear that I needed to expect the unexpected with Dawson. "Laredo? A woman?" His voice was low, and he focused on his meal to avoid my look of surprise. Perhaps he didn't care.

"Why would you say that?" I swallowed hard and directed my attention to the cup of coffee at hand. Cripes, for a professional assassin, I seemed an open book to this man.

He shrugged. "I read, watch television, and pay attention to things around me. Plus, I have the best IT man on the planet to search for information."

Dawson ordered three sandwiches to go. Even for the short time I'd been up, it didn't take long for my lids to droop. The droning engine and tires and my driver's lack of interaction left me no alternative. I mostly slept until we stopped for fuel, although he woke me to eat the sandwiches at different times and to take my medicine.

The truck stopped, and I raised my head. "Where are we?" I rubbed bleary eyes and looked around. It was like any other busy intersection with gas stations on all four corners. The dashboard clock read two-ten.

"Huntsville." We hurried for our gender-appropriate restrooms. He was coming out of the men's when I left the women's. "Hey…" He pulled a wad of cash from his front pocket and handed it over. "…for fuel and in case you need anything. I wouldn't mind an iced tea. Peach if they have it."

I stayed inside and bided my time until he finished with the diesel pump. I paid for it with the money he gave me. Waiting until we were on the interstate, I handed him the flavored tea. "How long until we reach San Antonio?" I planned to sleep through our passing.

"We won't. I turned north at Houston. We're on Interstate Forty-five to Dallas. We'll catch Twenty and stay on it until we merge with Ten east of El Paso."

I didn't attempt to show him the depths of my gratitude. I simply muttered, "Thank you."

"Hey, I live to serve." His deep chuckle would have buckled my knees if I were standing.

***

We listened to the radio and watched passing scenery. Dawson scored another positive in my book when the station he chose was playing 'seventies music. I waited until a break between songs before turning it down. "You were in the Army, huh?"

"Yup."

"Care to tell me about it?"

He didn't bother to look at me. "I'd rather not."

"Why? Didn't you get to travel and see the world?"

"You don't see much sitting in the bay of a transport plane." He didn't sound bitter or angry—his service simply didn't seem to be something he wanted to discuss.

"Oh." I was disappointed, hoping to learn more about my neighbor.

"Why don't you tell me about signing clients for The Company?"

I went silent for a minute, immediately understanding how he looked at time spent in the military. My kills were private. "What do you want to know? How it felt to sign my first client from my car while he sat on his porch and wondered what I was doing? Or the time I watched a man shoot his daughter up with something because she was too active and not listening? How he and his wife injected themselves and sat in a stupor while I walked in the front door and signed him from thirty-six inches?" I was quiet, lost in the unpleasant memories of a time when I sought my own form of justice. I almost signed the woman, too, for allowing her husband to drug their daughter. "Two men whose lives were worth a combined seventeen thousand dollars."

"Plus mileage."

"Wha…" I looked to find a sly grin on the face of my driver. "Oh, yeah. Plus mileage."

He chuckled, and it was real, causing me to join in. Except I couldn't stop—even when he looked at me with alarm. Somehow my laughter turned to tears I couldn't turn off. Instead of saying something, Dawson reached across the seat, unbuckled my harness and pulled. I slid awkwardly and snapped myself in the center with my right hand. His arm went around my shoulders, and I rested my cast on his thigh. I was unable to stop crying through it all.

"You are so damaged, my little dove." I felt his whisper, rather than heard it. With my head against his chest, I soaked his shirt with my tears. Dawson didn't complain or mention it. Instead he tightened his long arm.

\*\*\*

It was after eight when we stopped in Abilene. We bought meals at a fast food joint before finding a motel. Dawson checked us in while I waited in the truck. After he returned with the key cards, I locked the pickup and brought in our single bag of clothing. "I can drive, you know." We were sharing the burgers and drinks at the tiny table in our room. He looked as exhausted as I felt.

The gentleman who was my Idaho neighbor pinned me with that stare of his. "I know you can, but we don't need to take the chance, do we?" Despite his initial bluster, I noticed he never broke the speed limit, no matter where we were.

"Just wanted to make the offer."

He sat back in his chair, watching me eat. "What are you going to do now you're officially retired?"

"Teach, I hope. Find a fulltime job and get my own classroom."

"Will it be enough?" I swear the man didn't blink when he grilled me.

"Um…yes?" I wasn't sure of his question. "What is it you're asking?"

"You've led a life of thrills few could imagine, Jules. Is it something you can give up?"

Had he gone mad? "God, yes. You can't possibly think I enjoy this, do you?

"Probably not, but giving something up and enjoying it are two different things. You held the power of life and death in the palm of your hand. It's not something easily discarded."

"Consider it tossed away." I edged close to a state of anger.

"I was simply asking, little dove. Didn't mean to offend."

"Manny knows I'm done, and The Company understands it's over." I was adamant, sure in my decision, certain my old partner would honor our agreement.

Finished eating, I pushed back from the table, wanting a shower before bed. My clothes were dirty, including my underwear, but it didn't mean my body should be soiled, too. I stood faster than I should have, making my head spin and grabbed for the table. Before it could dissipate, Dawson was at my side, holding me. "You okay?"

"Yes, I'm…" I looked into his concerned face. Dawson's arm was around my waist, and all I could see were his lips. Of its own volition, my right hand found its way to his neck, pulling his face to mine. It took little pressure before our mouths met, his hands behind my back, drawing me against his body. It turned out something *could* make my stomach flip-flop more than his voice. It was the feel of his lips on mine.

"Oh, my little dove…" he whispered.

Chapter XIII

It took two and a half days from Abilene to Salmon. During those miles, I found Dawson capable of nonstop talking and learned much about his formative years. Only periods of service were left out unless the name of one of his team got mentioned. We compared childhoods, and while loving the way I was raised, Dawson's story beat mine hands down. Growing up in the same house in which his mother still lived, his was a carefree time of hard work and the mountains. Where Scotty rode a horse and packed in clients for a living, my traveling companion was raised in the saddle on the trail.

The farther we drove north, the colder it got. Mid-January had less snow than there might have been. As we left the city limits of Salmon, temperatures were hovering in the teens. Dawson pulled to the side when we reached my driveway and turned to me. "What do you prefer, little dove? Straight home to build a fire or Mom's to get Jake?" He glanced at the dashboard clock. "It's almost four. It'll be dark soon and won't do anything but get colder."

We were on the same wavelength. "I've been thinking about it. Drop me at the house and I'll build a smudge to warm the place. Can you meet me at Melissa's at six?"

He wouldn't let me enter the house alone, nor even first. Dawson unlocked the door and swung it open, waiting for any response from inside. When there was none, he stepped in and searched. "It seems clear." He came out of my bedroom with the little Colt and handed it over. My place wasn't freezing. Electric heat switched on if it dropped to fifty-five. After so long in the surf and sun, the lower temperatures were uncomfortable. I opened the cylinder and checked the loads before sliding the revolver into my coat pocket. Dawson asked, "Want me to hang around till you're ready?"

I needed time alone. "No, but will you wait to see if my Jeep will start?" My faithful Wagoneer barely turned over before catching. The powerful V8 engine still purred, and we left the garage door open so it could breathe while idling. I gave it a few minutes before turning it off, and Dawson walked me to the porch. I stopped on the second step and turned around. As I suspected, we were almost the same height. "Kiss me, you fool!" I'd always wanted to say that. Wrapping my right arm around his neck, I pulled him into me to work at perfecting our romantic expression. He backed me up the stairs before I pushed him away. "Down, boy. You go home, and we'll meet at six. Be there or be square." I shook with cold and scrambled in retreat to the comparative warmth of my house. Outside, I heard the rental Dodge cough to life and idle away.

Old, dilapidated, and dingy, my ramshackle dwelling was still home. Even cold and lifeless, it still felt good. While I wished for nothing more than to flop back in my familiar recliner, I retrieved an awkward load of wood from the back porch. Dawson taught me well, and the stove was hot in minutes. I retrieved a few more chunks of fuel before taking a bath.

The room was warmer when I traveled from the bathroom to my bedroom wearing only a towel. It was difficult to bathe while wearing a cast. I seldom felt completely clean. Dressing was difficult, too, but my old jeans, boots, short-sleeved blouse, and hooded sweatshirt never felt more comfortable. I was back, finally and forever home. I sat in my chair and enjoyed the simplicity and absolute silence. However, Jake waited at Melissa's, and the time Dawson and I planned to meet grew nigh.

The stove's firebox was filled one last time before I left, then shut down. Inside would be toasty when my boy and I returned. It was difficult not to hurry on the way to the Pelletier homestead. Melissa's road never felt longer, and I saw fresh tracks on it. His mother was lovely to be around, but it was nice to know Dawson was there before me.

It surprised me to see Bess's car when I turned into the parking area. She was usually at school until six or after. Our rental was next to hers. After shutting off the engine, I sat for a moment, mustering courage to climb the stairs and knock. I didn't travel three steps from my Wagoneer before the door burst open and my best friend raced out. "Jake!" He flew to me, ignoring my raised hand, jumping and putting his paws on my shirt front. He almost knocked me down with his exuberance. "Oh, you sweet boy, you can't imagine how much I missed you." My hug was tight and reeked of desperation. It took a few minutes to calm the excited dog, although he seemed sure we should leave for home. When he understood we were staying, he flew past me to the porch. I stopped after noticing Melissa and Bess watching.

To climb the nine steps was like approaching the hangman. Dawson caught Jake and brought him under control. Both women's eyes searched mine for what they could find. Melissa was the first to reach out and touch my injured cheek and jaw. Both took notice of my short and brown hair, and it seemed we broke into tears at the same time. These were my kind of women. They could weep for any reason, and I needed to get better at it. "I didn't think you were coming back," Melissa said through sobs above my head. "Dawson said we may never see you again."

I nodded, pulling her hair out of my face. She was so much taller and leaned over me. "I didn't think I'd be back to see any of you, either. It's so good to be here. You can't imagine how nice it is."

I was somehow passed from Melissa to Bess. She did little but cry and squeeze my aching body. "We're so happy to see you."

Dawson herded us into the warmth inside. Like my first time in her living room, I hunkered next to Melissa's woodstove. Jake was out of his mind with joy, running aimlessly through the rooms, continually stopping to make sure I was still there. "I'm making a beef stew for dinner." Melissa used a tissue from her pocket to wipe her eyes. "When Dawson called to say you were both home and would stop by for Jake, I made more. Can you stay?"

Her ability to cook made my mouth water. "Yes, ma'am." I was hungry and didn't feel like finding something to fix in my own kitchen. To see her obvious pleasure at my acceptance rewarded me as much as the meal. Removing my coat was difficult, and both women noted my holstered gun but said nothing.

Her idea of more—and mine—were two different things. I might have doubled what was planned. Instead, Melissa filled a three-gallon pot and baked dozens of homemade biscuits.

I ate my stew and leavened quick bread quietly, while Dawson and his mother caught up on news. He'd missed Christmas with his family for the first time except for his military service. I noticed

Melissa still had her tree up and a few presents were beneath it. Bess was quiet, eating her stew and glancing over her spoon every few seconds. "How did you break your arm?" She was casual with her question.

I chuckled. "Would you believe I was thrown from a twenty-two-story balcony?"

"No…" Bess was incredulous, and Melissa could only stare. I couldn't see Dawson's face—he was seated next to me.

"Gotcha!" I grinned at them. "Truth is, I'm pretty clumsy and took a hard fall." It was technically true. I *had* fallen—only after thrown from the height I'd mentioned.

Bess continued to press. "How did you injure your face? And why cut your hair and change its color?"

I froze. For moment I couldn't think, and a good excuse wouldn't come to me—nor a believable lie. In truth, I hated to even fib to either woman. "I can't tell you." I set my spoon aside and pushed my chair back. Dawson put his hand on my knee as if to stop me. "It was…it was just a case of closing out my old life to prepare for a new one…the one I've always dreamed of." His grip loosened, and he patted gently.

"That's how you got the cuts?" Melissa brushed her own face with the tips of her fingers while her gaze touched my healing wounds." I nodded. "And the arm, too. Am I right?" Again, I silently agreed. "Where were you? Can either of you tell us where you've been? It must have been south of here, because you're both tanned." I shook my head at her questions and assumptions.

"Only toward the end, Mom." Dawson said. "She was in a bad way and I went to help. Case closed, okay?"

"You were abused by a man, weren't you?" I could see Melissa swelling with indignation. "You went to break it off with someone, and he beat you…hurt you." I listened slack-jawed while she worked to create a reasonable story. In a way, it was better than anything I could have devised. I felt Dawson chuckle next to me. First his body shook, and then we heard him. Even Bess looked at her sister with alarm until Melissa took notice. "What?" She was more than a little indignant. "She went to break it off with a boyfriend…" she drilled into me with narrowed eyes. "It wasn't a husband, was it? Then he beat her... I just know it."

Dawson was forced to break in. "Mom...just stop. It wasn't anything like what you think, but it's difficult to explain. You know, national security and all."

"Oh, my..." Melissa sat straight in alarm. "...you're a spy? Is that why my Dawson helped you, because he was military?"

He gave a forward tilt of his head. "You're getting warm, so drop it unless anyone listening thinks you're a security risk." Her eyes got big and glanced around the kitchen. "You know how the government is. They can listen through the television if they want to...even if it's turned off."

It was all I could do to keep a straight face. Yet it worked, and Bess looked at me differently. While the two women processed what they learned, Dawson filled my bowl again. He included three more biscuits.

"I can't eat that much," My stomach was already complaining.

"You're far too skinny, little dove. Eat what you can, and I'll have Mom send more home with you."

I would have to put on weight to be considered lean. Upon weighing after my bath, what I saw frightened me though I'd stuffed myself for two weeks attempting to put on much needed weight. My goal was eleven more pounds to reach one hundred again. Then I would breathe easier. Perhaps another five by the following summer.

I almost finished the stew. In my best estimation, I ate two bowls, five biscuits, and drank a glass of milk. I rubbed my stomach after pushing back from the bar. Jake stayed next to me during dinner without complaint.

"Are you planning on returning to school, Julia? Does teaching still interest you?" Bess watched closely, presumably for a reaction.

"Oh, yes! I want to teach more than anything. It seems a lifetime ago when I had my own classroom in Astoria." I'd enjoyed the short, idyllic life experienced at the mouth of the Colombia River. Memories of the smell of salt water tidal flats rushed in.

"How long until you're ready to substitute again? We've been shorthanded with flu going around." She didn't sound enthusiastic.

"Not until the end of February or beginning of March. I'd like to have this cast off first. I'm sorry you have so many teachers out."

"March is soon enough, sweetie." She reached across the table and covered my hand with hers. "Do a good job and get along with the staff because there will be changes next year. Retirements, planned babies, and the like." Bess's smile was devious. "Besides, Thomas Howell has been asking of your whereabouts."

"That little worm?" Judging by the contempt in Dawson's voice, he was not a fan of Mr. Howell.

"He's a damned good teacher, young man."

"He's nothing but a tomcat, Auntie. If he put the effort into teaching he does trolling bars, I wouldn't argue your point."

"Enough of this. Can I interest anyone in chocolate cake?"

"I would." Dawson was clearly a fan of his mother's baking.

"I'd like one, too, although my jeans won't appreciate it this weekend," Bess said.

Melissa turned her attention to me. "Julia?"

"Oh, Lord, no. I'm too full." I leaned away to show how far my stomach protruded.

"Just a little piece then. I'll send more home with you along with stew and biscuits." She retrieved a beautiful slice from the counter, making me groan.

If a piece four inches to each side could be called small, she gave me just a little piece. Hers and my boss's weren't much larger, but Dawson's made up for us. It was closer to twenty-five percent of the cake. Catching his attention, I raised one eyebrow at the size. He grinned, his teeth covered in chocolate frosting.

Melissa wasn't any hungrier than me. "I forgot to mention, Julia. I have two packages for you. The UPS man left them a few weeks ago. Dawson asked me to watch for a delivery before he left, and I caught the driver the second day. I have them here for safe keeping. We've never had a robbery, but I would've felt bad if whatever you ordered was stolen from my son's porch."

As incongruous as it might seem, I'd forgotten about the shipped cash. Signing Wiggins and clinging to life consumed me after asking Dawson to accept and hide the deliveries in my root cellar. While trying to survive, I'd never thought of it again—I planned to earn a living by teaching for the next thirty-five years. "Thank you," I took a swallow of milk, searching for the right words. "It's work-related items and information on cashing out my retirement." I was getting better at walking the thin line between truth and fabrication.

"You don't have to do that, Julia. The school has a retirement program you're encouraged to roll it into. I know you're young, but let your money work for you rather than fritter it away."

"I have an accountant who takes care of finances for me, boss." It's difficult to explain, but to call her my boss gave me stability. "She's forgotten more than I'll ever understand about investments."

Dawson helped me load my Jeep after we finished eating. Two boxes of cash not much larger than an apple crate weren't light. Neither was the stew and biscuits for a skinny girl wearing a huge cast. Jake didn't need help. He parked his wiggly butt in the front seat and waited. "I'll stop in the morning to pack your stuff in." Dawson followed me to my Wagoneer while it warmed. "Leave it locked in the garage—the food will be frozen by morning. Don't touch the boxes. They're far too heavy." He opened my door and kissed me before I sat, stepping back to give me room.

My home was warm when I returned, but the fire needed wood again. It was past my bedtime. After locking both doors and checking all windows, I retired for the evening. Jake was on the bed waiting once more. He watched as I disrobed, slid into my pajamas, and placed the little Colt strategically on my nightstand. Only after I was beneath the covers did he use his claws to squirm and drag himself to my side. "Jake, you can't imagine how nice this is." I burst into tears and hugged my dog awkwardly. He groaned in return, trying to lick my face. I had no time to consider the future and Dawson or anything else. Instead, the long day and stress drove me into the arms of the sandman.

***

As tired as I was since rescued from the beach of the Grand Bahamas, my body seemed to know it was home. My eyes opened at 5:30, the same as most mornings of my adult life. Even when young, I seldom watched television, preferring an early evening with a good book. Sliding from bed and waking Jake, I drew on my robe and hurried to the stove. It had burned out, although the firebox wasn't yet cold.

Using wood stored inside the previous evening, it was quickly warming the house. I took the time to replace my cellphone battery, switch it on, and plug it into the charger. Messages or texts could be investigated after it was fully powered.

Without much in the refrigerator, I cooked pancakes and made coffee for breakfast. A radio station broadcast morning programs I liked, and I caught local and national news and weather forecasts among the music and chatter. I washed the few dishes, and after filling my cup with more coffee, opened my laptop. While it booted up, I checked my phone. Two messages were from Manny sent weeks before. *Received word client has been signed. Congratulations. Packages sent.* Another came a few hours later. *It was nice working with you, J. Enjoy retirement.*

There it was. I saw no indication they might back out of our verbal agreement. Of course, in the world of assassination, how good was The Company's word? Did they intend to try to force me to take more clients in the future? Only time would tell. After giving it more thought, I decided not to contact Manny. Our final communication before leaving for Missoula was to be our last.

Taking a deep breath, I accessed The Company's server to check on my overseas account. It didn't seem to work correctly, and after the third attempt, I received a website message. No longer did I have access to the server—meaning my account was off limits and unavailable. My guts froze knowing my hard-earned money was gone. Other than the cash still in my Jeep and what remained of the inheritance from my parents, all I worked for and saved was gone. I collapsed back in my chair and felt sick, then angry. How dare they take what was mine?

I clicked off the site and opened my email. I found a series of messages from both my overseas and US accountants and breathed a sigh of relief. The first stated they were instructed to empty and close my account and repatriate overseas funds. The second from my US accountant warned me of incoming monies and asked for instructions. Although it was a Saturday morning, I called her number to see how bad the damage was, should she answer. She did.

"Laura McKinney's office."

"Mrs. McKinney, this is Julia Hampton. I just returned home to find your email." Not sure what to say, I waited to hear her response.

"Oh, yes. How thrilling to receive a reward of this size, Miss Hampton!" Her excitement seemed positive. "Can you tell me how it happened?"

How what happened? Christ, Manny, what have you done? "It was nothing, Mrs. McKinney, really." For a moment, I considered ending the call, not sure what to say and afraid of implicating myself. Occasionally things work themselves out.

"Nothing? How can you say that? Saving the life of a child who'd been swept into the ocean has to be exciting. The report said it took place at West Palm Beach in Florida."

My sudden giddiness made me glad I sat. "Yes, ma'am." My legs shook in relief.

"A little over 1.25 million…how astonishing to receive so much. Yet what price can you put on a child's life? Can you tell me who the parents were?"

She'd inadvertently tossed me another lifeline. "No, ma'am. I'm not at liberty to discuss it. I signed a nondisclosure agreement. I'm not allowed to talk about it." I was faintly amazed at my smooth explanation.

Mrs. McKinney was gracious. "I understand."

We debated my money for an hour. She seemed to think I would want part of it in my personal account to spend. After I indicated it was all to be invested within a diversified but conservative portfolio, she promised to provide me with more information. Mrs. McKinney seemed determined to keep me a part of the decision making. However, she wanted me to realize the high cost of gifted money. I stood to lose a substantial portion in taxation if we didn't move quickly. Even if I lost thirty percent, combined with my inheritance, investable cash would measure almost nine-hundred thousand. She seemed to think it was possible to keep my losses in the eight to ten percent range. If so, my investments would be much higher.

Jake was one to laze in bed until his bladder forced him up. I thought nothing of it when he raced to the front door with desperation in his eyes. As he flew outside, I could hear an approaching vehicle. It was our rental truck, and I retreated indoors to escape the cold.

Dawson drove slowly after seeing Jake racing along the driveway and parked in his normal spot. When he knocked at the door instead of walking in, I smiled to myself at his manners.

"Come on in, sleepyhead. You too, neighbor." I grinned at Dawson and gave a quick stroke to Jake as he squirted between us to his food dish.

Dawson caught on immediately. "Thought you meant me at first. I've been up since before five." I gave him credit when he didn't attempt to sweep me from my feet. For whatever reason, I felt shy and introverted again. Perhaps it came with being on my home turf safe and sound with life back to normal.

"You beat me, although Jake got up only a few seconds before he ran out to meet you."

Dawson cleared his throat. "Jules, if you could follow me into town, I called the Dodge dealership and got an okay to leave the rental for pick up." He removed his coat and sat at the table after I filled an extra coffee cup. It was good to see the Colt on his belt again.

"Sure, if you don't mind bringing in the food your mom sent and the two boxes of cash first."

Dawson took a hasty sip and stood. "Toss me your keys and I'll get 'em."

He brought in the money first. The boxes were metal and heavy, and I found they were lined with a thick plastic sheathing and cardboard. When he returned with the second, the first was already open, and I was looking at more cash than I could imagine. The lid of the second hung unsecured when he returned with the stew and put it in the refrigerator. "Holy hell. Haven't seen so much money since the US government flew pallets of cash into Iraq."

"You saw that?" I was visibly startled, making Dawson grin. It was something I'd watched on the news.

"Yeah…" his grin turned savage. "My unit and I once blew through fifty million."

"What?" His statement didn't make sense. "You spent fifty million?" How could a soldier have and spend so much money? Did they steal it? I wondered if I should be worried about my hard-earned windfall.

Dawson snickered. "We got intel sayin' an incoming load of cash was gonna be jacked by insurgents. Before it left the plane, we planted the shipment with explosives. We not only detonated it when they stopped in a big warehouse, but seconds later a couple JDAMs from a waiting F16 struck, too." He used his hands to characterize an enormous explosion. I also noted once home, he was back to dropping "Gs" from some of his words. "Boom, no more bad guys." His story made me feel better about my neighbor's honesty. I chuckled about ruining so much cash until Dawson grasped my sleeve and drew me outside. "I suppose we should take it all out and make sure nothin' else was slipped into the boxes." It never occurred to me The Company might use my money to neutralize me. I nodded and followed him in.

Three quarter of a million dollars covered my table. Fifties and hundreds were stacked high. Taking over an hour to inspect, Dawson marched me out again to pronounce it safe as far as he knew unless contaminated with a foreign substance. He understood a hell of a lot more than I did about that sort of thing. The little I knew came from television shows and books. "Are you kidding?" I shivered from more than the cold, wondering if I'd already absorbed some terrible agent.

My neighbor nodded to himself. "Should've thought of it sooner. I'll contact Allen and see if he can send something to sweep it with."

"Sweep?"

"GPS, bugs, chemicals, perhaps biologicals."

I stared at the money as if it were poison. "You think…I mean…"

Dawson laughed. "We'll just check it for trackers. Chemicals would have already killed or made us sick by now. Bios would infect not only us but anyone we came in contact with, making its use unlikely. To be on the safe side, we'd better wash our hands with soap and hot water."

My stomach turned at the thought. "You really considered all this?"

He shrugged lazily. "Sure, didn't you?" I shook my head. "You don't seem to trust these folks, which gives me little reason to have confidence. I may call Allen and see if he could come over the hill and check the entire place. The garage and your Wagoneer, too."

"Do it. Do it right now." My anxiety rose. These were a syndicate who paid me to eliminate individuals they only knew from reports. One more death certainly wouldn't mean anything.

"Now isn't the time to panic, little dove. What's done is done. In the meantime, we'll replace it in the original boxes and hide 'em in your closet."

I followed him inside while I considered. "But I planned to store it…"

He didn't give me a chance to finish and held one finger to his lips as a warning. "No, the house would be best for now. If you're wanting to put it in the garage, we'll do it after trappin' any mice."

Shit, shit, shit! I was dumb. If there were electronic devices in my residence planted after I left for the Grand Bahamas, I almost gave away my best secret, the hidden cellar. If they did it sooner, The Company would know about my hidey-hole. We placed the money in the original boxes and stacked them in my bedroom closet.

"Would you start my Jeep while I dress?" I waited until he was out of my bedroom before closing the door. Turncoat Jake followed Dawson outside.

I was threading the Colt awkwardly onto my belt when they returned. Working with one hand made everything difficult. Assuring it was cinched tightly to keep the holster snug, I slung a hooded sweatshirt around my shoulders. It was a front zip, and I dropped a speed loader in my pocket. "Whenever you're ready, sir!" I played on the same respectful address I heard most of his team members use.

"I'd rather you didn't." His deep voice was mild, but I could hear displeasure he struggled to hide. "My name is Dawson, neighbor, or even farmer. Please don't use the military reference again."

It wasn't a first fight or even our first awkward situation. On our drive home from Florida were plenty abrasive moments when I could stay awake. It was an expression Dawson would rather not hear, although his team members used it frequently. I supposed it brought back memories he would rather forget. Nodding my quiet acceptance, I followed him outside, locking the door behind. It seemed strange to realize so much money was stored inside my humble shack.

Jake was beside himself with excitement when he realized we were going for a ride. The road was clear but icy in spots, and Dawson drove slowly knowing I would, too. My heater turned on high barely warmed the interior. Jake hung his head out the window until the end of my driveway before even he realized it was too cold. The dealership was across from the high school, and I followed the Dawson into the parking lot.

We waited only a few minutes for him to reappear after leaving the keys. "Whew…" He held his hands in the heat blowing out from the window vent. "…it's freaking cold out there."

"How bad is it?" I didn't have a way of checking the temperature with my old 'eighty-four Wagoneer.

"It was twelve when we got here. News said it should warm this afternoon and start snowing."

I slammed on the brakes rather than turn left and return home. "Snow? I don't have any groceries in the house." The age-old fear men and women have of hunger in winter clutched at me. "We'd better stop at the store before I go home."

"Can I buy lunch first if you have time?"

Taking a deep breath, I closed my eyes and let it out slowly. "For the first time in years I can do anything anytime I want." I grinned at him. "Let's eat." The Company yoke around my neck was never so evident until after its removal.

"Lunch first…then we'll find some groceries, all right?"

"Feed for my animals." The thought almost made me sick. Since arriving home, I'd not checked on either my chickens or rabbits.

Dawson read my mind. "Relax. I took your bunnies in their cages to Mom's. She's kept them in the barn. She also has an old coop, and there was plenty of room for your chickens after I patched a couple holes. I can bring them back anytime you'd like."

We went into the same lounge where I first met Scotty. Although before noon, it was a Saturday and bursting with patrons. Our server almost beat us to one of the few empty tables. "Your usual, hon?" She was younger than me, taller, and noticeably shapelier. I hadn't seen her before, but the woman and Dawson seemed friendly. Their chumminess made my hackles rise.

"No, coffee and BLTs for both of us." On our way home, he ordered for me more than once. Dawson checked with me to make sure he hadn't overstepped any hidden boundaries.

I nodded. "May I have a large glass of water, too?"

Our waitress's smile was beautiful. "Sure thing, sugar."

She turned and sauntered away, shaking her *thang* far more than needed. It was all I could do to not bare my teeth. Some women might have been thinking about hair pulling and face scratching. I was looking at the location where a bullet should best be placed.

"Friend of yours?" My voice was cool enough to drop the temperature twenty degrees.

Dawson was reading a message on his phone and looked at me with surprise. "What?" He glanced around the lounge. "I know almost everyone here. Who are you thinkin' of?"

"Our waitress. You know, the one flaunting her big boobs and even bigger butt."

He seemed taken aback. "Who, Allison? Christ, Jules, she was starting primary when I was graduating from high school. Besides, her name is Mrs. Allison Edwards." He winked. "You might have met her husband. Mike Edwards teaches middle school math for Aunt Bess." He did all he could to stop a small smile from appearing, but it grew, making my face warm.

I felt a trickle of sweat go down my back. "Oh, God, I'm so embarrassed. So, she's the famous Mrs. Edwards I've heard about in the teachers' lounge?" I covered my face to hide my shame. Before I could make a bigger fool of myself, Allison returned with our coffee and my water. Rumor had it she was the nicest woman in the world and perhaps the prettiest, with the best figure. I certainly couldn't disagree with the last two points.

A few minutes later, she swung by our table one more time. "Your sandwiches should be up in a few minutes." It suddenly didn't seem as if she flaunted anything when she walked away.

Dawson left our table to use the restroom. If I went to the women's I might not have returned in my embarrassment. My claws were extended for the first time in my life—and stupidly so. Our server's tip would be substantial to help make up for my evil thoughts.

"Miss Hampton."

I lifted my chin to see Thomas Howell standing next to me. "Mr. Howell. How are you?" I hadn't seen his entrance and assumed he came in after us.

"I see you're not alone by the vacated seat. Would you mind if I stopped for a moment?" He took the chair closest without waiting for a response. "We were told you were in an accident." His gaze left my cast and went to the injuries on my face. "Are you okay?"

"I'll be fine."

He leaned close enough to make my skin crawl. "Will you be back to substitute at school?"

"Not until my cast is off about a month from now." Dawson left the men's room, and it was frightening to observe—something I'd watched on nature shows. A shark hones in on its prey and knifes through water with schools of smaller fish parting to let it through. The predator picks up speed, and those around feel relief when it passes.

Dawson was no different. I knew he was a dangerous man, but until that moment, I didn't truly understand the magnitude. The instant he recognized the man sitting at our table, I saw a different Dawson. The crowd made a path for him, and he didn't slow when he reached our table.

Thomas must have noted my alarm and turned to learn the reason. The moment he saw my neighbor, his face paled, and he tipped the chair over in his haste.

"I warned you never again." Dawson's hands grasped Thomas' coat front and forced him rearward, then lifted and slammed him into a vertical beam. I feared Thomas Howell's feet were off the floor when his upper back and skull impacted the thick twelve-by-twelve. The sound reverberated inside the cavernous building. Stunned by the blow, he collapsed before Dawson could release the man to slump to the wooden planks below.

"I'm sorry...I didn't know." The teacher's eyes were glassy, and he held up a hand as if to hold Dawson at bay.

I heard a strangled cry, and a woman ran out. Not understanding anything going on, I waited until Dawson stepped back to allowed

Thomas to rise. It was obvious by the way Dawson set his feet that he was going to let Thomas stand before swinging.

A uniformed police officer may have entered for lunch, or perhaps the woman who fled summoned him, but he stepped to our table, and I held my breath. He gripped a can of pepper spray and focused his attention on Dawson. "Do we have a problem here?"

Chapter XIV

Dawson turned quickly, his eyes burning with rage until he saw the sheriff. As clearly as I did, the lawman saw the anger on Dawson's face dissipate—returning to the same lackadaisical man who left our table for the restroom. "Hey, Will. No problem here. Mr. Howell slipped, and I was offering to help him."

"Thomas?" the sheriff seemed to know both men. "Anything you want to add?"

"No, I'm fine." All of us noted the wooziness in his eyes. "It's all good." He turned without comment and left through the nearest exit to a rear parking lot. I tracked him from our window as he circled the building to his car in front.

"Dawson..." Will's words dripped ominous warning. "...no more. Do I make myself clear?" He stared at my neighbor until he got the nod he expected.

The sheriff turned away. Excitement over, the crowd lost interest. Dawson sat again, removing the ever-present Stetson and wiping his forehead with a sleeve. Allison brought our meal before he could explain. Her eyes were filled with pity when she set our baskets on the table. "Can I get anything else?" Her question was directed to both of us. My tablemate shook his head, and I followed his example. "I'll give you a few minutes before I return with a warmup for your coffee."

I wasn't hungry any longer but ate for no other reason than something to do. Dawson was quiet, and I glanced at him more than once to uncover the reason. He was staring into the distance, lost in memories.

The BLT was good, its hard toast making the inside of my mouth raw. I stopped for a sip of coffee and found I was thirstier than I thought. I switched to water, and my glass was nearly drained when I returned it to the table. "Are you going to tell me what that was all about?" The physical encounter concerned me because I couldn't forget the savagery on Dawson's face. My goal was to come across as nonchalant, although my guts still quaked.

"Nope." His anger flashed again. Others nearby were craning their necks to look our way, probably gauging my reaction or Dawson's. "Not here."

"More coffee?" Allison was quiet and reserved when she stopped again.

"Please." I slid my cup to where she could more easily fill it and watched her hurry away.

"Hey, Julia!" I barely had time to turn my head when Scotty came skidding in, taking the same seat Howell vacated. "Here to pay up? If memory serves, you owe me a dance but more importantly a kiss." He slapped Dawson on the shoulder. "Hey, buddy. Haven't seen you since Thanksgiving. Where've you been keeping yourself?" Scotty noticed the cast under my coat and stiffened. He was even more surprised to see my cheek and jaw when I turned my head. His eyes flicked from the cast to my injuries, and I could imagine the wheels turning. He didn't see an accident in his mind. "What the hell?" The loud, boisterous, and fun-loving man I was getting to know vanished. "Who the hell punched you?" He stared at Dawson. "Well? Is someone going to say something?" The muscles in his jaw bulged.

I waved my right hand lazily. "It was nothing. I took a fall while vacationing in Florida." Holding my cast up, I added, "You won't meet anyone clumsier than me, Scotty." I accepted his stare calmly without blinking.

He finally sat back, rigid and unyielding. "Dawson?" Scotty never looked away from me. A twitch developed under his left eye, and a dangerous side of the gregarious man emerged.

My neighbor backed my half-truth. "It's true. She took a bad fall. Lot worse than she lets on."

Scotty snorted in derision. "Would both of you stop treating me like a mushroom?"

"A mushroom?"

"Covering me in shit and keeping me in the dark." It was supposed to be funny, but Scotty wasn't laughing. He was far more serious than I might have suspected.

I shrugged and tried to laugh his suspicions away. "I don't know what to tell you then." My chuckle sounded fake even to me.

After the bill was paid, Scotty followed us to my Wagoneer. "A fist did that to your face, Julia. Don't try to bullshit a bullshitter." He closed the door after I rolled my window down. "Are you going to be okay?" His eyes darted to Dawson.

"I'll be fine, Scotty." I reached awkwardly and patted his hand where it rested on my car door. "Really. Thanks, but I'll be okay." He was still standing where we left him when we drove out of the parking lot.

***

Dawson was of little help while I shopped. He was quiet, answering questions with single words or grunts until I ignored him. When the cashier tallied my bill, I worried if there was enough money in my account. Most of it was in savings or invested. Noting my growing angst, he finally asked, "Got ants in your pants?"

"I'm not sure I have enough in checking," I whispered.

He stared back, cocking his head in confusion before a smile grew. "You're joking?" We were both thinking of so much cash stored at my home but none in my pocket.

"No," I whispered in desperation. "Do you have any with you?" He nodded, smug in his silent laughter.

The clerk finished, and I saw the amount. It was less than I feared, but enough to worry me. I swiped my debit plastic, entered the PIN, and held my breath, letting it out after my card was accepted. Dawson was already pushing one cart and pulling the other as I waited for the receipt. He stacked groceries in the back while I distracted Jake.

I held my tongue until we were leaving the city limits before reopening the can of worms. "Are you going to tell me about what happened back there?"

Dawson was staring out the side window. He sighed. "It was a long time ago."

"What happened with Mr. Howell certainly wasn't."

He didn't reply until we neared my driveway. "Take me to your place first so I can carry your groceries in." I was grateful for his thoughtfulness. Doing it alone would be difficult and time consuming.

Dawson locked my garage and brought in the last load when I came out of the bathroom. "I'll put coffee on if you're interested," He nodded and sat at the kitchen table. I took the time to fill my stove with wood while it brewed. We removed our coats, mine with Dawson's help, but not our Colts.

It surprised me when he spoke in monotone. "Thomas Howell is a couple years older than me. He moved to the area about a decade ago, a year or two before my discharge." He stopped for a moment and sighed. "Nancy Bickman and I went together through much of high school. I was convinced she was *the one*. She moved to Missoula and entered college after graduation. We tried to keep a long-distance relationship going, but it wasn't to be. I drove over to see her unannounced one weekend, but she was with another guy, and I turned tail for home. Two days later, I signed up for the Army and was on a bus heading for basic. We lost contact because I asked Mom not to give her my address."

My heart went out to him. "I don't blame you."

"I returned home after my discharge. Didn't take long before I happened to run across Nancy. It was the first time I saw her since watchin' her kiss the guy on campus. She was divorced but the same Nancy I remembered from school. One thing led to another, and we got back together. It didn't take long before I was in love again. I was so sure I bought the ring and prepared an elaborate surprise where I would ask for her hand. Mom was even willing to cosign for a house to be built where I live now."

Dawson took a break by getting the pot and filling our cups. "I'd met Howell since returning and knew him for what he was. I even warned Nancy after seeing him sniffin' around. She laughed and thought it was cute how I felt threatened. We'd talked about a life together, and she knew what I was considering. It was only a matter of time before I asked her to marry me."

I was getting a bad feeling where his story was taking us. "You don't have to…"

He ignored me. "It was a Saturday morning when I was ready to pop the question. I'd fibbed the night before and told her I'd be gone. Instead, I was setting up our perfect day. Her folks, along with me, Mom, Aunt Bess, and Scotty sneaked into her house about eight in the morning. She tended bar and normally slept late on weekends so it didn't surprise me when she was in bed. Leaving everyone in the front room, I tiptoed back there and opened the door to find Howell in bed with her. My entrance woke the pair, and Nancy burst into tears."

I wanted to make him quit talking but needed to hear how it ended. His face was cold as an eastern Idaho winter. "I saw enough killing in the service. If I didn't leave right then, there was gonna be more. I stomped through the living room and didn't stop till I was home. Mom said Nancy came running out naked as the day she was born trying to stop me. I guess things got pretty ugly. Howell tried to sneak out the back door, but Nancy's dad was waiting."

Dawson saw my quiet tears. His story was more painful than I could have imagined. I didn't need him to identify her; she was the woman who cried out and rushed from the lounge. It seemed odd when I thought back. Dawson must have noticed her, but I saw no indication of discomfort.

"Nancy tried to talk to me, but I've not spoken a word to her since that day. She simply doesn't exist any longer."

No wonder she behaved the way she did. "And Mr. Howell?" Knowing Dawson the way I did, the story didn't end there.

"We had words."

"That's it? You had words?"

Dawson stared into his cup during the recounting. He looked up after my question, making my eyes widen—his were colder than anyone's but the gray man. He opened his mouth to answer when we heard an engine outside. I was going to have more company. Glancing out, I saw it was snowing and retrieved another chipped cup from my cabinet. "Come in," I was filling it when the knock came. Jake came to press against my side, the big old wimp.

A glimpse to Dawson assured me his emotions were hidden well. When I motioned Scotty in, my neighbor's face indicated nothing of the terrible story. Scotty stopped short after closing the door and waited to learn the reason for my red eyes and tearstained cheeks. "Am I interrupting something?"

"Yes. Now get the hell out of here," Dawson said.

His reaction seemed to put Scotty at ease. He grinned and accepted a cup before sitting at the head of the table. I topped Dawson's and then my own without offering comment. Scotty blew over the top of his brew to cool it, and I could see his humor. "He told you, didn't he?" I raised one eyebrow and waited. "About Nancy and old Howell." For a tale as tragic and sad as the story Dawson recounted, Scotty's growing smile took me aback. I wasn't certain where the joke lay. Dawson wore a look of disgust when he glanced at our visitor. Scotty didn't seem to care. "Forgive me, old friend. I'm a pig, and we all know it. Your ex though, she sure as hell looked good in her birthday suit." He burst into contagious laughter, drawing a grim smile from Dawson and a chuckle from me.

"Yep, you're a pig," I said. Over his head, I could see the snowfall increasing.

I took the pan of stew Melissa sent and situated it on the wood cookstove. Choosing a cool part, I left it to heat slowly. Her biscuits went into the warming oven wrapped in a clean dishtowel. Leaving the boys to themselves, I took my cup and returned to the living room. Tipping my recliner back, I made myself comfortable with the book I was reading.

It took ten minutes of silence from me before they realized I wasn't coming back. Scotty followed me first and took a seat on the couch. Dawson didn't join us for another five. "You don't have a television? Christ, I'd go nuts

I couldn't concentrate on the novel and gave up after a half hour, setting the book aside. Dawson dozed on one end of the couch while Scotty snored on the other. Jake lay sprawled next to the stove. I rolled my eyes. I had only two men in my life, and both were sleeping. It looked suspiciously like Scotty was drooling a little. If I were a bit meaner, I would have used my phone to take a picture.

I needed to check on the stew and found my largest spoon to stir it. It was warming, and I dug to the bottom to help mix ingredients. Snowfall wasn't easing, and from the kitchen, it looked to be two inches on a fencepost. Neither of the boys woke, so I joined them in their slumbers.

My dream was the most vivid I could recall. The letter opener embedded in Wiggins' skull wasn't slowing him. I drove it in with my fist, pounding again and again, only to retreat in the face of his onslaught. Behind him were his bodyguards with letter openers protruding from their throats, and nothing could stop their advances. Behind me was the balcony with the pool a tiny speck thousands of feet below. Wiggins' hands went around my neck as he squeezed the life from me.

"No…" I struggled to reach my gun to stop the giant with a bullet. Only a firearm could halt him after the crude weapon lodged in his brain failed.

"Julia?" Someone called my name from a distance.

"Jules?" The voice was close and so familiar.

"No!" I screamed. Wiggins lifted my body to throw me into an abyss where the pool once lay. I fought to draw my gun—to empty it into his belly and chest. Both hands were around my throat when it came free of my holster, but somehow, he grasped the barrel and twisted. It hurt, causing a real pain in my fingers instead of phantom ailment, and my eyes flared opened.

Dawson held the Colt wrenched from my grip with my right hand still in his. The fear painted on his face as my dream ebbed was stark. I could still feel Wiggins' stranglehold and the feeling of abject terror and helplessness. Dawson knelt in front of me after setting the revolver aside. "Was it…?" He waited, hoping I knew who he meant.

I couldn't stop shaking and nodded. "Wiggins…he wouldn't quit, even with the letter opener buried deep. He dangled me from the balcony…about to let go…except there wasn't a pool," I said through sobs.

Dawson drew me into his arms to give reassurance and lend his strength. My reserves evaporated, and I collapsed into his embrace. Through my tears, I saw Scotty watch openmouthed. Dawson lifted me. Unable to stop crying, I didn't object to his carrying me to my bedroom. My terror hadn't abated, nor did Wiggins' fingers relax their grip. "Don't leave me." I scratched under my chin down to my collarbone to remove the unseen hands.

"I'm here, my little dove." He lay next to me, an arm resting across my ribcage. I held it as a life preserver, and he pulled me tightly against his body. Jake leaped to the bed, pinning me against my savior.

I took deep breaths to regain control. It was no different from mastering my pulse when shooting, and my pounding heart slowed its race. The warmth of two extra bodies combined with terror-induced fatigue caused my eyes to close. My last thought was of the iron limb keeping me safe.

***

I woke cold enough to scoot closer to nearby warmth. It drew me in, and with Jake shifting to press against me, I dozed again.

Someone—presumably Scotty—closed the bedroom door. With the woodstove and baseboard heaters in the living area and kitchen, my bedroom cooled drastically. I pushed on Jake in an effort to rise. If it were possible to slide from beneath Dawson's arm, I might not wake him. I struggled with the bulky cast. "If you're ready to get up, all you have to do is say so, little dove." The deep murmur in my ear made my stomach flutter and heart skip a beat.

I stopped my futile attempt at freedom—his arm didn't allow escape. "Why little dove?" I whispered, having wondered at the obvious endearment.

"You're a wounded and broken little dove." He drew me closer and kissed my cheek. Not as a lover but a friend. His coarse beard brushed my skin.

"Am I?" I'd not given it any thought.

"Are you what?"

"Wounded and broken?"

"More than you know. So much so you can't imagine." He pulled back after a second peck. I could feel his eyes on me.

His observations weren't bothersome. They were food for thought. As humans, we are rarely able to step aside and take an honest look at ourselves. We have a carefully constructed view of who and what we are, and seldom is it how others view us. My normal reaction to negative forces was to pull back and push the world away. "If I'm wounded and don't know it, how do I heal?" I feared it was a simple question with a complex answer and could not have been more wrong.

"By lettin' me help."

"How? What can you do?"

"Let me in, and you'll see." He nearly purred in my ear, so deep was his voice.

We were interrupted by a soft knock at the door. Dawson rolled to his stocking feet and answered it. Scotty looked in, fearful as a schoolboy at the principal's office. "Hey, I thought I heard voices." He bit at the inside of his lip, "Figured you might want to know the stew is hotter than a school girl on prom night."

I rolled my eyes at his chauvinist description. Besides, I spent my prom nights in my room doing homework. No one asked me to a dance in four years of high school. "We're on our way, Scotty. Thanks." I turned to my right side facing the door. Dawson came back to the bed with his friend only a step behind. "You know I'm not helpless, don't you?" I grumbled. They ignored me and assisted me anyway.

The stew was better than the first night. Dawson set the table, and Scotty stepped in to help. I found them waiting after I used the bathroom and washed my hands. Our bowls were filled with biscuits divided equally.

"Been having nightmares long, Julia?" Scotty waited until we were all halfway through our meal. "Are they always so real?"

"No, I normally don't have dreams I remember, let alone nightmares."

"This Wiggins character—who is he?" His tone was neutral.

I was gone to the Grand Bahamas so long I was unaware if Wiggins' death made the news in the states. "Did I say that? I don't remember." I was walking a minefield because Scotty wasn't stupid.

"Yeah, it was Wiggins, wasn't it, Pelletier?" He shifted to his friend for validation.

"Wiggins, Biggins, Diggins…could have been anything." My neighbor acted as if he held no interest in the question or answer.

Our meal was finished in silence. Sensing the uncomfortable atmosphere, Jake took his place near my chair. Dawson and Scotty ate seconds, but I waved off more. One bowl was all my queasy stomach could handle.

Having done it before, Dawson washed dishes while Scotty went outside to check the weather. It was cooling in the house, and I opened the stove to see how well it burned. Scraping the coals and larger chunks together, I left it open to get hotter. The front door slammed while I fitted more wood inside. I shut it down and walked the few feet back to the kitchen.

Scotty was frowning. "Six or seven inches and coming down hard. What's your plan for getting home tonight, Dawson?"

"Jules was going to drive me." Finished with the few dishes, he hung the dishtowel on a cabinet door and leaned his butt against the counter.

I made no pretense of not admiring my neighbor. He was quiet and relaxed…little seemed to upset him, even recounting the story of Nancy and Thomas. I found his attitude made him the most desirable man I could imagine. Seemingly in control of every situation, he was calm, collected, and considerate. He had every right to hurt Howell much worse than he did.

"Not this girl. At least, not tonight. Either you do it, Scotty, or we wait till morning. I can take him then. I don't have a lot of confidence driving in the snow after dark. It might be a little unseemly, but you're both welcome to spend the night. I have an extra bed and a comfortable couch. The roads should be easier to navigate in daylight."

Scotty opted for my spare bed after Dawson offered to take the couch. The boys brought in enough wood for the night and following day. Seeing an open door, Jake ran outside and did his business, hurrying back to where it was warm. It was nice to relax and watch things get done without lifting a finger. After the stove was loaded and closed, I stopped at my bedroom threshold. "I'm beat, guys. You're welcome to stay up as late as you'd like, if you hold any conversation to a dull roar, please. When you go to bed, open my door a foot or so. Otherwise, I'll freeze to death." With Jake nestled against my back, both the bed and I warmed quickly. Quiet voices murmured through the wall were enough to lull me to sleep.

An odd sound woke me, and I lay still, trying to decipher what caused it. Hearing the latch as my door closed, I waited for movement while I measured in my mind's eye the distance to the Colt. Feeling rather than seeing or hearing him, I knew Dawson stood at my bed's edge.

"Don't shoot me, Jules. I know you're awake. Your breathing changed," he whispered. It let me know he was exactly where I thought—perhaps a foot from the edge of my bed.

"What's going on?"

"The couch isn't as comfortable as you think. Would you mind if I slipped into the other side of your bed?"

"Not at all. Go ahead. Stay on the other side of Jake and keep your hands to yourself." Although he couldn't see it, I was smiling.

"Don't worry your pretty head, little dove. Your virtue is safe with me."

\*\*\*

How late the boys stayed up and talked before going to bed was obvious the next morning.

Jake overheated at some point during the night and moved to the foot. The area he vacated was filled with Dawson's still form. Waking first, I opened my eyes to perceive morning with enough light reflected off the snow outside my window to distinguish the extra body in my bed.

I rolled to my side and watched him sleep. His breathing was slow, shallow, and barely audible as he lay on his back. One arm, the closest to me, was thrown over his head. I edged closer, careful not to bump him with my cast, and studied his features from inches away.

Intent on his features as the morning light brightened my room, I couldn't help from reaching out. The room was cold, and goosebumps and hairs stood on my arm. Before my fingers could touch his cheek, I saw his eyes were open. After stroking his cheek and beard, I grasped his chin and turned his head to me. "Good morning, neighbor. Did I wake you?" My hand had a mind of its own as it stroked his face.

I heard the breath catch in his throat as our eyes locked. "You're beautiful." The reverberation came from deep within his chest.

His gaze was soft and made my chin quiver. "I've waited thirty years to hear that from someone besides my parents," I whispered, choking back tears.

He lowered the arm from above his head and carefully drew me nearer. My cast was all that held us apart. "It's true. Mere mortals are incapable of looking so exquisite when they first wake. You make it look easy."

I squirmed close enough to rest my cheek on his shoulder. "A girl could get used to your lies." I sighed. I could smell him, and although he needed a shower, it wasn't offensive. His was an aroma I grew to love more each day. My right arm went across his bare chest, and I could feel the wiry hair under my fingers.

Dawson lifted my chin. "You are exquisite, my little dove. It was the first thing I noticed when we met. Not only your physical beauty, but the inner grace shining through." Although we needed to brush our teeth, his lips tasted good when they touched mine. He pulled back after the gentle graze. "Even if impossible to comprehend the level at the time, I could see you were a dangerous woman whether you knew it or not. Beauty..." He kissed me. "...and danger..." He kissed me again. "...wrapped in sweetness. You are the perfect woman." His palm rested on my cheek.

We heard my stomach gurgle. He drew back smiling, but I wasn't ready to let go. Not allowing me to stop him, he pulled away and stood. Wearing only boxers, he was tall, lean, strong, and with scars I noticed for the first time. Whether from bullets, shrapnel, or both, it was up to him to eventually tell me. His clothes were in the front room, and he left me to dress. For a moment, I lay back and enjoyed the special minute we shared. I was about to throw the bedding off when he came padding back in with his clothes. Stifling my yelp into a squeak, I pulled the covers to my chin.

Dawson grinned at my reaction. "There isn't much under those blankets I haven't already seen." I watched as he battled to subdue a smile.

"That wasn't me. She was some other girl who was skin and bones."

"No," he said, pulling his jeans up and buttoning them. "It was the smartest, prettiest, and toughest girl I've ever known. She was definitely you." Taking a seat on the edge of my bed, careful not to sit on my leg, he pulled on his dirty socks and stuffed big feet into his boots. After lacing them, he stood and stared down. "She was and is a very beautiful woman." Giving me a last kiss, he quietly closed the door when he left.

The stove was roaring when I stepped out. Wearing jeans and an undershirt beneath a short-sleeved blouse, my feet were stuffed inside fluffy pink slippers with bunny faces and ears. I could see a thick layer of snow outside the living room window—something I didn't plan to venture into. I dampened the stove and hurried to the bathroom. After finishing, I went in search of Dawson with minty fresh breath. "Hey, you." My lips brushed his cheek as I passed where he was seated at the table. Coffee was on but not ready. An older gun magazine lay opened in front of him. "What would you like for breakfast?" My refrigerator was bursting with possibilities.

"Hotcakes and eggs?" Scotty was bleary-eyed when he stumbled in, occupying another chair at the table. They stayed up late, and he didn't appear to handle the lack of sleep well.

"Sounds good to me. How about you, neighbor?" I filled three cups with fresh brew, sliding one to each man, and keeping the last for myself. I searched for the new box of pancake mix after he shrugged. He didn't fool me—it was one of his favorite breakfasts.

Of course, Dawson helped. Trying to stir the mix by hand was awkward with a cast. A significant portion of the boxed mix and eight eggs were gone when we finished breakfast. Each man ate as much as I could have in three days. I made another pot of coffee while we remained at the table and digested our meal.

"Ready when you are." Dawson finished his cup and set it on the counter after a rinse.

Scotty nodded. The sky was clearing and it looked cold outside. "Let me start my truck and scrape off the snow. We'll leave when the windshield is clear."

The door no more than closed when my cellphone buzzed its alert of a message. It was on the counter out of my reach. Dawson was closest and handed it over. I unlocked it and checked to find it was a text. Shocked to see the sender, I read the four words making up the missive. Gasping before I could stop myself, I threw my phone across the table and scooted away.

"Jules?" Dawson was instantly wary of danger. I couldn't say anything and stared at my phone in horror. He took it to read what terrified me. It was from Manny, and the four words were the most paralyzing he could send. *Beware the gray man.*

Chapter XV

Scotty returned after stomping snow from his boots, bringing with him a blast of arctic air. Already shaking with fear, the cold chilled me further. "Truck's clear…you ready?" He was oblivious to my terror.

"Yeah, I need to get home," Dawson replied easily. "I'll be right out."

"Thanks for dinner and the bed…breakfast, too, kiddo." Scotty kissed my forehead.

I searched for saliva to wet my mouth before answering. "Anytime, my friend. It was nice to see you again." I wanted to stand and walk him to the door if not onto the porch, but I remained so terrified that my legs wouldn't hold me.

Dawson took a knee next to my chair after Scotty went outside. "I'll be back, okay?" I shook my head, unable to reply. My life was really and truly going to end and much sooner than I anticipated. The look on my face must have prompted Dawson to ask, "What does that message mean?"

I blinked rapidly, teetering on the edge of shock, and sidestepped his question. "Please stay away. Don't come back here. There's no sense in both of us dying."

He obviously understood nothing more than the seriousness by my reaction but helped me into the living room and into the chair closest to the stove, covering me with an afghan. My teeth chattered—I was fixated on Manny's text and unable to make out Dawson's words when he spoke again. The door closed, and I heard Scotty's truck tires squeak in the snow.

It took fifteen minutes before I regained control. Until I was dead, there was still hope. I hurried to my bedroom and retrieved Dad's Glock from my nightstand. Inside the closet was my rifle. I examined the firearm after scrutinizing the landscape from each window.

The M4 was stored with six spare magazines. It came with a standard ten round, and I purchased a half-dozen extras holding twenty. Mounted on the right-side rail was a red laser sight with a finger touch sensor on the trigger guard. On the left was the brightest tactical flashlight money could buy. It ran down quickly, but when the batteries were fresh, the white beam would compromise an enemy's eyesight for a short time. I needed only to press the rear with a fingertip to switch it on.

I was happy the rifle was scoped. An Eotech holographic sight, electronic life was a thousand hours, but I replaced the two double A batteries anyway. For me, it was perfect—no lining up front and rear irons or searching for the crosshairs of a standard duplex scope. Instead, I looked at a single holograph, placed the dot where I wanted the bullet to go, and squeezed the trigger. The laser worked best for close work.

It was difficult to lift the rifle to my shoulder while wearing the cast, and at least seven weeks remained until it could be removed. Now I feared it would be on my arm when my casket was closed. Still, I had to make sure every firearm I owned was fully functional and ready for extended use.

At noon, an odd sound intruded while I heated another bowl of Melissa's stew. It sounded like a jet or an eighteen-wheeler barreling at me—or perhaps an oncoming earthquake. In seconds, the whine of an aircraft I was sure was a helicopter flying low and fast reached me. Throwing a coat over one arm and my back, I feared it was an early attack, so I held the M4 awkwardly and ran outside. Almost slipping on a frozen porch, I slowed to see what direction it took.

It came screaming in, the pilot visibly pulling hard on the stick as it went into a tight turn, almost inverting the craft to bleed airspeed. The nose came up hard before the 'copter descended. A snowstorm was kicked up by its rotors before it settled gently a hundred yards behind my house.

I took up a defensive position behind a rear corner. I could read the model as a Bell 407 through the scope. Waiting as the engine powered down and blades slowed, I held the collapsible stock awkwardly to my shoulder. The door had yet to open, but I centered the holographic dot and slid the safety off.

A vehicle rumbled closer on my driveway. My eye never left the scope as Dawson's diesel approached at an angle where he couldn't see me at my corner hide. No matter, I was going to kill some trespassing son of a bitch when the 'copter door opened for a clear shot. Behind me, the diesel stopped, and a door closed before Dawson appeared from around the edge of my house. He seemed aware the helicopter had landed and marched directly to it. If whom I feared most turned out to be inside, my shot might need to be taken with Dawson in the line of fire. When the door opened, my finger crept to the trigger. No clear kill was offered with my neighbor between the occupant disembarking and my muzzle. It appeared the men shook hands before Dawson led him toward my house. It was an impossible task to make a positive identification under the thick hooded coat. Thrown over one shoulder was a large bag. "Stop right there." My voice was low and conversational enough not to throw my aim off. Yelled orders will shift the barrel minutely. The red dot of my laser was steady on his temple when I activated it.

I was forced to approach them at an angle, crab-walking with short, choppy steps. My broken arm was tiring, and I needed to lower it for a moment, holding the rifle for a brief time with my hand on the grip and recoil pad against my shoulder. The M4 is light, but supporting it with one limb was tiresome. In addition, trigger control dropped precariously.

I was within thirty feet before speaking again. "Drop the bag, hands up, and turn to face me." I was still crouched, ready to move any direction.

"Jules, it…" I could hear the worry and warning in Dawson's tone when it pitched higher than normal.

I didn't let Dawson continue. "Take the hood off. Now." My legs almost gave out when the squashed nose and leathery skin of Allen Fryxell became visible. Lowering the muzzle immediately, I hurried to them. "Damn it, Allen, you were a gnat's ass from being dead." The rifle hung from my shoulder on its one-point sling.

"Christ, Julia…" He clutched at his chest. "…if that's how you look when you're about to tap a mark, it's enough to kill by itself." He bent over, hands on knees and breathed heavily.

Dawson looked at me with pride, respect, and not just a little alarm. They both understood I wasn't one to shy away from pulling the trigger. If you're a client to be signed or a declared enemy, I won't lose any sleep. Both men followed me into the house where I double-checked the safety, setting my rifle on the table, and hung my coat on the back of a chair. It was much warmer near the stove, so I moved the M4 to the living room. I was filling the firebox again when they cautiously appeared.

"Been a long time since I saw that look, girl." Allen put his hands over the stove before rubbing them briskly. "It's normally an instant before someone's standing in front of the pearly gates."

Reaching to his shoulder, I pulled him low enough to kiss a cheek. "To what do I owe this visit, my friend? I'd love to know where you found that incredible machine out back."

He beamed with pride. "I bought it a few years ago. Got a hell of a deal. It makes sense for short distances when clients call with an emergency."

His answer appeared to amuse Dawson. "Horseshit, Al. You bought it because you like to fly like a racecar driver and needed an excuse."

Allen's sheepish grin was broad. "Yeah, that might be it, too." He turned businessman and withdrew a tablet and pen from a pocket. He wrote quickly and handed me a small sheet of paper.

*Dawson said you may have monitoring devices planted?*

I nodded and accepted the pen. *He's the one who thought of them. Perhaps located in a couple boxes I received while we were in the Bahamas.*

Allen didn't respond—going to work instead. Using a laptop from his bag, we waited while he booted it and searched through his tool kit. Never having anything to do with the world of spies and espionage, the work he performed was nothing like I imagined. After the computer was ready, he swept every inch of my house leaving no stone unturned. The electronic gadget he used was obviously connected to his laptop.

Dawson waved me into the kitchen and drew me close. "I called Al after I got home," he whispered. "You made one hell of an impression on him. He was gathering his gear the moment I mentioned you were in trouble again. I could hear him doing it while we talked."

"What sort of work does he do?" Our heads brushed each other's. It was difficult to grasp Allen was the man serving me drinks and other refreshments while I lazed about the pool at Wiggins' hotel. I knew he was also responsible for disabling the video feed, memory, and guest list of those who stayed. It seemed odd to find the man I tipped generously for a drink was worth a substantial sum of money. That helicopter wasn't cheap.

"Let's just say he works for anyone who can pay for his expertise."

"Can I afford him?"

Dawson grinned while we watched from the kitchen table. "Yeah, you'll be able to handle it." He chuckled. Allen disappeared into my bedroom. "He always looks for an excuse to fly his damned contraption."

Allen motioned us to follow him outside after half an hour. I shrugged into my coat and took my M4. He led us in the direction of his helicopter and stopped in snow a couple inches above my ankles. "Okay, we got four bugs, not including two GPS units with the boxes of cash in your closet." Allen winked at me. "Impressive stash, by the way." His grin evaporated. "I performed a radio frequency spectrum and electronically enhanced search of your entire home. It allows me to see into walls, ceilings, floors, and furniture to look for microphones, recorders, or transmitters. My equipment is capable of finding both active and quiescent monitoring devices. I found neither." He continued, "but there's a soft tap on your cell. Did I check your only one?"

"Yes." Burner phones were always discarded. My head spun to know my personal phone was wired to betray me. Somehow another person gained access to it and installed something.

"Is there anywhere else a tap might be located?"

"The garage and her Jeep." Dawson said.

"The good news so far is there have only been microphones, not cameras. Whoever this is didn't feel the need to transgress further. My guess would be this isn't a pervert, an errant spouse, or boyfriend. Someone is simply gathering information."

I still felt dirty and violated. "Where did you find the bugs?"

"Both bedrooms, the kitchen, and living room. Let's check the garage while we're out here."

Allen found two additional monitoring devices in the outbuilding. One in a wall, the other in my Wagoneer. He also located a GPS unit mounted on the Jeep's chassis. No matter where I went or what I said, The Company—or someone—knew about it. For once, I was glad to have removed the battery from my phone. Our conversations in Dawson's truck stayed private.

Allen dropped the offending gadgets in a box and took it to his helicopter. He left them with his equipment and returned to the house so I could fulfill my part of the bargain Dawson promised him. A home cooked meal. He sat at the table and watched while my neighbor helped me. "What's with the cash?" Allen gestured to my bedroom with his chin after I turned back to the table.

"Wiggins." I answered quietly.

"He was a big fish, but for one mark?"

"Besides a huge importer, he was my last hurrah."

"Her employers were potentially killing two birds with one stone." When Dawson was intense, his voice dropped an octave. He checked the biscuits in the woodstove oven and brought them into the kitchen. "I've been giving this a lot of thought. They probably didn't think she could sign her client. But it worked in their favor if she could incapacitate or kill him. Another employee could finish the job. If Wiggins turned the tables on her or the police arrested Jules, all the better. She's effectively out of their hair."

Allen's smile was one of humor. "I guess you showed them, didn't you? I'm surprised they paid off. But in doing so, there was an opportunity to introduce more eavesdropping units." He scratched the side of his squashed nose thoughtfully. "Kind of makes you wonder about the money, doesn't it?"

"You don't think its counterfeit, do you?" The idea never entered my mind until I asked. What I looked at appeared normal bills.

"I'd like to take it home if you don't mind." He smiled, one eyebrow raising to say the ball was in my court.

I shrugged. "Sure, but why?"

"Let's keep it simple and say I know people who owe me favors. These people know people. I can drop it off, and they can tell us everything there is to know about a particular bill. I can return it, replace it, or have a check sent to you."

My response was dry. "I'm not sure I could justify to the bank and government how I came up with three quarters of a million."

"It's no problem. I can write a check and say I purchased an item from you. Perhaps a painting, an old diary, anything on which we can place a value. So what if I was scalped by a savvy woman if I don't complain and am happy with my purchase? Who's to say anyone should become involved?"

***

Allen lifted off with ninety minutes to spare before dark. He would be over Montana and the Bitterroots in a quarter that time. My cash and the electronic device went with him. His plan was to drop the box somewhere in the Rocky Mountains as he flew home. I wondered if anyone would search for me so deep in the hills if the GPS units survived. He also removed the added hardware and made sure my cellphone was safe to use.

The door hardly closed behind us before Dawson asked the questions I knew were coming. "Beware the gray man. Who the devil is the gray man where four words scare the hell out of you?" I wasn't sure if he was angry at me or The Company, but he was on medium boil.

"It's who he is. He's the vague, dark, and dangerous one who found me in Los Angeles and recruited me for The Company."

"I don't understand why he's so damned scary to you."

"Because he's virtually invisible. You won't see or notice him before it's too late. He might as well be the wind. It wouldn't surprise me to find he's the one who planted the bugs."

"He's just a man, Jules."

"No, he's a ghost." It was impossible to stop my shudder. "A phantom none of us can see until it's too late. You don't understand. He's who they send to sign the most dangerous." He'd been the topic of many short conversations between Manny and me.

"Why not send him to the Bahamas if he's so good?"

"I've wondered about that but don't know." Running through the sequences in my mind, I considered what it was I did that the gray man couldn't. Why not send him instead, unless I was there to die?

Dawson saw my look of surprise. "What?"

"He was there. I thought I recognized him but wasn't sure. Now I am."

"The gray man? He was where?"

"The Bahamas. Probably waiting for me to sign Wiggins and then he would get my signature." My guts tightened, and I was in danger of losing my dinner. "There's a price on my head. I just know it." The idea was terrifying and made my head swim. Only I understood what it meant. The Company—or perhaps only one or two within— wanted me dead. I was no different from any client I was sent to put down.

"I'll put together a team—an army if we need it." I watched as Dawson became the leader his unit knew him to be. "Allen can spearhead the IT portion, learning who The Company is and where they're located. I can build a unit of ten to begin with, and we'll start taking down The Company one member at a time." His intensity was fascinating. "If you or I or both go down, we can make funds available so the fight continues."

"Let me try something before we do anything along the lines of what you're thinking." Using the speed dial on my phone, I switched it to speaker and propped it on the table. Raising an index finger to my lips, I indicated our need for secrecy. The phone rang three times before it was answered.

"Manny here."

"J." There was an uncomfortable silence while I waited.

He seemed upbeat. "Nice to hear your voice again. What can I do for you? Already bored with retirement?"

"Something a bit more personal than that, old friend. I can still call you a friend, can't I?"

"After what we've been through together, we're the best of comrades. What is it you need?"

"I need you to call the dogs off."

"Excuse me?"

"Call off the assassins."

The air went dead, and I thought our connection was broken. I waited silently until finally he spoke again. "I'm not sure what you mean. Is there something I'm missing?"

"If you don't know, it's time you found out. If I'm wrong, Manny, no harm, no foul. If I'm right…scorched earth…no one survives. No one."

"J, I'm not sure I understand—"

Assuming my suspicions were correct, I broke in before he could lie. "Doesn't matter if you understand or not. You'd be a piss-poor employee if you didn't. The Company doesn't know what it's unleashing if they're doing what I suspect. Hell, even I'm not sure I understand the ramifications. Your employer needs to be perfectly clear on this. It's the end for everyone whether I survive or not. If I don't, there won't be anyone around to stop the ball once it's rolling. Manny? It'll crush everything because no quarter will be given."

"I'll have to…"

I was angry and ready to play hardball. "Two words, Manny. Just two."

We heard him sigh. "I understand." The phone went dead. It seemed nothing changed with my old partner even after retirement.

Dawson listened carefully to the conversation. "I'm not following. Shouldn't Manny have known about the text? Didn't it come from his phone?"

I nodded. "Either he's lying about what he knows, or someone hacked him and sent the text to make it seem like it came from him. Maybe both." It was hard to believe my old partner would turn on me, but I presumed anything was possible in the world of assassination.

***

Dawson left without comment soon after my call ended. I saw the light in his truck come on and the door close. He was gone over an hour before returning. I wasn't sure if he was brave or stupid for going out after dark. In his arms were a soft case, shooting bag, and a bulging pack. Setting his equipment on the table, he opened the scabbard first. It was a rifle closely resembling mine, yet not the same.

I pointed to it. "What kind?"

"AR-10 made by Sig Sauer." He lifted it from the case and drew the bolt back, assuring himself it was empty. "It's their SIG716 Precision Marksman. It shoots the 7.62x51mm more commonly known as the .308 Winchester." He handed me a loaded magazine from his bag. "Twenty round magazines. This rifle shoots best with 168 grain match grade hollow points, but it'll feed anything. The scope is Zeiss." His face was cold. "This is the big brother to your M4."

"It looks like a brute." My diminutive gun now seemed like a rifle made for little girls.

"It's an animal."

Accepting the return of his magazine, he inserted it gently and seated it firmly with the heel of his palm. Drawing the bolt back and releasing it, he chambered a round before engaging the safety. Dawson leaned the rifle against the counter before fixing me with a stare. "Now tell me more about this gray man. I want to know everything you can remember."

***

No one can one hundred percent prepare for an attack that may come from anywhere at any given moment. My windows and doors were locked, but any entry can be breached in an instant. If caught while asleep, advantage goes to the attacker, and I could do very little. We drew the curtains knowing if we happened to look out or pass by, a bullet might be fired at our movement. I had shades under each, and we decided to pull them during the hours of darkness.

Exhausted, I was ready for bed. "It's late. How shall we handle sleeping arrangements?"

Dawson sat on the couch, watching as I closed the stove for the night. "You should sleep in the root cellar."

"You'll sleep…where?"

"The spare bedroom."

"Do you seriously expect me to leave you up here alone?"

"Someone has to stay with Jake."

Even meant as a joke, his comment made me angrier. "Either we both sleep in the basement or up here. Better yet, I stay here alone. This is my problem, my fight, and no sense in your being killed, too." If I were destined to die, I certainly didn't want Dawson or anyone else slain.

"How in the hell am I supposed to leave you here alone?" For a moment, I wasn't sure if he was going to attack me or walk out.

"Because I'm asking you to." I knew my whisper was hard for him to hear. It was difficult enough for me.

"I can't." His set angular features hardened.

"Why?"

"Because I love you, damn it."

I was elated. "That's why you should leave." God, I was tired of feeling this way around Dawson. Weepy instead of strong. What happened to J, the woman who looked her client in the eye and pulled the trigger without the slightest hesitation or compassion? The tiny brute who once drove a letter opener into the side of a man's head and gouged his throat open.

Dawson looked puzzled. "You want me to leave because I love you?"

"No!" I shouted, angry once again. "You need to go because *I love you.*" I was silent for a moment while we stared at the other. "I love you." My voice dropped to a more conversational tone. "I want you to live a long life even if it's without me. I couldn't live with myself if you're killed."

His voice softened a little. "Don't you think it's my choice to make?"

"Not if you're in love because you don't have a choice. It's a stupid emotion that compels us to do foolish things."

"Then I'm a stupid man being compelled to do something foolish. We'll get through this, Jules. You're smarter and tougher than you give yourself credit. Hell, you were thrown from a damned skyscraper and survived, then lasted another three weeks with injuries sure to kill anyone else. Tell me you're not tough."

I waved my hand carelessly. "Stupid luck. You know it's true. My good fortune isn't going to keep you alive."

"Fine." From the set of his jaw and shoulders, I wasn't winning the argument. "I'll take the nightshift, and you can have days. I'm not leaving, woman, and you can take my stubbornness to the bank."

My smile was tired and sad when I closed my bedroom door.

\*\*\*

Dawson looked as exhausted as I'd felt the evening before. When I rose at a half past five, I found him in the kitchen cooking breakfast.

Only the light above the range burned, and the shades were still drawn. His rifle leaned nearby against the counter.

"Here you are." He slid a plate across the table to stop in front of me. "Biscuits and gravy. Heavy on the pepper, light on the salt, two eggs sunny-side up. Coffee will finish brewing in a couple minutes." He stopped to consider. "I didn't hear or see anything. There's plenty of wood inside for the stove. Oh. After the gravy cools, could you please put what's left in the refrigerator, and I'll have it for my breakfast this evening?" He shuffled to the bedroom when I stopped him.

"Get back here, mister." My voice was as hard as I could make it. Although worn out, his eyes widened with surprise. I motioned to a spot beside me and watched carefully as he did what I asked.

"I'm not leaving." Judging by the stony inflection in his voice, he was still as unyielding as the night before.

I reached his collar. Pulling hard, I dragged the less-than-willing man to eye level. "If this is going to work, the whites of my eggs have to be cooked better than this." With a hand behind his neck, I drew his face to mine and kissed his mouth fiercely. We were grinning when he pulled back.

"Yes, ma'am." Standing straight and tall, his heels thumped together as he saluted. "I'll do my best from now on, ma'am." God, even his salute gave me goose bumps. My eyes widened with excitement as he leaned to me again.

His kiss was softer and gentler than what I demanded. Cupping my face and jaw in both hands, his lips were tender against mine. After a long one followed by three shorter, he finally pulled away. Taking his rifle from where it leaned against the countertop, he disappeared into *my* room! A moment later, Jake came scooting out, and I wondered if perhaps he got a push from behind. My boyfriend didn't plan to be awakened anytime soon.

***

Dawson slept longer than I might have thought. It was early afternoon before the door opened. His long hair askew, he ignored me on the way to the bathroom. He carried a small bag and a handful of clothes. I started the gravy and biscuits warming in the oven when I heard the shower. A new pot of coffee was almost perked. My timing was perfect. I finished plating his meal as he was leaving the bathroom.

It's a new day when I wake each morning—one I haven't had the opportunity to screw up. My being is filled with happiness the moment my feet are on the floor. Dawson appeared the exact polar opposite. He grunted when I handed him a cup on the way to the table. On the dish next to his biscuits and gravy were three scrambled eggs. Hot sauce and ketchup waited nearby. He sat and stared at his breakfast, and for a moment I thought he was falling asleep. "So how do we handle this?" Dawson looked up uncomfortably after posing his question. For the first time since we met, he appeared unsure of himself.

I'd considered the problem throughout the day. "I want him to come to me. I know the terrain around here well, and it's best to meet him on home turf. There's no way of telling—"

"No. You and me. How do we handle this…us?"

Our declarations of love weighed on my mind since being stated. I was sure he was fond of me before, and his attraction didn't seem fueled by lust. All we did was kiss and hold hands. It almost made me feel like a girl still in junior high. Ours appeared to be a relationship built one brick at a time. It didn't seem to be white-hot where we couldn't take our hands off the other. I was lost—having never been in love—and wasn't sure how to act. For so many years, I was positive my life would be lived alone, and my biggest fear was frightening him away. While I might be his wounded little dove, he carried his own share of formidable scars. "I was hoping you could tell me because this mutual love is a first for me." My lips were dry, and there was nothing in my mouth to wet them.

My attraction to him was something I avoided for months—even before leaving for Seattle and Yakima. From watching him stroll toward me to the way he wore his jeans and shirt made my heart pound. His voice lit a fire only a cold shower could temporarily control. Sometimes when we sat and talked, his gentle bass made me want to throw myself at him. His lean body, long black hair always gathered at the nape, and close-cropped beard were the source of constant daydreams. My future sat across the table, and I could see he was as fearful as me.

Dawson seemed incredulous—his wind and sun darkened face paled with concern. "Then you love me? It wasn't something you were just saying last night...you really love me?" He seemed surprised when I felt the same way about him as he did of me.

"My heart jumps when I see you. When you're away, the thought of how long it might be before you return makes me sick with dread. The idea of going through the rest of my life without you is terrifying. To touch, hear, smell, and be with you forever is all I can think of, Dawson. If this isn't love, I can't imagine what is." I hadn't noticed the tears until my nose ran. "I want to have babies with you, grow old and spoil our grandchildren together." Quite unromantically, I sniffed.

"Oh, my little dove, your healing has begun." He held his arm out and motioned me around the table.

Dawson scooted his chair back and made room for me on a thigh. When his hand slid around my waist, my right arm went around his neck, and my cast rested on the table. I pressed my face into his neck, his beard stubble bristling against my cheek. "I've never felt this way about anyone. My heart breaks when we're apart. When we're together, I fear it will explode because it's so full. When you found me on the beach in Grand Bahama, I couldn't imagine being separated again. I...there was just no way to tell you." After whispering in his ear, I put everything that was *the essence of Julia* into my kiss. Passion and lust were building before it ended, each trying to crowd out the other. My lids were heavy with the same desire I saw on his face when I pulled back.

"Jules," he said hoarsely, "I..." His lips were closed again by mine. Whatever he wanted to say, I stopped him. My body desperately wanted and needed him, but my mind wasn't ready. We first needed to be free of the gray man and The Company.

I slid from his thigh, filled our cups with coffee and pushed one across to him. No way was I going to temp either of us by doing anything but keep the table between us. Steam rose from his breakfast and cup. It made me think of how cold it must be outside. The insulation in the walls and ceiling of my home were less than adequate. Dawson directed his attention to breakfast, and I turned mine to the woodstove. I left it open to heat after filling it. With a broom handle, I pulled the living room window shade back. It was snowing again. I returned to the kitchen after closing the fire.

Dawson questioned me when I took my seat again. "How soon will he come? When you were sent out on assignment, how quickly did you leave after accepting it?"

"In my case, almost immediately. If he's anything like me, he's probably close. I don't mean right outside the house, although he might be. In Idaho at least." I bit my lip in concentration. "There's a chance he might refuse the job, but not likely. Signing me will likely provide a substantial payday and a feather in his cap." A thought suddenly struck me…the prostitute the gray man killed to protect my identity. He didn't think twice about signing her, although she was a freebee meaning nothing to him. "You've got to promise me, Dawson." He didn't nod in agreement but waited for my request. "If he…if he succeeds in signing me, you can't let him see you. He'll kill you as easily as swatting a mosquito. If he fulfills the contract when you're not here or nearby, don't go after him. He'll not only destroy you, but he'll include everyone else. Melissa, Bess, Andy, the kids…it doesn't matter to him." I stood to lean over the table. A little taller than him while he sat, my goal was to appear intimidating. "Promise me you won't put yourself in danger for no good reason if I'm gone. I want all of you to live long and healthy lives."

Chapter XVI

Dawson stared without blinking. For a moment, I thought he was considering my request until he took a long sip of coffee, leaned back, and chuckled. It grew until he roared with laughter. It kept on, making me more upset by the moment. He used a shirt sleeve to wipe his tears away and twice tried to drink his coffee but couldn't hold the cup still. Finally, he set it down and scrubbed his cheeks. After gaining control, he realized I was angry. Actually, I was livid. "You're serious?" He stared at me, wide-eyed.

"Damned straight I am."

His mood flipped as quickly as a light switch. "Then you can kiss my ass. Because if you don't kill him, I will." Dawson's outrage was immediate and made me step back. Fearsome to behold, mine crumbled in its face. He stood and leaned on the table, glaring across and jabbing an index finger at me. "If this goes wrong, I'll hunt the son of a bitch down and kill him anywhere I find him on this planet."

"No…" I shook my head.

Dawson wasn't having any part of my denial. "Where you sign clients nice and neat, I don't just kill the enemy…my job is to annihilate them. When I'm finished, body parts are strewn across the landscape." His voice deepened. The rumble I loved turned seismic. "Don't you ever give me shit about letting the enemy go. They're lucky I don't eat 'em after I'm finished." Had he spat on the floor in disgust, his feelings couldn't have been clearer.

\*\*\*

We lived with an uneasy truce throughout the day. A whole chicken was thawed, and after stuffing it, I baked the bird in my wood cookstove. Steamed vegetables and biscuits went with it, and I ate an apple because fresh fruit was something I craved again. Each of us read, and he spent time texting someone, perhaps more than one but didn't offer any explanation when he saw my interest.

"I'm going to bed," I announced, after letting Jake out a final time to do his business. It bothered me to let him go. With snow still

222

falling and temperatures hovering in the twenties, I didn't think gray man was outside. Even so, Jake deserved any protection I could offer.

"Okay." Dawson looked up from his phone. "I'll be on the job until morning. Sleep sound knowin' you're safe." His smile was warm with no sign of residual anger.

It was difficult to build enough courage to broach the subject. "I'm sorry about earlier. I had no right to ask that of you. Are we still okay?" I felt a lump in my throat from wanting to know but terrified of his answer.

"You're right. It wasn't a good subject, but I accept your apology." His voice was mild without backing down. Steel laced in his words.

"Are we good, you and me?" I feared everything was ruined, and it wasn't something I could stand because spending my life alone was something I'd grown tired of.

"Goes without saying." He set his phone aside, crossed the room, and pulled me to him. "An argument or difference of opinion won't make me stop lovin' you, Jules. You're what my heart searched for since I was born. To lose you now would be like having a part of me torn away." He kissed my crown. "I'll see you in the morning."

It snowed off and on for two weeks before an arctic blast struck. I'd seldom seen temperatures drop below zero. Mystic as were his powers, the gray man could hardly lurk with much deadly intent in our current conditions, so we used the respite to replenish the back porch with wood. Figuring the less ventured out, the safer we would be when the cold snap ended, we put two old towels on the floor for another stack of fuel inside.

When not working on something, my arm itched terribly under the cast. I used pencils, a dowel, even the handle of a flyswatter to probe for relief. Unable to stand the torment any longer, I asked Dawson to call for an appointment to have it removed. The soonest was in three days.

The temperature was seventeen below on the morning we set out to free my arm. Dawson filled in the time waiting for the Wagoneer to warm enough to put Jake in back by searching everywhere for watching eyes. I drove while Dawson rode shotgun. Actually, he cradled a rifle he called an AR-10. He left it under a blanket in the Jeep at the clinic parking lot and escorted me inside with the Anaconda on his belt and my dad's Glock in his pocket to hand off to me if need arose.

After scrutinizing a series of x-rays, the doctor agreed my arm healed enough to remove the cast, although he'd rather I wore it another two weeks and insisted on fitting me with a brace. Easily removed and adjustable, it afforded protection when I slept and could be set aside during waking hours. I was horrified to find my normally thin arm to be little more than a withered stick. Even with the doctor's assurance muscle tone would bounce back quickly, I could barely stand to look at it, but I was grateful for the chance to wash the stinking thing and scratch until my skin bled.

Dawson's vigilance was intense while we were home, but it increased dramatically during our excursion to town and back. Had he been wearing full combat gear in a Humvee within a war zone, he could not have been any less a soldier on patrol. His attentiveness went into overdrive when we entered my approach road. I wondered if he would make me crawl in the snow between my garage and front door.

Knitting and crocheting were two pastimes I enjoyed, but neither were much fun in a full-length cast. With it gone, I was able to resume my handicraft distraction when not reading. Before leaving for the Bahamas, I'd started a sweater for cold weather and now planned to finish it. A mixture of gray and sage green would match the coming spring terrain.

* * *

We didn't have a snowmelt until three weeks later. A warm wind arose, and within thirty-six hours, bare patches were visible around us, but the chinook didn't reduce solid white on the upper mountain. My arm regained a significant portion of its strength, and I was putting on needed weight. I was sure my clothes were fitting more snugly. No longer did protruding ribs or hipbones show in the mirror. Holding my breath and stepping on the bathroom scales after a shower, I opened clenched eyes and let out a whoop.

A flurry of activity sounded from the living room, and the door burst open. Dawson stood with his rifle shouldered, his eyes wild and searching for a target. Instead, he found me standing naked on the scale trying to cover myself with skinny arms and shrieking, "Get out!" When he'd backed far enough, I slammed the door and shouted a half-angry apology. "I'm so sorry . . . I didn't think!" I knew immediately he'd responded the only way he knew how, for which I was thankful yet no less embarrassed. Both of us lived on a ragged edge over an attack that might or might not happen. I'd not discussed it, but I wasn't ready to take our relationship to the next step until we were in a more relaxed environment, but like it or not, he got a clear view of everything I had to offer.

My wet hair didn't take long to fluff with a blow dryer. Still short as a boy's, it was growing enough to see two inches of blonde roots. I wrapped a towel around my torso and hurried to my bedroom. Dawson was seated on the couch again and didn't look up as I padded past.

When I returned dressed, I gave a weak smile in lieu of another apology, but it was Dawson who seemed most chagrinned. "Sorry, Jules." His eyes were downcast like a boy caught peeking through the wrong keyhole. "I heard you scream and figured he somehow got in there with you."

Since he was graciously letting me off the hook, I tried a haughty expression and said, "For your information, it wasn't a scream. You heard a cry of happiness."

"Then I hope to never hear you yell in fear. What were you so happy about...or should I ask?"

"I broke a hundred pounds!" I couldn't stop smiling. "One-oh-one point four to be exact. Next stop, one-oh-five." Most women fight too much weight. I waged my battle in a different direction. All it takes is a few days of no appetite, the flu or a bad cold, and I will drop five percent in forty-eight hours. It might take six months to gain it back. Even before my weight loss in the Bahamas, I was trying regain pounds after I was wounded.

"Didn't look like a whole hundredweight to me." His lips remained pressed together in a straight line, but I could see his cheek muscles under serious strain.

"I hope you got your eyes full, mister." I flounced to the kitchen in mock indignation.

"Not really." His conversational voice followed. "Wasn't much to see."

"What?" I stepped back to where I could give him a questioning stare.

"To tell the truth," he said, apparently having accepted as much blame as he intended. "I only had eyes for yours. Big as saucers they were, tellin' me what was going on, so I never looked lower."

"If there wasn't much to see, then what didn't look like it weighed a hundred pounds?" His giveaway to getting caught in a fib were two rapid blinks, and his way to defused the entire event was to raise his hands in surrender.

*\*\**

It was good to see the sun again. Patches of snow remained, and the ground was cold, but spring did its best to assert itself. During our time together, Dawson taught me to field strip my M4 and quickly reassemble it. The last tests were with blindfolds to simulate working in the dark.

My inherited Glock was simple to dismantle—it seemed to fall apart. Although he demonstrated the basics of his AR-10, he didn't offer to let me break it down. I surmised he felt he didn't want anyone—even me—to handle his rifle.

My phone rang for the first time in weeks. It was Bess. "Good morning, Mrs. Mueller," I said, good weather buoying my spirits.

"How are you, Julia?" I knew the call would eventually come. "Is your arm healing?"

"The cast is off, and my skin is better from where I reached under to scratch." I didn't tell her the worst damage was inflicted by my fingernails after I could use them.

She chuckled. "I broke my leg years ago and thought I'd die from the itch. I didn't envy you when I saw it on your arm."

"It was a spindly little sucker when the clinic removed the cast, but it's on the mend."

"How soon before you would feel ready to substitute?"

"Bess, I'm not sure…"

She didn't give me a chance to finish, her worry coming through clearly. "We have teachers out sick, two on maternity leave. I'm so shorthanded right now that it's difficult to keep the school functioning."

"Would you mind if I talk it over with Dawson first?"

Sudden humor filled her voice. "You have to clear returning to work with my nephew instead of a doctor?"

"It's complicated." I made it even more so by stretching truth to its very limits. "Since I did piecework for a civilian syndicate under contract to government agencies, Dawson reminded me of . . ."

"Safety concerns," he said when I hesitated too long.

"Did I hear my nephew? Be a dear and let me speak to him, will you?"

"Yes, ma'am." I held the phone out.

While he didn't quite snarl, he muttered in obvious displeasure. "Hello, Auntie." After a brief pause, he said, "Not so much Julia's safety *per se* but more for students in her classes." A long silence with a minimum of eye-rolling showed he listened respectfully until his jaw clenched. "Okay, Aunt Bess. Send the new manual. I'm against her working so soon under any circumstances, but she'll look over the details and get back to you." My man wasn't particularly happy when he ended the call.

"What new manual? What details?" I was bursting with curiosity. "What did she say to cause you to knuckle under?"

"The short answer is in recent years, spouses took kids against court orders, so a deputy is now assigned to patrol halls a half-hour before and after classes. Same at the high school. She locks doors, monitors closed-circuit TVs, and escort visitors."

"I remember a deputy passing my open door and closing it. That's it?"

"Aunt Bess says it's all in the manual. The best part is her chief engineer and head custodian is retired Idaho State Police. He and selected faculty are permitted to carry concealed. It could include you."

\*\*\*

I spent time on my laptop researching concealed carry options, and Dawson and I talked long after dishes were dried and put away. I was delighted how women's selections for discrete gun-toting were plentiful. I'd located shoulder holsters more resembling sports bras.

I'm sure one would work for my Colt revolver under a jacket, and Galco made a pretty leather purse with Velcro closures to secure Dad's Glock in my locked desk drawer. Tuffy Security sold a lift-seat storage locker to fit my M4 for the back cushion of my Wagoneer. Only the two of us needed to know I was armed to the teeth inside and outside of school. Dawson's hardline against me returning to work had visibly softened.

"I can't stay in the house forever, sweetie. At some point, I must reenter life, whether or not the gray man or someone else comes for me."

"I understand…"

Late as it was in our time zone, my phone rang. I answered after recognizing the number and put it on speaker before setting my cell on the coffee table. "J here."

"Manny. I need you to know I didn't send the text you received from my phone. Apparently, it was hacked."

My voice was even cold to my ears. "You've seen it, have you?"

"Yes, it's here. I swear it didn't come from me."

"Then someone sent me a warning. Is it true? Am I a client now?"

He sighed. "I don't understand what's going on. No one I've discussed it with seems to know anything. If they do, they aren't talking."

"Also, my mobile was bugged, Manny. Why am I being surveilled, and who's behind it?"

"I appreciate this isn't something you want to hear again, but I just don't know. I wouldn't eavesdrop when I can call you."

"I don't know either, my friend. One thing I am certain of…if you find out what's going on before I do and put an end to it, fewer people will suffer."

He sighed. "Whatever you have planned, don't do it."

"If the gray man or anyone else comes against me, hide, Manny. Whether you know it or not, he was in the Bahamas when I was signing the client. It tells me something's going on that probably isn't good for my health."

"You saw him? You're sure?" My heart fell when I didn't hear the surprise I hoped for. I hesitated—was it the gray man or someone who only resembled him? I was afforded only a momentary glimpse.

"You know who we're talking about. Tough to say with one hundred percent accuracy. In my mind? Yeah, he was there."

"Give me more time to learn what I can. Promise me you won't jump the gun and do something foolish."

"I'm not spending the rest of my life looking over my shoulder. Pass on the message, okay? If I don't get an all-clear fairly soon, I'll have no choice, and no one can stop events once they get going. It makes little difference if I'm alive or not."

"I understand." Dead air told me he ended our call.

Dawson was intense, not blinking when he leaned forward. "Is he telling the truth?"

"It's hard to say." I rubbed my face with both hands. "I'm sure of one thing. Manny's never lied that I know of. He always had my back no matter what. If he told me something, it always turned out to be true."

* * *

Being cooped inside was driving me mad. Dawson and Jake strayed outdoors to scout, but my larger protector insisted I stay within fortified walls and out of sight. My weight crept north of one-oh-three, and I was loving it. Standing in front of a mirror behind a *bolted* bathroom door after taking a shower, I was mastering the shimmy. Breasts a size I'd seldom dealt with jiggled for what was now only my own amusement.

I was barely dressed with my boots laced when Dawson and Jake roared through the back door. Spring mud stuck to their feet, and every step spread it across my floor. I was thankful it was hardwood instead of carpet, but I was unhappy until he explained. "A text came from Allen. Your cash proved to be legitimate. He's offerin' to write a check, or you can have it back. He doesn't care, so it's up to you."

I imagine everyone with my past has trust issues. When it came to money, my fear was the government or workers therein. However, funds sitting in a bank account begged for the attention of the unscrupulous who felt most deserving.

"The cash." I must have made an odd face, because one of his eyebrows raised. "I know it's stupid, but I don't trust banks or the federal reserve system to look out for my best interests. Having

229

money at home keeps the wolf from barking at the door." I tipped back in my chair and watched my boys take their places on the couch.

"If you're expecting me to assign blame, look somewhere else, lady. Folks today don't understand how close we all are to losin' everything. Not long ago, an article claimed many families are only a couple paychecks away from homelessness. It's tough to disagree when you see how everyone seems overextended."

"You don't think I'm being foolish?" Dawson's opinion was important to me.

"Oh, hell no. It's a lot of money, but I don't see why you can't keep it in a good place difficult to find. God knows we can protect it as well or better than most banks." He grinned and pointed downward. "I'll do a little construction before Al delivers it, but you have to promise not to kill me afterward."

His growing smile told me he joked. In the past, I may have bared teeth at such a reference to my former livelihood. This time, I only frowned.

"You've heard stories, haven't you? Over the centuries, the rich hired laborers to build something secret, and afterwards workers would be strangled to keep it strictly confidential. Hell, they probably still do it in some parts of the world."

"That's inhuman." I shivered and crossed in front of him to the stove a few feet from where he sat.

"Cold?"

"Freezing."

The next thing I knew, Dawson pulled me to his lap. "Let me generate heat for you." He held me against his chest with both arms. It wasn't the intimate embrace of lovers—he really was trying to warm my body. I shivered until he retrieved the afghan behind him. Between it, Dawson's body heat, and the woodstove, my shaking stopped.

"I'll be glad when this sunny weather thaws the ground. I'm tired of being cold."

By way of response. Dawson sniffed my neck after kissing it. "Mm...you smell nice." He nuzzled my throat, and I could feel his lips nibble flesh. If he wanted me at that moment, I was his. Never did I yearn so badly to be a man's woman, to belong to him as a mate.

The feeling increased during the following week when Bess called again. "Good morning, Mrs. Mueller."

"A very good morning to you, too, Julia. It's been five days, and we're even more shorthanded. Have you spoken with my nephew to discuss returning to work?"

"Yes. The pamphlet you sent calmed some concerns." Dawson shrugged but didn't utter a sound.

"Then you've come to a decision?"

"How soon do you need me?"

"The soonest you could come in. Next Monday morning at the latest."

"I'll be there." After a few amenities, I hung up and sneaked a look at Dawson. "I can't stay in the house forever, sweetie. If they want me dead bad enough, they could launch a missile through the front door. At some point, I must reenter life, whether or not the gray man or someone else comes for me."

"I understand…" I watched as his fingertips absently stroked the rubber grips of his Colt.

***

My voice was light and cheery, as was my mood. It was nice to be back. "Good morning, Mr. Howell." I noticed his eyes widen as I hurried past his room to the district office.

"I…g-good morning, Miss Hampton." He didn't bother to glance around before retreating into his classroom.

I was glad to see friendly faces greeting me. Students and faculty seemed to welcome my return. I knocked on Bess's door and heard her call, "Come in."

"Miss Julia Hampton reporting for duty, Mrs. Mueller." I couldn't help but grin. I'd been thinking of the first words out of my mouth.

"Seventh and eighth grade English and history, Miss Hampton. Perhaps for the rest of this week. Long term lesson plans have been laid out in case Mr. Windward doesn't bounce back."

I watched as her eyes moved over my body, searching for the telltale bulge. It was for naught. Dawson helped me choose my clothing for the day. I wore a three-piece pant suit, and my jacket covered a shoulder holster. The weather was still cold, and the shawl I surrounded my shoulders with worked to my advantage. Dad's

Glock hung under my left arm, and the right side balanced it with two spare magazines. Another was in my purse, three more were in the glovebox of my Wagoneer, where my M4 was hidden from sight. Even my .38 would be locked in the bottom drawer of my classroom desk, residing in a brand new Galco purse with a hideout pocket. I feared it was fanciful overkill, a gun battle with the gray man would be ended with one shot. "Is he sick?" I liked Mr. Windward. He was quiet and hard-working. Best of all, his kids loved him.

Her eyes flicked to the door before resting on me again. "Please don't pass this on. Mr. Windward was diagnosed with inoperable brain cancer. His first chemo treatment is this morning. Neither he nor his wife are sure how he'll feel afterward. I would ask you not relay this to anyone."

"Oh, God." I collapsed in a chair and stared at Bess. Earlier in the year, I'd heard Mr. Windward confide plans to take his wife on a surprise cruise after school year let out. He was sixty-seven and planned to retire before September. Remembering his excitement and intentions made me want to cry.

Mrs. Mueller was quietly compassionate. "I won't lie. This will be difficult if he loses his battle. He's taught here over thirty years." She was staring out her office window when the bell rang.

The day went smoothly—although with nicer and warmer weather, the young teens were a handful. Later in the evening, I received another call from the sub service asking for my availability. I worked the full week and finished in Mr. Windward's classroom. I felt bad when I realized Thomas Howell was absent from the teachers' lounge during lunch. The school was his place of employment, too. No matter how my farmer felt about him, Thomas shouldn't feel threatened there.

May—the last month of the school year—progressed, and I continued teaching middle school English and history. Mr. Windward was struggling with sickness from his treatments. Bess eventually approached me early in the month and offered a short-term contract as his substitute. On one hand, I was thrilled. On the other, heartbroken.

It was difficult to stay vigilant. Dawson reminded me of what I stood to lose each morning before leaving home. I never stopped in front of a window except to survey the school grounds and surrounding streets from one side. Sometimes, I watched from the front and rear doors, other times from shuttered windows. If the gray man lurked nearby, I hoped to spot him first. The entrances were locked during school hours, but to him, they may have well been thrown wide open. More than once, I spied Dawson performing his own recon around the school and town. It was something I didn't mention, and neither did he. He normally waited with dinner ready when I returned late each afternoon, acting as if he'd remained home all day.

"Have you planted your crops while I've been working?" I'd noticed my garden patch was tilled. Suspicious piles around the edges didn't look like dirt. I assumed it to be steer manure.

"Nope. Took most of the day to move my tractor and pick up a load of fertilizer. She's all tilled...looks good, doesn't it? It's still a mite early in the season. We'll likely pick up a few more frosts before month's end."

"Did you get your fields planted?" It was impossible to know less about farming than me. I rarely talked about it for fear I might embarrass myself.

The chicken he fried in peanut oil was second to none. I was amazed at the depth of flavor. Lots of steamed broccoli and a plate of freshly sliced fruit—it seemed someone spoke to Butch about my eating habits. They were in constant contact. "Nope." He didn't bother to look up while he mauled a crispy thigh.

"What?" I almost shouted my surprise. "Dawson, you can't put your life and livelihood aside while I sit and wait. How are you going to pay bills?"

He did me the favor of not smiling. "Same way I always do. Never said I raised crops."

"You told me..." I tried to remember exactly how he worded answers to my questions when we first met as neighbors. "You mentioned you and your mom owned a thousand acres of mostly bottomland...with tractors, tillers, disks, harrows, plows..." I stopped, not knowing enough about farming to know the different implements.

"Yep." He was smug, and I could see the humor sparkling in his eyes. "Except I didn't say I farmed, did I?"

I sat back and stared at my roommate with narrowed eyes, attempting to remember the exact wording. I could say nothing in my defense. "What do you do then? Is the Pelletier family incredibly wealthy with ties to the Rockefellers?"

Dawson was smiling when he took time away from eating and rummaged in the refrigerator. "I bought beer today. Want one?" He screwed the top from one and took a pull from the longneck. He grinned again after swallowing.

"Sure, why not?" I accepted a bottle after he removed the lid. "Well?"

He took his seat across from me again, apparently pleased with himself. "I'm a fulltime bodyguard and sometimes nurse to an ice-cold killer. Doesn't leave many hours in the day for me-time."

"You're not a fulltime bodyguard but you are one hell of a Nurse Ratched." His gaze didn't change. "So?" I held my hands wide. "What is it you do for a living?" Dad warned me about situations like this. I was in love with a man whom I had no idea what line of work he performed.

Dawson drank from the bottle again. "Investments."

"Could you be a bit more specific?"

"How's this for definitive? I gave all my money to Allen after we mustered out."

"He's an investor?" Dawson still didn't make sense.

"No...at least, I don't think so. I invested in his business. He didn't have any startup capital when we left the service, so I gave him every dollar in my bank account."

"So, you own half of his IT or whatever work it is he does?"

"Nope. Thirty-three-point three percent."

"Why so little if you provided the money?"

"Allen does the work...all of it...without any help or input from me. I don't deserve what he gives me."

"Wow." My head was spinning. Everything I thought I knew about him was turned upside-down. "How much did you give him? Or is that too personal?"

"I gave him everything. Most of ten years military wages, including combat pay. Money I didn't have time to spend. Mom was supposed to take care of it and use any she needed for the farm. I got home to find it untouched."

"You gave it all to our helicopter pilot."

"Yep." He retrieved another beer and offered it to me.

Not yet touching the one in front of me, I shook my head. "You make enough partnered with Allen to pay your bills?" A third didn't seem like much to me. I was used to receiving eighty percent.

Dawson nodded. "Plenty for me and Mom, with more left over for savings."

***

I breathed a sigh of relief when the final day of school let out. Mr. Windward wasn't doing well, and his wife was handling his retirement. When Bess appeared at my door, I wasn't surprised when she didn't offer me his position. Others substituted in the district far longer than me. Many were more qualified, and I certainly didn't expect preferential treatment. She did offer me work nearly every day the following school year if I wanted. Pay was far less than a salaried teacher but better than nothing. I was willing to wait and see if something more permanent opened. I wasn't going back to The Company for any amount of money.

Before leaving town, I stopped at the grocery store to pick up a few items Dawson forgot. I liked pepper, but he loved it, and we used almost twice as much as salt. I also preferred those little half-sheet paper towels he never seemed to find. Yet most of what I carried were fruits of all kinds.

With my basket filled and strolling to the check-out line, I saw movement near my Wagoneer. I passed the cashier and strode to the front windows for a better look. For only an instant, he turned and glanced at the store. It was enough. I set my basket aside and ran for the exit.

Using the entry wall for cover, I unbuttoned my jacket for easy access to my gun and peeked around the corner for my target, one that had already disappeared. A high school teacher walked in my direction, while I fumbled for my phone and made the call.

"Hi, honey. Are you already released from school?" For once Dawson's deep voice didn't affect my libido.

"He's here, Dawson." I took a deep breath to control my panic and pulse. "The gray man. He's here. I just saw him."

Chapter XVII

"Where are you?" Dawson's tone switched in the blink of an eye. His normally slow drawl disappeared, and the military commander reappeared.

"I'm at the grocery store." Still using the entryway corner as a barrier, I watched everywhere after the man disappeared like so much smoke.

"Stay tight. Retreat to the interior and take up a position allowing you the greatest visibility. Keep your back to a wall if possible. I'm on my way." I could hear him running as he talked.

Returning inside, I retrieved my basket and took it with me. My head was on a swivel. Both front doors and an emergency exit were in my lines-of-sight. If he entered, I would likely see him. My heart sank after I was spied by a coworker. We made eye contact shopping, and I saw no diplomatic way out. Of all the times, now was the worst.

"Miss Hampton!" Teresa Dotson was one of three fifth grade teachers. "Do you have plans for this summer?" Teresa's voice was chipper enough to make me want to slap the happy right out of her.

"Try to stay alive, Mrs. Dotson. Keep my head above the dirt line." I smiled in her general direction but not directly inviting her to stop. The gray man would have no qualms shooting her to get to me. Nor would it bother him to kill everyone in the store.

My flip answer didn't deter her. "Oh, Miss Hampton, that's what I love about you. You can make jokes about anything." Her titter belied an age much closer to retirement than mine.

"I might josh about many things, Mrs. Dotson. Staying alive isn't one of them." Taking only an instant away from surveilling, I winked at her. She giggled again and was still chuckling when she pushed her cart away.

It seemed a lifetime, but from my pocket came a faint ringtone. After fishing it out, I saw it was Dawson. My response was all business. "J here." I winced and grimaced. That name belonged to another woman I hoped was gone forever. Yet she automatically appeared in a time of great stress. Perhaps it was for the best—her services were needed in the worst way, and it was time to let Julia and Jules fade away and release the inner J if I wished to continue breathing.

"Jules…" He was kind enough to ignore my carelessness. "…I need you to use the emergency exit. Don't even consider your Jeep. Leave it where it's parked."

I hated the idea of going out. With my rifle left at home on my final day I didn't need to. "He's probably in back. The man disappeared like fog."

"He's not. Now hurry." He seemed certain, and I trusted no one like I did Dawson.

I left my basket and jogged to the rear. I took a deep breath and drew my Glock with little hope the gray man would allow me a shot. I pushed outside, and instead of a mortal enemy, Dawson waited in his battered old Ford. With the open passenger side next to the exit, I only needed to cross a dozen feet. I slid in, and we were away, leaving inertia to slam the door.

AR-10 was across his lap, he gunned the engine and tire treads grabbed at the pavement. He was taking us the opposite direction of home. To Challis—or perhaps south toward Pocatello or Twin Falls. "A young guy, maybe twenty-five, taller than me with a carrot top. Could he be your gray man?" Dawson turned onto a secondary street before we reached the southern town limits, slowing little if at all.

"No. He would be about fifty, brown hair, five or six inches shorter than you."

"There was a rifleman parked in the lot across the street. He was watching your Wagoneer. I think he was there to shoot you down if you ran to it." Dawson was matter of fact as he laid out our circumstances. He was so cool and calm, no wonder his unit held him in such high regard. I felt like a blubbering fool inside. Being prey was foreign to me.

We wheeled into a mobile home park. While I didn't know exactly where Scotty lived, it certainly wasn't inside city limits. Yet he waited next to a newer black four-door Dodge pickup with the windows heavily tinted. Dawson left his truck parked mid-street, and we leaped out at his urging. Scotty absorbed the sights of his friend armed with a rifle and me with a pistol in my hand. The Dodge idled, and he was all business. "Dad said don't worry about it. New trucks can be bought anytime." Dawson took a moment to shake his hand while my head was on a swivel. I expected a bullet to come our way any moment.

"Thanks, buddy. Tell William this means everything." Something passed in an instant between friends. "Don't come to us for any reason. I'm serious, Scotty. We'll call if we need anything."

"Julia…" I wasn't sure if Scotty wanted to punch or kiss me. Perhaps even he wasn't certain. "I don't know what you've got this guy into but take care of him." I agreed with a curt nod.

Although it was virtually impossible to see into the truck, Dawson made me slouch. Once we were out of town and driving north again, I sat up and buckled my seatbelt. Fumbling through his pockets, Dawson located his phone and made a brief call. "Ma? I want you to find Dad's shotgun and a handful of shells. Lock the doors and windows and hide in the basement closet. You might want to take a piss-pot, a bottle of water, and a sandwich or two." He was silent for a moment. "Yeah, it's really serious. Don't come out until you hear Jules or me calling you. Anyone else, shoot through the damned door…you hear me?" Listening quietly, he let Melissa talk. "Yeah, I'll tell her. Mom, I love you." The moment he ended the call, Dawson punched a second number. He flicked his eyes off the road long enough to make eye contact. "Mom said she loves you and to be safe."

Frankly, I was stunned. Melissa and I bonded quickly the few times we were together, yet for her to feel so deeply was surprising. Did I love her in return? Yes, I suppose I did—she was the mother to my soulmate. If God cared at all about poor sinner like me, perhaps we would have an opportunity to build a closer relationship.

Someone answered Dawson's next call. "This is an emergency, Allen. What we feared has come to pass. Jules is about to call a number. I need you to listen in and track the location. Can you? Yeah, five minutes…you have her information, right?" He must have heard what he needed and shut his phone. "Wait five and then call your handler. Once Allen locates him through your cell, he'll go to work. When this is over, it's only the beginning. Do you understand?" It was clear why Dawson drove slowly. We had calls to make before the mountains cost us phone service. Finding the first wide spot along the Salmon River, he pulled over but let the truck idle. We both watched the time on the dashboard. Finally, he nodded. "It's been six…make the call."

The distant phone rang twice before it was answered. "Manny."

"J here."

"Hey, it's nice to hear your voice!" He sounded upbeat and enthusiastic. "What can I do for you?" He chuckled. "Surely you're not broke yet."

No way was I going to cut him slack—men had been sent to kill me. "I wanted to give you another chance to tell me you have nothing to do with the gray man, old friend."

"Of course not. Why? Are you still worried?"

I spoke in monotone. "You were supposed to find information on your end."

"I'm still looking. So far, I've not found a thing. My gut tells me you don't have anything to worry about, J."

"Are you telling me the coast is clear? I don't have to watch my back for the next fifty years?"

Another chuckle. "Exactly what I'm saying. Enjoy yourself and live life to its fullest. Eat, drink, and be happy. Get married and fill a home with rug rats."

I was silent for a moment but not long enough for him to end our call. If Allen needed time, he would get it. "Would you tell me if there's something to worry about? If you hear rumblings concerning me, will you let me know?"

"Of course."

"Swear it to me."

"I swear it. On the lives of my family, J. I promise to have your back."

"You've always had it before. I see no reason to doubt you now, Manny. Besides, I've made ramifications clear should something turn awry, haven't I?"

"Perfectly."

"Okay, I hope this is the last time we have this conversation."

"I'm sure it will be. I can guarantee it." The phone went dead.

"What do you think?" Dawson was watching his rearview mirror. "He's always had my best interests at heart."

"Not what I'm asking. Listen to your gut. Was he lying?"

"Something's not right."

Dawson's cell rang, and he picked up immediately. "Did you get it?" Satisfaction on his face was my answer. "Good. Trace every call, get into his computer, and learn everything you can about his life. I want everyone he talks to, meets, and even knows casually. Find out if this thing is as big as Julia thinks it is, as well as everyone involved. If it is, and we go to war, I want to know the enemy. Then we take the fight to them."

*** 

We drove past North Fork and our driveways before turning onto a logging road. "Where are we going?" I wanted to get home as quickly as possible.

"To your place." He pointed south. "I live about three miles that way. Yours is another four." He glanced at my footwear. "Your shoes are going to be put to the test."

"I dressed for the last day of school...not hiking." They were flats to go with my outfit. I wore a long tan dress reaching my calves with a matching light jacket. My Glock was hidden beneath it.

We gained altitude as the truck growled its way up the steep gravel road. Finally, the spur he searched for leading south appeared. We turned and were forced to slow to a crawl. The course was filled with ditches and potholes caused by winter runoff. Switching into four-wheel-drive, Dawson picked his way through the worst of it. Logs, debris, and even small trees covered our route, yet we powered over it all. Finding it washed out before the end, he stopped and switched off the engine.

"We walk from here." He stashed keys above the sun visor where everyone looks first. "Don't lock the door. Scotty or someone will pick it up."

A beep emanated from my dress pocket. Checking my cellphone, I found it was low on power. I could do little but shrug. The final morning was busy. The thought of charging it was the last thing on my mind.

The road didn't end at the washout, and we fought our way on foot with Dawson leading. It was brushy, undergrowth crowding into the dilapidated bulldozed route. My dress continually caught on something, and Dawson turned when I cursed a branch for a tear. "Damn it! This is one of my favorites."

He didn't give me a chance. Handing me his rifle and drawing a folding knife from its sheath, he grasped the material at knee level. He cut his way around, lopping the skirt away with the razor edge. Glancing at his job, I was reminded of how white my legs were. Any Bahamas tan was long gone. The material was wadded and stuffed under the far side of a nearby log. Without a word, he reclaimed his long gun and took the lead again. His rifle ready at the new, awkward-looking port arms, Dawson moved with the confidence of a well-trained soldier and woodsman.

School let out at ten-thirty, and teachers were released for the summer at eleven if their rooms were clean and inventories finished. I spotted the gray man sometime before noon. Now on foot with miles in front of us, it wasn't yet one. It felt as if we'd been on the run for hours. The logging tracks ended, and we were hiking through steep unbroken forest without slowing.

Dawson's legs were long and made me jog to keep up. "Hey." My voice was low, and he stopped to see what I wanted. "Look at the cabin down there." Far below in the center of a meadow stood a small log structure. It was picturesque with a stream winding through the open flat. An unmaintained road stopped almost at its door. "Do you know where we are and how to get there?"

Dawson chuckled. "Yeah, I know how."

"Have you ever been to it?"

"Many times. It's my home."

"That's yours?" I glanced to where my finger still pointed and back to Dawson.

"Sure is. Mom's place is two miles east through the timber, almost out to the highway. Just a few more miles, and we'll be in the same area where you and Jake were lost and walked out of the mountains last Thanksgiving."

"You really know this area, don't you?"

My idea of who Dawson was seemed to change regularly. No longer was he a simple farmer—my neighbor was more a soldier-mountain man. It was hard to believe he lived in a place significantly smaller than mine.

"I've been all through these mountains on foot and horseback. Not often as far back as where Scotty guides, but yeah, I know this country pretty well."

***

We crouched at the edge of a small patch of timber ninety minutes later. Below lay my spread some mile distant. I knew Jake was inside waiting to be let out. At almost three, he would be forced to wait until dark—any accidents would be forgiven. Dawson studied the place and surrounding area through his rifle scope. We were on a heavily timbered ridge to the north of where I normally hiked the open country. A chilly wind blew down from behind us. "Anything?" I whispered. Neither of us had binoculars, but the high-quality scope on Dawson's rifle was adequate.

"Nope." Lowering it to his lap, he sat back. "I've got one magazine for my rifle, so I need to visit my place." He hesitated, the worry on his face plain. "Why don't you wait here, and I'll be back in three…four hours tops? Rest, keep an eye on your place, and I'll be here before you know it." The idea of being alone didn't frighten me. I was J. Yet Dawson leaving gave me pause, and he saw it. "Stay here, and no one will find you, Jules. Are you going to be okay? Or would you rather come?"

"Go." I waved off his concerns. "I'll be fine. Just hurry back before dark." I looked at the sky—it was clear and the temperature in the upper seventies. We needed to be inside before the downslope night wind cooled everything.

Although the consummate soldier, Dawson took time to give me a kiss. It surprised me, for when he felt danger, the man was nothing but professional. He pulled me to him and lifted my chin. Enjoying the kiss of a lover, I found myself molding my body against his. He tried to pull away but my hand slid behind his neck and head.

"My God." His eyes were wild and full of hunger when I allowed him to draw back. "Lady…" His growl reminded me of a wolf. "…when this is done…"

"Yeah? Then what?"

"I'm going to show you what it's like to be my woman. You understand?" I loved he was asserting himself as my man. The one I dreamed of throughout my life.

Time was drawing nigh for him to take me, for us to become one. Perhaps I'm old fashioned, but I needed to know my man wanted me. To hunger for me as a natural male needs a female. To make me his. Dawson's love was something I was sure of—reveled in—and the next step was our union. I needed his desire for me to make him ache. "I'm not sure I can wait until this is over." Many times over the past months I would have willingly given myself to him, and we had reached another such moment.

"We'll see." He crawled backward from where we watched and out of sight. I neither heard nor saw him after Dawson left my side. He passed into the timber as if a ghost.

Our war needed to end before it started. However, if The Company refused to stop, I suspected my time on earth was short. It was another reason to join with my man. I tried to imagine how it would be—would he take me as I desired—or would it be gentle? In the end, I didn't care, already craving his firm touch. If there was to be a future for us, The Company had to be stopped from pursuing me.

I could no longer stand the anticipation after two hours. If Dawson met with resistance, I felt sure I would hear gunfire. One nagging fear was his family. Mine could no longer be touched. The thought of Melissa, Bess, or any of their kin harmed was frightening. Following the direction Dawson took, I found the timbered ridge dropping toward my home. Using it as cover, I soon found myself crouched inside the trees some two hundred yards north of my house. It was difficult to believe The Company sent someone there, but I saw the gray man, and Dawson located another shadow watching my Jeep in town.

I was certain my way was open, when a flash caught my attention to the east. Nothing moved but my eyes until I saw it again. Not far away, a strange male sat, his right flank exposed. I backed away until out of sight and drew my Glock—a round chambered and seventeen more ready in the magazine.

While I might not be the bravest, smartest, or best shot, my strength was patient stealth. Taking one step at a time, my attention was on approaching the seated man from his rear. It was almost a half-hour before I could see over a small rise. He wore a camouflage hat, shirt, dungarees, and boots. Pulled tight against his shoulder was an AR15, almost the same as my own long gun, configuration the only difference. The man wasn't a hunter except of human prey. He was at my home to kill me.

A short step, lower my weight slowly, lean forward, and prepare for the next. While most of my focus centered on the seated man, I never lost track of my surroundings. Stopping once when I saw one hand slowly reach his hat, he scratched an itch beneath the brim. At thirty yards, I was able to see his red hair hanging. I guessed it was the same man Dawson identified in town. My sights never left his upper back. Place a foot gently and feel for breakable debris beneath before easing down. Once comfortable with weight dispersion, I repeated with my opposite foot. Within seven paces before he glanced around, I was looking over the sights when we made eye contact.

To his credit the red-haired man never made a sound. He twisted to bring his rifle up. I shot him twice beneath the armpit before I broke into a sprint. He collapsed, slumping to the ground. I didn't slow as I passed his corpse and fired one more to the side of his head. The fight was brought to me, and I had no remorse. The enemy would give me no quarter, and I planned to return the favor.

I felt the concussion from a near miss as I left the timberline. My house lay not more than a few hundred feet. Once outside of the trees and surrounded by sage reaching my waist, I stopped to reconnoiter before finishing my sprint. A bullet drove the air from my lungs before a second went over my head. I fell to my knees, emptying my G17 in the direction the shot originated from. Ejecting the magazine while trying desperately to catch my breath, I fumbled for another. Pressing it home and running the slide forward, I searched for the shooter.

The shot came from the direction of my house or a nearby patch of brush twenty feet across and twice as long. It was a damp area and sometimes a trickle ran to the wet weather creek going through a culvert under my road. Keeping the area trimmed seemed pointless, and now I wished I hadn't been so lazy.

Still gasping, I crawled back the way I came to the safety of thick conifers. The rifle lying next to the corpse seemed godsend until I realized one of my bullets hit the action. It was inoperable, and I left it behind to backtrack farther. I was still armed with thirty-four rounds for my handgun.

Blood was soaking my back. I couldn't reach it, but the wound seemed restricted to one side. Not coughing blood, it was time to reenter the fight. I was battling for my right to live, death the only other option.

I worked my way south, mindful of blood loss. It took forty-five minutes to travel beyond my house to where I could view the front. Having passed the brushy patch, I didn't expect a shooter to still be there. No cars were parked, and I crouched to watch my surroundings. My hearing had been compromised by gunfire, and I was forced to rely on eyesight. The high-pitched ringing in my ears was painful. Already it felt as if a rib had broken. Where at first the wound was a burning pinch, pain now radiated outward. If I didn't know better, my side and back felt like I'd been skewered by a spear. Used to hunting alone, my biggest fear was for Dawson. He must have heard the gunfire and perhaps feared the worst. I didn't worry about him losing his head. According to Mandy, the man had been in more firefights than I could imagine.

Movement called my attention to the untended thicket. I was wrong—my shooter was still there, but now a camouflaged figure crawled from the edge closest the timberline. At sixty yards, to take a shot was chancy, but since the target accommodated by coming straight to me, I inched back, keeping undergrowth between us and bided my time.

Motionless in a far wooded background, tree bark camo served well, but it tended to highlight items as it neared in sage and grass. I made out a soft knapsack, and even the rifle was mottled green, brown, and gray from its stock out to its muzzle. Concentrating through pain the sniper inflicted, I grew nervous because of something out of kilter—strangely like looking in a mirror—until I realized a left-hander low-crawled toward me. Vegetation thinned, and lefty pushed up in a sudden break to the "safety" of the timber where I waited. At less than twenty yards—almost running into me with rifle at port arms—I realized the full impact of the eerie mirror-effect. It was a younger woman about my size. She stopped, desperate to bring her rifle to bear before three bullets from my Glock tore through her chest. Pitching onto her face, she struggled to all fours and tried a shaky lurch to where her rifle lay. A shot to the crown from three feet put an end to it. Ejecting the partially emptied magazine, I slammed in a full, slid the spare into its carrier beneath my arm, and holstered my nine-millimeter to enthusiastically claim her firearm. I found an all left-handed Browning semi-auto for hunting wild pigs. Ironic and bitterly disappointing. I had no chance to get used to various opposite operations and in-my-face case ejection. Even its ammo proved useless to me—a foreign custom cartridge somewhere between .22 Hornet and 5.56x45mm NATO. The good news was her bullet hitting me was a small full metal jacket which I hoped meant minimal damage. With eighteen ready in my pistol, I was prepared to storm my house. Two down and how many more to go? I'd expected only the gray man, and Dawson surprised me when he was sure a shooter waited with my Jeep in his sights— but he was right. The Company employed lone wolves, or so I thought. Was I an anomaly along with the man who recruited me into this business in that we worked alone, but others were sent out in teams? Food for thought should I survive the present attack.

I worked past the brushy patch and inspected the machine shed and garage from a distance. Both front and rear doors of my house appeared untouched. No vehicle in sight told me my attackers hiked in or were dropped off. The gray man worked alone, which meant other assassins, possible members of the young woman's team, or an entirely separate set of assailants lurked close by. I needed to find a way into my house.

Should I attempt to rush my front porch, it would be a long, exposed sprint of a hundred yards from where I stood. Then mount steps and across to the door. It was locked and using my key would take extra time. A marksman at any reasonable distance would have an easy shot. Not willing to chance it, I reversed course through the timber to where I could watch the back again and study my surroundings. After thirty minutes without seeing movement, it was time.

I'd left my handbag in the Wagoneer and only took my debit card and keys into the grocery store. Holding the backdoor key in my left hand and the Glock in my right, I crashed through the sage, fearing each step to be my last until reaching the porch.

I stepped aside as the door swung in. I could see only Jake who appeared alarmed when I came in an unexpected entrance, but his attitude told me no one was inside. With all the gunfire outside, he was keen to have me with him. He followed me to each room, wriggling from head to tail. When I stopped in my bedroom, he hopped onto the bed and watched as I disrobed. I didn't leave the Glock behind when I hurried into the bathroom to check my wound in the mirror.

It was in a place I couldn't reach except with the tip of a finger. The bullet entered below my shoulder blade leaving a tiny hole and exited a few inches away in the direction of my spine with more ragged edges. In between was swollen and angry. I cleansed the area of drying blood with a wet washcloth wrapped around a tongue depressor. It still seeped fresh ooze, but both holes were relatively small. No evidence of tumble, and I could find no remnants of lead, jacket, or bone fragments on the cloth. Fears of a damaged rib lessened, although it wasn't outside the realm of possibility. I packed the area with disinfecting balm using a clean depressor. Not able to apply a bandage, I carefully fastened a clean bra and allowed it to cover the wounds. I groaned in pain while dragging on underwear, jeans, and a tank top. Glancing through windows on the way, I ran for my bedroom where I changed into clean socks and hiking boots.

With my Glock stowed in the shoulder holster under my arm, I belted the .38 around my waist. Six loose rounds went into a front pocket, and I pulled a light flannel shirt over weapons and extra magazines. Even from up close, I would appear unarmed.

Jake whined his need to make a bathroom run. I checked my M4 and flipped on the electronic scope and laser switch before letting him out. Loaded with a twenty-round magazine, I slid two more into the rear pockets of my jeans. Checking windows for movement first, I opened the back door and let him out after giving it some thought.

I didn't believe anyone would shoot Jake and risk giving their position away. Even so, I watched carefully as he ran to check his markers, urinating to let encroachers know he faithfully did his duty.

I wondered about Dawson again upon Jake's return. My neighbor should have returned even if his hike was longer than he expected. Had he been anywhere close, he would have heard the reports. What should have been a four-hour round trip was now closer to five. The timepiece over the stove indicated almost eight o'clock—it would be dark in an hour. Remembering my dead phone, I found it in my discarded dress pocket and plugged it in. When enough power trickled in, I switched it on while allowing it to charge. No new texts nor voice mail showed.

Feeling a panic build, I went through Dawson's pack and box of gear. At the bottom was something heavy, and I pulled out a carton of fifty .44 magnums—more ammo useless to me. Continuing my search, I found another large item and drew it out. Staring in surprise, I realized in my hand was a way of tipping the scales of justice in my direction.

The box read: *ATN PS15 Night Vision Goggles.*

Chapter XVIII

Pitch darkness meant I was ready to leave. Four texts to Dawson weren't returned. It was imperative I not be seen, so in addition to black boots and clothing, I located my black knit stocking hat. An earlier trip to the local salon trimmed my locks, and I drew it down to cover my blonde tresses. A few disagreeable curls were tucked under with a finger.

While allowing Jake out a final time, I adjusted the head straps to mount the night vision unit and ate an apple and a handful of grapes. After my pup returned, I switched off the only light inside to plunge my home into darkness. I was shocked upon turning the system on and swiveling down its rubber shield around my eyes. While not as well-lit as midday, I could see objects fairly clearly. One restriction made using it difficult—I was required to turn my head in the direction I wished to view. Peripheral vision was nonexistent.

My black hoodie covered my .38, and the shoulder harness for my Glock was moved out over the top. It was my primary sidearm with the Colt as a more concealed backup. Stowing two extra magazines for the M4, I was ready—if it was possible to be adequately prepared for a battle to the death.

I raised the goggles and cut power. "Jake," I soothed, squatting next to where he lay on the couch watching me. His front feet were crossed as though royalty. "I'll be here again as quick as I can, okay?" I patted his head and smooth coat. "Maybe Dawson and I will be back for good this time. Would you like that?" In the low light of a waning moon, I saw his ears perk at our neighbor's name. Kissing him on the muzzle, I hurried to exit from the rear. Adjusting my head-straps a final time, I swiveled the goggles down, switched them on again, and the night came to life.

Holding my rifle by the pistol grip with muzzle low, I cracked the door far enough to see outside. My backyard and the mountain rising above were brighter than I could have imagined. If a man or woman were waiting, I could have easily located either one.

The optics gathered moonlight, and night became day after I stepped out. Turning my head awkwardly, I searched again for enemies. Not able to see movement, it was time to work my way east to Dawson's place.

I wished I knew better where I was going. The journey should have taken little more than a couple hours in the daylight. Learning to use the goggles, it was over three before I was standing at the timber's edge. Light shone inside Dawson's cabin across the meadow.

While I desperately wished to sprint to check on my man, J was in complete control. Patience was key when dealing with The Company. Each of us who signed clients had a personal way of performing the job.

Thirty minutes practice with goggles in tandem with the compact long eye-relief scope helped to confidently train its red dot on Dawson's single west window. Although rarely taking my attention away, I didn't neglect my surroundings.

Nocturnal animals prowled nearby, and it was exhilarating to observe them as they would see me in near total darkness. Mule deer browsed; owls swished by searching for rodents—I could hardly believe my enhanced eyes when a bear entered the far corner of the meadow before shuffling into the pine again. As the minutes ticked into hours, a long-tailed cat crossed my neighbor's driveway to disappear into the undergrowth. It didn't dawn on me until moments later that I'd caught sight of an elusive mountain lion. A shiver and a predatory smile accomplished pride in realizing I'd joined the mountain food chain at its top. With the secrets of the night no longer hidden from me, nothing was safe when I prowled. Nothing and no one.

Although early summer, it grew significantly colder as the night wore on. I was sure of movement inside the tiny cabin. However, the light never switched off, and I soon doubted myself. I pulled the sweatshirt hood over my head and hunkered down against an old pine stump. It was just high enough I could lay my rifle across it, assuring a steady rest. I was unable to determine the distance to the cabin—it might have been two hundred yards or perhaps four hundred. Looking across the flat rather than from high on the mountain was much different. Add tenebrosity while using night vision, and it was impossible to be sure.

When humans are most tired—both mentally and physically—it is time to act. If anyone but me remained outside, the night owl had yet to show hide nor feather. I was confident no one was nearby. Judging by the moon, it was after three, perhaps closer to four.

I slowly picked my way across the meadow and found my first guess was closest. Instead of two hundred yards, it was closer to two-fifty. Closing in on the lighted window, I was forced to switch off the goggles and push them up—too much light blinded me. I waited a few moments for the black spots to disappear before looking again.

A man I didn't recognize was seated at a small table directly in front of me. If he should be awake and on guard duty, he failed miserably in the attempt. A second also appeared asleep on a couch at the north end of the room. Dawson's rifle leaned against the wall along with a semi-auto handgun near the seated man's hand. With two killers already put down at my place, the men weren't long lost friends stopping by to visit.

Dawson lay on the floor with his hands behind his back. I supposed they were zip-tied. Plastic took less room and proved more easily carried than handcuffs. For a heart-stopping moment, I feared he might be dead until a leg straightened. Whether he reacted to a dream or was simply uncomfortable, I was relieved when he moved.

I couldn't think of any reason for Dawson to be held except as bait. If so, a third member of the team was nearby. My greatest fear was the gray man, but I couldn't imagine him being part of a group with the two slackers inside.

Slipping to the front, I carefully tried the door while flattened against the wall, only to find it locked. I squatted next to the building and adjusted the goggles over my eyes before switching them on. I checked my surroundings carefully and stood after reasonably certain no one waited nearby. If they could see me, it was only because they used the same technology. Creeping the perimeter of Dawson's house, I was flabbergasted to find it powered by solar panels. We'd seldom talked about his place, and the modern science was a surprise. While I knew he no longer lived with Melissa, it was her I thought of when we spoke of his home. Power cables entered a small anteroom extending from the side, and I tried the door. Like many equipment add-ons, I wasn't surprised it was unlocked because it didn't lead to the main interior. Twisting the knob and pushing inward, I stepped back to bring my short-barreled rifle up. My heart pounded while fear-induced sweat trickled down my spine. The wound on my back faded to unconcern.

A bank of six batteries inside the tiny room connected to a wall-mounted inverter. It was the first one I'd seen in person but recognized it immediately. From there, I had only to trace the line to locate the shut-off switch. Throwing the main breaker carefully, I cringed at the sound much louder than anticipated. I heard no exclamations nor movement inside and hurried back around to the west window. The room was pitch black, yet I could see both visitors clearly. Switching my gaze to Dawson, it took a moment before realizing he'd changed positions. Instead of lying on his side with his back to me, he faced the window. I stared intently before noticing his blink. Leave it to my man to realize what went on around him. It was his home, and anything out of the ordinary would alert him. Squatting again, I spent a minute or longer observing my surroundings. First with goggles alone, then combined with my rifle scope. If people lurked nearby, I simply couldn't find them.

It was now or never. Standing again, I chose to kill the sleeping man in the bunk first. Raising my rifle scope awkwardly to the night vision goggles, it took a moment before I was prepared.

"Hey, wake up!" I heard Dawson's voice. "Lights are out. Somethin's wrong." His voice was raised, waking the sleeping men. What the hell? Why would he warn them of my imminent attack?

The answer was immediate. A third man stood from where he was seated beneath the window and blocked out my chosen target. He held a rifle, and I couldn't have seen him where he was. His muzzle pointed at Dawson, sentencing him to an immediate death.

My first round was loud in the silence of morning. It went through the back of the once-hidden man's skull, and he collapsed. Both remaining combatants swung their guns to me the moment they realized an attack was underway.

When my first target dropped, my rifle was already trained on the second next to the table. I moved the muzzle a few inches, and he went down at the bark and bright flash while I swung to the third. Time was of the essence, and it was up to me to stop him from killing Dawson. My third round went off before I was prepared. His cracked at the same moment, spraying me with glass. I was lucky to wear the goggles or might have been blinded. How he missed, I'll never know. Even outside the cabin despite my ears ringing, I could hear him gurgle for oxygen. I kept my rifle trained on him while he fought to live, a battle ultimately lost.

Dropping to one knee, I spun around in anticipation of an attack. I was at my most vulnerable during the fight—should the gray man have been nearby, my life would be over. "Dawson? Can you hear me?" The window and frame were badly damaged and would need replacing. I stayed on my haunches, prepared for another battle. The collapsible stock was tight against my cheek, and the scope helped me in locating possible movement.

"Yeah, I can hear you." He sounded angrier than injured.

"Can you open the door?"

"Give me a minute, and I'll try." I could hear him struggle to stand and eventually fumbling at the door, but I kept my attention focused outward. "It's unlocked, J. You'll have to twist the knob to open it. It's pretty stiff, and I can't get it to turn."

Chills ran down my spine. Dawson never called me J, yet it was true. I was working in the death business again, and it was my pseudonym during those past hours or days. It bruised my heart to hear him use it. He was standing inside, anticipating my entry. I could see he was blind in the absolute blackness waiting for my help. "Scissors?" It was safer and easier to snip his binding than to use a knife blade.

"Top drawer to the left of the sink."

They were exactly where he said. His restraints were cruelly tighter than needed, and he let out a grunt when the pressure relented. "Thanks." He rubbed his hands and wrists, trying to restore blood flow.

"Are you all right? Have you been injured?"

"Just a bruised ego." He didn't say more, and I didn't press. He rustled behind me, and I glanced over my shoulder to see what he was doing. "Got 'em," he grunted. From the bottom of a drawer, he drew out another pair of goggles. "They're old but still function."

The ones I wore looked like a pair of small binoculars affixed to my eyes with a harness around my head. What he put on was a combination of binocular eyecups and a monocular held by similar headbands. "How did you know I was looking in the window?" My time was split watching him and the open door. My question was answered when he switched the unit on. I could see green around the eyecups.

"The glow. It wasn't much, but I happened to catch it when you moved your head. I've been exposed to it enough in combat to recognize it immediately." He checked his rifle after holstering the Anaconda. I knew the reason he fingered the butt of the revolver was to alleviate anxiety by feeling it was there and securely in place. "We need to get out of here before it's light. No telling how many more there are." He swung a pack onto his back and shuffled next to me at the edge of the doorway with his rifle, ready to move out.

Now that he was free, I wasn't sure of our next step. "Do you have a plan?"

"Neither of us have a vehicle, and Mom's still in the basement closet. I think we should take to the hills."

"Not without Jake, we're not." He was my boy, and I was responsible for him. It wasn't a duty I took lightly.

"All right, we'll swing by your place and see if we can get to him." Dawson was as fond of Jake as me. They bonded over two years of housesitting and sometimes living together. "If we can't..." He shrugged, but I could sense his sorrow.

Dawson didn't understand. My dog was everything to me, and no way was I going to let the gray man or anyone else take him away.

\*\*\*

Dawn broke before we reached my place, and our night vision units were switched off and stored in Dawson's knapsack. Nothing was encountered on the return hike other than mule deer. We were almost to the timber's edge when we nearly stumbled over the first body. I hadn't mentioned my skirmish because we remained quiet as possible except for brief whispers. He turned to me with a raised eyebrow. "One of yours?"

I nodded and pointed. "Another over there." It made me feel better to find nothing fed on them. The thought cropped up when I saw the bear and lion. "Wait here."

I left Dawson to watch the rear of the house while I scouted the front. Nothing was changed—the young woman's body lay where I left it. Neither corpse meant anything to me. They were no different from roadkill along the highways, yet when I noticed a beetle about to reach the remains, I stomped it rather than let nature begin its work so soon.

Dawson was still squatting when I returned. "I didn't see anything. Cover me until I get to the porch." I didn't give him a chance to answer and eased into the opening. With the rifle butt against my shoulder and watching through the scope, I hurried to the back. Taking a position to observe both the door and hillside, I saw Dawson sprint.

God, he was my Adonis. Hair pulled back and beard growing longer, Dawson's mouth was little more than an angry line across his face. Watching him come, I understood why our fighting men and woman were feared in combat. His pack bounced slightly as he ran—focused as he was on our surroundings and the rifle in his hands. He wasn't breathing hard after reaching my side. I left him to view our surroundings while I unlocked and swung the door in. As it opened and I pulled back, Dawson stepped onto the porch with his rifle shouldered. He went in first, and I was behind, taking a position just inside. Jake barely slowed as he passed our neighbor on his way to me.

"All clear." Dawson inspected each room with the proficiency of a SWAT team. I never learned how, and it was enlightening to watch. I closed and locked the door before releasing my rifle to hang from its sling. My phone was still on the charger, and I checked it for messages. None there, so I disrobed in my bedroom. Jake came in with Dawson behind. I was down to my underwear with my back to him. "Christ, Jules, what the hell happened?" His cool fingers touched the area around my wound. It felt hot and weepy.

"How bad is it?" Since being wounded, I'd taken little time to consider it. Although my back and side were stiff, it didn't hurt all that bad.

Dawson unhooked my bra to slide from my shoulders while he examined me. "You need a doctor, honey. There's an exit wound, but the bruising tells me the bullet damaged the edge of your latissimus dorsi." He pushed, making me wince. "It might have glanced off a rib."

"It's a bullet wound. We can't go to a doctor. Law enforcement would be all over us."

He knew it better than me. "Don't shower. Take a bath with a washcloth in the sink. Let me make a call, and you holler when you're finished. I'll clean it up." With the door cracked open, I was able to hear his side of the conversation. I assumed it would be Melissa, but it wasn't. "Al? Yeah, it's me. Hey listen, we've got trouble. I'm going to need some antibiotics and…" He moved into the kitchen to watch the front, and I couldn't hear any more. The door opened and closed, but his low rumble still floated reassuringly to me. He must have let Jake outside to water the sage.

Dawson was done with his call, and Jake was inside again when I finished with my whore's bath. While I wanted a shower to wash the sweat trickling down my back, it was better than nothing. The sink was refilled with clean water when I called for help wearing only panties. "I'm ready." I'd leaned over the sink when he opened the door. I knew he could see my profile, but the light from the single bulb was best for his examination. I rinsed the washcloth and held it out. "Could you get my back, please?"

His touch could not have been gentler. My neck and shoulders first—avoiding my wound as he made his way down. Stopping at my waist, he reached around me and rinsed the cloth again. The water turned a cloudy red. As he repeated the process, his ministration caused me to wish for a way to call the gray man and ask for an official timeout. Instead, I interrupted his next rinse, and he dropped the cloth in the water. Pulling his hand to my breast, I enjoyed its strength and roughness. He cupped and massaged, barely pinching my nipple before I felt his breath on my neck. His kiss buckled my knees while I gripped the porcelain.

His lips were soft and the course bristles of his beard exciting. I heard a moan and knew it was me. Dawson's fingers left one breast and stretched across to the other, giving it a tug before releasing me.

He kissed my shoulder again before whispering in my ear. "Soon, honey. Not yet but soon." I groaned when he pulled back, not able to trust my legs enough to relinquish a white knuckled grip on the sink. He was right. We had things to do, places to go, and people to kill.

***

"Mom isn't happy." Halfway to the ridgetop, we could see my home a mile below. Jake was joy personified to hike with two of his favorite humans. Since cleaning and dressing my wound, it ached while wearing my daypack. Dawson found a comfortable place for us to rest while still able to see in every direction.

"You called her?" I sat beside him with my wounded side away. Leaning my head against him seemed to give me a brief respite.

"Yeah, we talked long enough to see if she was okay. No one came in the house…or at least downstairs. She's tired, hungry, and sick from the smell of her bucket."

His news buoyed my spirits but made me sad. "I'm so sorry. All because I moved into the area."

"You have to live somewhere, and you carried out your work far away. You didn't invite this trouble. Someone sent it without your permission. Anyhow, Mom's fine, and I'm okay because of your skills. We have five dead you handled alone. At this point, I'm not sure where it's negatively impacted my life. I even got to vacation in the Bahamas." His arm avoided my shoulder and went around my waist. I felt him kiss my crown. The midday sun shone, but the wind chilled me. I was sleepy and found it difficult to keep my lids open. Going without shuteye was something I was capable of, but like any girl, required my fair share of hours in the sack. No sleep the previous night was catching up. I fumbled in a pocket for my phone. "Do you have a signal?" Dawson watched as I held the cell out hoping for at least a bar. The best I could do inside my house was two.

I was surprised. "Three bars. I guess we have better line-of-sight up here than I thought."

From the distant highway leading north to Missoula, a car slowed and rolled into my driveway. Jake returned from his explorations and threw himself to the ground next to me. I set my phone aside and raised my rifle to watch. Dawson already stared through what appeared to be expensive binoculars. I'd never known a pair of

Swarovski's to come cheap. The vehicle stopped next to a small grove of willows. Even at such a long distance, I could see someone exit the driver's side.

Setting my rifle aside, I pushed a button to active a number on my cell. I put it on speakerphone while battling the wind. "Manny here." I could hear the careful guarding of his voice in the wind.

"Hello, Manny."

"J?" He sounded surprised.

"When we meet, those will be the last two words you'll hear in this lifetime. Surprised to find me still alive?"

"Yeah." I wasn't sure in the breeze, but there might have been regret in his voice. "We hoped to move your body to California by now. I gave my word and meant it when I promised to bury you with your family. If it sets your mind at ease, I continue to stand by my pledge."

"It does, but let's talk about your body instead. Where would you like it buried? I'm coming for you when this is over. You know that, don't you?"

He didn't sound worried. "My plot is already purchased if you were somehow able to locate me."

"You're going to need it, old friend. Let's talk about *your* family. Do you have graves bought for little Michael and Juanita? Or your wife, Rosita?" Oh, yes, Allen was coming through with information. He and Dawson spoke multiple times before we left my house.

His silence went long enough I thought our link severed. When he finally answered, Manny was badly shaken. His voice cracked. "You can't. Those are my babies, my life, J. Leave them out of this."

I was proud of my control. "You should've left me alone. I would have taught school, retired, and eventually died of old age. Now you've opened the can of worms I warned you about. What happened here is a mere skirmish, Manny. The war has barely begun, and you've already lost five with another walking into my sights."

The person walked like a man and was closing in on my house. Dawson set his binoculars aside and shouldered his rifle. It would be virtually an impossible shot. Sharply downhill and at such long range—a mile or more—we would need better equipment than we possessed. Most people don't understand, many accomplished shooters included, a bullet arcs less when shooting steeply uphill or down. Gravity affects it far less than shooting horizontally. Dawson adjusted both elevation and windage knobs.

"Can we talk about this…negotiate a sort of truce?"

His comment made me laugh. "I thought we had one. You promised me we did. Then you broke it. Your word means nothing, Manny. Yours will be only the first death of many. The Company and you fired the opening salvo, so this war is on you. Although it hasn't been offered, I expect no quarter given because I'll offer none."

"Let me talk to them. Maybe I can work something out." His voice raised, albeit minutely, and I could almost taste fear through the receiver.

"Famous last words, and I've heard them before. Don't you understand? Because of you, it's a battle to the death."

"I'm very sorry…"

"Too little, too late. You can run, but you can't hide. No matter where you go or how fast, when you least expect it, me or someone else will be there. You've signed your family's death warrant by not listening. Right now, my only question is deciding how far to go. Your parents in Albuquerque…your brother and his new wife in Tuscaloosa…where do I draw the line? Clue me in, Manny, how far do I take this in relation to your extended family? Into Mexico?"

"J…" It hurt to hear the terror in his voice. I'd once relied on him for my safety and well-being, and he'd never let me down.

"Your employers…tell them I'm coming. Let them know I'm on my way and none of you can stop me. Only when I've filled the morgues with bodies, or they've run out of toe-tags will I consider a halt. Unless I'm left alone."

"Money? Do you want more money?" He was the voice of desperation.

My laughter was bitter. "Cash means nothing now. I've been forced to kill too much in the last few hours, Manny. Not to sign a contract and take evil off the streets…you have me killing real people now."

"All right, if that's the way you want it."

Dawson raised his rifle, and I braced for the roar. "No, this is the way you get it because of your duplicity." Laying the phone on a thigh, I plugged my ears. The man was in my backyard as he searched for a way in.

Dawson fired once and held off shooting a second time until he regained his sight picture. The concussion caused me to close my eyes, but when I opened them, the man was still alive. Jake leaped to his feet and ran a safe distance to escape the thunderous clap. Having obviously missed him, Dawson squeezed the trigger rapidly and emptied the magazine. I watched as the prowler sprinted in the direction of the timber on the northeast side of my house. He was going to find a nasty surprise. Bodies left behind would bloat in the afternoon heat.

I lifted the phone again. "Did you hear? That's the sound of a war you started. Imagine shots directed at your wife, kids, parents, sibling, or even friends. You have family, and he who hath family, hath hostages." I knew the quote was butchered but didn't care. I would take a few moments and look up Francis Bacon another time.

Manny always ended our calls, and the present one had run its course. "I'm coming for you. Nothing you do can stop me." My voice lowered as I whispered my promises and hoped he heard them over the wind. "I'm coming, Manny."

I ended the call before he could answer, and it rang almost immediately. Muting it, I slid the phone into a side compartment of my pack. Fear stirred him to anger, and I would not give him the opportunity and satisfaction to rage at me. He knew where I stood, and it made me feel good that he should know what was coming. Would I really go through with it and take it out on his family? It should have bothered me when the thought didn't. If the war went on long enough, yes, they may necessarily have to die.

Dawson replaced the spent magazine with another. After laying the rifle across his lap, he used his binoculars to view the terrain below us.

I couldn't see while I sat with eyes squeezed shut and plugged ears. "How close did you come?"

"The first was a near miss. Damned near got 'im. Your gray man," he added. "A little too much wind drift for the distance. Otherwise he'd be dead."

"You saw him?" I almost whispered my question.

"Yep."

"Are you sure it was him?"

Dawson removed the binoculars pressed against his face and looked at me. "No, I'm not absolutely certain. He matched the vague description you gave." He offered a grim smile. "I sure as hell hope it wasn't the meter reader."

I shook my head. It hadn't been long since I received my bill. "No, not Terry. He stopped by a couple weeks ago."

"Let's go, then." Dawson stood, slung his pack, and reached out to give me a hand. I looked at it, then back to my house. It didn't seem right to leave the gray man where I knew him to be. My opportunity might never come again. Dawson saw me waffling, unable to make up my mind. "C'mon, Jules…"

I chewed at a cracked place on my lip. "I may never have a chance like this again." J wanted to charge down the mountain and finish it. We could fight on my home turf.

"Or have a better opportunity of getting yourself killed, young lady."

His tone was sharp and enough to end my indecisiveness. "You win…we'll do it your way." Wiping my butt free of dirt, I waited for him to lead the way. Before we moved on, his eyes were piercing, drilling their way into my head. He must have found what he searched for and turned away, taking us deeper into the mountains. According to Dawson, we weren't fleeing.

We were leading the gray man into what I hoped would be a trap of our choosing.

Chapter XIX

I knew almost nothing about the gray man except for stories, other than he was nondescript and a master at signing clients. Was he comfortable enough in the outdoors to follow us into the backcountry? Or would he simply bide his time until we grew weary of waiting? Salmon was the only place I knew him to be outside of a big city.

Dawson wasn't sure the gray man would give up pursuit, even though he'd been stymied twice at performing his job and narrowly missed by a hail of gunfire the second time. "He's going to be angry, Jules. Not only did you give him the slip in town, he was almost killed today. Either he's concerned and no longer wants the job or angry because he's a step behind. An educated guess tells me it's the latter."

I used a little hop to bounce my pack higher and tighten the shoulder straps. Water, a couple of sandwiches, and a few blankets because I didn't own a sleeping bag left my knapsack light and easily handled. Still, the miles we traveled wore on me. No sleep and running on adrenaline the previous twenty-four drained my energy. Although officially reaching one-oh-five and much stronger physically, I wasn't conditioned to hump a rucksack up the side of a mountain. On the other hand, Dawson acted as if he did it his entire life. I guess he did in one way or the other. Between the stories he told me of growing up and then joining the army, much of his life was spent with a pack and rifle. Never was he the genteel farmer I once imagined him to be. We stayed a hundred feet or more below the crest but continually pushed upslope. Always the consummate soldier and woodsman, he effortlessly kept us from needless exposure. Farther above stood a larger mountain our ridge would intersect.

Dawson called a halt when we dropped into a small depression heavily wooded on three sides. He could see my strength reserves were depleted, although we'd stopped to allow me rest far too often.

The main peak towered over us and would take little more than an hour to reach. If the end of a prominence hadn't blocked my line-of-sight, Gibbonsville would have been visible to the east.

"We'll ride out the night here." Dawson tossed sticks and rocks from a small flat area. "You're about done. Time to rest, little dove. We can make better time in the morning." Although he didn't mention it, my guide needed sleep, too.

I was worried, wishing to have been in better shape. More miles between us and the gray man would be beneficial. "Then what?" Understanding his plan, I pitched in to help make a comfortable spot to sleep.

He stopped to stare. "We hope he follows us until we kill him. If he gets the chance, he'll do the same to us."

We spread our blankets and shared the meal I'd packed: two peanut and jelly sandwiches each plus a baggy of dogfood for Jake. He waited patiently on the blanket for a handful. After wolfing it down, my boy waited for us to share the crust of our bread. As one who loves it, I didn't provide any but a last corner bite. Dawson either didn't care for the outer part of his bread or felt sorry for a soft-eyed pup.

I put two sandwiches away for the following morning. Jake licked his chops and didn't blink while he watched. After the water bottles were safely stowed, he finally stretched out on the blanket next to me. My boy was tired from the climb. If we traveled the eight miles Dawson estimated, Jake tripled it. "Can you tell me more about your conversations with Allen today?" I asked.

We faced where our back trail was best watched after getting comfortable. "Figures he knows more about The Company than any single person inside. While Al can't name all the players, he's identified much of the upper hierarchy who pull the strings."

"Manny?" I knew the answer in my heart but needed to hear the words. "Is he directly involved in labeling me as a client?"

Dawson was silent, wiping imaginary dust from the receiver of his rifle. He was aware of the soft place I carried in my heart for a one-time friend who always had my back and saved my life at least once. Until now. "Sounds like he made the ultimate decision. If nothing else, he played a large role in your assassination attempts. He sent both teams you've killed."

The knowledge was more painful than I imagined. "Do you know where he is? Has Allen located an address?" Jakes head came up from where it rested, and he growled.

"San Diego, California." The voice behind us was cheerful before we heard the wisp of parting underbrush against clothing. Dawson jerked reflexively to lift his rifle. Like me, he knew the gray man would sign us without mercy. "No, I wouldn't do that, Mr. Pelletier." My farmer relaxed and waited.

Somehow, my enemy almost beat us to where we stopped. It was my fault for not being in better condition. Dawson could have been a dozen miles farther into the mountains if I hadn't held him back. Our capture didn't surprise me—the gray man was more machine than human. I instinctively knew he turned and ran directly toward where the bullets were originally fired from. He couldn't feel fear— that would make him mortal.

My biggest worry come true wasn't the loss of my life—it was that Dawson would perish because of me. "Now what?" My rifle lay close at hand, but with the gray man behind us, it was impossible to bring it into battery. Dawson's lay across his lap pointed in the wrong direction.

The voice remained ebullient. "Now I sign you."

A chill went through me. I could only hope the gray man was satisfied with our lives and didn't feel a need to attack the Pelletier family. They did nothing wrong.

Dawson shook with a rage I could feel. "Could you first explain why?" he gritted. "All Julia wanted was to teach. She wasn't a liability."

The gray man chuckled, although I could hear no humor. "I have no interest why The Company chose this route…but me? Money, Mr. Pelletier. Who could guess this scared little skinny girl I brought into the organization not so long ago would be worth so much? Make no mistake, J. Never has there been such a lucrative contract. Believe me, because I've taken the best jobs around the world."

To know he traveled the globe to sign clients didn't surprise me, but I needed my curiosity satisfied before he killed us. "You were in the Bahamas, weren't you? When I signed Wiggins?"

His dry laughter grated. "I thought you identified me at least once. Guess I was right. The Company sent me to fill the contract if you couldn't. Judging by what I saw of the aftermath, they shouldn't have underestimated you. Girl, you may be the most bloodthirsty killer The Company has fielded. Me? I sign them for money. But you? You enjoy it." Disgust oozed from his tone.

The gray man was wrong. I was sure of it. Rather than argue, I shrugged lazily. "They left me no choice. You were there for me, weren't you?"

His flash of anger surprised me. The gray man didn't have emotions, or so I thought. "Where in the hell did you disappear to? After flying from your balcony, I never could find you. Believe me…I looked."

His admission offered a glimmer of hope. He wasn't fail-free. He could make mistakes, too. "I was busy hunting you." The lie was easy. I shifted, anticipating a bullet tearing through my brain at any moment, but I needed to look him in the eyes.

Nothing changed. Still blending into everything around, the forest as much as the city, he was every bit as nondescript as I remembered. In his hand was the same suppressed pistol he brandished before, similar to my work gun. It wasn't holstered or pointed at the ground—the muzzle didn't waver from my forehead. I continued to twist and didn't stop until my left side faced him.

He gestured slightly with his free hand. "Toss the rifles." I reached slowly to grasp mine. "Easy now, girl. I'm guessing you'd like to enjoy these last few moments." I threw it with fingertips to land only a few yards from where I sat. He stood at no more than twenty feet. "Your turn, Mr. Pelletier." Dawson complied, taking care to not hit my rifle with his. The pistol bore remained trained on my head. "Now, where was I?"

He appeared to enjoy himself. Personally, I never wanted to speak to my clients. It seemed no different from a farm kid naming the family steer, knowing it would be slaughtered in the end. "I was explaining how I hunted you in the Bahamas." Past feeling fear—the anger of a treed mountain lion built.

His politeness was infuriating, knowing he was there to kill us. "Oh, yes. First, since Mr. Pelletier can't seem to keep from touching his belt gun, I'd like him to lob it in this direction." I guess he didn't like the reaction he got from Dawson. "Careful...I'll sign Miss Hampton now rather than later if forced."

Dawson was angry and I supposed terrified for me. For a moment, I thought he might take his chances and fight. To toss away his last line of defense was tantamount to surrendering and embracing death. I caught his eye and nodded to follow directions. The corded muscles in his neck bulged further when he gave up the Anaconda.

"Your Glock, Miss Hampton. Over here, please." It hurt to pitch Dad's pistol to the side. I was sure my father was watching, sad in the knowledge I'd soon be with him, Mom, and Meghan. The gray man's response was smug. "You see? This's why you are where you find yourself...and why I am where I am. You stood no chance against me in the Bahamas. You were good at harvesting stupid sheep, but when it comes down to it, you're nothing but a simple killer." He was right, but perhaps he didn't know of my altercation in Yakima or of the man and woman lying dead a few thousand feet below us. Not to mention three more at Dawson's cabin. None were easy. "You're worth a lot of money...more than any five clients I've signed. The Company has never seemed so frightened of anyone." He smirked. "In this case, just a scared little girl."

Perhaps it was time to make him angry. "Fine, let's finish this. I'm tired of your nasally whine." I leaned to stand, twisting farther, not at all ready for my death—let alone Dawson's. "First you'll want the magazines for my Glock." Using my left hand, I reached under my arm and grasped them, lifting both to toss in his direction. As I hoped, his eyes were momentarily drawn to the two objects.

Sweeping the diminutive revolver from its holster high on my belt, I drew while tossing the spare 9mms. My .38 bullet caught him squarely in the chest. He wasn't anymore ready than a casual shooter would have been. However, rather than drop, he turned and disappeared into the brush before I could follow up! Forgetting everything but my target, I gave chase. The jack pines were thick, and I paused for a moment, deciphering his flight. Like any animal with a lung wound, he would be forced to retreat downhill.

Three bullets drove through the brush at me. They made no noise, except when two furrows cut in a tiny trunk while a third sliced away a small limb. All came within a foot of me, clean misses by any measure. "Down, J!" I automatically dropped to a knee and glanced over my shoulder. Dawson aimed his rifle about to open fire at our unseen target. I fell to my stomach. As quickly as the trigger could be squeezed, the magazine emptied its rounds into the foliage. Rather than fumble for another in his knapsack, Dawson exchanged his gun for mine. "Get back," he commanded when he pushed past where I lay. "Stay with Jake." With my rifle at the ready position, he was swallowed by pine boughs.

Stand down and stay behind? Who the hell did my Captain America think he was dealing with? The direction he took led down a steeply timbered slope. I retrieved my Glock and holstered both handguns before a check on Dawson's rifle. He'd already shown me simple basics of his AR-10, so after retrieving a magazine from his pack, I seated it and chambered a round. The four-to-twelve power variable scope was turned to its lowest setting.

Like any predator, my partner pursued our prey to quickly run him down. The hillside was almost vertical where they disappeared. If the gray man continued on the same path, he would eventually find himself at the bottom of a narrow canyon. After suffering a grievous wound, his chances of survival ruled out taking any route except the way we came up. Yet the way he fled wouldn't get him back. Perhaps I could use Dawson giving chase to my advantage.

Jake appeared from the trees on the hill above me. He stopped, cautiously looking about before taking tentative steps in my direction. While shotgun fire didn't bother him, reports from rifles and handguns frightened him. Rather than waste time trying to coax him closer, I flew down the hill we recently climbed. If I calculated right, the gray man would break from the timber below unless Dawson caught him first. Light slowly faded the farther down I went. Certain the gray man would cover huge distances even gravely injured; I didn't stop until reaching a rock promontory. From there, I could see a mile or more beneath me.

Finding a comfortable place to sit, I used my knees for a rest. Dawson's heavy rifle served to steady the crosshairs when I leaned into the stock. The light-gathering ability of the scope was surprising, giving me an unexpected advantage. A gentle breeze blew into my face, bringing with it the warmth of the valley bottom and fragrant scent of sage. I took a moment to worry about Jake alone on the mountain. Perhaps he would stay near our gear left behind.

My greatest fear was the gray man emerging without Dawson in pursuit. Our quarry was canny enough to lie in wait to kill the man I loved to affect an escape. If mortality forced the killer to push on to reach help, Dawson stood a greater chance of survival. Although I expected my target to show at lower levels, I didn't neglect glancing over my shoulder. It wouldn't do to lose my life by underestimating him.

Twilight was giving way when movement caught my eye. I was sure it was the gray man exiting the trees. He stopped and looked over his shoulder before cutting across the slope below. The rock mass where I situated myself stood at least three-hundred yards above him. Settling my cheek against the stock, I increased the scope power to seven. I took the safety off, drew a deep breath, and started my trigger squeeze. Knowing the bullet would impact high, the crosshairs were held low shooting at a steep angle targeting his hips. He stopped to rest with tall sage between him and where I prayed Dawson would appear when the trigger broke.

My initial response was to the rifle's recoil. Like any practiced sharpshooter, I was surprised when it went off and bit my tongue after leaving my jaw relaxed. Pain bloomed in my mouth while I struggled to reacquire my target. The sage where he stood was recognizable, yet no body was visible. I waited—any slack taken out of the trigger—hoping him dead or bleeding out. Movement twenty feet beyond where he disappeared caught my eye, and I trained crosshairs on it. The gray man was crawling away, struggling to disappear into the sparse vegetation! Settling the scope's crosshairs at his rump, I remembered to close my mouth before squeezing the trigger. Recoil and muzzle blast startled me a second time, and I opened my eyes to him stretched out face down.

The trip from the rock outcropping took longer than I hoped. Winding my way along its edge, I warily descended to the sage, holding the shortened collapsible stock to my cheek and shoulder. This was the gray man, and I refused to take chances. Darkness closed, making my job much harder, yet I didn't allow myself to hurry and invite a bullet in my guts. Rather, I hunted as if I expected a wounded bear to charge.

I could barely make him out when I located the body. He lay prone with one arm outstretched and the other twisted beneath his torso. I expected him to roll over and open fire until I noticed his gun three feet from his hand. Not willing to chance it, I drove another bullet between his shoulder blades, and the muzzle blast worsened the ringing of my ears. I worked my way around to where his gun lay. Slinging my rifle, a quick check showed me only three rounds were absent the gray man's weapon. I could breathe easier knowing he hadn't hurt Dawson. Although it was overkill, I used the man's own work gun for a final four rounds into his skull.

I heard a noise over the shrill ring in my ears before seeing movement. Something was finding its way through the sagebrush. The moon gave off illumination enough I could make out Dawson when he closed to within a hundred yards. He wasn't yet sure where I was, and I watched while he hunted. He hadn't bothered to switch on the light mounted on my rifle's fore-end and give away his position. I waited until he closed to twenty-five yards before saying anything. "Over here," I called. The muzzle of my own M4 in his hands automatically swung toward me before he recognized my voice.

He stayed quiet until reaching where the gray man lay at my feet. He squatted, peering at my kill as if to convince himself of what he saw. "Huh, figures," he grunted. "You let me birddog him and picked him off from above, didn't you?"

"Sorry. Couldn't chance he might escape." While the former was a white lie, the latter was the absolute truth. I couldn't let him get away. Remembering my cell in a side pocket of my jeans, I tapped the light app and bathed the area with its glow. "Are you okay?" I asked.

"Yeah. Are you?" He continued after I nodded. "Bastard took me for a hell of a hike. Left a crappy blood trail, and I struggled when it got dark under the timber." He toed the body with a boot. "Doesn't look like he's going anywhere. Head for your house?"

No matter how exhausted I may be, it was time to return for my dog. "We have to go back for Jake. I left him on the hill." My speech was thick with a swollen tongue.

"You don't reckon he'll pick up our trail and follow if we hike out to your place?"

I shook my head. "Don't know and don't care. Jake depends on me, and I'm not leaving him alone up here." Wolves frequented the area, and my four-legged friend wouldn't stand a chance against a single lobo, let alone a pack.

We switched rifles because I preferred my carbine version. The battery in my phone ran low long before I hoped. Turning the flashlight mounted on my rifle to its faintest setting, we used it for short bursts to keep from running out of power. It seemed half the night was gone before I heard Dawson over my ringing ears. "This's it. Should be down here…" He swung off the ridge and into the swale where we originally planned to camp. I turned my flashlight to high and saw my buddy huddled in the center of our blankets.

He lifted his head at our return but didn't stand. Our gunfire scared him enough I was afraid he might flee. "Jake!" I hurried to where he waited, unsure of our intentions. "It's over, little guy." My hug seemed to reassure the pup, and he wriggled in my arms, doing his best to lick my face after I knelt.

Dawson sat next to me on the blankets. "For now." Jake treated him to the same excited welcome, giving me a chance to switch off the light. It was impossible to distinguish anything, so I turned it to low again.

"We're going to be out of light in a few minutes, sweetie. We'd better make ourselves comfortable. Jake, move." The excited pointer ran a few yards to pee while we situated the blankets and packs.

"Here." Dawson tossed a blanket to me and wrapped himself in the other. "Be daylight quicker than we'll be ready. I imagine tomorrow will be a busy day."

I checked the time on my phone before powering it down. "It's a few minutes after midnight." Our return to Jake required many long rests. Following Dawson's lead, I found a comfortable place and stretched out next to him before extinguishing our light. Our guns were within reach, and I felt Jake curl against my stomach in the nearly total darkness. Expecting to fall into an instant exhausted sleep, I was surprised to find myself wide awake listening to Dawson's quiet snore.

A new J was born with the gray man's death. One who didn't sign drug peddlers. Instead, her ruthlessness would be directed toward any who had a hand in naming her as a client. My hidden smile was cold when I considered my most recent kill. Another awaiting his turn for the same was Manny, and if attempts on my life didn't end, he would be only the first in the next phase.

***

Morning turned into a whirlwind. Finding an area where we could receive a signal on my nearly dead phone, Dawson contacted Allen who we heard, then sighted shortly after an hour. He came prepared, and I suspected our request wasn't his first rodeo when it came to tidying messes. After locating it again, we wrapped the gray man's corpse in a tarp and stowed it in the luggage bay. We left it deep in the mountains where scavengers would make short work of it. The bodies around our homes were disposed of in the same manner. While a team of forensic specialists wouldn't be fooled, our cleanup seemed reasonable.

Allen left for home, hoping to draw as little attention as possible to a large helicopter frequenting the area. Jake was happy for him to go—he wasn't pleased at flying, but I certainly wasn't leaving my pup behind. I preferred wolf packs to dine only on the meals we left.

It was difficult explaining to Melissa why she spent so long hidden in her basement. The poor woman was stiff from sleeping on cold concrete and looked worn out. Dawson and I waited in the kitchen for his mom to finish her shower and dress. It was painful watching her hobble, knowing I was responsible for her aches. Sixty-seven summers young, the basement floor must have been excruciating to sit and lie upon. Her son was the first to broach the impending subject. "No one came in the house?"

"Not that I heard, honey. If anyone did, they were quiet as a church mouse." She limped to the refrigerator, searching for something. "Either of you hungry?"

She slid free a pot roast leftover with potatoes, making my mouth water and stomach gurgle, and I didn't give Dawson a chance to answer. "Starving."

Melissa turned to see us nodding. She clucked to herself and turned the oven on. Tossing in a handful of carrots, she covered the pan and put it inside to warm. Dawson and I were sitting at the bar observing her work when she hung the dishtowel and confronted us. "No more bullshitting an old woman. Won't one of you tell me what in the hell's going on? Why have I been cowering in the corner of a basement closet afraid to be in my own home?" She didn't have to lift her voice to express displeasure.

"Mom..." Dawson said, twisting in his seat while trying to formulate a believable reply.

"Don't 'Mom' me, boy. I asked for answers, not keys to the universe. I've taken a stick to your ass before, and I'll do it again...even in front of company. Now, humor me with some sort of plausible explanation. No more lying..." She made deliberate eye contact with both of us. "...from either of you."

She deserved her answer from me. "The Company I worked for has been trying to assassinate me." What else could I say? Melissa deserved a truthful account. "Dawson's done his level best to keep me alive."

"Damn it, Jules..." I could see he wasn't happy with my revelation. He nodded to his mom who waited—although not patiently. "It's a fact. Her previous employer has been... difficult."

I choked at his choice of words. "Difficult? Most organizations send out a severance package when an employee quits. Not teams of killers."

Melissa bristled with indignation. "What sort of work did you perform, young lady? Anything to do with last Thanksgiving?"

I wasn't going to lie. "Yes, ma'am."

"Well?" She held her hands out, waiting for one of us to go on.

"I agreed to one last assignment after retiring. They forced me back and planned to see I didn't survive it." I reached out and fondly covered Dawson's hand with mine. "Your son saw to it they weren't successful." When I glanced back to Melissa, I could see the worry behind the glare she fixed me with. It was difficult to find fault with her anger.

"Why haven't you contacted the law…or have you?" She saw my hesitation. "Your work hasn't been legal, has it?" It wasn't a question.

"Legal?" I chewed my lip, searching for the correct answer. Not to merely pacify Melissa—also one factually correct. "Perhaps moral, but no, not legal in the eyes of the law."

"You've drawn my son and family into your problems, haven't you? That's why Dawson asked me to hide. They were coming for us, too."

I nodded. "My greatest fear. Except the person I dreaded most is no longer in the picture." No other as deadly as the gray man could exist. No, I was wrong—there was at least one. She looked back each time I glanced in the mirror. By forcing me to continue in their employment and now battle for my life, I was no longer only J. My lids drooped with memories, knowing I meant what I said to Manny. No one around him was safe, including his family— perhaps especially those closest to him. To stop The Company in order to protect Dawson's kinsmen and my life—I was more than willing to accept the ugliest of tasks.

My lips were pressed into a flat line as I considered my plight and future. I could smell and taste Manny's death. It was one I would see through to the bitter end no matter what it took. Yes, the gray man still lived—he survived within me.

Melissa and Dawson were staring when I wrenched myself into the present. While her eyes were wide as she considered me, there was something else. Fear certainly—I could smell it on her as if I possessed the powers of an animal. I must have shown a certain amount of sadness, too. She'd glimpsed the face of J if only for a moment. Dawson was fascinated after already exposed to what I was. But I hoped he also saw Jules whom he knew loved him without reservation.

Melissa set our plates and silverware on the bar. "What happened? Will there be more? Should I warn our relatives to move away?"

"No," I shook my head. "I'm planning to send a message very soon to show them the error of their ways."

"Can you do it alone?" She used a trivet for the pan and dished for us without asking. "You don't need my Dawson any longer, do you?" Her voice was calm and assured, yet I could hear pleading undertones. She was a mother begging for the safety of her son.

I nodded, sure of myself. "I can do it alone." But could I? Had I grown to rely too much on my farmer-warrior? Was it time to sever the string that bound us and fly on my own again? Would such a decision take him and his family out of The Company's potential crosshairs? Perhaps it was time to find out how reliant on others this new woman was.

Chapter XX

My target thought anonymity had been achieved by obscurity in humble surroundings. Possessing enough wealth to afford the top suite in this city's tallest high-rise with the priciest of modern security, the clever quarry chose the extreme opposite place to hide—a dilapidated three-bedroom, two-bath residence in a poor part of town. Instead of ostentatious rent-a-cops, this neighborhood was shunned—including by routine police patrols—due to the presence of gangs. No doubt some thugs who considered themselves dangerous collected "protection money" from my victim.

One safety network was as useless as the other once a lioness marked her prey and stalked closer.

School was about to start back in Idaho. Only seventeen days until Bess planned for me to substitute for the district. I'd spent my summer scouting, hunting, and preparing to harvest my prey while careful to avoid detection. I was a killer who would not be stopped. The Company would rue the day this teacher took them to school.

My thick blonde hair was short again—very close-cut in a boy's style. I combed it over left to right from a distinct high part. Although its hue was normally very light, two months in the sun bleached it platinum. My bodyweight surprised me when it climbed to one-oh-seven. Even with my fair skin, I was tanning rather than burning on daily runs with Jake. With swarms of beautiful people teeming in southern California, I wasn't surprised when few noticed me. They weren't supposed to. Though wearing a skimpy one-piece swimsuit in the hot west coast sun, I didn't turn heads.

It didn't matter—I was whom I had become and didn't feel a need to be recalled. Perhaps my body would someday be fed to scavengers, too, lost to the world and remembered by few.

Wearing loose tan cargo shorts and a tight matching tank, I left a short-sleeved blouse unbuttoned and hanging over it all to cover my work gun. Shoved down the front of my pants, I could grasp it and draw quickly. My little Colt was left behind—a trail gun to kill varmints and save lives. No, this job called for my suppressed Ruger.

Two weeks to find my target—six more to watch and learn patterns. I tracked and observed from between blades of grass as any good hunter, except my greenery in an urban environment were streets lined with parked cars, homes, and pedestrians. I observed my prey carefully like any hungry lioness, determining its habits and desires before leaping. Nothing could go wrong to send the necessary message to powers-that-be. I wanted it both blunt and explicit.

The disembodied voice in my ear was distinct. "Now, G-dub. He's using his work phone and two computers as we speak."

Over the past forty-two days, Allen and I learned my prey sent his young out or to bed when he grazed. Technology was his form of browsing, and my toothy smile was ugly when I started my silent charge.

"Exiting my vehicle." I was getting to love blue-tooth. Knowing the importance riding upon it, Allen patiently walked me through its use. When Dawson referred to me as the gray woman to his team mate, Allen shortened it to GW, which he pronounced Gee-Dubya, and finally settled on G-dub.

The initial attack phase was smooth, and I worked my way to the backdoor of the run-down home. Parked two blocks away, fifteen minutes passed before I was ready. "In place and waiting for go." My voice was low.

"He's off the phone but still on the computers. Go when ready."

"Affirmative, I'm moving in now." Although faced with my possible death, I was more excited than fearful.

The screen door was loud. I listened to it many times while scouting, and I stopped to spray its hinges and spring with a penetrating solvent. Waiting a moment while it leached into rusted cracks, I opened it enough to coat the house door hinges. Setting the can aside, I pushed inward, counting on a soundless entry. My teeth were bared in the knowledge my prey's throat was exposed. This kill was important, perhaps more so than any during my employment with The Company.

I drew my gun as I stepped inside, not before. I was tempted to check the chamber—I'd done it a half-dozen times already. Instead,

I slid the safety off and prepared for the second phase, a way I hoped to set me free and allow the next chapter of my life. Alternatively, it might bring about my death. Choose to ignore it, and I was worm food. A hungry lioness always acted.

The room I entered was the living area. It was clean with a child's toy left on the end of one couch. I glanced at it—the stuffed pink kitten a little girl carried for weeks. She was the youngest at around four.

To my left was the kitchen and beyond it a dining area. To the right, a hallway, bathroom, and bedrooms. I listened carefully and detected the tap of computer keys. Rather than find myself blocked in a corridor without an avenue for escape, I first swept the kitchen for danger. From there, I checked the dining room but found nothing. Taking a deep breath, I squared my shoulders and stared in the last direction. I was the apex predator who slowed her advance as she edged forward, each step muted by a worn but clean carpet.

The door was closed when I located the source of noise. Standing to one side, I tested the knob with a slow, firm grip. It was unlocked, and I slowly pushed inward. A phone chirped to announce an incoming call, and a familiar voice answered as I peeked through the doorway. His back was to me. Two laptop computers were in use, and he shifted slightly in his chair while he gave a greeting I knew well: "Manny here." I stepped inside, closing the door without catching the latch. I waited in silence against wood-print panels for him to finish. "Hey, Alec. Is Joseph with you? Good. Your client is in Tucson, Arizona. Male, 36. I'll text you the address. This one isn't a bottom feeder and pays seventeen-five. He goes by Pablo Herrera. Call or text when he's signed." He listened for a moment before giving his answer. "Soon, my friend. I see another on my list paying over thirty. I'll try my best to point you in his direction. First we'll see how good of job you do signing this one."

As he tended to do, Manny ended the call without fanfare and went to tapping a computer keyboard, presumably texting the address Alec and Joseph needed. After finishing the missive, Manny leaned back in his creaking office chair. To our left was a small refrigerator. He bent to the side and opened the door. I wouldn't have expected him to be an Orange Crush fan. Sensing something different, he turned his head and froze when our eyes met. Mine peered over the sights on my Ruger. The barrel was steady as a sandbagged rest.

He immediately knew who he faced, and his absolute shock completed me. Manny sagged into his chair. A tongue gone suddenly dry tried to lick pale lips. His eyes never left mine, and trying to fake calm, he opened the soda and took a long swallow, but blood showed where he'd bitten the inside of his mouth. At last, he gulped and croaked, "J."

I nodded and stayed silent, allowing him a last few moments of heartbeat. He turned the chair to face me squarely. Anyone else would have already been signed. This was Manny, who at one time was responsible for my life.

When he had nothing more to say, he shrugged, and the lioness lunged. "Goodbye, Manny."

The bridge of the nose and brow of an adult man is thick bone, so I directed my bullet an inch higher. The custom brass catcher snagged the empty case, and the slide loaded a fresh round. His head fell against the backrest, and his mouth relaxed to slowly open. Fingers on his right hand twitched while I waited. Then a foot. Seeing no more signs of movement, I advanced to stop at his bent knees.

His features were slack and pupils dilated, all indicating death. While I worked for him—with him—my trademark was to make sure I completed the job. Four rounds to his temple, and my career with Manny ended.

Two computers were open and running—another two sat on a shelf. On the desk were a brace of mobile phones and one in his shirt pocket. Cells went into my cargo shorts. The laptops were closed, and I put them in a neat stack, looking about for a bag. I found an expensive leather one big enough for all four. I slung it over one shoulder and gave a last look to the room. Nothing I could see remained to collect for Allen. He'd been firm that I needed to secure all electronics and deliver them to him.

No one appeared to watch when I stepped across the threshold, pulling the door closed. After a brief hike to my rental, I loaded the satchel of electronics onto the rear seat, and returned to my apartment.

***

I'd left hours ago on my lone mission. Before inserting my key in the front door I'd locked behind me, I eased the heavy bag to the stoop and gave an agreed pattern of knocks while saying aloud, "Jake's my best boy." Any other signals meant I was under duress.

When I heard eager paws against the door, I pushed in with the hardware liberated for Allen and crouched at my pup's level for kisses to let me know all was forgiven.

Jake had been sad when I'd left him behind, but Dawson was wild-eyed with fear and anxiety. I hurried to the living room where his pacing wore a trail into the carpet.

He'd gone livid when I insisted on working alone. Like all men, he wanted to be the protector, the one who guarded his woman. It was admirable and one of the reasons I felt so strongly toward him. He was the only person on earth who could make me feel safe. However, both of us knew confronting Manny was my task alone. Dawson argued, begged, and finally thundered his anger when I departed. Relief radiated from his body when I entered was palpable.

"It's done?" His bass poured over me like a spring rain—pure and cleansing with resonance I loved. I wondered how long it would take before the tone no longer made me go weak in the knees. My fondest wish was it would never happen.

I nodded. "For now. I have three phones and four laptops for Allen. We'd better pack and start back to Missoula." Dawson worried me—he hadn't welcomed me into his arms since my return.

I'd learned what a deeply romantic and loving man he was. Our couplings were everything I hoped for and more. When we weren't out surveilling, much of our time was spent in bed discovering what the other liked. Perhaps the most thrilling aspect of my lover was his pleasure when he first saw me. His gaze—softened by love—showed me the hunger I longed to see. I planned to spend my life nurturing and feeding his desire until the end of our days.

"Already done," he said. "We'll toss everything in my truck and leave the rental at the lot. This time tomorrow…we'll be at Allen's."

We could accomplish about eighteen hours of drive time over twelve hundred miles if we took turns. Allen needed the data and information we possessed as a possible means to help stop The Company's pursuit of me—perhaps even take it down if they entered my life again.

"Honey?" I needed to feel his strength and protection. Dawson didn't say anything. Instead, he opened his arms. The killer within me was gone, and left behind was just Julia—his Jules. The gray woman hid, waiting, biding her time. When and if the need or call came, she could step into her role at a moment's notice. Now Julia needed to feel all the warmth and love of her chosen mate.

"What do you think?" he asked. "Is it over?" My ear pressed to his chest; lower register reverberations caused my heart to skip a beat.

"I hope so. I'm ready to be a school teacher again. Just regular old Julia Hampton. Work from eight until four and grumble about afterschool projects I'd rather not participate in."

He'd listened patiently while I talked incessantly about working the next thirty-five years until retirement. I wanted nothing more than the monotony of common life. Jake pressed against my leg, whining and eager to be a part of our bond. "Is it an unequivocal requirement for you teach as Julia Hampton? Could it be something different? Maybe start with a missus?"

"I'm not changing my name—even for The Company." I pushed back, holding him at arm's length. "I'll wear Dad's name until…" What he suggested finally sank in, and Dawson smiled when my eyes opened wide. "Are you asking…I mean, are you saying…" I couldn't bring myself to verbalize the question.

"Vegas is on the way, and it wouldn't take but a few minutes. We can renew our vows after we get home if you'd like." He watched my reaction carefully.

"Say it. Please, Dawson, say it." Every girl who aspires to someday be a princess and rescued by her white knight wants to hear the words. He made my wish come true.

"Julia Marie Hampton…" Dawson dropped to one knee, holding my hands in his. "…would you do me the honor of becoming my wife and spending your life with me?"

How can a simple query be so powerful? It is what most men look forward to someday ask and what every little girl growing up wishes to hear. Even knowing what the question would be, it still knocked the wind from my lungs. "Yes, Dawson. I'll be your wife until the end of our lives." I helped him to his feet so I could look up. It wasn't right to look down at a man over a foot taller. "I will never, ever let you regret this day."

***

"I understand congratulations are in order, Mrs. Pelletier."

I didn't notice Thomas Howell standing inside his homeroom door as I passed. I was asked to substitute on the second day of school. Even with the brief time I spent working in the building previously, entering again was a breath of fresh autumn air. His voice caused me to stop and turn. "Thank you, Mr. Howell." I felt certain he meant it.

A student whose name I couldn't recollect called to me. "Hi, Miss Hampton."

"Hi to you, young lady, but I'm not Miss Hampton any longer. It's Mrs. Pelletier." My heart swelled with pride. I loved my new name, Julia Marie Pelletier. Melissa and I were already discussing dates for a formal wedding. My husband didn't care. In fact, Dawson expressed surprise at her reaction after hearing we married in Las Vegas. She seemed as happy as us.

A text arrived from a strange number not long after we left Nevada—one I never expected. A single word spoke volumes and gave me reason to be optimistic: *Truce?* I waited less than a minute before answering with a thumbs-up emoji. Perhaps I would live a long life.

Farther down the hall outside her office, Bess greeted students as they passed. I stopped at my door to unlock it and glanced her way one last time. My husband's aunt was watching from fifty feet away. She appeared genuinely friendly when our eyes met, and she broke into a broad smile. Grinning back, I took a deep breath and entered my room for the day. Yes, life was good—exactly as I hoped it would be.

So long as The Company didn't reawaken the gray woman.

CPSIA information can be obtained
at www.ICGtesting.com
Printed in the USA
BVHW030723260919
559226BV00008B/13/P

9 781945 181689